Race Track

The Blind Spot of Privilege

Reed Fromer

Race Track
The Blind Spot of Privilege

*This book is dedicated to all those who fought,
and are still fighting, for affirmative action –
those who understand that "equality" is not
a facile slogan uttered in a vacuum but an imperative
that demands ongoing scrutiny and struggle.*

*Special thanks go out to Jacki Fromer and Carol Larson
for their diligent contribution to bringing the
technical components of this literary project to completion,
to Irving, Jon, and Dave Fromer for their
inspirational examples of putting one's artistic
creativity to use in the service of social progress,
to my wonderful wife, Gina Fromer,
for her unending support through this and
all my other undertakings, and to
my son, Devin - to whose generation the task
of instilling a more inclusive and
empathetic ethos is entrusted.*

Chapters

Author's Introduction

"The fortunate man," observed Max Weber, "is seldom satisfied with the fact of being fortunate. Beyond this, he needs to know that he has a right to his good fortune. He wants to be convinced that he 'deserves' it, and above all, that he deserves it in comparison with others."

Weighing in on how that "need" can affect one's perception of concepts and events, Upton Sinclair wryly noted, "It is difficult to get a man to understand something when his salary depends on his not understanding it."

In this book, I've constructed a parable to examine the phenomenon that caught the attention of both the prominent sociologist and the progressive author: the inability of so many people to recognize an unfair circumstance when the unfairness happens to work to their advantage. Throughout what I would call my politically cognitive years, I've harbored a fascination, and maintained sort of an informal study, of this psychological trend – mostly as it relates to a specific arena of our society and our political system.

I spent well over a decade gathering anecdotal and historical data, formulating what I thought were some pretty strong arguments, and nurturing aspirations to write a book on the subject of racism – with a focus on the logic and motives behind the fiercely contested countermeasure known as affirmative action.

Like Weber, I would marvel at the lengths to which people are willing to go to convince themselves that any favorable position they hold can *only* be attributable to their "meriting" it – that if they're "up here" (wherever "here" may be on the ladder of society) and someone else is "down there," then it *must* reflect a corresponding difference in intelligence, or work ethic, or determination. And like Sinclair, I'd observe how evidence to the contrary – evidence that the spoils of society might not tend to drift to the most deserving recipients, but rather to those who enjoy certain built-in advantages – can become absolutely, inalterably *invisible* to those who prefer not to see it. (Notwithstanding Sinclair's choice of the word "salary," the incentives in question aren't limited to economic gains. It could just as easily be ego, social standing, religious convictions, or a philosophical worldview that makes the inconvenient realities so hard to "understand.") The utter refusal of some to recognize disparities that aid their own advancement is my focal point in this book.

The obvious question would probably be "Why take the risk of relying on a parable, which readers may or may not understand? Why not just go ahead and write about what you're really writing about?"

I never found myself at a loss for words in any effort to build a straightforward case for affirmative action. The problem was, by the time I felt secure that I had sufficiently honed and coordinated my arguments in written form, I found that the arena in question had been labeled by our nation as a topic that no longer exists, a subject area that no longer calls for discussion. This had, in fact, *always* been the position of a certain segment of the political spectrum, but with the election of Barack Obama to the Presidency in 2008, it became clear that the mainstream had likewise bought into the notion that we could now take discussions of racial disparities off the table. We heard the refrain *ad nauseum:* How could racism still be any sort of hindrance to minorities if a black man could become President? (Anti-racism activist Tim Wise has noted that it would be equivalent to argue that India and Pakistan *must* have eradicated patriarchy and subjugation of women, given that they've both had female heads of state.)

Commentators who continued to raise concerns surrounding racial injustice were said to be "harping" on the matter, or playing a "card." It was even suggested, in certain quarters, that those who had the temerity to insist that this particular problem still existed *were*, themselves, the source of the problem – "the *real* racists," as we've heard in perpetuity. It seemed, therefore, that the chance to argue the case directly to any widespread, receptive audience had passed me by. I had developed a sound, thorough, convincing argument – on a topic that no one wanted to hear about anymore. (Bear in mind, this was before the regression of our society's commitment to racial equality sprung into hyperdrive and reached such a nadir that a whole new sociopolitical movement became necessary merely to convey the idea that black people's *lives* were not expendable trivialities.)

Searching for an alternate angle, it struck me that while I was ruminating over my original, would-be nonfiction endeavor, I often turned to a particular argumentative tool: sports analogies. I would gravitate repeatedly toward sports-themed illustrations ("Suppose you had a football game in which ..."), and drift into deeper and deeper layers of applicable comparisons ("Now, let's go further and assume that there's *also* a special rule in this football game that says ..."). During the period when I still

4

envisioned my end product as more of an academic essay, it nagged at me that this reliance on symbolic equations was pulling my writing into some not-very-academic-sounding territory. At the same time, I had to recognize the flipside: The analogies were *fun*. They were exciting to formulate, and entertaining to read afterward. And they made the points they were intended to make, at least in my eyes.

So, in the end, I decided to take one of those athletic metaphors and run with it (no pun intended, I promise). In doing so, I envisioned an American society just as we know it, with a sporting world *almost* identical to the real-life version. I merely inserted one little twist. I picked out a specific facet of track & field that we take as a given, as an automatic procedure, and posed the question: "What if this particular mechanism never *occurred* to us? What if, somehow, we just never thought about doing it?" That fanciful "what if" became the basis for the parallel universe of this story. Outside of that, everything is just regular ol' life in America in the early 1990s.

The natural objection to the scenario I'm presenting is that it's way too far-fetched, that *nobody* could ever miss something as obvious as the detail that, in this story, has managed to escape the attention of an entire society.

I can only offer this response: Yes, they could. I've seen 'em do it. I've spent well over thirty years watching vast numbers of my fellow Americans overlook a phenomenon that should be *every bit as impossible to miss* as the oversight depicted in the pages that follow. I've heard one of my society's most blatant, egregious, in-your-face, and impactful social maladies described repeatedly by one side of the political aisle as an *imagined* problem – as little more than a hallucination brought on by a persecution complex. The only way I *could* offer a fitting parallel to that mindset was to veer into theater-of-the-absurd territory.

There's your full disclosure: The central premise of this story is going to demand a complete and total suspension of your disbelief. Because I've mixed that premise with the familiar realities of American life, it's possible that some readers will find the juxtaposition somewhat jarring and incompatible. They'll resist the notion that folks who hold jobs, raise families, attend school, go to the movies, and participate in sports could possibly be so clueless about what's right in front of their eyes.

My response would be, "Someone actually thinks that's unrealistic?"

CHAPTER 1
"Wilkersons Can't Run the 400"

"Dad, the track & field tryouts are tomorrow," said Kevin as he sat down to dinner. He paused a moment after this announcement, to feel out the vibe of the room. He had been playing out a whole range of prospective outcomes in his head, a variety of ways his parents might respond once he made his intentions clear. In the best case scenario, the mere mention of "track & field" would inspire a wave of nostalgic storytelling from his father about his youthful days as a discus thrower, which would put him (and, ideally, Kevin's mother as well) in a positive, receptive mood toward whatever news bulletin would follow.

"Uh-huh. And … ?" responded his father in a passive tone.

With the best-case scenario effectively nipped in the bud, Kevin decided there was no point in holding off any longer. There wasn't some easy angle to come at this. "And, uh … and … I think I'm gonna try running the 400."

The cat was out of the bag. Now, he knew, his parents' reaction would reveal a lot about their level of faith in him. Not so much in his abilities – he was actually pretty secure about that – as in his judgment.

His father offered no immediate verbal response but just sat quietly and pensively at the table, nodding almost imperceptibly. Kevin took this as a good initial sign, on the whole scale of possibilities. His mother, though, instantly dropped what she was doing in the kitchen, and came and stood in the dining room doorway, looking at him intently. It was the same look she had given him when he was seven, and had asked her if he and his two friends could take turns skydiving off the roof into the backyard, using her umbrella as a parachute. Here, once again, she looked as though she was trying to peer past her son's mane of blonde hair and through his skull, to assess whether or not he had an actual brain behind it.

"The 400," she finally said, as though simply repeating the name of the event made her point. "The 400-meter dash. The quarter-mile. That's what you're going out for?"

"Yep," said Kevin, trying to exemplify the confident look and delivery of a "can-do" mindset, which he hoped would quickly spread to his folks, by osmosis or something. It didn't.

"Can you tell me something, Kevin?" asked his mother. "Can you tell me why, every once in a while, you get this urge, this obsessive need, to set yourself up for failure? Where does it come from? There are so many areas where you know you can succeed. And you know very well that I'm not one of those stuffy parents who says that sports aren't a worthwhile focus, or anything like that. You *do* belong out there tomorrow. I would be the first to support you. But to pick the 400, out of all the choices – I mean, an athlete like you could make the track team in almost any of those events. You're fast enough to run the 100 meters. Why not go out for that? Or you could do the longer one, the – what is the longer distance, 2,000? I know you've got the endurance for that. You could come out a winner in so many events, Kevin. But no, you've got this uncontrollable impulse to go and pick an event where you know you've got no possibility of success. *Why, Kevin?*"

"Because it doesn't make sense, Mom," Kevin said, quickly coming to terms with the fact that there really never was any mystery as to how his parents would react. No, this was destined to be an uphill battle from the start. "The more I've thought about it, the more it just … I dunno, it just doesn't feel right. Why *shouldn't* I be able to compete in the 400?"

His mother answered slowly, firmly, and deliberately, as if the reality wouldn't sink in if she relied on a normal, conversational tone and cadence: "BE – CAUSE … OUR LAST NAME IS WILKERSON."

Given what they all knew about the nature of running events, and about the historical record of their outcomes, her answer should have ended the discussion right there. It was common knowledge at every level, from youth sports to high school to college to semi-pro competition: People with alphabetically late-ranking names simply could not compete in the 400-meter dash. Its demands just didn't coincide with their athletic capabilities. This was such an absolute, such a given, that it was laughable – and almost heretical – to suggest otherwise. If your surname was Washington, or Young, or Warner, or Valdez, it was understood by all that you just didn't have what it took to keep up in races of that distance. Kevin was as familiar with the statistics as anyone else. But he wasn't quite ready to surrender the argument.

"Here's the thing, Mom," he said, "there's always a certain amount of talk that goes around leading up to these things – y'know, leading up to any competition. People make predictions, who's gonna win this event, who's gonna win that one …"

Mrs. Wilkerson nodded and gestured for him to continue.

"So some of the buzz has been about the guys who are, like, 'guaranteed' to win the 400. They're practically calling it a done deal, saying it'll either be Simon Addison or Billy Lloyd Beech."

"What's your point?" asked his mother.

"Well, the thing is, I'm faster than them. I've been in P.E. with both of them for two years, and – plus, y'know, guys get into pick-up games at lunch, or after school, or whenever. No matter what game we're playing, if I have to catch up with them, or outrun them, I can do it. They're never too fast for me."

"Like I said," continued Mrs. Wilkerson, "*what* is your *point*?"

"My point, Mom, is that I should be able to beat them in the quarter-mile. If I'm a faster runner·than them, and they're the fav– I mean, supposedly the favorites, I should be able to win the race."

"You may *be* faster than them in a football or soccer game. Look, I'm sure you're faster in badminton and ping-pong, too! And probably Monopoly and Chinese Checkers! That doesn't change the fact that you are *not* about to beat them in the 400, no matter how much you seem to want to cling to this pie-in-the-sky fantasy of yours. It's just not something that's meant to happen!"

"Okay, Mom, okay … I got it. Point taken. I'll think about it some more, and I guess I'll make a decision during school tomorrow."

Finally, his father chimed into the conversation – not so much because he had anything profound to add to the mix as because he sensed that he'd be hearing about it later on that night if he didn't back up his wife. "I appreciate that you have that confidence inside you, Kevin," he said. "I really do. And it's going to serve you well in other areas in life, I'm sure, but this is one situation where … well, you know what the facts are. I don't want to discourage you, but … I just want you to be realistic about this."

"I think I can pull it off," said Kevin. "I got one of those pedometers – y'know, like an odometer for runners and hikers – and with that and my stopwatch, I've been timing myself over a range of distances that I've calculated as pretty close to 400 meters, and my times are better than ever."

"You do what you think you need to do," said his mother, exasperated. "I can see, pretty clearly, that I won't be able to talk any sense into you on this one. You'll have to learn the hard way about the importance of knowing your boundaries."

"Be realistic. Know my boundaries. Got it," muttered Kevin, adopting a tone of voice that was intended to show a *little* hint of bitter sarcasm, but not blatant disrespect. He got up to leave the table.

"Some things are the way they are, Kevin," said his mother as Kevin paused to listen before heading out of the room and toward the hallway, "and we wouldn't be doing you any favors, as your parents, if we didn't try to drive those realities home when you don't seem to grasp them on your own. This is one of those realities: Your name starts with a W. Not an A, not a B, not a D, or an F, or even an H. Your name is Wilkerson, and *Wilkersons can't run the 400.*"

CHAPTER 2
Gym Lessons

"Wilkersons can't run the 400." "Wilkersons can't run the 400." The phrase echoed in Kevin's mind as he lay in bed, like in a cinematic nightmare where a torturous refrain from an earlier scene in the story keeps replaying itself in the protagonist's head (always with heavy reverb), tormenting him as he writhes back and forth across his pillow, unable to block out the sound. Kevin figured he wasn't likely to be getting any sleep for at least an hour. So instead of writhing, he sat up against the headboard and sorted through the many thoughts competing for dominance in his mind, every one of them surrounding this far-reaching desire of his.

Kevin, again, was no stranger to the conventional wisdom he now found himself about to try to undercut, to knock from its pedestal. He was fully aware that, as a "late-name" athlete, his ambitions flew in the face of everything the sporting world knew to be the basic truths of competition. Nobody named Wilkerson had ever won a 400-meter dash as far as anyone knew; nor had anyone named Vernon, or Ulrich, or Yates. This was not some peculiarity associated with James Monroe High School, with the largely rural community of Richardson Park (which the school served), or with the state of Illinois. If anyone with a low-ranking name were to emerge victorious in the quarter-mile *anywhere* in the country, it would be beyond an anomaly; it would be a headline-grabbing freak occurrence.

The ironic thing was this: As Mrs. Wilkerson's recommendations to Kevin reflected, late-namers were not even remotely deficient as athletes in general, or even, more to the point, subpar as runners. They tended to do every bit as well as their "early-name" peers both on shorter runs, such as the 100-meter or 120-meter dash, and on significantly longer runs, all the way up to marathons. But whatever combination of swiftness and resilience it was that allowed them to triumph a fair amount of the time when it came to those events, those qualities invariably let them down on the once-in-a-blue-moon occasions when they had the audacity to try the 400 meters. Late-namers just *could not* win it – no matter how much an individual's running speed in other competitive settings might seem to suggest that he or she could.

You could comb through the archives of any track & field organization, and the winners of the 400 over the decades would stay in accordance with the most predictable pattern of early-alphabetical surnames: Bradley.

Alcott. Anderson. Caldwell. Emerson. Brown. Avalos. In the Monroe High School gym's lobby, which housed many of the trophies and awards won by Monroe teams or individuals through the years, Kevin had often paused to admire the plaque honoring an iconic figure in the history of the track team – the great Max Aaronson, who had gone undefeated in both the 400-meter dash and the 250-meter hurdles throughout his four years at the school.

The hurdles, by the way, happened to be another event where late-namers had enormous trouble getting into the winners' circle (although, even then, not as much trouble as on the 400). The 200-meter dash yielded similarly skewed outcomes. Numerous experts surmised that there must be some sort of a symbiotic relationship between the various events within the range of 200 to 500 meters, judging by the unmistakable tendency of certain runners to excel across the board in those events – and of certain others to fail miserably in them.

The same curse crept into play when it came to the relay races, but in a very esoteric fashion: Late-namers could be valuable members of four-person relay teams – *as long as they weren't the lead runner.* They could be the second one to carry the baton, or the third, or they could be the one taking it for the home stretch, and your foursome would likely have as good a chance as anyone else out there. But if a late-namer was your initial runner, forget it. Your team would have no remote possibility of taking first place – a moot point, anyway, because no coach would be clueless enough to arrange things in that order to begin with. Certain pockets within the Monroe sports community, in fact, still remembered the mishap that, it was widely agreed, had cost the school its chance at victory in the relay four years before Kevin began his attendance there.

The relay team at that time consisted of four outstanding sprinters – all seniors – named David Aldrich, Will Graves, Willie Jasper, and Kendrick Turner. Naturally, Aldrich was the lead runner, followed by Turner, Graves, and Jasper. In that sequence, the combination had always yielded great success, dating back to their sophomore year. But it all fell apart in the most dismaying fashion on what was supposed to be the climactic triumph of their high school careers. In the spring of 1986, when the line-ups for the championship match were submitted by the school to the track meet officials, something had been altered: Either someone had made a careless error in transcribing the names of the respective competitors, or – most people suspected – a computer in the Monroe Athletic Department or at the league administration's office had been hacked.

Whatever the explanation, the card that ended up in the officials' hands had *Turner* listed as the lead runner, with Aldrich second. The Monroe coaches raised an impassioned protest, but the officials wouldn't budge. The relay team had to run in the sequence indicated on the official roster, and the feared outcome inevitably prevailed: The mere switch of positions between Aldrich and Turner ended up adding crucial seconds to the team's usual time – and, correspondingly, costing them the match.

A few observers pointed out that Dave Aldrich, accustomed to being the lead runner, was probably underprepared in the art of receiving the baton from a teammate, which could have interfered with their momentum. But the video of the race clearly showed no mishandling of the exchange between Turner and Aldrich. It had been flawless, in fact. No, the eventual consensus was that Kendrick Turner – certainly through no fault of his own – was simply thrust into an untenable position, one that demanded capabilities that people like him just didn't possess. It was just a fact of life, an irrefutable, reflexive truism: You don't put a late-namer in an early-namer's role and expect the same result.

Kevin had been particularly intrigued when he had first heard about the relay fiasco of '86, although at the time he couldn't articulate exactly what aspect of the ordeal grabbed his attention with such compelling pull. As a relay team member in his own right (third pole position) on the junior varsity track team during his sophomore year, he had found himself dwelling on the story with an inordinate level of fascination, pondering and evaluating it from multiple angles.

Just like the presumed gulf between his own odds in the upcoming 400 and those of Simon Addison and Billy Lloyd Beech, Kevin found the conventional assessment of Kendrick Turner's abilities inadequate, misconceived, and contradictory. He had even made a moderate effort to discuss the matter directly with Turner, on an occasion when the recent grad had been summoned back to Monroe by the track coaches to help mentor some of the younger sprinters. (Evidently, the stigma of that relay loss hadn't dampened their appreciation of his overall athletic prowess). Unfortunately, the demands of Turner's visit didn't afford him the time for a one-on-one interview, and Kevin was left to wrestle with his doubts about the whole affair on his own.

Kevin had noticed another interesting statistical detail while looking through the school records mounted on the walls between the trophy cases.

In the early years of competitive running – at least, the early years in which the results were recorded and preserved for posterity – the mid-distance runs appeared to have a noticeably wider range of winners' surnames, as opposed to in recent years. Forty or fifty years prior to Kevin's freshman year at Monroe, the names were predictably skewed toward the beginning of the alphabet, sure, but not with the same lockstep consistency. Dotting a landscape of Bensons, Clarks, Andersons and the like, there was also a Nelson, an Oberlander, two Jaffees (probably related to each other, thought Kevin), a Lohman, a Waldron …

Wait – a *Waldron?!* The presence of a "W" name on a list of 400 winners was a sight that would make any passerby, including Kevin, do a double take. But no question, the accolade was right there, imprinted on the steel plate in the same gold lettering as all the others: "1942 – Burt Waldron."

That was long ago, however, and in more recent decades the disproportionate results had become much more pronounced and unvarying. In fact, in the school's preceding 25 years of boys' track, the *latest*-named quarter-mile winner was a Kirk Gantz, who had broken the ribbon 18 years back. Along similar lines, the girls who had won the 400 over that stretch all had names starting with H or earlier. The prizewinners included a Cordelia Hawthorne, a Margie Hayes, and 19 winners in the A-to-D range, a few of them with multiple victories.

Kevin had gone as far as to point this out to the head of the athletic department about a month earlier, not so much in a spirit of protest, but merely as a small-talk item of interest. Did anyone else ever take note of, and bring to the school's attention, the recent decades' gradual but undeniable increase in early-name exclusivity in the quarter-mile? Had anyone thought to look into this ready-made opportunity for some data-driven research? Could there be a physiological explanation for it? Had early-namers somehow managed to increase their average foot speed dramatically over the '70s and '80s, to the point where even the "mid-namers" weren't able to keep up as they once could?

Tom Ackerman, the athletic director (and, in his own earlier years, a two-time district champion in the 400 himself) seemed largely disinterested in the actual content of Kevin's inquiry. But admiring the student's intellectual curiosity – or, more accurately, recognizing the importance of *appearing* to admire it – he offered a halfhearted attempt at a sociological explanation. It wasn't so much that anyone's running time grew faster or slower, he assured Kevin. More likely, it reflected the mid-namers gradually coming to the realization – as most late-namers had figured out years earlier – that they just didn't have the ability to measure up to the early-namers when it came to the 400.

"Over time," said Mr. Ackerman, "they came to terms with their own limitations. Once the truth sank in that this wasn't where their strengths were, they turned their attention to other pursuits. The smart ones, anyway."

"But Mr. Ackerman, you can see these names right here. It wasn't always the case," Kevin persisted. "If you go back far enough, you've got at least a few mid-namers on the list … and then, about 20 or 25 years ago, you just stop seeing them. There must be some reason for the change. It's too obvious, the difference, to just be – y'know, like, random chance…"

"Well, you've gotta consider, Wilkerson," responded the gym teacher, "that recruitment also had a lot to do with it. The early-namers didn't *always* win, but they won enough of the time that the competitive high schools and colleges could see that a fellow's name carried a lot of weight. If you wanted your school to come out on top in the 400, or the 200, you wouldn't go *looking* for a kid named Nelson or Jones – let alone a Williams or a Young. It wouldn't make sense, practically speaking – not when there might be twenty kids in the A-B-C range dying to run for your team. If you were looking for the next Max Aaronson, you'd go where you knew the skill was strong, and that was at the beginning of the alphabet. So … after a while, you just stopped seeing more than one or two mid-namers in the quarter-mile or the hurdles. And when you did see 'em, they'd always lose. So if you were a smart coach, you wouldn't go in such a … y'know, a counterintuitive direction. If you had late-namers who showed athletic potential, you'd steer them to the quick sprints, or the long runs, or the field events, or you'd put them as your second, third, or fourth guy in the relays, where they might be able to handle the load."

"Wonder how this guy Waldron managed to win back in '42," marveled Kevin.

"Well, now, that's interesting – I actually *do* know something about that one," said Mr. Ackerman.

"Did he run for you?" asked Kevin.

"Uh, no, Wilkerson, I wasn't actually coaching 50 years ago," responded the 44 year-old Ackerman.

"Sorry," murmured Kevin, making a mental note to do the internal math the next time the figures were available. "But can you tell me what happened?"

"Well, it was a little bit before I was born," said Ackerman, "but the story was kinda quirky, so it's been passed down through the department over the years. I don't know if I have all the details right. I know that it was kind of a depleted field that year. The way I hear it told, our three best runners of the 400 meters were out. One had an injury, and two others had both left school during their senior year to enlist in the Army and fight in World War II. I think our rival school had some similar issues. So Waldron wasn't exactly facing the toughest competition."

"That was it?" Kevin asked incredulously, wondering how such a mundane story could merit being "passed down through the department over the years."

"Well, no, there was another funny thi – well, it wasn't *funny*, certainly. That's a bad choice of words. Out-of-the-ordinary – that'd be a more decent way to put it."

"Yeah?" said Kevin, perking back up.

"Uh-huh. See, around thirty minutes before the meet was scheduled to start – just as the visiting team's bus, or whatever they traveled on, was arriving – an earthquake hit this whole region. It wasn't one for the record books, but it did a fair amount of property damage. One thing it did was, it jarred loose a whole section of the spectators' stands and sent it toppling onto the running track. On the other end of the field, meanwhile, a big light tower was broken off from its base, and fell onto the opposite side of the track, like a tree falling across a road. It was really a lucky thing that no one was seriously hurt. But they didn't have any sort of equipment on hand that would help them move either of the obstacles."

"And it would've been too big a hassle to switch the location to the other team's school?" Kevin surmised.

"Right, exactly," continued Mr. Ackerman. "It was something like 90 minutes away, so it would've been getting dark by the time everyone drove there – and their school didn't *have* any lights for nighttime competitions. They needed to carry it off then and there. Remember, it was the championship meet, and there was no way to reschedule it within the last week of school, before everyone took off for summer vacation. But the track was unusable."

"So what'd they end up doing?" Kevin asked.

"Well, someone pointed out that the football field was a hundred yards long, of course, from goal line to goal line. As it happened, it didn't sustain any damage. So they moved the running events there, and set things up so that the runners would duplicate their tracks until they'd gone the right distance. So, for example, on the 400 – and I'm thinking they hadn't gone metric yet, so it was the 400-*yard* dash back then – they had the runners touch a tape at one goal line, turn and run back the other way, and then two more times, until they had run exactly 400 yards. Obviously, it wasn't the ideal way to run the race. I mean, sprinters don't train on a regimen of stopping suddenly and changing direction, so they were forced to adjust on the spot. I think they had to improvise in a whole variety of ways and work out, y'know, makeshift set-ups for a lot of the other events, too. Nobody was really happy about it."

"Except maybe Burt Waldron," offered Kevin.

"Well, again – the really good runners were out of action in any case," Mr. Ackerman was quick to remind him.

"Maybe the track has something to do with it," Kevin ventured to suggest, reasoning to himself that if the one occasion when the track *wasn't* the venue for the 400 happened to coincide with the one victory by a late-namer, the two anomalies might not be totally unrelated.

Yet as he introduced the possibility, an eerie sensation crept into him, as if he was violating a taboo of some sort by veering into this area of thought. He couldn't think of any logical reason why it *should* be off limits, but there was no denying the feeling of tension that had taken root. So he forged ahead, somewhat timidly: "Maybe … maybe it wasn't a coincidence …"

"Maybe *what* wasn't a coincidence?" Ackerman asked abruptly.

"Maybe – maybe the change in how the race was set up had something to do with a guy with a 'W' name having an actual chance to win."

"What do you mean, 'having an actual chance?' Are you saying he *didn't* get a fair chance the rest of the time? That really sounds like what you're implying," responded Mr. Ackerman.

"I don't know – I mean, I don't know anything about Waldron, obviously, or how he did the rest of the time. It just seems like –"

"We all run on the same track, kid," the A.D. said, seizing control of the reins of the dialogue. "We all start the race on the same line, and we all finish it on the same line. And if you're the fastest runner out there, you win the race, and if you're not, you don't. What could be more obvious, a more fair competition, than that?"

"But –"

"But what?" blurted the A.D., suddenly sounding agitated and defensive. "You think, what … that there's some kind of … some sort of *conspiracy* going on against the Waldrons, the Wilsons and Washingtons, and – oh, yeah, and the Wilkersons? You guys have trouble doing well in an event, so you think there must be something wrong with the event *itself*. That's the *only* way it can be explained, right? It couldn't *possibly* be that maybe you just haven't worked as hard as some other runner out there, could it?"

"That's not what I'm saying, Mr. Ackerman, no. I'm just saying that the … the law of averages would –"

"Law of averages? In *sports?*" Ackerman let out a little guffaw of disdainful disbelief. "Let's see … would that be the same law of averages that would make short people do just as well as tall people in basketball, if it were really a law? Does it make everything nice and equal like that? If you tried taking on Mike Tyson in a boxing match ten times, does your 'law of averages' say you should expect to beat him in, oh, I dunno, two or three of those ten fights? 'Cause that's what's *fair*? That's your share of things? Well, yeah, that'd be great. There's just one problem: You know as well as I do that you'd get knocked out before you could land a single punch, and that it would happen in ten fights out of ten, in twenty out of twenty, and in a hundred out of a hundred. The same thing would happen to me, and to anyone else here. That's why *he* gets to be the heavyweight champ, and *we* don't!"

"But I'm not talking about trying to –"

"We're all responsible for our own outcomes, Wilkerson – and for knowing what's within our reach, and what isn't. If you don't do well at basketball, do you blame the basket for being too high? No, you work at it, and learn to shoot better – and if you *still* can't hit a shot, maybe you conclude that basketball just isn't your game."

"But if –" Kevin tried futilely to get a word in, but Mr. Ackerman was on a roll, relishing every bit of the teachable moment that had fallen into his lap.

"If you can't hit a baseball out of the infield," he went on, "do you blame the bat, or the shape of the infield? Do you say, 'Well, the shortstop was in the wrong place – otherwise I would've gotten a hit!' Do you do that? No, you practice your swing, you develop your hand-eye coordination, you build your arm strength, and maybe – *maybe* – you'll do better next time."

"Right, Coach, but that doesn't answer the –"

"And *so,* if you have trouble keeping pace with the others in the 400 meters, what do you do? Do you blame the *track*? Is that going to be the excuse? Or how about this: You train harder! You monitor your diet, your exercise, maybe your sleeping habits. You look for flaws in your stride, and work to correct them. You care enough to take the steps that give you a better chance at winning. At least, that's what *I* would suggest! But if that's too much of a burden for you, I guess you can just go around whining that someone must be rigging things to stop you from succeeding."

CHAPTER 3
Marriage and its Side-effects

Kevin had replayed that dialogue with Mr. Ackerman in his mind so many times in the month since it had taken place that he was sure his internal recitations of the exchange were word-for-word accurate. As commonsense as the coach's admonition sounded on the surface, there was still something that didn't feel right about the whole deal. Kevin continued to ponder the oddity of Burt Waldron winning the 400 on the football field, rather than on the track. He thought about his many opportunities to go up against Simon Addison and Billy Lloyd Beech in one competitive setting or another, and his consistent ability to hold his own against them in matters of foot speed, regardless of the distance in question. He thought again about the legendary Max Aaronson and his dominance in the late 1940s. He pored over the collapse of Kendrick Turner and the '86 relay team, and searched for an angle to explain the receding numbers of mid-namers on the 400 meters' component of the Wall of Fame.

Now, as he still sat up in bed, weighing and juggling the wide array of arguments in relation to his determination to try the quarter-mile the next day, another historical anecdote popped into his head. In his eyes, it seemed to poke the most undeniable hole in the determinist position that his mother had invoked that night. It was the story of Helena Antonelli, or, variously, the story of Helena Vardell.

They were, in fact, one and the same. Helena Antonelli, who had gone to Sacred Heart in nearby Springfield, had been recognized as one of the fastest high school runners in Illinois. She even attained some national recognition, earning a "Face in the Crowd" mini-profile in Sports Illustrated. (Kevin only knew of this after the fact; he was just two years old when she graduated.) Numerous colleges had recruited her for their track and field programs – as well as for basketball, in which she also starred.

Miss Antonelli opted for Michigan State University, where her athletic exploits matched the dominance she had shown in high school. She routinely won titles in the 100-meter dash, the 200-meter dash, and the long jump, and earned a starting spot on MSU's varsity basketball squad as a freshman. Then something happened: She met a fellow Spartan named Ronald Vardell, fell in love, and got married toward the end of her sophomore year. Coming from a traditional Catholic background, it was unthinkable that she wouldn't take her husband's name. So she came back for her junior year as Helena Vardell.

Two weeks into the Fall semester, the women's track season began. Suddenly, Mrs. Vardell found herself getting blown out in the 200 by the exact same runners who could never keep up with her in the past. She was losing, in fact, by almost the same margins as her earlier victories. Naturally, people attributed it at first to the well-known relationship between surname alphabetization and aptitude for the 200 – until a Lansing sportswriter named Steven Yablonsky pointed out that Helena Vardell was, biologically speaking, the *same person* as the Helena Antonelli who had run everyone else into the dirt the previous two years.

After coming to grips with the validity of that observation, the locals began to offer other theories, almost all of which centered on the possible effects of marriage on Vardell's performance. Maybe settling into domestic bliss had "dampened her competitive fire." Maybe the obligations of her role as a spouse had diverted her time and energy from the training routines that had served her so well in the past, and falling behind her rivals was the inevitable price of that shift in priorities. Or had she gotten pregnant, and simply wasn't showing yet?

All of this speculation was nipped in the bud when Yablonsky's subsequent column alerted his readers that Vardell's performance in all of her other athletic endeavors hadn't dipped in the slightest. Her times in the 100 and distances in the long jump were as outstanding as ever, in no way fitting the profile of someone who'd forfeited her competitive edge. Later on, his argument was bolstered further when basketball season tipped off and Vardell took her dominance on the court to even higher levels. It was only the 200 where Helena Vardell seemed to have lost that Helena Antonelli magic – nowhere else.

So people scrambled and probed for alternate explanations, suggesting that there was some sort of deep-seeded psychological link between a late name and the tendency to crash and burn in the mid-range races. A fellow sports columnist, Jordan Elgin, drew a comparison to another well-documented phenomenon: There were certain major league baseball players, wrote Elgin, who had consistently been among statistical league leaders during regular-season play, but then would invariably seem to lose their ability to hit on the occasions when their teams made the playoffs or got to the World Series.

These specific players – Elgin cited a few recognizable names, along with the relevant batting statistics – would routinely cruise through the regular season in high style. But bring on the playoffs, and they would inevitably transform from a reliable cog in the team's success to a useless "hole in the offense." They would appear overmatched and uneasy, and their batting averages would plummet to depths they had never exhibited up to that point. So, Elgin concluded, the increased pressure of high-stakes competition clearly affected the comfort level of those specific players in a detrimental way, while other players – quite possibly with less innate ability – could make the transition to playoff action with no trouble.

That, he proclaimed, must be what happens when a late-namer steps up to the starting line of the 200 (or 250, or 400) alongside earlier-named rivals. No one can fully explain it, but it's *there* – an insurmountable "wall" that forms in the psyche of a late-namer and makes the victory impossible. The fact that it even happened to *this* runner – this young superwoman who had demonstrated such superior ability back when she was an early-namer – only served to confirm the intrinsic depth of this characteristic. "There's something in the make-up of certain individuals," Elgin opined, "that brings out the best in them at specific times – and, conversely, the worst at other times."

The only one who didn't seem satisfied with Elgin's theory was Steven Yablonsky. The two sportswriters even engaged in a minor journalistic skirmish for a couple of weeks, challenging each other's arguments in their columns. (Their rivalry, interestingly enough, dated back to their days as track athletes in Southern Michigan.) Elgin suggested that the resistance of his compatriot to make his peace with the ordeal of a fellow late-namer stemmed from misdirected personal frustration, with a sub-component of jealousy: "When Mr. Yablonsky asks, 'Why? Why?' " he wrote, "someone needs to alert him that the answer is 'Y! Y!' "

Yablonsky responded by writing that Elgin "has this strange idea that anyone who disagrees with him must be suffering from 'E-ness' envy."

When Kevin first heard the story of Helena Vardell – around the same time as his exchange with Mr. Ackerman – he went to the library and looked up the articles from twelve years earlier, when the whole debate occurred. He found his own misgivings mirrored, and powerfully reinforced, by Yablonsky's words: Just like Kevin, the Lansing writer couldn't put his finger precisely on it, couldn't pinpoint it in a microcosmic sense – but something was *just not right* about the whole set-up with the mid-distance races. Steven Yablonsky knew it. Kevin Wilkerson also knew it.

In contrast to Yablonsky's reasoned arguments, Jordan Elgin's explanations all seemed incredibly shallow and evasive, like he was grasping at any pseudo-intellectual straw to avoid looking at the obvious.

But what *was* the obvious? What factor, evading the detection of quite literally everybody, was throwing such a wrench into reality as any sane person ought to recognize it? Performance can vary, sure, thought Kevin – but a person can't simultaneously be the fastest runner and *not*-the-fastest runner in a group. And dedicated athletes like Helena Vardell and Kendrick Turner were being established as exactly that by some quirk in the nature of these specific track events. Yet the way of doing things simply perpetuated itself, without objection or question. Not a single red flag seemed to have gone up in reaction to the statistical peculiarities, outside of lone-wolf voices like Yablonsky's.

Suddenly it hit Kevin that he wouldn't have a snowball's chance of winning *any* race if he went into the tryouts on three hours' sleep. So he said goodbye for the night to Simon Addison, Billy Lloyd Beech, Tom Ackerman, Kendrick Turner and Dave Aldrich, Helena Vardell, Steven Yablonsky, Jordan Elgin, and – putting aside the question of whether or not either of them were still alive – Max Aaronson and Burt Waldron.

As he re-adjusted his pillow and lay down on it, he directed his mind toward subject matter as far from the sports arena as possible, trying to settle on a thought that would stand the best chance of putting his internal rumblings to rest. He drifted in quick succession through an outing the previous summer on his cousins' cruiser on Lake Michigan, the scene in *Ruthless People* where Bill Pullman tries to rob Judge Reinhold at the ransom drop, a recent science project that he had gotten back with a perfect 100%, and his girlfriend Jessica's beautiful, welcoming eyes. Settling on the second of these four options, he soon drifted off to sleep with a smile on his face.

CHAPTER 4

Tryouts 1992

The track & field tryouts were a lengthy, involved ordeal at Monroe – so much so that on the designated day, the school made a special arrangement for students who had indicated their interest to be released from their afternoon classes. So by 1:20, Kevin was out on the athletic field along with about 180 other students, A.D. Ackerman, Head Track Coach Eric Shogren, twelve assistant coaches, and about 40 parents who had volunteered to help facilitate the tryouts. A good number of additional parents and other random spectators looked on from the stands.

Because of the potential reaction – not "controversy," exactly, but at least a fair amount of eye-rolling – that Kevin's choice of event might spark, he had deliberately avoided making it public, not even breaking the news to his closest friends. Not wanting to be doused in the ooze of another "be realistic/know your boundaries" lecture, he hadn't called his parents during the day to confirm that he was going ahead with it. The flipside of this secrecy was that not a single one of the spectators was there for the purpose of supporting him.

The only one he had confided in was Jessica Mather, his girlfriend of about seventeen months. Kevin, though initially drawn to Jessica (predictably enough) by her looks, relished their relationship even more at this point for the honesty that characterized it. Jessica was someone he could count on for emotional support and, at the same time, objective input on any relevant subject. He knew that she was not the type to humor him or subordinate her opinions to stroke his ego, and that suited him well. If *she* had been the one to tell him that the 400 meters was a foolish pipe dream – well, he probably would have gone ahead with it in any case, but at least he would have pondered the pros and cons more thoroughly before reaching the same preordained conclusion.

She had commented, when Kevin had raised the prospect a couple of weeks prior to the tryouts, that no, it didn't seem like a very realistic goal. But she added that the long-time absence of any late-namers in the race might work to his advantage. "It'll trip them out when they see you, that's for sure. It'll really mess with their heads. They'll figure you wouldn't have signed up if you didn't have some special strategy to overcome – y'know, the whole history of the thing. Maybe it'll psyche them out, and throw them off their game. As long as you're not going in with any pie-in-the-sky hopes, it's worth a shot." After a brief moment of thought, she added, "Can you imagine what the reaction's gonna be if you *do* win? You'll be a legend, kind of like a … like a pioneer! It's worth it just for that one-in-a-million chance – I mean, uh, not that …" She cut herself off as it struck her that "one in a million chance" wasn't exactly the phrase most likely to boost her boyfriend's confidence.

In that same conversation, she offered to sign up as an interested participant herself, so she could get out of class to come and cheer him on. As much as Kevin would have liked that from a selfish standpoint, they ultimately concluded that it wasn't worth the risk of her getting in trouble for cutting class, should it emerge that she wasn't trying out for anything. So on the big afternoon, she remained in precalculus and he stood out on the field feeling very alone, despite the many familiar faces that populated the crowd.

He had, of course, been humoring his mother the previous night when he promised to "think about it some more." Well, he *had* thought about it some more – almost exclusively, in fact, throughout his morning classes – but there was never any wavering, any question in his mind, as to his ultimate intentions. Even his opening choice of words, "I think I'm gonna try running the 400," was euphemistic. He had already signed up for the event two weeks earlier. He didn't "make a decision" during school, as he had likewise promised. He merely reaffirmed the decision he had already made. He was there to become one of the four runners who would represent Monroe High in the 400-meter dash. That was his agenda, nothing more and nothing less.

His mother was correct in her contention that Kevin could make it onto the track team in any one of a handful of events. There was no question that over a 100-yard stretch, he was one of the two or three swiftest runners in the junior class, a distinction that would probably hold true if you added the seniors to the mix. But his wasn't strictly all-or-nothing cheetah's-burst speed. In contrast to most of the sprinters, he could also pace himself for the long run, comparable to those African hunting dogs that catch their prey by pursuing it endlessly and tirelessly until it keels over from exhaustion (at which point the whole pack jumps on it and rips it to shreds). Years of multi-seasonal soccer had fortified his endurance, and making the team as a distance runner, while nobody's guarantee, was well within Kevin's capabilities.

But Mrs. Wilkerson was right about another thing as well. Kevin often seemed to gravitate toward whatever battle promised to be the toughest. He never liked to take the easy path. Whenever there was a topic-of-your-choice essay in English or social studies, he would deliberately opt to write on a subject that was completely foreign to him, rather than (along the lines of most classmates) picking a subject that was already an area of personal interest and would therefore require far less research. Told that something was beyond his reach, that "something" would suddenly become the front on which a ravenous urge would start to burn within him.

So it was with the 400, which was now set to take place in about five minutes. As Kevin finished stretching and working to release the tension in his joints, he peered around at his fellow contestants, all similarly engaged. He came into brief eye contact with the presumptive favorites, Simon Addison and Billy Lloyd Beech, and then glanced over at Tristan Downing (in his junior year, like Kevin, Simon, and Billy Lloyd).

The remaining entrants consisted of a highly touted sophomore and three seniors. One of the three, Tony Carson, exchanged a casual nod of acknowledgement with Kevin as the two vaguely recognized each other from youth soccer a few years earlier. The other two seniors were not familiar to him at all. Given that they didn't know his name, his presence meant nothing out of the ordinary to them. But the respective looks on Simon and Billy Lloyd's faces both testified to the incongruity of Kevin Wilkerson in this field. Simon colored his curiosity with a hint of disdain, sort of a "What the hell does this clown think he's doing here?" look. Billy Lloyd, on the other hand, didn't look judgmental – just intrigued. Tristan, meanwhile, had been facing a different direction the whole time and hadn't seen Kevin.

The moment had come. "All runners for the boys' 400-meter dash, report to the starting line for your lane assignments!" blared the voice of an assistant coach through a megaphone. Verifying that everyone was present, they set about assigning the lanes in the customary fashion: alphabetically by last name, working from the innermost lane to the outermost.

"Lane one: Simon Addison!" Simon gave a self-celebratory fist pump, as if egging on a crowd that had shown up specifically to watch him, and ran with exaggerated high-knee action to the starting block on the innermost lane.

"Lane two: Quentin Baker!" Quentin, one of the two seniors Kevin had never met, took a pass on the theatrics Simon had offered up, and jogged, business-like, to his spot in the second lane, right beside the first runner. His low-key dignity – specifically, its contrast with Simon's showboating – earned some moderate applause from the crowd. The six remaining runners took note and planned accordingly.

"Lane three: Billy Lloyd Beech!" Billy Lloyd, who at 6'4" stood almost a head taller than Simon and Quentin (and who had treated his middle name as an integral part of his first name since second grade), sauntered over to his position, immediately to Quentin's right.

"Lane four: Vince Cancelliere!" The lone underclassman in the line-up, who had dominated the JV field as a freshman the previous year, made his way to the fourth lane to test himself against the more seasoned track veterans.

"Lane five: Anthony Carson!" As Tony Carson made his way to the track and stood beside Vince, Kevin recollected what he could of the playoff match between their teams about four years earlier, in the under-14 age group. That was the game where he had received a deflected ball just across midfield, gone on a tear down the right sideline, and fed a perfect centering pass to Gilbert Ramirez, who headed it past the diving goalie. Later in the game, Kevin also assisted a score by Mikey Jorgensen. It wasn't enough, though, as Tony's team scored two goals over the final fifteen minutes to win 3-2.

"Lane six: Mitchell Carson!" This was the other complete stranger to Kevin.

"Lane seven: Tristan Downing!" Athletics served as a refuge of sorts for Tristan, who dealt with serious academic struggles. Kevin's awareness of this – not that it was front and center in his mind at this particular moment – had led him at times to reflect, humbly and appreciatively, on his own wider array of options. Here Kevin was, for example, deliberately choosing an event strictly for the personal challenge of it, and the most formidable challenge at that. If he did lose, as everyone (except him and maybe Jessica) expected, he would still wake up the next morning as a solid student with an A-minus average, a supportive home environment (on most fronts, at least), a fulfilling romantic relationship, and a lot of viable options concerning his college education and his life beyond that. What would it be like, he wondered in reference to his schoolmate, to know you *didn't* have those luxuries? To feel like *everything* – your self-respect, your sense of accomplishment, your future prospects – hinged on whether you could win *this one* football game, this one basketball game, this one track meet?

It'd be a totally different reality.

"Lane eight: Kev –" The assistant, not having read the names until that moment, was caught by surprise and stumbled over the announcement. He quickly collected himself and completed the line-up: "Kevin Wilkerson!" As Kevin strode toward the outermost lane and stood there, shoulder-to-shoulder with Tristan, a detectable murmur ran through the pockets of onlookers in the nearby portions of the field and the stands.

Kevin did his best to block out the uneasiness that was taking root among the crowd in reaction to his participation in the 400. He was aided in this effort by an unexpected interruption of the preliminaries: Mitchell Carson left his starting block in lane six and approached the facilitators to argue that Anthony Carson, because he went by "Tony" on a day-to-day basis, should rightfully be alphabetized *after* him and that, correspondingly, the two should switch lanes.

It took about 90 seconds to put the matter (along with Mitchell Carson's fledgling career as a political agitator) to rest. The assistant coach in charge, making clear his disgust over this petty disruption of the proceedings, obligatorily asked Tony what name appeared on his student I.D. card. Tony, more amused than annoyed by his classmate's shenanigans, insisted that it was, without question, "Anthony," and he unhesitatingly offered to run over to the bleachers and retrieve the card from his sports bag. The assistant, itching to move past the non-incident, told Tony not to bother – he'd take him at his word – and then firmly told the still-griping Mitchell to "get your ass back in your lane, before I track down your birth certificate and change your last name to Zuckerman."

Kevin gladly welcomed the opportunity to be something other than the center of attention at this particular moment, and he chuckled under his breath at the irony of runners obsessing over a detail – lane assignment – that everyone tacitly treated as if it bore no relation to success or failure. He thought to himself: *If this were just a concern about propriety, there's no way in hell they'd be making this big a deal out of it. There's something ABOUT these lanes, and this alphabetical set-up – there's something we're all just agreeing not to talk about. That's why Mitchell Carson's raising a stink – there's something PRACTICAL at stake here, and he knows it. Tony knows it, too.*

Now the race was ready to begin. The eight boys assumed their take-off positions, shoulders lowered, bracing their feet against the starting blocks that were installed right alongside each other, from the innermost lane to the outermost. Kevin turned his head, almost imperceptibly, to take a final glance at the seven competitors lined up in a neat row to his left. *I know I'm faster than them,* he reaffirmed to himself. *I'm the fastest runner in the field. There's no question about it.* Almost instantly, though, the conflicting thoughts resurfaced: *But so was Kendrick Turner, and so was Helena Vardell ... NO, Kevin! Get that out of your head!*

He quickly assembled as many urgent, here-and-now imperatives as he could muster up, to prempt his doubts about the integrity of the event. He thought, *Legitimate or illegitimate, honest or rigged, you're not going to win a damn thing if you stumble coming off your block, or if you're out of rhythm, or if you trip over your own feet. Make sure your own house is in order. Don't give them any alibi if things don't go ... if they ... if ... Aaronson starts with TWO "A's," not one, so he would've always been guaranteed that inner lane– STOP THINKING ABOUT THAT! It's got nothing to do with your life, which right now is about winning this race! And you're GONNA win it! You're gonna win it 'cause you've had P.E. with Simon and Billy Lloyd and Tristan and you KNOW you're faster than them. Nobody made this decision for you. You chose to be here. Be ready. When that gun goes off, you –*

BANG!

Had the starting gun sounded even two seconds sooner than it did, it would have knocked Kevin out of the running right then and there. He would have been in the midst of his sea of ruminations, mentally and physically unprepared for the signal. Fortunately, the "be ready" directive in his mind came just at the critical moment, and he quickly assumed a quantifiable lead over the competitors running in the lanes to his left. His stride was sure and consistent, his breathing measured and durable. His arms pumped like pistons, driving him forward.

At the moment he approached the curve at the north end of the track, he held an advantage of somewhere between five and six meters over Simon Addison and Tony Carson, his nearest pursuers. Far from having used up his reserve of energy in building that lead, he felt ready to turn his speed up a notch. Kevin Wilkerson was well on his way to claiming first place in the 400-meter trials.

Then, the next thing he knew, he wasn't.

Kevin's shift in position happened too quickly for him even to detect its occurrence. As the eight runners reached about the thirty-degree mark of the curve in the track, Kevin suddenly found himself trailing the seven competitors he had been leading less than two seconds earlier. As the curve continued, he found himself – and, for what it was worth, the runners in the lanes closest to his own – falling farther and farther behind the leaders. He knew beyond any question, from the physical feel of things, that his pace hadn't slowed. And it hardly seemed conceivable that Simon, Quentin, Billy Lloyd, and Vince had *all*, coincidentally, chosen the exact moment when the track began to curve to kick into some otherworldly high gear. Yet as Kevin continued veering to his left, it looked and felt as if the others were advancing three steps for every one that he took. The more he pushed himself, the greater the distance grew between him and the projected winners.

By the time Kevin reached the 150-degree point of the arc, all considerations about his relative speed in P.E. had been rendered meaningless. The question of which Carson should rightfully have been in the fifth lane was an equally moot point. Tristan Downing would have to search for some other opportunity to enjoy the feeling of success that evaded him in class. All the runners in lanes five through eight were nonfactors; their presence in the event counted for absolutely nothing.

The moment Kevin emerged from the semicircular portion of the track and arrived at the straight segment across from where the race had begun, he began slowing to a passive jog and, within a few more steps, stopped running altogether. There was no purpose, no hint of motivation for him to finish the race – the fact, unacknowledged as it was, was that there hadn't *been* a race. Kevin had come out of the curve trailing by such a ridiculous length that he couldn't discern which specific runner, at that same moment, was beginning to lead the others around the second curve at the south end, on his way to breaking the ribbon.

Glancing indifferently ahead at his fellow also-rans, he saw Mitchell Carson, similarly, suspend his effort and retard his velocity as soon as it became clear that he had no chance to win. Tony Carson and Tristan Downing, in contrast, dutifully completed the course at full exertion – but the result had long been decided by the time they arrived at the finish line.

All these details, along with the question of who had won the race, were not the least bit important to Kevin. He was disgusted beyond words – not with his performance, but over his absolute certainty that he had participated in a complete and total farce. He felt not like the loser of a competition, but instead like the victim of a scam – like a laboratory mouse that had successfully completed a maze, only to find that what had *looked* like a path to freedom at the end of the labyrinth was in fact a deceptive backdrop, a mirage. A set-up. A lie.

A couple of minutes after the conclusion of the race, the order of finish was relayed to the announcers' booth and subsequently rang out from above the bleachers: "We've got the results for the boys' 400-meter dash. First place: Billy Lloyd Beech!" The announcer paused a moment as the spectators applauded and Billy Lloyd, who had relied on his lengthy strides to overtake Simon and Quentin at the last second, waved to them in appreciation.

The announcer continued, "In second place: Simon Addison!" Still clueless as to how his preening prior to the race had been received, Simon pumped a fist in the air and pranced around a bit – before realizing that the applause had died down rather abruptly, and quickly adopting a more reserved stance.

"Third place, and the 400 meters' sole representative of the Class of '92 for the upcoming track & field season: Quentin Baker!" The spectators, gratified to see at least one senior make the team, added a little extra volume to their cheers for Quentin.

The announcer resumed: "Fourth place, Vince Cancelliere! Congratulations, Vinnie, and welcome to the varsity track team!" The young runner reacted with a satisfied smile and two clenched fists, amply pleased with his showing but not wanting to appear full of himself. A sizable cheer, comparable in volume to the one for Quentin, went up in honor of Vince. Kevin, however, heard none of it. He was already two blocks away, determined to put as much distance between him and the Monroe campus as possible.

CHAPTER 5
The Circumference Formula

Jessica's 7th-period Spanish class let out at 3:10. By the time she made the trek across the campus, twice intercepted along the way by friends, and arrived at the dual playing fields, it was around 3:30. Both fields were still packed with athletes, coaches, and spectators. Both were still bustling with activity. Knowing that the 400 tryouts were long since finished – although she didn't yet know the result – Jessica nonetheless headed directly toward the running track, figuring it was where she would stand the best chance to find Kevin.

Once there, she scanned the area three or four times without any luck. Then she caught sight of Tristan Downing, who was now waiting to compete in the long jump at 4:00. Jessica knew Tristan very well through an entirely different avenue. She had been working with him for three months as a volunteer for the school's peer tutoring program. Wanting to know how things had turned out, and what sort of demeanor to expect from Kevin whenever she finally managed to catch up with him, she approached Tristan with arched eyebrows, assuming an inquisitive, *well, how did everything go?* expression.

Tristan was momentarily unsure whether she was asking about his result or Kevin's, but he quickly realized it made no difference. The answer was the same either way. He shook his head and offered a thumbs-down gesture, then nodded in empathy with Jessica's disappointed body language.

"You happen to see where Kevin went?" Jessica asked.

"Nah," said Tristan. "I wasn't payin' attention. I've still got another event to try out for, in about 20 minutes. I'm not sure whether he stuck around for a little while, or he might've went somewhere right after the 400 ended. I really don't know." In any other context, Jessica would have pounced on the improper grammar of Tristan's "might have went," but it seemed like the least important concern under the sun at that particular moment. She gave Tristan a supportive pat on the shoulder, and resumed scanning the field and the stands for Kevin.

An assistant coach, seeing Jessica standing there without athletic gear on, asked her what her business was on the field. When she responded that she was "just looking for someone," he politely alerted her that only competing athletes, trainers, and facilitators were allowed to be there.

Apologizing to the man, and concluding that Kevin might feel similarly unwelcome as an extra body amidst all the official activity, she took one final glance through the bleachers before heading off toward Kevin's house.

Not finding Kevin at home or anywhere en route, and verifying with Mrs. Wilkerson that he hadn't shown up and gone back out, Jessica grabbed her bike from home, took her best guess at the odds, and made her way toward McMillan Creek.

Near the terminal point of a local hiking trail was a serviceable expanse of flat ground along the edge of a stream. A quaint little footbridge over the water, a gentle cascade about five feet in height, and a veritable dome formed by the tangled branches of the surrounding trees combined to give the area a picturesque look and a serene, meditative atmosphere. It was a popular spot for small-scale picnics, with two tables installed by the community for that purpose.

But from the local teenage population's perspective, McMillan Creek had another distinct selling point. There was a naturally formed enclave, perpetually shaded by the trees above, with a steep incline that obscured it entirely from the view of anyone on the approaching footpath.

This established it as an ideal make-out spot, assuming one had the wherewithal and the endurance to transport the requisite mattress pad or thick blanket the full length of the hiking trail. Hidden away in the little nook, one would be – well, more typically, *two* would be – entirely safe from unexpected intrusion.

With little competing noise, it would be easy to hear the sound of any individual or party descending the last stretch of the path toward the picnic area in plenty of time to avoid unwanted exposure. In the early 1980s, many teenage moviegoers in Richardson Park exchanged knowing smiles when they heard the horny students of the fictional Ridgemont High talk about going to "The Point," with the implications of what-you-do-once-you-get-there understood by all. McMillan Creek was "The Point" within their rapidly expanding realm of experience.

Jessica had no remote illusions right now, however, that Kevin might have romantic thoughts on his mind. She knew that the creek also served for locals as a refuge from the frustrations and inequities of daily life. It was a place one could go to "get away from it all," a place where one could be alone with one's thoughts in a setting that offered no element of conflict or corruption. It met that need well enough to be worth the 25-40 minutes, depending on one's walking pace, that it would take to get there.

Bikes were not supposed to be on the hiking trail, and the inevitable sparring between bikers and hikers, revolving around the first group's alleged disregard for safety and the second group's alleged monopolistic urges, occasionally worked its way into the letters section of the local paper. Jessica respected the rules as a general principle, but right now she was in no mood to lock her bike on the rack and drag herself along a predominantly uphill trail, only to find out (if it turned out to be the case) that she had guessed incorrectly as to her boyfriend's whereabouts. Besides, she had no plans to zoom recklessly past any startled pedestrians – and it would probably be pretty sparse, in any case. The weekends were when most foot traffic occurred. So she pedaled past the rack and on toward McMillan Creek. She only encountered two hiking parties along the way, each consisting of two people, and neither in the mood to scold a bicyclist that evening.

Approaching the creek after about eight minutes of riding, she was relieved when she peered down toward her destination and saw Kevin there, sitting atop one of the picnic tables, with his feet on one of its attached benches and his elbows on his knees, staring out toward the woods on the opposite side of the stream.

Jessica was just about to call out to Kevin when he heard the noise of her bike, turned, and saw her approach on the elevated path. He greeted her with a wave, and turned back to the direction he had been facing. Jessica knew not to feel slighted at his failure to crack a smile when he saw her. It was abundantly clear that something was bearing a heavy weight on his mind, something deeper than simply not having won the race. She dismounted from her bike and walked it down the winding descent to the picnic ground. When she reached Kevin, he extended his arm to welcome her. For about a minute, they just sat silently, his arm around her and her head leaning on his shoulder, each of them waiting for the other to say something.

Finally Jessica took the initiative: "So, uh … I didn't hear exactly what … I mean, I know it didn't … well, like, what happened? Did you feel like you were off your game?"

"No!" Kevin responded emphatically, while deliberately looking away to make it clear that he wasn't directing any of his frustration toward her. "Nothing like that; not even close! I was on, all the way. I was kickin' everyone's ass for the first part of the race, and then something happened – it happened right after we started going into the curve. And it wasn't me;

I know it wasn't. I *know* it. I was going just as fast – I'd say even faster – than when I built my lead at the beginning. But there's something about those lanes that doesn't … I mean, I can't figure it out, but there's something that shifts things away from … from a fair set-up. It's not right. It felt like I was having to go twice as far to get to the same place."

Another stretch of silence followed, this one for about ten seconds. Then Jessica spoke up again.

"What if you actually were?" she asked.

"What if I actually was what?" responded Kevin.

"You said it felt like you had to go twice as far to get to the same place."

"Right," Kevin said, in a tone that was half response and half inquiry.

"Well … what if that was actually true? What if the outer lane really *is* longer than the inner ones? I mean, now that I think about it, if I imagine looking down on the track from a bird's-eye view, the outer lane sure *looks* longer."

A matching image of an overhead view of the track instantly surfaced in Kevin's mind, and he could see exactly what Jessica meant. But it was so radical a suggestion – in terms of its implications in relation to the entire history of the race – that he had enormous trouble processing the concept.

He shriveled his forehead. "Wait – you think it's actually longer, *physically* longer? I don't think that could – I mean, how could they do that, set it up like that, without noticing?" Even as Kevin raised this objection, he could feel the geometric reality of the situation quickly assuming an authoritative presence in his brain. In fact, as he began to take it in, Jessica's hypothesis seemed to gain more validity every half-second. But again: How could such a blatant flaw be overlooked, not just by one school or one district, but by an entire sports world? *That* was the part that was impossible to assimilate. "It couldn't be that simple," he continued to protest. "Somebody – *some*where – would've caught it and fixed it, if what you're saying is right."

As he continued to voice his resistant reaction, Kevin could tell from Jessica's pensive look that she was formulating a new, important thought on the matter. She took about five extra seconds after he finished speaking and then asked him, "Kev – what's the circumference of a circle?"

"The distance around it," replied Kevin.

"No – well, I mean, yeah, that's right, but how do you find it?"

"It's pi times the radius squ– no, that's – uh, it's pi times the diameter."

"Good. Now think about where *you* would be running – I'm talking about in the lane you were in – right at the point where the track starts to go into the first curve."

"Got it," said Kevin, still unsure where this math lesson was going.

"Now picture the same thing at the point where the curve ends, where the track straightens back out. In *your* lane, remember. And then, picture a straight line drawn from one point to the other."

"Okay, but I don't–"

"Wait, hold on; just bear with me, babe. Now do the same thing with the points that the guy on the inner – who was on the inner lane?"

"Simon was there. Simon Addison."

"Oh. Okay, so picture where Simon would be at the start and at the end of the curve, and draw the same imaginary line for him – y'know, like if it cut across the soccer field and met back up with the track. Now, think about it: That second line's a lot shorter, isn't it? Like, I'm thinking the distance between his two points is maybe *half* as far as the distance between yours, right?"

"More than half, but yeah, it's definitely way smaller. So you're saying, that would mean if you took … if you …" Kevin's eyes widened, and his mouth fell open. "Oh, you have GOT to be kidding me."

All the pieces began falling into place: Jessica's imaginary lines were the respective diameters of circles, and multiplying each one by a constant value – 3.14, or however far out you took it – wouldn't change the ratio of one to the other. It also wouldn't matter that straight segments were in play in addition to the semicircular components. Those stretches didn't aid or hinder anyone. But regarding the arced portions, the relationship was inescapable: A longer diameter meant a longer circumference, and that meant a longer distance to run. Kevin's absolute worst suspicion now stood confirmed. More accurately, a fact so scandalous that it lay a good distance *beyond* anything he had allowed his mind to suspect now stood confirmed.

In a flash, all the mystery surrounding late-namers and their struggles was eviscerated. Every lane in the 400 yielded a distinct distance from the universal starting line to the universal finish line. Kevin, and quite likely Tristan Downing and Mitchell Carson, had run a 400-meter dash that was actually *longer* than 400 meters. Either that, or Simon, and probably Quentin Baker and Billy Lloyd Beech as well, had run a 400-meter dash that was shorter. His "W" had denied Kevin a fair shot at exactly that.

In the ensuing second, in the rapid-fire manner in which one's life supposedly flashes before one's eyes during a near-disaster, all the other puzzles resolved themselves as well. Max Aaronson, as fast as he probably was, still wasn't necessarily faster than everyone else. He simply never had to face a fair competi-tion. His path to the tape was invariably shorter than those of all the other runners. Conversely, Burt "Football Field" Waldron had won in '42 because it was the only time he, or anyone with a comparably late name, *had* been given an evenhanded opportunity.

The revelations continued. Because lanes for the relay races were assigned by alphabetizing the *lead* runners' names, the Monroe team of '83-'86 had always enjoyed the built-in advantage of a shorter route than their opponents – as long as David Aldrich was the lead runner. When that mysterious computer glitch moved Kendrick Turner ahead of Aldrich, it resulted in the team being bumped from the familiar comforts of the shortest lane and confined instead to the longest – an unexpected impediment that their collective speed couldn't overcome.

The same cause-and-effect explained Helena Vardell's unprecedented struggles in the 200 during her junior year at Michigan State. The star runner hadn't "lost a step" by settling into marriage – it was her surname change that moved her from an inner-lane cakewalk to an outer-lane slog.

The distinction between the events that effectively negated late-namers' chances and those that didn't crystallized in the same second. A late name wouldn't hamper one's chances in the 100-meter dash because there was no curve in the utilized portion of the track.

The longer-distance runs, meanwhile, maintained their legitimacy because runners weren't restricted to an assigned lane. Regardless of where your starting block was, you could navigate your way to a favorable position along the inner boundary of the track, provided you did it safely.

But all of the races that featured the combination of curved segments and confinement to specific lanes amounted to a built-in act of sabotage perpetrated against the outermost runners – and, by extension (and thanks to another unquestioned tradition), against alphabetically challenged athletes.

It followed that the preordained outcomes *would* spiral into a self-reinforcing pattern, wherein late and mid-namers – as Tom Ackerman had indicated – would ultimately shy away from events where they had no chance. Where Ackerman went wrong was in his contention that the lack of success stemmed from a lack of *ability*. Runners in the stigmatized demographics had not "come to terms with their own shortcomings." Nor had the teams' declining interest in them been based on other runners being more highly qualified. Rather, they had merely lost their motivation to participate in a contest that was rigged against them – even if they couldn't pinpoint exactly what form this rigging had taken. Schools improved their odds not necessarily by finding the fastest runners (although, to be fair, speed *was* still an important part of the mix), but by building around runners who would receive a gift-wrapped boost toward the finish line. In this light, everything made perfect sense.

And yet, at the same time, it still made no sense at all. Because, in effect, this discovery implicated *everybody*. It suggested an inability to grasp reality at the most basic, fundamental state, and pinned it on *every single individual* who had ever organized, participated in, officiated, watched, broadcast, or written about these particular events. Even for the lone voices in the wilderness who had caught on to the fact that there *was* a fundamental problem, such as Steven Yablonsky (and Kevin himself), the notion that it could inhere at such a foundational, rudimentary level was too unsettling to take in. That explained why Kevin still found it so hard to swallow, no matter how self-evident the reality was, now that Jessica had alerted him to it. "There's *got* to be something we're overlooking," he said.

"I really don't think so." Jessica's assured tone conveyed that it was way beyond a matter of opinion by this point.

"But that means that for years – hell, for *hundreds* of years – not *one* person's been smart enough to notice this! That's just impossible. I mean, for starters, I'd really like to think that *I'd* be smart enough to catch it. But if this is as clear as it – as it sure seems like it is – I just don't think there's any way it could get by *everyone* like that. You couldn't have something this obvious that not a single person notices."

"Hey," said Jessica, "you know it took 200 years or so before women were allowed to vote, right?"

Kevin was so completely thrown by this seeming non sequitur that trying to factor it into his thought process felt comparable to tying his brain in a knot. Scrambling to find some way to make contextual sense of it, he seized on what seemed like the least-worst interpretation.

"You're ... you're telling me that if they'd let women in on deciding how these races were set up, that one of them would've caught the mistake?"

"No, babe, you're missing the point. That's not what I'm saying."

"Well, I don't – I'm not following the – what *are* you saying?"

Jessica took a few seconds to formulate her thoughts to her satisfaction before explaining, "I'm saying, Kev, that ... that just because something might be totally obvious once it's brought to your attention, and I mean *so* obvious that, like, how-could-anyone-with-a-brain-in-their-head-miss-it – that doesn't mean that something like that can't still go for a long, *long* time without being noticed. It's happened in all kinds of situations all over the world. That was just the first example that came to me. I mean, look – if someone right now stood up and said that women shouldn't be allowed to vote, we'd think he was nuts. Take any one of these guys who've been running in the primary – Jerry Brown, or Bill Clinton, or Paul however-you-say-it – Songus, or Ta-songus, or whatever. Now, what would happen if one of them were to say, like in a debate, that voting should be limited only to men?"

"He'd be laughed off the stage," replied Kevin. "Booed out of the auditorium."

"Right," agreed Jessica, "and he'd be history; his career would be finished. Also, look at the places, today ... you know how there're still a few countries in the Middle East where women can't vote. And we talk about *them* like, 'See how backward they are?' I mean, that's one of the main things we cite when we talk about ourselves being so far ahead of them, so much more 'civilized,' or whatever word we use."

"So you're saying ... ?" Kevin gestured for her to get to the point.

"Well, *there's* something that's so obvious you'd have to be completely out to lunch, totally clueless, not to see it, right? But for the whole first half of our history, that was the normal assumption! That was what everyone, or at least everyone who had any say in things, understood to be true. You didn't hear anyone questioning – well, actually, y'know, there probably *were* people who questioned it, but they were ignored, shoved out of the discussion. The guys we talk about as the most brilliant minds, the most advanced thinkers in history – Jefferson, Madison, Ben Franklin – each one of them was totally at home with the idea that women didn't have the tools, didn't have the common sense, to be trusted with a vote. The genius inventors and scientists, the great writers – none of them saw a problem there. I mean, *there's* an idea that's so obvious that we're like, 'How could anyone not be smart enough to get it?' Well, but there you have it: None of *them* were smart enough to get it. Or again, maybe some of them *did* get it – Mark Twain probably did, and Frederick Douglass – but they couldn't influence things enough to change them. It was just the way things were, just like this is the way things are in this situation."

"I still think someone would've caught this one," said Kevin.

"Force of habit, babe, force of habit – that's the way a lot of things are decided in this world," said Jessica. "When something's a pattern, when it's just accepted, then for most people, the easiest thing is to fall into line, into what everyone says is the way it's supposed to be. It's hard as hell to break through that, no matter how obvious it is – or how obvious it *should* be – that something doesn't add up. That's how it is: Most people just go with things. Either they train themselves not to question anything at all, or they twist their own thinking to justify the set-up they live in, to sell themselves on the idea that it makes sense, somehow."

"So you'd probably have to put the founders having slaves in that same category," offered Kevin, seizing the opportunity to give his mind a little side trip from the imposing weight of its new knowledge.

"There you go – perfect example," agreed Jessica. "Saying, 'we're gonna build a country where all men are created equal,' and at the same time, you're owning other human beings. *That* sure managed to get by them, didn't it? Lotta folks still haven't figured it out."

"I guess they justified it, though, by telling themselves the slaves weren't really, like … full people, not totally human. That's how they handled the contradiction, or … tried to cover it up," Kevin theorized.

"But that's total bullshit," said Jessica. "Not just to us, looking at it today – *they* knew it, too. Deep down, they *had* to know it. 'Cause they had all kinds of laws making it illegal to do stuff like teaching the slaves to read. Right there, you're admitting they're human, 'cause – well, who else but a human *can* learn to read? Frederick Douglass called them on it. Just about a month ago we read this one speech by him where he pointed that out. He totally nailed their asses on it. He said, basically, 'You notice they've never bothered to make a law against teaching a horse to read, or teaching a cow to read. See, they don't need those laws, because no horse or cow is *gonna* learn to read!' So, he was saying, if they're insisting that the Blacks weren't fully human, why would they be worried about them trying to do things that only humans can do? So look, there's another one, right there! Smartest guys in history – we're told – and they couldn't catch something that obvious."

"Well, it's like you said: They twisted their own thinking so the set-up would make sense."

"Right," said Jessica, "and it's not just political stuff where they do that, anyway. How many centuries did it take those medieval doctors to figure out that using leeches to make the patients 'bleed out the disease' wasn't making them any better – that it was killing them, instead? But that was what everyone said was the way to go, so they went with it. They didn't let the facts get in the way of … of tradition. Force of habit, babe. I think we've got a case of that here."

"Well, *I'm* not okay with just 'going with it,' and letting this one go on another hundred years," said Kevin. "If no one else is gonna take the lead on it, I've gotta do something about it."

"It's a big bite to – to bite off," his girlfriend warned.

"Yeah, I know; I'm still not sure how well I'm handling it myself."

"What are you gonna do? Talk to the track coach, or Mr. Ackerman?"

Kevin's mind was instantly flooded with the memory of his jarring exchange with the A.D. back in February. He recalled how contentious Ackerman's tone and demeanor had become at the even the most tentative suggestion of some built-in impropriety in the track. He really wasn't feeling much of an urge to subject himself to another expedient lecture on self-reliance.

"Nah, you know what?" he responded. "I think it's bigger than that. Ackerman runs the department as far as the school goes, but I dunno if he really has any pull. And Shogren definitely doesn't have any say in things. He'd be even further down the ladder. I think I need to go to the top, talk to Mr. Paige."

"For real? You think he'd even make time for an issue involving sports?" asked Jessica doubtfully.

"Maybe not, but this – I need to bring it to someone's attention who's up high, who's got the power to change things … if he can see the point we're making."

"We?"

"Well, the point *I'll* be making, but I'll give you the credit for catching what the problem was."

"Umm … not sure I want that …" muttered Jessica.

"Okay, well I wasn't tryin' to – I mean, let's not get hung up on – I mean, whatever. You want me to say I figured everything out on my own?"

"Just don't make it sound like you're there 'cause *I* sent you."

"No, of course not – they'd know better anyway. I'm the one who's all into sports to begin with."

Lurking beneath this casual banter about shared versus solo credit was the mutually recognized reality that this was a far bigger deal than reporting to the principal that one of the drinking fountains wasn't working. Kevin, were he to proceed, would be embarking on an all-out challenge to what had been considered eternal common sense by the entire establishment. He would be informing them that they were all oblivious to the physical fact that had been staring them in the face for decades.

Jessica, thinking on her feet as always, steered the subject in a new direction. "There's two things we need to do first, before you go talk to anyone," she said.

"What?" Kevin asked.

"First, we need to actually go and measure the lanes. Between our dads, we should be able to scare up enough measuring tape." Mr. Wilkerson and Mr. Mather were construction workers on the same crew. In fact, the two teenagers had originally become closely acquainted through a company picnic, rather than at school. "Whatever meeting you set up, you gotta go into it *knowing* that your facts are right. There should be a time over the next few days when the track's not being used. We can stretch the tape down the middle of the outer lane – we need the cloth type, not the metallic, so we can curve it. And we'll need to weigh it down with rocks or something, so it won't blow away. We'll get a sense of how long that one is, and then we'll go to the inner one and do the same thing."

His girlfriend's enthusiasm, the vicarious charge she was clearly getting over an issue that would've meant nothing to her life if not for his connection to it, brought the first hint of a smile to Kevin's face since the tryout. "Okay, I'll gather up as much as I can," he said, "and we can go back there on … maybe on Thursday evening, when the girls' soccer practice is over. It's usually pretty empty – does that time work for you? And what's the other thing?"

"The other– yeah, that's cool," she said. "The other thing is the tough one. You gotta have some idea of what to *do* about it. They're not gonna listen for long, or be too receptive, if you just say, 'Hey, I discovered this problem; you guys need to fix it.' You're saying it's not fair, then you need to think of some way they could *make* it fair. You can't just throw it all in Paige's lap and walk away."

Suddenly, and not coincidentally, Kevin felt very tired – not physically so much as mentally. "Let's catch our breath on this. Gimme a day to think about it," he said, as if addressing an authority figure who had just given him an assignment. "By the time we connect on Thursday, I'll come up with something. Let's take a little break from this."

Hearing this suggestion, and reading the visual cues as well, Jessica nodded, hopped down from the table, and began walking over to where she had leaned her bike against the incline. Kevin followed, and then stopped abruptly. "I think I might have an idea," he said. "Tell me if this sounds too crazy."

Jessica nodded inquisitively.

"What if ... what if you adjusted the finish lines to make equal distances for everybody? You could measure it real precisely, do the math, and then move the finish line for each lane farther back toward the curves – y'know, like, the farther out the lane is, the closer the line would be ..." He gestured with his hand to indicate an incremental staggering of the finish lines. But Jessica was already shaking her head.

"It'd be a disaster," she said. "It wouldn't work. You wouldn't be able to tell who finished in first place, 'cause you'd have to be watching all these different lines simultaneously. I mean, you could have, I guess, computerized sensors or something that would tell who won, but nobody would like it. There'd be all kinds of controversy, arguments over who got to their line first."

"Yeah, you're right," he said. "Well, okay, just a first try ..."

Once they zigzagged back up to the hiking trail, Jessica climbed on her bike and pedaled slowly enough for Kevin to jog alongside her. It was dark by the time they arrived back at the small parking lot at the head of the trail. Unable to follow his own advice, Kevin had been tossing prescriptions of all varieties around in his head throughout the trip back.

"How about this ..." he finally ventured. "You're totally right; every runner has to finish on the same line. But ..."

"But what?"

"But ... it might be okay if we didn't all *start* on the same line."

CHAPTER 6
The Principal's Principles

Allen Paige, the principal of Monroe High, was a man of short stature and what could be characterized as unimposing looks. In his adolescence and early adulthood, he had borne the further burden of a nasal, high-pitched speaking voice, which he had spent years conscientiously modifying to avoid ridicule. In summation, he fit the conventional image of a nerd – although the term wasn't yet in common usage during the early 70's, when those traits were most in evidence. Sharing his name – to the ear, though not on paper – with eventual NFL Hall-of-Famer Alan Page only exacerbated his social struggles at that stage. It didn't help that Allen Paige spent those years in Chicago and Alan Page played for the rival Minnesota Vikings. (The association began to feel more agreeable to the young educator when the all-pro lineman was traded to the Bears in 1978 – and even more so when he later segued from the football field into the legal profession, ending up on the Minnesota State Supreme Court.)

Mr. Paige was not the most personable of administrators; he had ascended to the leadership of Monroe High (from his origins as an English teacher) mostly on the basis of his organizational efficiency and his financial acumen. Vice Principal Kay Holland and Academic Dean Murray Ingerman handled most affairs involving students, and Kevin had a good rapport with both of them. But the magnitude of his proposal was such that he knew it would ultimately require the backing of higher authority – someone whose reach could potentially extend (as this matter extended) beyond the Monroe community.

"I really don't have too much time to deal with this – uh, this – well, I couldn't quite figure out *what* you wanted to talk about when Mrs. Gowland relayed your message to me," said Mr. Paige when Kevin was ushered into his office and sat in the chair facing his desk. "You're saying – I'm just not clear on this. You're saying there's a problem with our track? Something's wrong with our running track?"

"Well, no, sir, not *our* track specifically," said Kevin. "There's, like, a problem with … with *the* track. I mean with all of them. With the whole arrangement of the – of some of the running events. There's a flaw in the system, a real basic one that I think needs to be looked at."

"Well, uh … good thing you brought it to our attention," said Mr. Paige with a feigned tone and expression of serious concern. Then, reassuming a look more befitting his genuine reaction – total bewilderment, mixed with impatience – he inquired, "What is it that you're talking about?"

"Well, sir, you know how we start all the races at the same starting line…"

"Right," said Mr. Paige, wearing a look that asked, in effect, what could be less controversial than that.

"And we all run toward the same finish line…"

"I don't have time for you to bring me up to date on the obvious, Mr. Wilkerson. Please get to the point."

"Well, the problem is, with certain events – the 400 and 200-meter dashes, the 250 hurdles, and a couple of others – that creates an uneven set-up. The runners aren't going the same distance, so the result isn't legitim–"

"What do you mean, 'aren't going the same distance?' " interrupted Mr. Paige. "Everyone starts on the same line and finishes at the same line. How does that add up to people not going the same distance? I don't get what you're trying to say."

"Well, Mr. Paige, it has to do with the curves in the track – with the fact that it's an oval. A curve makes the outer lanes longer than the inner ones; it's a bigger arc on the outer part of the track. That's why the problem doesn't come up on the 100 meters – it's short enough that you can run it using just a straight portion of the track. And in some of the longer runs, you're not restricted to a specific lane. So with those events, every runner has the same distance to travel, and the fastest runner over that distance wins the race. But with–"

The principal cut in: "The fastest runners in the 400 and in the 250 win those races too. That's what a race *is*. That's kind of the point."

"No, but sir, in the 200, 250, and 400 distances, whoever's put in the outer lane – in any of the further-out lanes – is being forced to run a longer path to the finish line. And since they assign the lanes by alphabetizing your last name, that means certain people aren't being given a fair chance."

" 'Certain people?' Can you be more specific, please?"

"Well, sir, doesn't it seem strange that nobody with a last name starting with a letter that's late in the alphabet *ever* wins the 400, or the 200? But they – we – do just fine in other racing events? That doesn't suggest that something's not quite right about the set-up?"

"Getting a little greedy, aren't we?" countered Mr. Paige. "You just acknowledged that there are all kinds of events where you have no problem competing. But the fact that there's just this *one* – or a couple – that you *don't* do well in, that tells you there must be something wrong with the event itself? That it must be rigged against you?"

Kevin was suddenly noting the discomforting similarity between Mr. Paige's choice of words and the lecture he had received from Mr. Ackerman. At the very moment this realization was dawning, things turned almost surreal, as the principal, right on cue, launched into the athletic director's choice comparison: "Think about it, Kevin – you don't see a whole lot of five-foot-two guys in the NBA, do you? But do you hear them whining, 'it's not fair; the basket's too high?' Or complaining that they're not getting the same 'fair chance' to dominate as Michael Jordan?"

Kevin couldn't believe what he was hearing. *What is WITH these guys? Do they all get handed the same script or something? And what makes them so damn edgy about this? They all go from zero to sixty in a half a minute when you bring this up! What the hell's going ON around here?*

"No, you *don't* hear them saying that, do you?" Mr. Paige answered his own question. "Now, why is that? Well, see, maybe they know something we don't! Maybe it occurs to them that they do well in some areas, and aren't so strong in others, and that they should focus on competitions where they have a chance. They do just fine as jockeys, or as – as – uh, in gymnastics. *And*, if they work hard enough, and perform well enough, they can make it in basketball, too – like that Bugsy guy in Charlotte."

Had he not been so flustered, Kevin would've pounced on Mr. Paige's inadvertent reinforcement of his point: You could cite a real-life example of a five-foot-three man playing pro basketball quicker than you could find a late-namer who'd won the quarter-mile. By this point, though, Kevin was engaged in a massive struggle just to keep his mind properly oriented. He was stunned by how quickly the dialogue had drifted a mile off topic. Desperate to steer it back to the central issue, he opted to dial back the element of his protest that could be perceived as "playing the victim" and returned, instead, to the strictly technical aspects of the argument.

"Sir, I didn't come here to talk about basketball, and I'm not here to complain about not winning a race. I'm trying to help make the race a real measure of – I mean, something that really tests people over the same distance. Right now, we don't have that. When the track goes around a curve, the outer lanes stretch longer. They're forcing certain runners to go *farther* than 400 –"

"That's an optical illusion, Mr. Wilkerson. You're making assumptions because it appears that way – because the outer lane *looks* longer. But you don't understand as much as you think you do, and you're not considering the implications of this, umm … this accusation you're making. You're implying that the organizers of these athletic contests actually throw people into an unfair set-up and then go around pretending they haven't."

"With due respect, sir, that's exactly what *has* been happening. Not just here, but everywhere, and for years, even for decades. I had trouble coming to terms with it myself – I mean, you're right; it seems too far-fetched to think that they could just overlook this for so long. But I went ahead and measured some of the different lanes with cloth measuring tape, and they're not the same length. They're not even close."

"Oh, you *measured* them," said Mr. Paige in a tone of completely unfettered sarcasm. "Well, that should put the whole matter to rest. Because of course your methods were scientific; you know you couldn't *possibly* have recorded the lengths with anything less than total accuracy."

The discourteous manner of Mr. Paige's speech caught even the principal himself by surprise. Becoming suddenly aware that he wasn't setting the best example of civil discourse for his student, he took a moment to collect his thoughts, and tried to make sure that his next statement sounded more like an actual attempt to engage in dialogue.

"Okay, Wilkerson," he said, "let's assume, for just a moment, that what you're saying is true. Let's grant the benefit of the doubt that there's this glaring, blatantly unfair arrangement that somehow evaded the detection of everyone in history until you discovered it …"

"Actually, sir, it was Jessica Mather who figured it out first." As Kevin said this, it sunk in how thoroughly the whole discussion had been turned upside-down. Citing Jessica's contribution should rightfully have stood as the ultimate act of chivalry, as the honorable determination to give credit where it was due. But in the context of where this meeting had gone, it sounded instead as if he were trying to shift the blame.

"Fine, until … until Jessica Mather discovered it. But you're the one bringing it here, and telling me to fix a problem that no one *knew* was a problem until this moment. The question is, what do you suggest we do about it? Do we need to scrap the oval tracks and construct straight ones for all the races?"

"Sir, no, of course not – I know that's not feasible. I'm not gonna suggest something ridiculous like that."

"Well, then, what? Is it about breaking tradition, and giving *you* the inner lane now and then, if you're convinced it gives its occupant such an unbeatable edge?"

"No, I'm not asking for that either, sir. I'm not looking for an unfair advantage over anybody. I just want it to be an honest competition – even if I'm not involved with it at all."

"Well, *do* you have any ideas as far as that goes? You've brought up this supposed problem; are you prepared to help look for a solution to it?"

"Actually, sir, I do have an idea. We could ... I mean, the organizers ... what they could do is alter the starting positions for each runner, to compensate for the difference in how long the lanes are."

An onlooker, going by the expression on Mr. Paige's face, would just as likely assume that Kevin had said, "Oober-gloober the pencil sharpener with a green piffle-bump's nose hairs."

"Come again?" said the principal.

"What I'm saying, sir, is that – okay, let's say that, once we measure the distance from the starting line, where it is right now, to the finish line, we find out that in the second lane, the distance is, say, 4.3 meters longer than it is in the first lane, the inside one. So you'd make up for that by having the runner in that lane start the race 4.3 meters further up, so they'd end up having the same distance to go to the finish line. And then so on, with each lane: The closer to the outside you'd be, the further ahead your starting block would be, so that all the distances would even out." Out of his pocket, he fished a small diagram he had prepared and showed Mr. Paige a depiction of staggered starting lines.

"*That's* what you came up with?" asked Mr. Paige in disbelief.

"Sir, it would work, once people understood why it was being arranged that way. Every runner would have a chance to–"

"I need to be the one speaking right now, Wilkerson," interjected the principal, "before this gets out of hand. Now, I just need to ask you: When you were formulating this idea of yours, did you ever stop and consider how absolutely *ridiculous* an arrangement like that would look? Did you think about what a laughingstock someone would be if they suggested that certain runners need a head start in order to compete, and certain others need to be penalized, because some folks aren't getting enough wins?"

"That's not what I'm suggesting, Mr. Paige."

"Whattya mean, it's not what you're suggesting?! You just suggested it! You said the runners in the outer lanes should get their starting positions bumped forward – I was *here*; I *heard* it."

"But that's not a head start, sir, technically, because– "

"How is it not a head start, if you're starting ahead? That's exactly what it is! And how are you going to explain to the runner on the inner lane – not to mention the people coming to see the race – that he has to start *behind* everyone else, because otherwise he's going to be too dominant? How is that fair to him?"

"Sir, it's fair because it's – the guy on the – he's not dominating because he's running faster; he's dominating because his path to the finish line is shorter!"

"But is that *his* fault? Did *he* design the track? Did he get to decide what his last name was going to be? Why does he have to be punished for that? Don't you see what you're proposing? You're trying to manufacture an equal outcome by changing the rules, instead of by improving your own effort!"

"Not an equal outcome, sir; just an equal chance. That's all I'm asking for. I mean – okay, you said, 'You don't criticize the basket for being too high.' But if I got in a basketball game where the other team got to shoot at a regular ten-foot basket, and my team had to shoot at, like, an eighteen-foot hoop, don't you think I'd have some cause to complain?"

"Yes, you would. Absolutely, you'd be entirely justified. But you're overlooking one thing: Nobody would *do* that, Wilkerson. People set up sports events so they can find out who gives the best performance in a competitive setting. And they want those results to be accurate and meaningful. Nobody's interested in a competition that's set up unfairly."

"I'm not accusing anyone of doing this deliberately, sir. I'm leaning toward the thought that it was just, like, an oversight, back when they first got these things going. Somehow, it got by them at the start, and then they just stuck with it through force of habit."

"And that's been *okay* for people, hasn't it? I mean, somehow, people have managed to observe this exact arrangement for a long time now without it jumping out as some unbearable violation of their sense of fair play. Doesn't that kind of tell you something? Do you realize you're crediting yourself with being the *first individual in history* to notice this flaw in the system – something that managed to elude everyone else? If it was as clear as you're insisting that this was a rigged game, don't you think we would have *heard* something before now? Wouldn't we have heard somebody, somewhere, voicing some opposition to it?"

Kevin, feeling as though he was about to keel over from pure exasperation, said, "Sir, I hope I'm not being disrespectful here, but I think you'd have to agree that your reaction to *my* bringing it up hasn't been exactly, y'know ... receptive. My guess would be that it probably *has* been brought up, but whenever it has, the person who saw the problem just got shouted down, or ignored, or outvoted or something, and they ended up deciding it wasn't worth the hassle. Sir, most people don't like to change things. They're real ... resistant to looking at things in new ways. But that doesn't mean they can't still be wrong sometimes. A lot of things were just accepted for a long time before someone pointed out that there was ... I mean, someone had to tell people that that the sun didn't go around the Earth, or that women should be allowed to vote. It's gotta start somewhere."

"Gosh – just when I thought we couldn't come off any more arrogant than we were sounding already," said Mr. Paige. "So it's starting to look like it's all about securing our place in history; is that it? Aristotle, Susan B. Anthony, Kevin Wilkerson ..."

"Mr. Paige, I'm not trying to put myself– wasn't it Copernicus, sir, not Aristotle?"

"Don't be a smartass!" shouted Mr. Paige, as Kevin made a mental note not to waste goodwill – especially when it was in such minimal supply – by trying to prove points in peripheral subject areas.

Mr. Paige, determined to wrap up the visit with a hint of the civility that had evaded him throughout its entire duration, resumed speaking. His tone was quiet, yet firm. "Now listen, Wilkerson," he said. "I have responsibilities running this school that I have to get back to, and those responsibilities *don't* include telling a century's worth of athletes and coaches and judges and sports fans that they don't know an honest competition when they see one. My suggestion to you is this: If you can take even a tiny percentage of the energy you seem prepared to throw into this crusade, this need to convince everyone that they're incapable of seeing reality, and instead put that energy into your own determination to improve out there on the track – I feel pretty confident in saying it'll result in a big payoff for you. That's how the real winners in history have done it. When Jackie Robinson ..."

Oh, give me a break, thought Kevin.

"... broke in with the Brooklyn Dodgers, he faced a world of adversity, a lot more going against him than you could ever even begin to imagine. But he didn't complain; he didn't run to the authorities and cry, 'it's not fair!' He toughed it out. He fought through that adversity. He performed at such a high level that no one could deny him his just due. Because he understood one thing – he understood that *life* isn't always going to be fair."

This from the guy who, five minutes ago, was freaking out at the notion that we might even THINK of doing something "unfair" to the guy on the inner lane, Kevin marveled to himself. A few seconds later, the additional thought occurred to him: *And wait a goddamn minute – isn't that EXACTLY what Jackie Robinson's famous for? Going to the authorities and telling them the shit wasn't fair?*

"You do the best with what you've got. Sometimes you win, sometimes you lose, and you learn to handle it either way. This is a free country, not a communist system. That means a lot of things, one of which is that we're all responsible for our own outcomes." Once again, Kevin felt the twinge of a familiar script. "That's part of the reason you hear people speaking in sports metaphors so often. It's because these sports events hold up a mirror to the way things work in our society in general. In most arenas, somebody's going to come out on top, and it'll be because that individual cared enough, and worked hard enough, to get there. If someone wants everything to be guaranteed equal and balanced, they should go to Russia or someplace where that's the basic line of thinking behind the system."

"Well, Mr. Paige, I hear you, sir, but I'm still not gonna – I'm – wait, but didn't they just switch *away* from being communist over there?"

"This meeting is over!" declared Mr. Paige, as Kevin made a mental note to do a better job remembering his previous mental note.

CHAPTER 7

Wake-up Call at Greenfield

Until he was thrown off course by the revelation that his principal had apparently missed the recent dissolution of the Soviet Union, Kevin had been on the verge of declaring that his commitment to fairness was not going to be derailed by one discouraging encounter. As it stood, he left Mr. Paige's office in a galvanized state, more convinced than ever that his assessment and prescription were logically sound and that it was strictly a matter of finding the right set of ears to listen to his argument.

It took just a few days, however, for him to notice his energy waning in relation to the issue. Within a week he had to admit to himself that he was feeling stifled, not out of any misgivings about the cause's validity but by the simple practical matter of where to go next. He began to wonder whether there might be some mysterious combination of genetic traits that made one a successful activist – whether, had he been someone else, he would have known by pure instinct what avenues to pursue and what tactics to use.

He also had to bear in mind that this stretch of his academic career – the concluding months of his junior year – stood to be the most crucial in relation to colleges' assessment of his applications. He knew that right now was when he could least afford to let any sort of political engagement sidetrack him from his practical imperatives.

So he decided to resume his efforts after the semester ended, when he could delve into the logistical demands without sacrificing his chances of landing a scholarship. Even as he reaffirmed his intentions, though, he had no real clue how to map out a game plan.

In fact, the issue might have been laid indefinitely to rest, except that about three weeks after his meeting with Mr. Paige, Kevin was working on his trig homework at about 5:30 on a Monday evening when the phone rang.

"Hello?"

"Hey, Kevin – that you?"

"Yeah? Who is it?"

"It's Billy Lloyd."

"Oh! Uh … hi! What's … what's goin' on?" Kevin and Billy Lloyd Beech had always been on respectful, casually friendly terms, but had never had any real social connection. Though both would certainly be ranked among the elite athletes at Monroe, they specialized in different team sports (Kevin in soccer, Billy Lloyd in basketball), which reduced their opportunities to bond within one arena or the other. The upshot was that Kevin had no remote idea why Billy Lloyd was calling him.

"I gotta talk to you, man – it's pretty important," said Billy Lloyd. "You got any wheels?"

"Uh … I'm pretty sure I can borrow my dad's truck," responded Kevin. "What, you wanna meet somewhere?"

"You know Pierre's Deli? How close are you to that?"

"It'll take me about seven or eight minutes. Is that good for you?"

"How about I see you there in fifteen."

"Okay, sure," said Kevin, whose curiosity had increased tenfold during the eight or nine seconds that it had taken to arrange the specifics of the meeting. As marginal as their association was, Kevin had been around long enough to know one thing about Billy Lloyd Beech: He was a serious person. If he said that the matter he needed to discuss was "pretty important," it wouldn't turn out to be something trivial – much less any kind of prank.

Kevin put his shoes on, grabbed some spending money, retrieved the key from his father, pulled out of the driveway, and made his way down the road toward the little hub of shops and business that included Pierre's Delicatessen.

Although it had only taken him ten minutes, not fifteen, to get to Pierre's, Kevin saw Billy Lloyd's lanky, towering figure already waiting at one of the six tables when he walked in the door. Billy Lloyd gestured toward the counter.

"Grab whatever you want," he said. "I got it."

"You sure?" Kevin responded with a quizzical expression.

"Go for it."

Still totally mystified as to the agenda of the meeting, Kevin got a turkey sandwich on whole wheat bread and a bottled water. From the table, Billy Lloyd waved to get the clerk's attention and gave him an I'll-take-care-of-it gesture, which the clerk acknowledged. Kevin put the food on a tray and made his way over to join his schoolmate. "Thanks a lot, man, 'preciate it," he said. "So what's up?"

"I wanna find out about this – this, uh – whatever the thing is that you're trying to do connected with the track, and the 400. Something happened, and, uh … I wanna get involved."

This was a significant bit of news to take in so quickly, especially given the truncated status of Kevin's own advocacy. Kevin stammered over his response, and didn't even think to ask the obvious question of how Billy Lloyd had come into the knowledge of his protest. "Well, that's – I mean, that's great, umm … I appreciate it an' everything; it's just that – well, I don't know that I could say *I'm* really 'involved' in it right now. I've kinda dropped the ball on it, at least until I can figure out some other angle. I talked to Ackerman and Mr. Paige, and both are like talking to a brick wall; nobody wants to listen. They just go into this freaked-out, circle-the-wagons mode the minute you bring up– but wait, you said 'something happened.' What happened? What's the situation?"

"The track's not even," said Billy Lloyd. "The way it's set up, you don't have a fair race. That's what you've been saying, right? You were trying to tell them that the outer lanes are longer than the inner ones – literally, like physically longer, is that right?"

"Yeah, that's the issue," confirmed Kevin. "It's not even close, from one lane to the next – I went and measured them. But again, nobody … well, wait a minute. How did you know I brought any of this up? Who told you?"

"Nobody told me, not directly," said Billy Lloyd. "I overheard Ackerman talking to Coach Shogren about it. I was just nearby, stretching before practice, and I heard him tell Shogren that you'd gone to see Mr. Paige. I was kinda curious, so I stayed close and tried to pick up as much as I could. He sounded pretty pissed off – almost like he thought you were accusing him of something. I couldn't quite piece the whole thing together, from what he was saying right there. But then we had a meet at Greenfield on Friday, and I figured it out."

"Yeah? What – how – tell me what happened."

"So we're there, right, and we're waiting to get our lane assignments for the 400. And when the names were called, you won't believe what happened: The Greenfield line-up was *all* A-names – all four of them. There was an Atkins, an Archerfield … umm … I forget the other two, but they were all A's."

"Damn … so you ended up running in the farthest lane to the outside," Kevin offered in conclusion.

"Well, no – almost," clarified Billy Lloyd. "Cancelliere was in the eighth lane; I was in the seventh. But it didn't matter. I was running even with all the other guys until we went into the curve, and then I started dropping behind by this crazy distance – but I know I wasn't going any slower. By the time we came out of the curve, Simon and a couple of the Greenfield runners were, like, a mile ahead. And I know Simon's not that much f– what am I talkin' about; he's not faster than me at all! I'm faster than him!"

"Right," said Kevin, "but until this meet, you were always running the 400 just a lane or two away from him. You never had that big a distance between you – between where Simon started and where you did."

"That's right," said Billy Lloyd, "and we always finished right around even with each other. But the moment I get moved out a few lanes, he's suddenly twice as fast as me?! That doesn't make any kind of sense. So I knew something was wrong with the set-up. I mean, it felt like I … like I was …"

"… like you were having to go twice as far to get to the same place," volunteered Kevin.

"Yeah …" said Billy Lloyd, whose look somehow managed to express both shock and relief at Kevin's acute awareness of his ordeal.

He picked up his story: "So here's what happened afterwards. The whole bus ride back to Monroe, I was feeling like shit. I felt like – not just disappointed, but more like somebody had conned me out of something. It was that kind of feeling. I felt, like, *violated.*"

Kevin nodded, affecting an empathetic expression that said, *I've been there, pal, I've been there.*

"But that's not why I'm here," said Billy Lloyd. "It's what I started thinking about later on that night."

"What was that?"

"Well, I knew that my loss wasn't legit, and at first, that's what was eating at me. But the more I tripped on it, and turned it over in my head, it started to sink in that there were races I won, too – and they had the same set-up. So that meant *they* weren't real either! And that felt even worse, when it hit me that I wasn't winning those races any more legitimately than I'd lost this one. *None* of it was a real measure of anything. What kind of sense does that make?"

"Somehow, they've managed to make sense of it for a long time," said Kevin wearily.

"Yeah, but that doesn't work for me. I don't want a win to just be handed to me – the hell with that. I'm a damn good runner, and I should be able to beat the other guys over a fair distance, on an even playing field."

Kevin, making a strong effort to sound conciliatory rather than judgmental, said, "I hear you, man, and … and that's great. Funny, though

… it took being on the other end of the stick to put two and two together, didn't it?" As Billy Lloyd nodded sheepishly, Kevin continued, "I mean, you know from P.E., and other situations, that Simon Addison's not twice as fast as you. But you know the same thing about both of you guys, and how fast you are, in relation to *me*. You've had all kinds of experience with how fast I can run – and Tristan too, while we're at it. So … how'd it seem believable that we'd both finish a mile behind you, back at the tryouts?"

Billy Lloyd, momentarily looking about as small as a six-foot-four teenager could look, peered off into space and mumbled through clenched teeth, "I just told myself you had an off day."

Kevin responded with a you-should've-known-better look, which was promptly met by an I-know-I-deserved-that countenance from Billy Lloyd.

"I know, man, I know. It's – it's all true; you're right about all of it," he acknowledged. "It should've been something that made me say, 'Hey, wait a minute,' but I just kinda didn't think about it. I guess it was easier just to go along with things."

Kevin's eyes widened a bit as he thought to himself, *Damn. My girlfriend should be a freakin' psychology professor.*

Trying to steer the storyline back in a direction where he could once again position himself in a more admirable light, Billy Lloyd said, "But that ends now, all of it. I'm not gonna be part of a rigged game. Simon and Quentin might be okay with it, but I'm not going for it. So now, the question is, how do we fix it? I heard Ackerman say you had come up with some sort of idea, but what I got was all second-hand, and I'm guessing he probably wasn't talking about it in a … in an honest way. I never really knew what the suggestion was."

Laying aside the fact that he had tabled his efforts for the time being, Kevin explained the concept of staggering the starting positions as a countermeasure against the lane disparities.

Billy Lloyd wrinkled his brow. "That'd look pretty weird," he commented. "I mean, I guess I can see where it does what it's supposed to do and everything, but you'd have a hard time selling people on it."

"I know," said Kevin, "but I have this sense that – or, well, I *had* this sense, until I talked to Mr. Paige – that once people had the situation explained to them, they'd make the adjustment. I mean, people want a fair competition. They just haven't quite caught on that … that this is what it would take to create one."

Although Billy Lloyd's facial expression still didn't suggest complete acclimation to the idea, he said unhesitatingly, "Well, if that's the way it's gotta be, that's what we'll have to go for."

As much as Kevin would have liked to feel his momentum re-energized on the spot by Billy Lloyd's matter-of-fact resolve, his better instincts suggested a reality check. "But I've already tried," he said. "I mean, I'm not sure who else to go to, or whether anyone's gonna listen. People are so invested in the way things have always been, and I don't know if the reaction's gonna be any different than it was with Ackerman or Paige."

"We'll talk to Ed Markbreit," said Billy Lloyd.

"Who the– who's that?" Kevin asked, even as the last name sounded vaguely familiar.

"He's the head commissioner of inter-school sports for our district. He's a pretty big mover & shaker; he's got the power to get changes made where they need to be. He's seriously, like, y'know, 'in there.' I don't – I've never verified whether it's true or not, but I've heard he's a cousin of an actual NFL ref."

THAT'S where I know the name from, thought Kevin.

"And he's a good guy," Billy Lloyd went on. "If he sees that this situation's gotta be looked at, he'll get things rolling. Guaranteed."

"Wait – you're going too fast for me. What's our connection to this guy? What's our in?"

"My dad. He and my dad have known each other for–"

"Oh, man, that's right, I forgot! Your dad's the president of the school board or somp'm like that, isn't he?"

"Well, not the president right now, but he's on it – he had a term as the president, back when my sister was a senior. They rotate every couple years. But he's built up a lot of really good connections, and he can get Markbreit to listen to us."

Billy Lloyd paused for a moment, and then resumed in a very serious tone, "It's gotta mainly come from *me*, though. You're gonna have to bring me completely up to speed on the whole deal, so I could explain it just like it was my original idea, and then I'll make the pitch."

Kevin was a bit thrown off by this stipulation – not out of any sense of territoriality, but purely because he didn't understand the reasoning behind it. "Umm, alright, I … uh … I'm okay with that, but why? Why do you say it has to be you?"

"Two reasons," said Billy Lloyd. "One is, he knows me. And like I said, he's an honest, upright guy, and he'd credit you with making the point if you made it – but he'll be more receptive to it coming from me at the beginning, 'cause he knows I wouldn't come at him with just any bullshit. If my dad tells him I have something he needs to listen to, he'll take me seriously. It won't be just some stranger off the street."

Kevin gave an understanding nod, guessing that the second point would be the more important reason.

"But it's the second point that's the more important reason. Coming from me, he'll know there's no 'personal gain' angle." Billy Lloyd made air quotes as he spoke. "Think about it: My last name starts with a B, right? I couldn't possibly be doing this to swing some advantage from a new arrangement. I'm in a better position – I mean, if you put aside the Greenfield meet – I'm better off with the way things are right now."

"Oh, man – I gotcha!" said Kevin, nodding again in immediate and complete agreement. "That's – Damn! I didn't even think about that, but that's huge. You're totally right; it's got more …more, uh … more integrity if it comes from you. There's no way it's gonna look like someone who was just frustrated about not winning the race. If you make the case, they'll know it's all about trying to set things right … 'cause you'll be pushing for a setup that'll actually make it *harder* for you to win, not easier. Oh, wow … this is pretty big, what you're talkin' about doing. You're really sure about all this?"

Billy Lloyd nodded as if to say, *as sure as I've ever been about anything in my life.*

"Now, I don't mean," he assured Kevin, "that I'll go to Markbreit, or whoever else he might want to bring in on it, without you. You should be there for any meeting, 'cause this is your deal, ultimately, and you'll still know more than me about how to make the argument. But let me kinda be the front man on it – we'll get farther that way, I'm tellin' you."

"Yeah, no, that's – you're totally right," agreed Kevin, who felt like a huge weight was being lifted off his shoulders. More precisely, he felt like there had been *two* huge weights on his shoulders, and one of the two was now being lifted off. He still faced a daunting, uphill fight, but at least now he had acquired an ally in the struggle (assuming Billy Lloyd wouldn't get cold feet when it mattered). "So when do you think we should try to hook up with your dad's friend?"

"I dunno; it might take a little while. He's out of town a lot," said Billy Lloyd. "I have this feeling we ought to set our sights on the '93 season, and not so much right now. That'll give us the chance to work through any hassles that someone might try to lay on us."

"That makes sense," said Kevin. "It's not like they're gonna suddenly alter the rules right in the middle of the track season anyway. This is a long-term change we're talking about, a ... a reform we're tryin' to get going here, and it's not gonna happen overnight. But you're not thinking of waiting until the fall, are you?"

"No, no – nothing like that, no. I just meant we might not be able to go see him *tomorrow,* or within the next few days. I'll talk to my– you know what, actually? I should arrange for *you* to explain the situation to my dad. Would you be okay starting there?"

"Sure – whatever you think is the right way to go at it." Knowing that Greg Beech was a prominent lawyer, Kevin instinctively began translating his array of internal arguments into terminology and phrasing that (he imagined) sounded like legalese.

"And I don't have to front for you on that," Billy Lloyd assured him. "My dad'll listen to you if I tell him you've got something to say. I'll take the lead once he connects us with Markbreit."

"Fair 'nuff," said Kevin.

As if on cue, both boys took a brief recess from the conversation and sat quietly, pondering the magnitude of their upcoming endeavor. "We'll be takin' on a lot of history," observed Billy Lloyd.

"Yeah, we will ..." Kevin concurred. "But that's how changes get made. Look at it: Martin Luther King, Susan B. Anthony ... umm ... Galileo ... well, hey, you've been reading Thoreau in English just like us, haven't you? The whole junior class has the same line-up in American Lit, right?"

Billy Lloyd nodded. "Yeah. We did sections of *Walden* and a few little clips from *Civil Disobedience.*"

"Well, there you go. Civil disobedience. That's what it takes," declared Kevin. "Someone comes along and tells the – tells their society that they've been getting some detail wrong. And they make a strong enough argument that people start to wake up. Well, *some* people wake up; you're never gonna get *every*one on board."

"King, Susan B., Galileo, and Thoreau, huh?" responded Billy Lloyd with a muffled chuckle. "Geez ... maybe they'll be naming schools after us, one day."

"I doubt it," said Kevin, pretending to consider the prospect in complete seriousness. "This isn't *quite* at the same level. Those folks were dealing in some pretty deep, far-reaching issues. But hey, maybe they'll name, like

… a gym after us somewhere, or a field."

Billy Lloyd smiled in amusement. Then, suddenly, his expression took on a slight alteration, suggesting that a mildly disconcerting thought had interrupted his enjoyment of the light exchange.

"What?" Kevin asked.

"Should it worry me," Billy Lloyd thought out loud, "that all four of the people you mentioned got arrested?"

"I dunno," Kevin answered honestly.

CHAPTER 8
The Pitch

True to Billy Lloyd's projection, it would be well over a month before he and Kevin managed to obtain a conference with Ed Markbreit. In fact, it took twelve days before Greg Beech even had the available time to meet with his son and this new associate.

The fledgling activists both knew that this lapse in time was more of a blessing than a setback, because it gave them time for Kevin to tutor Billy Lloyd in the logic and intent behind the staggered starting block concept. It also gave them ample time to discuss what they both recognized as the biggest challenge they faced: *How do you launch a presentation that inevitably stands to insult your audience?* That was the uneasy prospect they both came back to again and again in their planning process. Whoever happened to be on the listening end when they made their argument, that individual would in effect be receiving the message, "Here's something you've been too dumb to notice."

Of course, the bluntness of that indictment might be tempered by the presenters' humble acknowledgment, "… and until a few weeks ago, *we* were too dumb to figure it out ourselves!" But on the other hand, they would be crediting themselves with having caught the discrepancy before their listener. Clearly, that message, that dynamic within an exchange, was one that both Allen Paige and Tom Ackerman had been unable to absorb without feeling threatened.

Billy Lloyd assured Kevin repeatedly that Markbreit would be a completely different animal, that he was self-assured enough to be able to say, "Okay, on this one matter, this one detail appears to have gotten by me" without imploding. That didn't mean for one second, however, that there could be anything awkward or ad-libbed in their approach. Meeting once a week during their shared study period from 10:15-11:30, they gradually formulated an outline for their intended presentation, which they then developed into a more thorough dissertation. They came fairly quickly to a consensus as to which points to emphasize. When a certain aspect of the sales pitch had them both befuddled, Kevin would catch up with Jessica during lunch or after school and ask for her opinion. She was always happy to weigh in, despite having ceased any pro-active role once she had helped measure the lanes.

During this preparatory stretch, Billy Lloyd was still obligated to the track team for several more meets – a commitment he fulfilled, but with a reluctance and a sense of disillusionment that increased exponentially with every outing. He collected two wins, two third-place finishes, and a fourth-place finish among those competitions, but at his subsequent sessions with Kevin, his demeanor showed no variance in relation to his most recent outcome. He saw his wins and losses as equally empty and meaningless.

He confided that he would have quit, in fact, were it not for long-term practical considerations along the same lines as Kevin's. He had to think about his future. Although Billy Lloyd would have the relative advantage of not needing any financial assistance, his athletic achievements still represented his best shot at maximizing his range of college choices. Recruiters would want an explanation as to why a star athlete would take it upon himself to abandon his team in the middle of a track season, and those inquiries probably wouldn't serve as the most opportune moments to launch into reformist oratory.

An additional incentive for Billy Lloyd to play out the string – one that Kevin had to reassure him wasn't childish – was his desire to deny his ego-crazed teammate Simon Addison the satisfaction of victory whenever possible. Simon's self-adoration, his tendency to treat any positive outcome for himself as a reflection of some innate superiority, had always grated on the nerves of Kevin, Billy Lloyd, and most of the other top-tier athletes. But now, with the added awareness on Billy Lloyd's part that a good number of those triumphs weren't legitimately earned, the pompous posturing was becoming all but unbearable.

Billy Lloyd relayed his aggravation to Kevin: "It feels like you're in a spelling bee, and some hot-shot punk spells a word wrong, but he wins the contest anyway – because someone went and bought off the judges. So you already feel ripped off. But *then*, like that's not bad enough, you have to watch him go in front of audiences and lecture them on how 'if you just study and work hard like *I* did, you can be a champ just like me.' You just wanna throttle the guy. It's gotten to a point now where if I can't beat him, I'd rather see someone from the other school win." Kevin understood the feeling.

They also shared the unequivocal conviction that Simon couldn't be trusted. From the very start, there was never any consideration of trying to enlighten him to the reality of the situation. They had likewise determined up front that they didn't know Quentin Baker or Vinnie Cancelliere well enough to try to recruit either of them. Maybe the senior and the sophomore would be the types to put integrity and reason over adherence to custom (and personal gain), and maybe they wouldn't – but it didn't make much sense to reveal one's agenda to a virtual stranger who might take an adversarial attitude. It was worth noting, Kevin pointed out, that Baker and Cancelliere were hamstrung right along with Billy Lloyd when the Greenfield team stacked its roster. Baker, ordinarily in lane two or three, was pushed to lane six, while Cancelliere was shoved all the way to the outermost lane. And both, of course, had finished that race in far worse standing than usual as a direct result. Kevin, not having been there, asked Billy Lloyd, "Did either of them come out of it feeling like something didn't add up?"

"Not that I heard, no," said Billy Lloyd. "It was just the regular, 'Oh well, better luck next time.' But remember, it took *me* until later – until later on that night to start putting the pieces together, to really get the extent of it. Still, I didn't hear anything from Quentin or Vinnie afterwards, either – nothing at practice, or at the next meet. But I mean, we don't really talk too much to begin with. I don't think we need to waste time worrying about them – it's not like we need anyone else's help to make the case. We know we're right about this; it's just the question of how to communicate it."

As they continued honing "how to communicate it," they agreed that it was crucial, right from the onset, to acknowledge the improbability that such a colossal and enduring oversight could even exist. It was clear that they would have to say, up front, "We *know* how hard this is to take in, to accept. But facts are facts, and logic is logic, and there are times when a little detail manages to slip by *everybody,* even the best and brightest, and – well, we seem to have stumbled on one of those times." They also knew that the case would have to be so foolproof, so far beyond counterargument, that the listener would be spurred into a readiness to go and make the same pitch to subsequent audiences.

They harbored an odd gut feeling, one that each boy had arrived at intuitively, and independently of the other. Kevin and Billy Lloyd both anticipated that the biggest bridge to cross was not demonstrating that there *was* a problem, but rather making the case that the problem demanded a response. After all, the fact of the lanes being uneven was undeniable; it would immediately become clear to anyone who bothered to grab some measuring tools and duplicate Kevin and Jessica's legwork.

What promised to be the hard part was overcoming the "if it ain't broke, don't fix it" mindset that they were likely to run into – wherein someone might admit the technical point of unequal lanes, but would sooner sweep the issue under the rug than go through the logistical and political ordeals of altering an entrenched system. Mr. Paige had made at least one accurate statement: People *had* managed to make their peace with this skewed arrangement for years. The sports establishment had set up a completely illogical template in which otherwise dominant runners were inescapably knocked out of the competition by virtue of their names. Yet in the face of this, traditionalists (like the sportswriter Jordan Elgin) had been perfectly willing to scour the earth to find any explanation but the accurate one. They had gone to the effort of concocting an entire pseudo-science, a whole array of expedient psychological theories, rather than opening their eyes to the basic, glaring flaw in the system. And theirs had been the prevailing view. How do you make a case for the urgency of a change when it so clearly *hasn't* been looked at as any sort of urgent matter?

So they concluded that any intellectual or moral pitch would likely be insufficient unless it could be coupled with a practical motivator. What was needed was an appeal that went beyond the simple do-it-because-it's-the-right-thing imperative. As Jessica had noted, history showed that a certain path merely being "the right one" was never a guarantee that people would choose to take that path. To stand a chance, they had to build a case that the event *itself* – not just its integrity – would benefit from the proposed changes.

In one discussion, they found themselves drawing an analogy to various movies in which, at the climax, the protagonist would give an impassioned speech on some ethical issue, appealing to the conscience of a roomful of predatory capitalists. At the conclusion of the oratory, there would always be a few seconds of awkward silence – and then one or two of the audience members would slowly start applauding, followed by others, and still others, until finally you'd see an entire room of corporate sharks standing and cheering wholeheartedly for a course of action that none of their real-life counterparts would consider even for a second.

They agreed that endings like that, while intended to warm the heart, were patently ridiculous. "People don't just reverse their whole way of thinking like that," said Kevin. "The board members are always like, 'Gosh, I just never *realized* that poisoning little bunnies and squirrels to test our chemical products was wrong, until you pointed it out to me!' Changing people's minds is never just … some sort of cakewalk. It doesn't happen that way."

"Right," said Billy Lloyd, "but what *would* make it believable – or, at least a *little* more believable – is if the person talking to them makes it hit home in a strategic way. Y'know, like if they point out, 'This is not just the right choice; it's the only way to save our asses!' It's gotta be put out there like, 'It's all for the good of the company!' That's how we've gotta come at it with this."

"Well, I think we can do that," said Kevin. "I mean, look at the tryouts. They had *some* suspense, of course, 'cause there's the question of who'd come in first, but half the field didn't have any part in it. That's not a good competition. If someone was there pulling for me, or Tristan, or Mitchell Carson, or – well, basically, anyone but you, Simon, or Quentin – their emotional involvement would've been out the window by the time the first curve ended. Even Cancelliere – sure, he made the team, but there was never any way he could've come in *first,* unless all three of you guys ran the worst race of your lives. So you've got eight guys racing, but for all except two or three of them, they're basically just filling up space. The only thing they can take away from it is, 'Well, maybe I'll be in a better lane next time.' And that should be the *last* thing a guy's worried about after losing a race. Now, compare that to something like the hundred-yard dash, when you've got every runner – I mean, unless someone really sucks, and doesn't have any business being out there to begin with – coming close to the finish line around the same time."

"So it'd have the effect of creating better finishes," Billy Lloyd concluded the line of reasoning. "More guys actually coming down the stretch with a chance to win – *that's* an angle we should come at it from. You'd be making things fair, *and* you'd be making the race itself better for everyone – for the fans, especially."

"Yeah – once they get past their gut reaction, the first time they see it," clarified Kevin. "And we gotta keep in mind, bringing them around to that understanding is not gonna be easy at all, even if it feels like it should be automatic. Hell, if an academic geek like Mr. Paige can't see the math behind it, neither are a lot of other people gonna see it. They'll wonder why so-and-so is 'getting a head start,' or why so-and-so is 'being made to start way back there.' They're gonna resist, even when they see the ending getting more exciting, 'cause their idea of what's 'fair' is all distorted, all messed up. Things have been like this for so long, everyone just makes it their reality."

"Right ... and then that 'reality' starts to be the– well, y'know, it reinforces itself. It builds on its own expectations," theorized Billy Lloyd. "Once people get it in their heads that 'these folks are good at doing this particular thing, and those folks aren't,' then it makes perfect sense to them when that's how the results keep turning out. They assume it's just, like, the natural order of things. 'Course ... it's easier to do that, I guess, when you're *in* the group that everyone thinks are just naturally the winner types." He affected a guilty look and gestured toward himself as he spoke. "When you're on the receiving end of a privilege, you kinda have the luxury of not having to think about it. Of not ... of not having to *notice* that it's a privilege."

"Such integrity!" Kevin announced in a light-hearted but sincerely admiring tone. "Insightful, and totally objective thinking – very rare these days."

"Well, shit, if I'm gonna pull the rug out from under myself, I gotta score a few points for it somewhere," muttered Billy Lloyd.

By the time they met with Mr. Beech, they had scrutinized, edited, and memorized every detail so thoroughly that their primary concern, now, was making sure their delivery wouldn't come off as too academic and scripted. They wanted their presentation, in addition to stating its case eloquently, to have a comfortable, conversational flow to it, and they monitored each other during the formulation phase to catch and revise any line that sounded too stuffy and over-rehearsed.

Because Mr. Beech's domain was law and not sports, they constructed their initial presentation around points of logic and consistency, opting to save the supplemental, it'll-make-for-a-better-event angle for Commissioner Markbreit.

Kevin had, of course, educated his cohort in the meantime on all of the anecdotal examples that pointed to the inequity of the track layout. He told him about the snafu with Turner and Aldrich in the relay, he took him through the ordeal of Helena Vardell (including the journalistic sparring between Steven Yablonsky and Jordan Elgin), and he even went back to the 1942 quirk of fate in which Burt Waldron escaped the curse of the outer lane courtesy of an earthquake.

All of those oddities, persuasive as they were, bore less of the burden of making the overall case once Kevin and Jessica had verified the varied lane distances. That, on its own, should rightfully have been enough; the rest was merely garnish on the salad, so to speak. The one illustration that they agreed to keep front and center, though, was Billy Lloyd's own experience at Greenfield High. More than anything else, that was what swiftly and soundly put the lie to all of the sociological and psychological theories about speeds and surnames.

Those theories, after all, had constantly sought to establish, or to confirm, that the inability to prevail in certain events was an innate shortcoming associated with late-namers. But Billy Lloyd Beech wasn't a late-namer. Billy Lloyd Beech was an early-namer – who had consistently achieved the success that went along with that trait. According to the conventional wisdom, that success was a pure reflection of his abilities. If those abilities were intrinsic, the Greenfield team wouldn't be able to negate them simply by fielding an "A"-saturated line-up. But they *were* able, on the other hand, to use that exact strategy to negate his chance of competing for a victory. It clearly pointed to an outcome that owed itself to some key factor other than ability. To believe otherwise was to suggest that Billy Lloyd momentarily forgot how to run, and then promptly recovered the requisite knowledge by the time Monroe hosted George Marshall High the following Tuesday – when he was back in the familiar environs of lane three.

Leaning on that improbability as their primary anecdotal weapon, but relying more heavily on the basic numbers and measures, they sat down in Greg Beech's study and made their first collaborative pitch for a new arrangement of the starting blocks. Kevin did most of the talking, and Billy Lloyd chimed in judiciously, sensing when a certain additional point might reinforce the argument in terms his father would appreciate. As they spoke, Mr. Beech listened intently, jotted down a few notes, and withheld his questions until he gathered that the boys were done.

When he did ultimately speak, Kevin and Billy Lloyd felt a swift rush of relief that his response posed no challenge to their fundamental claim. His first comment jumped right into the realm of potential remedies, which stood as a reaffirmation in their eyes. By opening a discussion of solutions, he was implicitly agreeing that there *was* a problem to solve. So that first hurdle was finally cleared, momentarily exorcising the brush-offs Kevin experienced in his two prior adult encounters – and it felt good.

The primary concern voiced by Mr. Beech, one for which Kevin had braced himself, was the likely resistance of the masses to the idea of abandoning a nice, linear, universal starting line in favor of a skewed, tiered set of individualized starting positions. He alerted them that, fair or not, a new arrangement would prove a tough adjustment for the aesthetic sensibilities of most viewers, and he suggested that the boys put in a little more time brainstorming about alternate ways of addressing the problem. "I'm not saying there *is* a better answer out there, necessarily," he admitted. "I certainly can't think of anything off the top of my head. But I just want to urge you to try to – to really make sure you've exhausted *all* the possibilities, in case there may be some way of getting things right that won't send too much of a shock through the system."

As Kevin nodded appreciatively, he marvelled, privately, at how smoothly and in stride Mr. Beech had taken the essential component of the pitch. *Why wasn't his reaction stronger?* Kevin wondered. *This was something pretty profound, pretty jolting we were telling him – and he's seen as many of these races as the next guy, especially with a son so involved in it. Why didn't it throw him, to find out right here and now that he was watching a bunch of rigged contests and never noticed? Or wait – is it possible, maybe, that he already DID know the deal was unfair, and he just didn't have the time or energy, he couldn't make it a priority, to speak out about it? Maybe this step we're taking is one that he knew someone needed to take – just not him. Geez. If that's the case for Mr. Beech, maybe it'll be true for other folks too. Maybe there'll be a few more reasonable people out there than I thought.*

As he processed this train of thought, Kevin remained tuned in to the practical advice that Mr. Beech was offering. When he felt like it was his turn to speak again, he promised that he would put some additional time into digging up and assessing all options – although he reiterated that he *had* gone over the situation with a fine-toothed comb (several combs, actually) and didn't expect to stumble on a better prescription than the staggered starting lines.

"But Dad," cut in Billy Lloyd, "what about it, overall? I mean, even if we can't come up with some other idea, do you think it'd be worth bringing this to Mr. Markbreit? You think he'd – would he feel like it's worth looking into?"

"I think he'd want to hear this, yeah," responded his father – in a tone that echoed Billy Lloyd's own assurance when he had first mentioned Markbreit's name to Kevin at the café. Not only would the commissioner be willing to "hear it," Mr. Beech was saying; he would treat it as a matter of consequence, as something to take seriously. "It'll take a little time, I'm sure, before we can secure an open date. It might not happen until you're out for the summer, realistically. But I'll get in touch with him. I've gotta hand it to you. You boys have really done your homework on this. Again, I'd like you to put some more time into trying to come up with different options to deal with the discrepancy. But you've made an argument that's not going to be easy for someone to refute, if they look at it honestly."

"*That's* the big question," muttered Kevin, gesturing with his hand to acknowledge the word "honestly" still hanging in the air. "But sir, I wanna tell you, either way, I really appreciate your support on this. I don't know that I would've had the energy to pursue this whole thing if Billy Lloyd, here, hadn't stepped in and gotten involved. I owe you guys a lot."

"A little premature," cautioned Mr. Beech with an appreciative smile. "First let's see how things turn out."

Two days later, Billy Lloyd caught up with Kevin at school and informed him, excitedly, that a meeting was scheduled for June 7th. "You're still gonna be around after school lets out, right?" he asked him. "Your family doesn't go away or anything, do you?"

"Nah, I'm good," said Kevin. "I'll mark it down. This is great news, man. Should we ask your dad for any tips? He could … maybe help us … strategize …" Kevin's voice trailed off as it occurred to him that Mr. Beech had already made his contribution by arranging the meeting, and that one shouldn't get greedy with someone else's time or intellect.

"No need," said Billy Lloyd calmly, grasping that Kevin had already backed off the suggestion himself. "He said, basically, just tell it to Markbreit like we told him."

At this point, their confidence was high enough that they agreed to limit themselves to one final "pre-meeting meeting," to reconfirm their points of emphasis closer to the date, and to determine to what extent they wanted to inject the enhancement-of-the-event angle that they had previously discussed.

Beyond this, they officially declared themselves to be on hiatus, which enabled them to throw themselves into the home stretch of the academic year with little distraction.

Billy Lloyd picked up one more unsatisfying victory amongst his final three meets of the track season. His cumulative outcomes almost secured a spot in the district-wide track & field finals, but he was glad, in fact, to have fallen just short. He was so ready for the tainted season to end that when it did, he told Kevin it felt comparable to getting paroled after a prison term – or like finally recovering from a five-week flu bug. "I feel like I can *breathe* again," he said.

On June 2nd, the 1991-1992 school year ended. Five days later, Kevin returned to the Beech family's home, where the meeting with Ed Markbreit was to take place. Greg Beech facilitated the introduction between Kevin and the commissioner and led the two of them, along with Billy Lloyd, into his study. The moment his son and the two guests were seated, he began to head out of the room. "I'll be downstairs if anyone needs anything," he said.

"Wait – I thought – you're not staying?" stammered Kevin.

"You don't need me," responded Mr. Beech. "You've got this." He directed a subtle wink toward Billy Lloyd, and exchanged a nod with Markbreit as he departed – a tacit conveyance that things were in good hands.

"So what can I do for you?" asked Markbreit in a sincere and respectful tone, as soon as he was alone with the boys.

"Well," began Billy Lloyd, "we realize this is gonna sound crazy, almost inconceivable ..." and the pitch was in process. As per the plan, the roles were now reversed; this time Billy Lloyd handled the bulk of the presentation, with Kevin interjecting when he saw the opportunity to strengthen a point, to fortify a given plank of the proposal.

Two weeks later, Kevin received a phone call. "Kevin, this is Ed Markbreit," said the recognizable voice. "I wanted to let you know that I've put together an exploratory committee to look into this – this issue that you brought to our attention. It's still a little early to promise any particular outcome, and I don't want you to spend the whole summer on the edge of your seat, but I'd say there's a strong likelihood we're going to take you and Billy Lloyd up on your recommendation."

"Thank you, sir," responded Kevin.

CHAPTER 9
Ackerman's Ambush

As August segued into September, the Presidential campaign was in high gear, with the war-weary incumbent swiftly losing ground to the upstart Governor of Arkansas (while legions of third-party loyalists still clamored for a populist Texas billionaire to re-enter the race). The 1992 NFL season kicked off, with Thurman Thomas, Troy Aikman, Jerry Rice, and other stars gearing up to drive their teams toward Super Bowl contention. Larry Bird, after winning the Olympic Gold with the historic Dream Team, had just announced his retirement from the NBA. Clint Eastwood was riding the crest of his most highly praised film in years, *Unforgiven.* Communities in South Florida were recovering from the wreckage of Hurricane Andrew, and a powerful earthquake and tsunami were preparing to unleash even greater devastation on the people of Nicaragua.

Yet to Kevin Wilkerson, Billy Lloyd Beech, Jessica Mather, and about 180 others entering their senior year at Monroe, world events remained generally remote. Even the upcoming election was relegated in most of the students' eyes to a backdrop, largely seen as something occupying the time and attention of other people, in distant communities. Sure, some of them might voice preferences for Bush, or Clinton, or Perot – "preferences" that in all likelihood were just perfunctory echoes of their parents' politics – but their immediate concerns were closer to home and less cosmopolitan. This was the start of what they saw as their official transition to adulthood, the school term when the road to their respective futures would take its key turns and twists, and when they would get a good idea of what the upcoming few years might have in store for them.

Kevin had made a conscious decision not to stake his emotional health on the final call of the committee delegated (at least, supposedly delegated) by Ed Markbreit to look into the starting-block matter. Not having heard back from the commissioner for the remainder of the summer, he made no follow-up calls, and he urged the same patience on Billy Lloyd's part. They had done their job; they had made their case, and now it was out of their hands. Kevin would live with whatever the verdict turned out to be – and with whatever form of communication would be used to relay it to him.

He bore in mind that his entry into the 400 the previous semester had sprung from his inborn urge to challenge barriers – his addiction to uphill fights, as his mother would have characterized it – and not from any practical consideration. It had always been soccer, not track, which stood as his primary vehicle for pursuing a college scholarship. And should his athletic resumé need any additional padding (which it most likely wouldn't), he could, quite simply, follow that original parental advice and opt for a winnable track & field event, one that didn't entail a late-name handicap. He was undecided, in fact, as to his game plan surrounding the 1993 track season even in the event that his prescriptions were put into play. He might end up steering clear of the 400 altogether; there was no guarantee that he would necessarily *want* to be the test case of a new arrangement if and when it came into effect. Again, he told himself, his motive in all this was to bring integrity to the competition and legitimacy to its outcome – not to increase his own chance of winning it.

So the status of his proposal was nowhere in his mind, really, when he gathered in the gym with about 160 other students at the kick-off assembly for the fall sports season. This was a mandatory orientation for anyone intending to participate in one of the fall-semester sports, which included football, boys' soccer, girls' volleyball, boys' and girls' lacrosse, and co-ed cross-country. The student-athletes would get all the requisite details regarding practice times, game schedules, equipment needs, and academic expectations. This meeting was designated for varsity teams; the junior varsity and freshman squads would assemble for the same purpose the following afternoon.

Kevin and the rest of the varsity soccer players sought each other out as the gym filled up, and formed an unofficial team section as they seated themselves in the stands. Having attended daily practices since two weeks prior to the start of school, and for the most part enjoying two or three years of affiliation with each other already, the varsity team was a close-knit group with a strong sense of camaraderie. They had suffered a 2-1 loss to Burbank (on what many thought was a questionable awarding of a penalty kick) in a semifinal match the previous November, but they were highly favored to take the district championship in the fall '92 season. Kevin (or "Wilks," as the rest of the team called him) was one of the main forces behind this success; as the center midfielder, he was a veritable "coach on the field," mentoring, resituating, and exhorting his teammates throughout the game. He had been elected co-captain of the varsity team for the previous season, an honorific rarely achieved by a junior. With the same titles scheduled to be handed out in about another week, just prior to the first league game, there was no doubt that he – probably along with goalkeeper Seth Langdon – would be entrusted with that leadership role again.

He listened obligingly to a stream of information that was mostly superfluous or irrelevant to him; either he already knew the instructions being conveyed, or they dealt with sports other than soccer. Though entirely necessary, the assembly cut into practice time, and Kevin was anxious for it to end so he and his teammates could hit the field.

He was glad, then, when Mr. Ackerman resumed his spot at the podium following the lacrosse coaches' briefing and said, "Okay, so that should pretty much wrap things up …" Kevin readied himself to rise from his seat and head out, only to hear Ackerman continue: "… except for one other thing we need to bring to your attention. Now, this could wait until later, because it doesn't pertain to any fall sport. However, since a pretty good number of you are also involved in track and field in the spring, it makes sense to give you a little heads-up about it now."

The students, intrigued by the minor buildup, settled back into their seats. Kevin's pulse, meanwhile, was racing a mile a minute. *Holy shit! This is it – we're gonna find out right here and now,* he thought. *And they must've gone ahead with – well, with SOMETHING, at least, 'cause he wouldn't be making an announcement if things were just staying like they were. Here it comes! Okay, Kevin, relax. You know there's gonna be some kind of reaction to what he says. Just take whatever happens in stride.*

He found himself suddenly wishing that his comrade was present at the orientation, but Billy Lloyd didn't play a fall sport, and consequently had no reason to attend.

"It's been brought to our attention," said Ackerman, "that certain running events – uh, that there are allegations that some of the running events have not been giving all of the competitors a … totally equal chance." He enunciated the last three words of the sentence as if to put them in quotes. "So … so in the interest of being completely fair and even-handed, the athletic commission is, uh, going to install a new wrinkle in the set-up for a handful of events: the 200 meters, the 250-meter hurdles, the 400 meters … and, umm, from what I understand, possibly the relay races."

Kevin couldn't recall ever having heard such a flat, monotone delivery of important news – of *any* news, now that he thought about it. The A.D. spoke in the uninspired, deflated tone characteristic of a politician who's just been caught in a scandal and is now announcing that he's umm, retiring from office to, umm, spend more time with his, uh, family. Without the slightest change in inflection, he continued:

"Because the runners in the outer lanes in certain races have had difficulty keeping up over the curved portions of the track, the commission has decided to experiment with a different ... with an alteration in the starting position of each runner, as a way of ... making up for it." Again, he phrased "making up for it" so as to convey the definitive message that this was *someone else's* idea, not his. "So starting with the tryouts in March, the starting position in each lane will be set up a little bit ahead of the one to the inside of it. In other words, the farther out your lane is, the farther ahead you'll get to begin the race – on the particular ones I mentioned. Whether they decide to implement this with other events in the future is, umm ... hasn't been determined yet."

Already a wave of uncomfortable, muffled commentary was sweeping through the stands: a few voices blurted out variations of "What the hell?" and "Why do they gotta do that?" but the predominant reaction was confusion on the whole concept. Most of the athletes weren't 100% sure *what* Ackerman had just told them.

Of course it occurred to Kevin that clarity was probably the last thing the unsupportive A.D. wanted. *Could he GET any more vague and uninformative?* Kevin wondered. He noticed very quickly that what should have been a moment of pure triumph – not that it would have been his style to gloat or over-celebrate – was not feeling in any sense like a positive experience. Then Ackerman took it to the next level.

"And while we're bringing this to your awareness, I thought it was important to give credit where the credit's due. You should know that this new policy, this first step in the direction of justice, has come into being thanks to the tireless effort of one of our own, right here at Monroe – Mister Kevin Wilkerson." He gestured toward the soccer contingent within the audience.

The collective vibe in the gym at that moment was comparable to that of an open mic in a café or nightclub just after someone has concluded a really terrible performance. People weren't sure *how* they were supposed to react. While pockets within the crowd offered some mild, obligatory applause, the discontented dialogue increased its volume a notch. Again, random voices emerged from the pack, asking questions like "What does he think he's doing?" to no one in particular. (None of these gripes, it should be noted, came from within the soccer team, which held Kevin in high enough esteem to know that if he, in fact, did whatever it was the A.D. was crediting him – or charging him – with doing, there must have been a sound reason behind it.) A large majority of the attendees remained in an awkward state of limbo, not sure how to interpret the announcement or how to feel about it.

Kevin, on the other hand, had one thought, one very pertinent question, front and center in his mind: Why had Ackerman credited him as the sole advocate, the lone initiator, of the new policy? Why "Kevin Wilkerson" and not "Kevin Wilkerson and Billy Lloyd Beech?" Markbreit *had* to have relayed to him that it was two boys, not one, who sought out his audience and made a strong enough case to convert the commission to their cause. In fact, it had been Billy Lloyd who took on the role of spokesperson when it counted the most. What possible reason did Ackerman have for failing to mention his involvement?

Then, in another instant, it crystallized for Kevin, as he remembered his own statement back at Pierre's Deli – the one about it "having more integrity" coming from an early-namer like Billy Lloyd. Ackerman's agenda, in no uncertain terms, was to obscure that reality, to portray this *not* as two students' concern for a contest's integrity but rather as a case of one malcontent whining about the race being too hard for him. That was precisely what Ackerman wanted the students to glean from the announcement: Our little Kevin, here, lost a race, and didn't think it was fair, so he went and got the rules changed to help his chances next time. Nothing to do with the farcical records, the incongruous outcomes, or the years of self-perpetuating alphabetical stratification – no. This was about a loser and his resentment toward the winners.

As Kevin sat in stunned silence, he saw Mr. Ackerman surreptitiously make eye contact with him from the podium and give a smug little nod, as if to say, "You built this bed, pal; now you can lie in it." Kevin knew exactly what was up. And Ackerman knew that Kevin knew. *And,* Kevin knew that Ackerman knew that Kevin knew.

Kevin, in no mood for tacit or telepathic messaging, shook his head at Ackerman and mouthed the words, "You son-of-a-bitch ..."

Ackerman maintained eye contact for another second or two, then turned back to face the general center of the stands and said, "Alright everybody, it's time to head out. Have a good practice; make sure you've gotten all the info you need. Let's give 'em hell out there – make this a great fall season for Monroe, right across the board."

"Hey Wilks, what the hell was that? What's he talkin' about?" whispered fellow midfielder Jesse Irving, who was rising from the adjacent seat.

"Nothing; it's – don't worry about it. I'll tell you later," responded Kevin, tersely.

It would be misleading, and overly severe, to describe the various exchanges to which Kevin was subjected over the following couple of weeks as "fallout." Though he was approached with some regularity, it was most often by fellow athletes who were merely looking for clarity. What *was* that change that Ackerman was talking about? Only a handful of these inquiring minds belonged to likely participants in the affected events anyway; naturally, they wanted to know if whatever-it-was-that-went-down meant that they should be training or strategizing in a new and different manner.

Kevin dealt with all the pestering by carrying around two small diagrams in his pocket – both color-coded, one showing the track set-up as it had always been, and one showing the arrangement they could now expect to encounter in the spring.

He did his best, as he guided one listener after another through the visuals and the logic, not to sound belittling, not to take on a tone of "Okay, let me explain this in a way that your brain can maybe kind of figure it out." It was hard, though, and he could feel his delivery becoming progressively more agitated and impatient with each repetition of the lecture. He soon took to apologizing up front for "sounding like a kindergarten teacher." But kindergarten *was*, rightfully, the grade level by which something as rudimentary as this – a simple fact of one line being longer than another – should have been well within everyone's grasp.

To Kevin's gratification, nearly all of those who came at him in a spirit of honest inquiry *did* emerge with a clear grasp of the concept, and at least a tentative acceptance of it, once he had explained it. It didn't feel so much like winning an argument, for the simple reason that the "argument" had never taken place to begin with. There was no valid reason for anyone to assume a defensive posture; time and again, Kevin heard variations on the generic admission: "I never thought about that before."

There was the problem, however, of those who *weren't* inclined toward honest inquiry. Heading this list, predictably enough, was the one who stood to lose the most – and who was apparently now committing himself, alongside his lacrosse duties, to the additional "sport" of making Kevin's life miserable.

Kevin did what he could to avoid Simon Addison's company.

Unfortunately, the two happened to share class periods for chemistry, economics, and P.E., making it impossible to eliminate interaction altogether. Simon's ribbing began in the first P.E. class following Ackerman's announcement. As the teams were formed for flag football, Simon blurted out, "Wait a sec – they've got four varsity players, and we've only got two! That's *not fair!* We should get to start with a ten-point lead!" He made sure to glance Kevin's way at least three times over the short duration of this mock protest. Marty Jankowitz, one of the varsity football players to which he was referring – specifically, a 260-pound lineman – told Simon to shut up and get in position for the kick-off.

Not content with relegating it to the athletic realm, Simon carried the derisive act into chemistry class as well, suggesting to Miss Searles that, because he hadn't done as well as he'd hoped on the previous week's quiz, he should get a five-minute head start on this one. Miss Searles, wearing a look that was equal parts confusion and reprimand, told him to sit down and be quiet.

"Okay, okay," he acquiesced. "Just tryin' to make sure everything's fair and even for everybody – right, Wilkerson?" With only a handful of their classmates being fall athletes and thus having been present at the orientation, the majority of them sat in complete bewilderment as to the subtext of Simon's gag. Like in a humorous movie scene, at the mention of "Wilkerson," their heads all rotated to look at Kevin. He reacted by gazing out the window and flicking his hand in a dismissive gesture toward Simon, akin to brushing off an annoying insect.

The fact that it wasn't winning him any new fans didn't dampen Simon's enthusiasm for the routine. If Kevin was walking in the hallway and happened to pass by a group that included Simon, his tormentor would pretend to have been in the midst of ruminating on the upcoming track season (extremely implausible, given that it was still well over five months away), and would lament, as if in mid-sentence, "... of course, it's gonna be harder this time. They're giving these big head starts to some of the others, so I'm gonna have a lot more to overcome. Some of us have a bitch of a time gettin' credit for our accomplishments." On the couple of occasions when this happened, Kevin made sure to show no hint of reaction as he walked on, leaving Simon's compatriots to wonder why the subject matter had changed so abruptly.

Although he was successful at hiding it when any third party was present, Kevin had to admit to himself that the stream of abuse *was* getting to him

– as was his certainty that the school official who would be entrusted with installing the change was steadfastly against it, and seemed intent on undermining a smooth transition.

The fact was, by portraying the new format in its first public unveiling as Kevin's sole handiwork, Ackerman had seized control of the narrative. With complete say over how the innovation was to be introduced – but needing to at least *appear* impartial – he had chosen the strategy of pinning it on the person who could most easily be suspected of self-serving motives. Having no comparable megaphone, the best Kevin could do was to alert fellow students on a one-to-one basis as to the real intent, and the real personnel, behind this effort. Jessica, on-point as ever, referred him to Mark Twain's observation that a lie can travel halfway around the world while the truth is still putting on its shoes.

Kevin did fill people in on Billy Lloyd's role, as well as Ed Markbreit's, when they approached him with larger questions about the concept. In such a limited and after-the-fact context, though, alluding to a partner inevitably tended to sound like passing the buck. It shouldn't have, but it did. It echoed, to a degree, the unease Kevin had felt in Mr. Paige's office just after crediting Jessica with her discovery. Even with the merits of the argument clearly on their side, mentioning that someone else was also involved couldn't help but come off like a sort of alibi, along the lines of "Well, I wasn't the *only* one playing ball in the house …"

Billy Lloyd himself leaped into the fray the moment he heard what had happened at the assembly, telling any set of ears he could solicit that this had been a two-person effort and that Kevin "shouldn't be getting all the credit." His use of the word "credit" was consistent and deliberate, a way of conveying the message that this was a *positive* undertaking, not something for which anyone – least of all Kevin – should have to apologize. Of course, since his name had gone unmentioned in the original announcement, it would have made no logical sense for any of the athletes to seek out Billy Lloyd Beech, as opposed to any other random student, for comment on the matter. So he had to manufacture his own chances to broach the subject – even as Kevin was growing increasingly weary of the subject's persistent intrusions on his time.

Any respect that either of them had held for Tom Ackerman was firmly a thing of the past. They had each gotten along fine with the A.D. over the bulk of their first three years at the school, but his character had never been put to the test (within their scope of awareness) prior to this. Though it was a moot point, they were sure that Ackerman's quickness to defend the status quo traced back to his having ridden his own early name to two district championships. "He's just like Simon; it's the same deal with both of them," Billy Lloyd commented at one point. "He got his victories, and he needs to feel like it's – like he got them by being *better* than everyone else. The idea that he might've had an unfair advantage ... he never let that cross his mind, and it's like he hates you, now, for introducing that whole train of thought."

"Well, it's like you said, last spring," Kevin rejoined. "He had the luxury of not having to think about it."

Kevin, unfortunately, *didn't* have the luxury of not having to think about the upcoming track season. His mind kept churning out scenarios about how it would be perceived if he were to run, and win, in one of the events that his efforts had helped revise. The more he thought about it, the more the truth settled in: His role in creating the new arrangement would carry too much weight. There was no way that a victory in such circumstances – legitimate as it would, in fact, be – would be treated as anything other than a compensatory gift that Kevin had finagled for himself. He decided by the end of September that the 400 was out of the question. He would run in the 100 meters when the time came, or maybe do one of the field events like the long jump or the triple jump, but it wouldn't work for him to be both the reformer *and* the groundbreaker in any of the modified mid-distance events.

*Some*body had to fill that latter role, though. That was also beyond question. If these changes were installed and still nobody with a late-ranking name stepped up to compete – or if the late-namer who did compete wasn't up to the task – all the old myths would be validated. The Ackermans, Elgins, and Addisons of the sports world would immediately say, "See? It didn't make a difference. Even when we gave them this huge advantage, they didn't have what it takes."

What this meant was that he needed to find a recruit, a stand-in – someone with a similarly late name who would have both the athletic ability to win the 400 *and* the poise to face down whatever second-guessing and taunting would emerge from the crowd. Kevin stood prepared to coach his hypothetical protégé on both fronts: First, how to maximize his speed over the distance in question; and second, how to respond, firmly and unapologetically, to the challenges that he could expect to face afterward.

He was at a loss, though, in terms of who the fitting choice would be.

His intimate knowledge of the strengths and weaknesses of the entire soccer squad, and some vague awareness of who were considered the best pure athletes on the football team, enabled him to compose a list of prospects – which he then whittled down to the names that started with T or later in the alphabet. The list was short to begin with, and quickly became shorter as various obstacles and conflicts came into play.

He knew, for example, that the two ideal candidates among his soccer teammates, Dallas Tompkins and R.J. West, wouldn't be going out for track because they were committed to baseball in the spring. Conrad Vance, a speedy wide receiver on the football team, might have been a viable contender – if it weren't for the fact that he was going to be spending March and April in Portugal as part of a senior-year exchange program. Kevin approached a couple of other athletes, Mark Urban and Braden Winchester, who simply weren't interested. Billy Lloyd, meanwhile, reached out to Jeremy Wood, a fleet-footed basketball teammate, who similarly declined. "They know it's gonna be scrutinized," Jessica reminded Kevin when he vented his frustration to her, "and they're just not ready to carry the load. It's too heavy a responsibility for them."

Running out of ideas as far as his own crowd was concerned, Kevin was beginning to think he would have to turn either to the ranks of the girls (which he didn't oppose in principle; he just had no idea who to ask) or to the lower grades – the freshmen and sophomores. The possibility of finding a hidden gem among the underclassmen certainly existed; Vinnie Cancelliere was hardly the first athlete in history who had managed to make a varsity team as a sophomore. Maybe there was another Cancelliere – or, as the circumstances demanded, a "Yancelliere" or "Zancelliere" – waiting to be discovered.

The problem was that the logical person to consult regarding the most promising younger athletes at Monroe would be one Tom Ackerman, and Kevin wasn't about to tap that resource. On top of that, freshmen and sophomores could only sign up for varsity spots once they had gone unclaimed by the upperclassmen, so there would be a definite risk in staking one's hopes on a runner for whom there might not *be* an available space when the time came. Of course, the J.V. track team would serve as a fallback showcase in such a circumstance, but nobody really paid any serious attention to that, or to its outcomes. So Kevin soon found himself retreating from the underclassman option, and limiting his search to the realm of untapped older candidates. It was beginning to feel somewhat futile, right up until the beginning of October – when the answer dropped right into his lap, from an unexpected trajectory.

On September 30th, Head Coach Joe Lawford gathered the soccer team together at the end of practice and informed the players that the varsity team was going to gain an addition the next day, a junior whose family had just relocated to the Richardson Park area from San Francisco, where he had played for Lincoln High. The players, naturally protective of their team cohesion – and individual playing time – reacted with a flurry of questions ranging from the basic "What's his name?" and "What position does he play?" to the more apropos "How do we know he's good enough?"

"Well," said Coach Lawford in response to the last question, "remind me: How many of you made the varsity your sophomore year? Just one, right?" The players nodded, as the coach gestured toward Seth Langdon. "And Seth, here, was a specialist – the varsity team happened to have a desperate *need* for a good goalie."

Jesse Irving, figuring out where the coach was going with this, concluded, "So you're about to tell us this guy made varsity as a sophomore?"

"Good guess, Irv, but no, not quite. He actually made the varsity as a freshman." An audible gasp went up from a few players. "He backed up the left winger and the left and center mids. Then last year, his sophomore year, he was a starter from day one, and made third team all-city. And this is at a school with about 400 more kids than ours." This reassurance had the ironic effect of putting the players even more on edge – particularly the starters on the left side of the offense, who each experienced the same instantaneous reaction: *Oh, shit – they're calling in some ringer to try to take my position from me?*

"Now, regardless of what awards he might've piled up, nothing's gonna be handed to him," Lawford continued, aiming to assuage their evident insecurity. "He'll have to earn his playing time just like anyone else. But you all know, I'm going to go with whatever line-up and whatever rotation I think gives us the best chance to win. The main thing is, when he shows up tomorrow, I absolutely expect, and I have no doubt, that you guys will make him feel welcome on this team." He made sure to pass his intense glare over the whole squad as he spoke, stopping a moment longer on the two or three players who might need to have the point driven home most emphatically. He also gave a final, summative nod to Kevin and Seth, to tell the co-captains, in effect, *you two are in charge; anyone gets out of line, it's on you to deal with it.*

As the coach surveyed the team to confirm that his message was being received, the uniformity of white faces and blonde-to-light-brown hair – reflective of a student body that was about 98% Caucasian – made one additional detail seem prudent to mention. "By the way, just … just so you guys aren't caught off guard," Lawford added, "the guy's Japanese."

Immediately, about six players asked simultaneously, "Does he speak English?"

"Yeah, he speaks English! Jesus Christ!" Lawford shouted in response. "I meant Japanese, like – his *ancestry*, you know what I mean? He's an American, who speaks English just like the rest of you! I said he's coming from San Francisco, not Japan! Dammit, guys, *think* before you ask stupid questions!" As he walked off to collect some stray soccer balls, he muttered audibly, "Geez, good thing I gave you the heads-up – you guys *really* would've embarrassed yourselves!"

R.J. West called out to him, "Hey, coach, I didn't hear – what'd you say the guy's name was?"

"Uh, it's Mike," responded Lawford from a slight distance. "Mike Yamasaki."

"Yamasaki?" Kevin repeated inquisitively.

"Yeah."

"With a Y?" asked Kevin.

"Yeah, of course! What're you – what's that got to do with anything?"

"Nothin', it's cool," said Kevin. "It's all cool; we'll make him feel right at home."

CHAPTER 10
The Outlier

The next day, Mike Yamasaki showed up – with the tools that had vaulted him onto the Lincoln High varsity soccer team on full display. In the 35-minute scrimmage that concluded the practice, he repeatedly outran his challenger to the loose ball. He sent a consistent stream of beautiful centering passes from the left offensive corner into the goal area. His ability to predict the flow of play and to move in anticipation of where the ball was likely to go was the stuff of Coach Lawford's dreams. When a teammate gained possession of the ball and looked around for possible passes, he would almost invariably see Mike already waving to him from a wide-open region of the field.

Perceiving that Kevin, as the center half, was the primary ball-handler, he even took the initiative, unfazed by being the new kid on the block, to talk strategy with him early on: "Okay, so if you get the ball and someone's about to start pressuring you, what do you think's the best – like, would you rather have me slide back to a lateral position most of the time, to give you more options? Or should I just assume you'll be able to get a solid feed up the wing, and kinda be ready to break on it?"

By the end of his initial practice, Mike had won over his new teammates – with the marginal exception of the incumbent left wing, Jay Marcivius, who was already resigned to the likelihood that he would now be coming in off the bench (unless, he started pondering … unless *he* could potentially beat out Jesse Irving for the starting spot at left half).

Kevin, of course, brought a dual agenda to practice. As a team leader, naturally he wanted to assess Mike's facets as a player and ascertain how and where he could best help the team. But just as surely, he was privately scouting for his surrogate when the time would come to run in the footraces. He watched Mike most intently not during the scrimmage or the drills, but during the three laps around the field at the start of practice and the wind sprints at the end. He liked what he saw.

Of course, he had no need, or inclination, to be hasty. It wouldn't be the best form to tell a sixteen year-old, within two hours of having met him, that your aspirations involved anointing him to shatter a century-old barrier. That probably *would* inspire him to demonstrate how fast he could run, but not in the direction you were hoping. So Kevin made a deliberate decision to get to know Mike first, to establish a bond of trust – which, conveniently enough, coincided with his obligations as team captain.

When Kevin made it back to the locker room, after helping Lawford put the balls and pylons away, he joined an informal group interview of the newcomer already in progress. Mike was filling in the other players on the basics. His father, an electrical engineer, had been transferred by his company to supervise a project in northern Illinois. He had one younger sister in sixth grade, he was the third generation born in America and English was his parents' language as well, and no, he didn't have any experience in martial arts.

With that one borderline exception, the few questions that revolved around Mike's ethnic background stayed in respectful territory. Given the monotone demographic of the community in which they'd spent their entire lives, the players couldn't help but feel a slight sense of the exotic, of the "foreign," personified by the new associate. Still, bearing in mind the coach's admonition on the previous day, they chose their words and questions extra carefully, repeatedly reiterating to themselves, *Don't say the wrong thing; don't make yourself look stupid.* Kevin stayed true to that approach, but did go as far as to inquire of Mike, "Does it feel weird – I mean, coming from San Francisco, where there must be thousands of – well, y'know…to a place like this, this, like, 'sea of white?' Does it feel like a real adjustment? Or is it just – like, something you don't trip on?"

"Well, you know what's funny about that is that *this* – right here, being part of the soccer team – isn't really different for me," replied Mike. "I mean, you're right – the Sunset District, where we lived, is a real heavy Asian population, and there were all the different – y'know, Chinese, Japanese, Korean, a lotta Filipinos – huge crowd at Lincoln. So, yeah, being here, where you got – what is it, about six or seven Asian students? It's gonna take a little getting used to, maybe. But what I was saying was, even with the numbers, most of them weren't focused on sports. So that kinda set me apart from the beginning. Just like here, I was the only Asian member of the team – even on the JV, where I started off my freshman year before they switched me up."

"What drew *you* to the game?" Jay Marcivius asked.

"Well, I always went to school in the Sunset," said Mike, "but my parents' work situation – my mom's a home care nurse, and the summer when I was about eight, she got appointed to take care of some patients in the Mission District. So they had to set it up for me to go to one of the rec centers there, so I could get picked up on time and everything. Well, the

Mission is the Latino community, and man, you're talking about folks who live and breathe the game. With some of those kids, it's *everything* to them. I mean, they could've just finished their soccer game, and you ask them, 'Whattya want to do now?' Find an available field somewhere, and play *more* soccer! So that was the activity, day in and day out, and, I dunno, I just took to it. It felt like a good fit. So from that point on, I pretty much did soccer camps all summer, and it just kinda became my thing. But just about all the other kids were white or Hispanic – maybe one or two black guys, here and there. I had to get used to being the outlier in the group. So this is a more familiar scene than you'd think."

"Outlier?" echoed Steve Grenier, the team's would-be comic. "Sounds like somebody who tells you he's realized he's gay, but he's just making it up."

The locker room went silent. After a second or two, Seth Langdon spoke for the team: "Groaner, that didn't even come *close* to working. One more of those, and you get an extra two laps tomorrow." Grenier offered a half-apologetic shrug in response.

"Nah, the outlier was – it was from – don't you guys remember statistics?" implored Jesse Irving. "When we were doing the mean, median, mode – all that shit we were supposed to find for a set of numbers."

"Right," said Kevin. "An outlier was a number that was, like, a mile away from the others in the set. Like if you had 8, 7, 6, 50,000, and 9, the 50,000 would be the outlier."

"Yeah," recalled Jesse, "and the thing about it was, if there was an outlier, it messed with the average! Remember that? It threw it all outta whack. There was that one about if the workers in a – if, like, the 10 workers at a factory each make $18,000 a year, but the owner takes home $11 million, then, y'know, he shouldn't go around bragging that the whole workforce makes 'an average' of a million a year. It's *his* pay that's throwing that all off and making the average so much higher; everyone else is just barely getting by. That's why we figured out that the *median* would be a better measure in that situation, 'cause it – because … are we getting a little off topic?"

"Nah, it's no biggie," Mike assured him. "Hey, look, it'll fit everyone's expectations perfectly: Just go home and tell 'em, 'We had a Japanese guy join the team today, and he got us all talking about math and statistics in the locker room afterwards.'" Everyone laughed, and Steve Grenier made a mental note to study Mike Yamasaki's timing and delivery.

Over the ensuing couple of weeks, Kevin worked on striking the right balance to earn Mike's respect, which would be needed when the time came to enlist him in his quest. He made a concerted effort to make the newcomer feel welcome on the team and (when the opportunity presented itself) at the school in general. Being in different grades, they didn't share any classes, but if Kevin saw Mike in the cafeteria or during leisure time on campus, he would beckon for him to join whatever group he happened to be engaged with, and would introduce him around.

At the same time, he guarded against appearing desperately friendly, omnipresent, or ingratiating. Jessica had cautioned him against "coming off like someone trying to establish his liberal credentials by seeking out token cross-cultural connections." Kevin had no remote clue what these words of advice meant, but he did his best to adhere to them anyway.

The immediate dividends yielded by the new presence, and clear upgrade, in the line-up helped create a natural comfort in association. By the end of Mike's third practice, Jay Marcivius had been effectively "Wally-Pipped" – the sports-world colloquialism for permanently losing one's job to a new phenom, named for the Yankee first baseman who missed a game with an injury and was replaced by a rookie named Lou Gehrig. Mike was slated to start the next game at left wing. Dallas Tompkins, the team's strongest shooter, reaped the greatest benefit, with his scoring opportunities increasing about threefold in Mike's first game. The Monroe Mustangs had been undefeated at the point of Mike's arrival, but with him, their margins of victory promptly increased to a much more comfortable range; instead of 3-1 or 1-0, they were suddenly winning by scores of 4-0 or 6-1.

The players tended to assign nicknames to most of their own ranks. Usually, it merely involved a corny variation on the player's name – alongside simple abbreviations like "Wilks" and "Irv," they referred to Jay Marcivius as "Shivers," Sterling Larkins as "Skylark," and Sean McBride as "McGroom." In a few isolated instances, though, a nickname would relate to a player's specific skill area. Left defender Cody Orbach, known for his fearlessness in approaching long, mile-high punts from the opposing goalie and heading them back upfield, was "Bouncer" – a name that reflected both the literal bouncing of the ball off his head and the more figurative connotation of clearing trouble from the scene. ("Groaner," the name assigned to Steve Grenier, had the enviable distinction of being both a play on his name *and* an assessment of his comedic instincts.)

It was along similar lines that, from unknown origins amongst the squad, Mike's patented centering pass soon became the "Golden Gate Bridge." In short order, that segued into Mike being anointed "Golden Gate." (Steve Grenier put some feelers out on "Yama-soccer," but found that it didn't catch on.) The moniker took some getting used to on Mike's part; early on, he felt the need to pull Seth Langdon aside to receive some assurance that the "golden" part wasn't some veiled allusion to his skin tone.

"Ahh, no, man, that's nowhere in their minds," the goalie promised him, laughing. "That's no part of it. Nah, it's just their only reference point for San Francisco – the first thing they identify it with, that's all."

"Umm … okay," muttered Mike. "Guess it beats 'Rice-a-Roni …' "

While the newcomer soon came to take the nickname in stride when hearing it from other players, Kevin nonetheless refrained from using it in his own dialogue, on the off chance that it still might rub his projected recruit the wrong way. This fell into a broader pattern, for Kevin, of treading carefully – eventually, it began to emerge, perhaps *too* carefully.

For even as the feeling of unity and shared accomplishment carried off the field and onto campus life for the players, Kevin nonetheless found himself procrastinating when it came to broaching the subject with Mike. He would continually tell himself that he would absolutely, positively, pull Mike aside after *this practice* and introduce the topic to him – only to find a reason to put it off when the moment arose.

Though he didn't think of himself as superstitious, he couldn't deny that a nagging "don't mess with a good thing" mantra was repeating itself in his head, warning him against inviting in any kind of awkward element that could, in some unforeseeable way, jinx the positive flow that the team had going with Mike. Plus, Kevin continually reminded himself, track season was still a long way off – although that wouldn't be the case indefinitely, as Billy Lloyd reminded Kevin on more than one occasion.

It took a pure coincidence, a serendipitous moment, to convince Kevin that he had waited long enough. Early on a Saturday afternoon, he was at Sports Authority shopping for new socks and shin guards when he happened upon his intended protégé, there for the same purpose. After the two shared a few obligatory (and celebratory) comments regarding the previous day's 3-0 triumph over Marshall, Kevin impulsively asked, "Hey, Mike, are you in any kind of hurry?"

Mike shook his head. "What's goin' on?" he asked.

"I just wanted to talk to you about – well, there's an idea I wanna run by you, see how you feel about it. We could zip over to Subway, or the frozen yogurt place; I'll treat."

"Yeah, okay," responded Mike receptively, assuming the content of this idea would relate to the team in some manner – to game strategy, or a tweaking of the line-up. When they had each made their purchases and gone out the front door, Kevin pointed toward the various culinary options in the mall, inviting Mike to name his preference. "Swirlies is fine; I could go for a yogurt," indicated Mike. "That okay with you?" Kevin nodded, and they made their way across five storefronts in the mall. Mike got a small blueberry cheesecake with mixed-fruit topping, filled a paper cup at the drinking fountain, and joined Kevin at the table. "Thanks a lot, Wilks," he said, raising his bowl in acknowledgment. "So what'd you want to talk about?"

Kevin, despite having played out the exchange countless times in his mind, found himself suddenly tongue-tied. The weight of asking someone to play a central role in this systemic transformation was much more imposing than merely stating the case in favor of the transformation itself. "Umm, I was gonna ask … ummm … what are you thinking of doing in spring?"

The vagueness of the question elicited a puzzled frown from Mike. "Whattya mean, 'what am I doing?' I don't – I mean, I'm *here*, in school, and …" His voice faded out as he waited for clarification.

"Well, right – no – I mean – do you ever do … any spring sports? Like, I'm kinda tryin' to recruit some good runners for the track team."

Almost immediately, Mike shook his head in discomfort. "I don't think so, man."

"Well, why not?" asked Kevin, making sure to speak in an inviting tone, not a coercive one. "I mean, you've got such great form; I've made a point of checking things out during wind sprints and drills. You and Terry and Dallas are, like, the fastest runners on the team."

"*You're* the fastest runner on the team," corrected Mike.

"Well … yeah, maybe," said Kevin, trying to deflect the conversation from any discussion of his own role in the mix. "But you mean, you've never thought about it?"

"Nah," said Mike. "I mean, it's just . . ." Again, his voice trailed off.

"It's just what?" asked Kevin.

"Well, I'm not a hundred-yard dash guy. Y'know, you've got those guys with longer legs, a thinner build; I wouldn't really be able to … I mean, the heats, the distances where I'd do the best, the ones I think would play to my strengths, would be the ones in the middle ranges – the 200, or maybe the 400. And – well, of course those are out of the question."

"*Why* are they out of the question?" asked Kevin – not to solicit information he already knew, but rather to steer the dialogue in the direction he wanted it to go.

Mike angled his head a little, and peered across the table as if suddenly harboring doubts about Kevin's cognitive abilities. "Well, *you* know. I mean, of all people, you would have to know – *WIL*kerson ... "

He gestured toward Kevin with both hands, as if presenting an exhibit or a piece of evidence. The subtext was unmistakable, whether one's training ground had been Northern Illinois or Northern California: *We both know what sort of machinery we're up against,* Mike was conveying.

Kevin was already speaking more fluidly and confidently, satisfied that his pitch was starting to take its proper shape. "I know what you're talking about," he said, reassuring Mike that he wasn't out to lunch on the matter. "No one with a 'Y' name or a 'W' name ever wins those events. But why *is* that? Do you just figure that you're not as fast as those ... those Andersons and Bakers, and the guys who win 'em? Are they all just better runners than you?"

"*No,*" responded Mike, with both a tone and an expression that suggested he'd be a colossal idiot if he believed that.

"So you know," said Kevin, continuing to guide the exchange, "that it's more about the set-up than about actual skill and speed."

"I'm not stupid," said Mike, whose matter-of-fact delivery jolted Kevin with the reminder that he, along with nearly everyone he knew, evidently *was* stupid until about nine months earlier. Echoing his first visit with Greg Beech, Kevin felt the point being driven home once again that just because a problem has gone unaddressed doesn't necessarily mean that it's gone unnoticed.

Bracing himself for the firestorm the suggestion could unleash, he asked, "But if you knew – if you could see that they had this rigged set-up that made it impossible for you to compete, why didn't you say something about it?"

"Oh, gee – thanks, pal," reacted Mike, more in amusement than annoyance. "I mean, at least we're not putting any pressure on anyone here, are we? This way that they've done it for a hundred and somp'm years, which *they* obviously have their reasons for keeping it that way, even if they don't make a goddamn bit of sense to me – *I'm* supposed to be the one, *me,* personally, to take on city hall, and tell them they've got things backwards? Wow – yeah, ya know, I would, but I'm kinda going through this transition period right now: It's called 'life.' So, like, maybe if I didn't have anything else to worry about. But hey, what about you? You're in the same boat. Why don't *you* say something about it?"

"I did."

Kevin said this so calmly and resolutely that Mike knew instantaneously that the story·didn't end there. Kevin didn't just "say something about it" – Mike had no iota of doubt, judging by the serene smile on Kevin's face, that he had *done* something about it, too.

"What are you talking about?" asked Mike, trading in his confrontational tone for an intrigued, almost deferential one.

Trying to condense things without sacrificing crucial content, Kevin relayed to Mike the events and discoveries that had led to his interest in the young prospect. He told him of the inconsistencies that had first aroused his suspicions, his own disastrous tryout in the 400 and his subsequent enlightenment courtesy of Jessica, the obtuse reaction of Mr. Paige, Billy Lloyd joining the ranks, the sale of the concept to Ed Markbreit (with a sidebar to explain what the concept *was*), and the lifeless briefing by Tom Ackerman at the fall assembly.

With each chapter, Mike's attentiveness became more evident. When the saga was complete, Mike looked slightly to one side, arched his eyebrows, and mouthed, "Wow ..." Turning back to Kevin, he said, "So this is – I mean, they're really gonna implement this? You know that for sure?"

"It was announced; that's all I know," Kevin reiterated. "At a certain point, I'm gonna make another call to the commissioner, to Mr. Markbreit, just to check in and confirm everything ... and also, to make sure that they'll have some, y'know, neutral officials there to make sure things get set up right. Ackerman's not on board, as far as his whole attitude, and I think he'd undercut the change if he felt like nobody was watching."

Uh-huh," said Mike, "and your reason for not doing it – I mean, not running yourself is ... what? You're worried people would look at it like that was the whole motive, your whole reason behind everything?"

"You got it," affirmed Kevin. "That's it, exactly. That's why Ackerman made sure to put it out there like it was all *my* doing, not something that Billy Lloyd was in on with me. It wouldn't work if I were the one to – if the result was a victory for me. But I can't just walk away from it, either.

It has to be – there needs to – there's gotta be an actual *effect*. If the same old names turn up, or if we put someone out there who's gonna lose by a mile anyway, they're gonna say it was all just a huge waste of time and energy. They'll say we were kidding ourselves the whole time – that this proves people like us don't have what it takes. It'll make the commissioner look bad, too, and I seriously can't let that happen."

He paused a moment, and then explained, "But, you see, Mike, winning the race is just half the battle in this one. It's just as important that when you *do* win the race – I mean, well, y'know, who*ever* it is that wins the race – that they know how to answer the bullshit questions they're gonna have to face. There's this asshole Simon Addison, a senior who thinks he was born on page one, and he's never gonna let this go. But he won't be the only one. People – some of them'll say you had an unfair advantage, that they had to 'help' you win. You need to be able– geez, listen to me; I'm jumping the gun again! I'm sorry; I don't mean to keep saying 'you.' I'm just talking about what's gonna happen when somebody does – when someone breaks through on this."

"No, it's cool – I understand how you're using the word," Mike assured him. "So, you need someone who can tell them, basically, 'Screw you, up yours, go to hell, I ain't apologizin' for shit.' "

"Well – yeah, e-e-e-essentially, I guess, but ..."

"I didn't mean in those exact words," said Mike.

"Okay," said Kevin, exhaling heavily.

"I think I could come up with some good – some pretty good comebacks," said Mike. "I mean, we're all going the same 400 meters – for the first time *ever*, maybe, but doesn't it kinda come down to that? And hey, if this Addison guy complains that I'm getting some special treatment by having the line moved to the right place, I can just tell him I'll switch lanes with him if he thinks it'll help. We can have our own, off-the-record race, and he can choose any goddamn lane he wants."

Over roughly the last ninety percent of Mike's brainstorm, Kevin was floating in the stratosphere. Mike hadn't yet given him a word-for-word pledge, "I'll do it," but for all intents and purposes, that was precisely what he was telling Kevin. The moment Mike abandoned the conditional tense by saying "we're all going ..." Kevin was overwhelmed with excitement, knowing that he had his answer. Still, it would be bad form to forge ahead without confirmation.

"Wait. So it sounds like you're saying ... it's – like you're interested in giving it a try. Is that – I mean – does it sound like something you wanna do?"

"It's like you said," responded Mike. "*Some*one has to."

"Oh, man, I can't even tell you how much I hoped you'd be up for this." Unashamed about revealing the depth of his emotional investment, Kevin leaned his head forward until it came to rest on his clenched fingers, and kept it lowered for a few seconds before looking back up. "And I'll do whatever I can, anything I can, to make sure this pays off for you. I'll work with you. This is what needed to happen. First of all, I knew you were smart enough to know what to say if–"

Kevin caught himself as he noted an uncomfortable reaction from Mike, and quickly clarified, "I'm *not* stereotyping; I've been around you enough to know that you had enough goin' on upstairs to handle this. And look, you're already ahead of me – I hadn't even thought of that idea of offering to race Simon, or whoever, on different lanes. But that's the key, like you said. Not feeling like you owe anyone an apology if you win."

"That's part of what makes it … well, it kinda – in a weird kind of way, it reminds me a little of something in my family history," said Mike.

"What's that?" asked Kevin, genuinely interested – although, as appreciative as he was feeling at that moment, he was quite prepared to affirm the uncanny similarity even if Mike were to go on to equate the situation with a special recipe from his favorite aunt's cookbook.

"Well, it's also about people who, when you … when you take steps to make something fair, they treat it like it's a pain in the ass."

"Uh-huh," said Kevin, whose countenance urged Mike to proceed.

"See … my grandfather was interned during World War II," Mike began.

"Yeah? What line of work?" Kevin asked.

"No, not an 'intern,' " Mike corrected him. "He was *interned.* He was caught up in it when they rounded up all the Japanese Americans on the West Coast and threw them in prison camps, 'cause they thought they'd be, like, loyal to Japan instead of America."

"Oh, right! God! I don't know anything about that, but I know it – I mean, that it happened," said Kevin. "That was crazy! They just assumed anyone might be a spy, huh?"

"Yeah," said Mike, "but you notice, they only did it to one group, right? I mean, remember, we were fighting the Germans and the Italians, too, but nobody started locking up all the German Americans, or all of a sudden saying that people with Italian names should be treated like enemies."

"Interesting point … wonder what the distinction could've been," responded Kevin, adopting a deadpan tone and affecting a slight roll of his eyes to assure Mike that yes, he did know exactly what the distinction was. He thought back to his discussion with Jessica about the inconsistent standards of the Founding Fathers, and concluded, "Boy, you learn a lot of things over the years that kinda get in the way of your – your patriotic, uh …" He left the sentence incomplete, unable to find the right abstract noun to finish it.

"Well, yeah, that'll happen," concurred Mike, "but later on, when people began to come around a *little* on race issues and stuff, well, then it started to feel kind of embarrassing that – y'know, that all this had happened. So they started coming up with some arrangements to compensate the ones who'd been put in those camps – the ones who were still alive, anyway."

"When did this start happening?" Kevin asked. "How many – how much later on?"

"As far as I know, not until the late '70s," responded Mike. "So we're talkin' about these – these reparations finally getting to the victims, like, 35 years after the fact. But they did it; they followed though. They tracked down the ones who were still around, and gave them somp'm like twenty thousand dollars each."

"Did your grandfather get his?"

"Yeah, he did – but, really, *we* got it. He didn't have his kids – and that was really just my mom, and a brother who died real young – he didn't have them 'til later. He was already 54, I think, when my mom was born. So by the time this award came, he was around 82 or somp'm like that, and near the end of his life. So it wasn't like *he* was gonna go out and party with the money. He did what anyone would do; he passed it on to his daughter, and her family."

"You would've already been around by that time, right?" asked Kevin, doing some quick subtraction in his head.

"Yeah, but I was just two or three. I didn't know about any of it when it was actually going on. I learned about all this stuff later – a few years ago. But this is where it ties in. My dad said that, when the decision was made to give these payouts, these awards, there were actually people, like newspaper columnists or whoever, that tried to argue that it wasn't fair."

"That what wasn't fair?"

"They said it wasn't fair that these awards were being given, because – well, just like I was telling you in our case, a lot of the folks were too old to do anything with the money except give it to their kids. And *they* hadn't been the ones – the next generation, they hadn't been put in the camps. So some people had the nerve to freak out about that. They were like, 'Why should *these* people get anything?' It's funny; I'd be ready to bet they never once wrote a column – or they wouldn't have, if they'd been around back then – talking about how it's unfair to grab someone who's never broken a law, or … shown any disloyalty to their country, and just throw 'em in prison 'cause they're the wrong race. But the moment someone gets – y'know, comes into a benefit that they couldn't see themselves getting, *that's* when they suddenly notice things not being all perfect and equal."

"Damn – that *is* starting to sound a little like this," remarked Kevin.

Mike nodded. "And, see, this was the dumbest thing about it, my dad pointed out. They act like what happens at one time, or to one generation, doesn't have any effect on what comes after it. Like everyone starts with some … some sort of blank slate that's got nothing to do with anything before them. When those folks were taken to those camps, everything they had – all their property, all their possessions – got confiscated by the government. They just *took* all their stuff from them; maybe some of them got some of it back after the war, but probably most of them had to start from scratch. So that was money, or property, that their kids *would* have inherited, right? If it hadn't been stolen from them, basically? I mean, sure, there would've been all different levels of … of what they would have earned, and what they would have passed on. But it's not like hauling my grandfather off to a prison camp and taking all his stuff had 'nothing to do with me,' or with my life."

Kevin chimed in eagerly: "Right! And wait a minute – who's gonna – I mean, since when are you supposed to feel guilty about it if your parents come into some money when they're already gettin' up there in age? Those people complaining – I mean, like any of *them* would've turned down their own inheritance! They wouldn't have cared *when* their parents got the money, or how it ended up coming to them. They would've taken it in a heartbeat! Why should your mom and dad be the only ones who're supposed to go around feeling like they got something they didn't deserve?"

"It gets worse, though," said Mike. "I mean, it gets … crazy, really. There were a few writers – again, this is just stuff I heard from my folks – who said that the whole compensation thing was a bad idea because it didn't 'look good' that a bunch of payouts were just going strictly to Japanese people."

"Are they *kidding*?" asked Kevin in wholesale disbelief. "Who the hell else were they supposed to *go* to?"

"Yeah, that'd be my question," agreed Mike, "But that's pretty much how they said it. They said, basically, a lot of things go wrong for a lot of people, and it's gonna rub folks the wrong way if 'certain people' get big awards and others don't. Like we were being singled out for some special favor."

"And no one pointed out the little detail that they didn't *put* anyone but the Japanese into those prison camps?!" Kevin asked.

"Yeah, I know; good point. Somehow, it got by them," muttered Mike.

Kevin began to role-play, in mock self-pity: "Hey, I sprained my ankle once – where's *my* twenty grand?" Instantly, the familiarity to his own ear of his tone and content struck him. "Aw, man – you know what? That's *exactly* what Simon Addison would've said, something just like that! Only he would've been serious, like it was an actual – I mean, he would've thought he was making some kind of a statement about *you,* not about … about those newspaper columnists."

"So he's good at noticing when it's not – when stuff doesn't work out in his favor," Mike concluded.

"Right," said Kevin. "As long as everything goes his way, then everything's just, y'know, the way it was supposed to be. You know how you could have a little kid who – okay, like, let's say someone brings in one cookie for each kid in a class, or something. He's like the kid who thinks he should get all the cookies for himself, and when you tell him, no, he'll get the *same* as everyone else, he starts screaming, 'It's not fair!' It's the same thing you'd hear from a little kid, just like that: 'Fair,' to him, means he gets to come out on top."

"Well, then, we'll have to give him something 'unfair' to complain about," said Mike. "I'm pretty sure it could– oh, shit!" He jumped up from his chair, looking at his watch.

"What's the problem?" Kevin asked.

"Now I *am* in a hurry," said Mike. "I gotta get to my sister's piano lesson by two; she forgot her bus money, and I have to connect with her. But listen, we'll talk on Monday, and get this whole thing rollin'. I'm good. Thanks again for the yogurt." He ran out the door and disappeared to the left of the front window.

Damn, thought Kevin as he sat alone at the table. *I oughtta be a talent scout, or a company recruiter or something. I've got this real gift for meeting the right people.*

Later that afternoon, he called Billy Lloyd and gave him the good news.

"That's great, man; terrific," said Billy Lloyd. "Now, you understand, I'm still gonna kick his ass when the time comes, right? I mean, just makin' sure you keep that in mind."

Kevin had momentarily forgotten that, unlike him, Billy Lloyd would still be an entrant in the 400 when spring arrived, and – with the systemic flaw corrected and a legitimate outcome guaranteed – would now have even greater motivation to win. He took a moment to re-orient himself.

"Well, if you do, umm … more power to ya," he finally said. "At least you won't have to second-guess yourself this time."

"That's the whole idea," said Billy Lloyd.

CHAPTER 11
Taking Care of Business

Verbalizing it to Mike served as a reminder to Kevin that he had, in fact, intended to touch base with Commissioner Markbreit – but had been hemming and hawing for quite a while, mulling over what to say (and even what medium of communication to use). Now that his chance encounter with his projected groundbreaker had proven a successful catalyst to get that ball rolling, Kevin figured it was similarly time to stop putting off this outreach call. He obtained Markbreit's fax number from Billy Lloyd, and then composed and sent a note requesting that the commissioner call him when he had the time. He received the call about two weeks later, on the 18th of November.

"Mr. Markbreit! Hi! Thanks for getting back to me."

"Of course. I'm sorry it takes so long. You guys have a pretty big game coming up, don't you? You and the soccer team?"

"Yeah, we're in the final – we're hosting Hillside on Friday, and if we can hold 'em off, it's an undefeated season. Monroe hasn't ever had that before. I mean, as far as the soccer team."

"That's fantastic, and I want to wish you guys good luck. I'm hoping, tentatively planning on being there to see it. But I gather that's not what you called about …"

"Uh, yeah, no. I just felt like I should check in with you, to see if things are still looking good for the new arrangement we talked about, and … I guess, to see if there's anything I can do to help. I know, probably not, but I just thought it'd be worth asking."

"Yeah, no, I think we're actually in pretty good shape," responded Markbreit. "We've taken all the necessary measurements for each of the affected events, and we'll be on hand to make sure everything's set up according to our specifications."

"Oh, good – I was hoping there'd be, like, interleague personnel taking care of all that, making sure things were done right," said Kevin.

"Having some doubts about our own sports director's trustworthiness?" Markbreit asked, sensing that Kevin was waiting for him to open the door to the subject area.

"Well, I don't like to – I mean, I would never accuse Mr. Ackerman of trying to – like, to sabotage it or anything, I just … well, you could tell from the way he announced it back in September, you could see that his heart wasn't in it."

"That's not something you'd ever have to worry about, in any case," Markbreit affirmed. "The set-up for any event, and the enforcement of the rules, that's always the responsibility of the league. It's always handled at that level. We'd never entrust that to a school itself, or to the athletic director. That's a matter of policy, right across the board."

"Okay, yeah – I mean, I figured it was," said Kevin, who in spite of his statement of confidence was feeling much more at ease having heard the commissioner's words of reassurance. "If you don't mind my asking," he went on, "have the other A.D.'s gotten on board with the idea? What's the overall reaction been?"

"It's been mixed," said Markbreit. "The whole range. Some of the directors actually favor the idea a lot – like Jack Wohlford at Marshall and Stephanie Turlock over at Burbank. But then, some of the others, like Don Cranston at Greenfield and Jerry Ambrose from Redfern, aren't too happy about it. And then, a few are kind of in the middle on it – like Garrett McCaffrey over at Hillside."

"Oh. Okay," said Kevin.

"But we're hoping the holdouts will come around, eventually. Quite honestly – and I don't know if this makes you feel better or worse – Ackerman's been the toughest nut to crack on this one."

"I don't doubt that," chimed in Kevin, "and I don't think you can count on Mr. Paige to bring him around on it, either." He quickly thought to add, "Well, you know, that's why I'm taking myself out of the running on those events – the ones that're impacted."

"You are?" Markbreit sounded genuinely surprised.

"Yeah … I just decided it would look – well, that too many people would look at it like I was just doing it for myself if I came out and ran in the same event. I want to make sure people understand it's not about that. It was never about me being pissed off that I didn't win. I'll still be there. I'll do something, some event that's not affected by the change. And I've worked things out with this younger guy, a junior who just transferred to Monroe. I think he's gonna run in the 400. I'll kinda be his trainer."

"That was a really wise decision," said Markbreit. "It takes away any ammunition someone might have against you. Billy Lloyd's still going to run, though, right?"

"Oh, yeah, definitely," Kevin confirmed. "He's ready to go right now. There's no issue with him."

"Well, tell him … uh …" Markbreit went quiet for a moment, then resumed. "You know, now that I think about it, yes, there *is* something that both of you can do. I would've thought of this further down the line, in fact, and gotten in touch with both of you."

"Sure, what is it?" Kevin asked receptively.

"Well, I'm sure you realize that a change this big, it's going to garner a good deal of media attention. You and Billy Lloyd, you've already shown that you can make the case for why this had to happen – you made a foolproof argument to me, which got us to this point. What's important is that I can count on both of you to be available on the tryout day, when this is first put into effect – to be accessible to the reporters, ready to answer any questions, no matter how dumb some of them might be. You're prepared to continue being the front men for this, in other words – can I assume that?"

"Oh, yeah, absolutely, sir," Kevin assured him unhesitatingly. "And the kid who's gonna win the – well, who's *hopefully* gonna win the 400 – he'll be a perfect front person for the whole deal himself, too. He caught on to where I was going before I really even finished spelling it all out."

"That's great," responded Markbreit. "Glad to hear it."

"But how's anyone gonna know to ask *us*, specifically?" inquired Kevin. "I mean, if Mike – that's the guy I'm working with – if he goes ahead and wins the race, obviously they'll seek him out. But how will they know that Billy Lloyd and I have anything to say about it – especially since I won't be running in those events? Is someone gonna, like, steer them in our direction?"

"They're reporters – it's their job to find that stuff out," said Markbreit. "Of course, they'll ask a wide range of respondents – other runners, coaches and trainers, probably some random spectators. But they're going to want to track down the "Ws" of journalism – you know, who, when, why – and they'll follow up on their leads ahead of time, so they know who to look for on the tryout day. Trust me, it'll be a busy day for you, and it *may* pull some of your focus away from whatever event, or events, you do decide to enter. Are we okay with that possibility?"

"Yep," responded Kevin. "You got it. We'll be ready for whatever they throw at us. We'll probably even rehearse a little, between Billy Lloyd, Mike, and me, just so we don't get caught off guard."

"Sounds like a plan," said Markbreit. "I have to take care of some other business now, but unless something unexpected comes up, I'll see you at the match on Friday."

Friday arrived, and evidently, something unexpected *did* come up – as Kevin pretty much expected it would – but after quickly scanning the stands and the V.I.P. boxes alongside the announcers' booth, and not seeing the commissioner, Kevin put that aside and gave a quick wave of acknowledgment to his personal cheering section, which consisted of Jessica, his parents, his aunt Joanie and uncle Rich, and Marvin Bartolomeo, a co-worker on his father's crew who had coached Kevin in the youth league a few years earlier. Then, turning his back to the stands, he set upon gearing his energy solely toward the task of rallying the team around its ultimate aim.

"Alright, EVERYONE IN!" he yelled forcefully, as the referee indicated that they were within about five minutes of kick-off time. Except for Seth Langdon, who continued making saves in the goal on balls tossed by an assistant coach, the varsity players abandoned their passing and juggling warm-up drills and ran to form a huddle around Kevin by the bench. Coach Lawford nodded, authorizing Kevin to handle the pep talk.

"We *know* we're the best team!" Kevin declared unequivocally. "And there is NO excuse for us not to play like it! We can talk all we want about a bad call last year, but if we had taken care of business, the game wouldn't have *been* close enough to be decided on some bullshit like that! So we're gonna TAKE care of business this year! We want it the most, we've already beaten this team once, and we didn't even have our Golden Gate Bridge goin' for us when we did it!" He gave an appreciative glance toward Mike as he spoke, then paused a moment to allow Seth to join in the huddle.

"We're stronger now than we were then. We all know that. But it's not gonna count for a damn thing if anyone's planning to go out there and give less than this team needs from you. That's *not* gonna happen – every one of you, you're gonna be *there* for your teammates. If I get the ball, if Irv or Terry gets the ball, I want us to have at *least* three options from the moment it's there at our feet. You're not waiting for the game to come to you; you're anticipating, every moment, asking yourself, 'Where does my team need me to be?' All right? All right?! ALL RIGHT?!" The team started to echo the phrase, raising their collective voices to a crescendo. "Let's DO it!! Get out there and stick it to 'em! Let's kick some ass!!" Kevin yelled, as the players high-fived and made their way out to their respective positions.

It didn't take long for things to begin feeling fairly secure. A mere nine minutes following the opening whistle, Mike outran the Hillside right defender to a loose ball in the corner, pivoted, and with his strong left foot lofted a centering pass that soared over the mixed clump of players in the goal area and landed about twelve feet out from the right post, where Dallas Tompkins advanced and slammed a right-footed shot past Charley Grant, Hillside's all-league goalkeeper.

About fifteen minutes later, Kevin got his opportunity. As he retrieved a ricocheted ball about twenty yards behind the midfield line, he saw that the aggressive Hillside defense had made the collective mistake of intruding a few steps past that line and onto Monroe's half of the field. He affected a big windup and feigned a pass toward Mike, who was momentarily lingering across midfield in an offside position. Confident that they were about to see the pass go through, see the lineman raise his flag for offside, hear the referee's whistle, and be awarded a free kick, the opposing defenders relaxed their posture for a split second – during which Kevin promptly tapped the ball to his right, adjusted his balance, and launched a long leading pass toward the completely abandoned *left* side of Hillside's defensive half, where Sterling Larkins tracked it down a good twenty-five yards away from the nearest defender, dribbled it about ten additional yards, and nonchalantly slipped a low shot under Grant's reach. The Hillside stopper and left fullback erupted over the lack of an offside call, but the linesman covering their defensive half verified for the referee that Sterling hadn't yet crossed midfield at the moment when the ball left Kevin's foot, which negated the possibility of such a violation. And Mike hadn't been a participant in the play, which made his illegal position irrelevant. The goal stood, and Monroe made it to halftime with a 2-0 lead.

Things grew a little tenuous when Hillside's rangy attacker, Harley Gilliard, capitalized on his height advantage over the 5'8" R. J. West to head a corner kick past Seth Langdon's dive and narrow the score to 2-1, just six minutes into the second half. Coach Lawford ordered Kevin and Terry Cressman to focus primarily on defense from that point forward, to guard against an equalizing goal.

At the eighteen-minute mark, though, the Mustangs regained the breathing room they desperately sought. In a nicely poetic turn, the third goal came courtesy of Jay Marcivius, the deposed starter who was now relegated to playing roughly fifteen-minute stretches each half, when Mike needed a breather from all his sprinting up and down the line. The Hillside defense had just foiled a Monroe attack and gained possession of the ball. Sterling and Dallas began their obligatory retreat, and Jay turned as if he was about to head back toward midfield, too – but then he suddenly spun back around and darted into the path between the right back and the stopper, having correctly anticipated that the former was about to feed a casual pass to the latter (whom the defense ordinarily relied on to launch the ball downfield). Catching both defenders entirely by surprise, Jay intercepted the pass, dribbled twice, and blasted the ball into the upper right corner of the net.

He was immediately buried in a dogpile of appreciative teammates, and received a second round of high-fives eight minutes later, when he returned to the bench as Mike re-entered the game to play out the remainder.

As the last few minutes were winding down, with the 3-1 victory looking securely in hand, Coach Lawford began subbing out the marquee players who were finishing off their varsity careers – in increasing order of prominence, that meant midfielders Jesse Irving and Terry Cressman and left back Cody Orbach, then Kevin, and finally Dallas Tompkins – so they could receive their due applause from the crowd for helping to bring home the championship and an undefeated season. (Mike was kept in the game because he was still a junior, and Seth because replacing the starting goalie in such a circumstance could be perceived as rubbing the result in the opponents' faces.) As each substitution took place, the announcer went all out to emphasize the departing stars: "Now entering the game, Sean McBride replacing KEVIN WILLLL–KERSONNNNNN!" The crowd responded accordingly. It was a transcendent moment, one that each of the players knew they would carry with them for life.

Two weeks later, on Friday of the first full week back from the Thanksgiving break, the Fall Athletics Award Banquet was held in the school's multi-purpose hall. Kevin attended with his mother and father. The array of fall teams and their respective individual honorees were acknowledged in roughly ascending order of their relative success. The football, volleyball, and lacrosse teams announced their most valuable players, along with special awards for inspirational play, team leadership, or improvement. Thirteen players across those various teams were recognized for making first-team or second-team all-league. The honors in cross-country included the biggest accolade to this point in the evening, highlighting the accomplishments of Erin McBride (the older sister of Kevin's backup at center half), who had achieved the district's best numbers among the girls.

Everyone present knew, of course, that the sequence would climax with the coronation of the soccer champs. Kevin applauded as his protégé Mike Yamasaki received the Tiny Arnold Award for inspirational or courageous play. (The award was named for an undersized but impactful soccer player who starred at Monroe in the mid-1970s, before tragedy struck in the form of a fatal motorcycle accident about a month prior to graduation.) Kevin then joined Dallas Tompkins and Cody Orbach on stage as it was announced that the three of them had made first team all-league – and remained there as the room erupted over the announcement that Dallas had been voted Most Valuable Player of the entire league. Dallas' first response, before the hysteria had any chance to die down, was to beckon and shout for Mike to return to the stage. "Golden Gate! Get back up here! Get a handle on this prize! C'mon! C'mon, I didn't do it by myself, man!" After a brief hesitation, Mike acquiesced and came up once more, to the cheers of the audience, and joined Dallas in hoisting the MVP trophy up above their heads.

Then came the time for the official consecration of the championship itself, which would include the unveiling of the trophy to be housed in the gym's front lobby, the handing out of honorary certificates to all team members, and the awarding of smaller replicas of the trophy to the team captains. As the players began making their way from their respective tables toward the staircase on the right side of the stage, Kevin descended those same stairs to assume his spot alongside Seth at the end of the queue.

Joe Lawford proceeded to check the inscription on the top certificate in the stack and offered a few laudatory comments about the corresponding player before announcing his name. Jesse Irving, knowing from the content of the introduction that it referred to him, promptly made his way to the center of the stage to receive his award and shake hands with the coach and the athletic director. Next up was Jay Marcivius, still basking in the glow of a full week of accolades for that third score (and further buoyed by the awareness that, with Jesse graduating in June, the starting left half position would be his to claim in the fall). The acknowledgments continued – Steve Grenier, Todd Smith, Ruben James West – as Lawford made his way through the randomly ordered stack, surreptitiously altering the sequence at a couple of points so that the captains would be summoned last.

As each name was reeled off and applauded, and as Kevin and Seth progressed closer to the middle of the stage, the thought began staking out its domain in Kevin's mind: *How is he going to do it? What little trick is Ackerman going to pull to try to sabotage my moment?* He sensed, with virtual certainty, that there would have to be *something,* some little dig. It wouldn't be anything detectable to the crowd, nor even to the coach and the players in the immediate vicinity. In some mode of conveyance decipherable only to Kevin, though, Ackerman would get his two cents in. Kevin implored himself not to react in any overt manner when the inevitable took place. *Rise above it,* he commanded himself. *This is your night, not his.*

Finally Coach Lawford was speaking of Kevin, complimenting his vision on the field, his advanced understanding of the game, and his leadership skills. Having learned previously from Kevin that he was focusing his collegiate search within a local geographical range, he concluded, "We know that some university in this region is going to reap a great windfall for their soccer program when they offer this young man a scholarship. Let's hear it, just one more time, for Kevin Wilkerson!"

The crowd offered up a final round of applause. Its decreased volume, relative to the earlier response to the all-league announcements, didn't reflect any drop-off in enthusiasm, but merely corresponded with the lateness of the hour and the attendees' rapidly waning energy. A decent number of the families associated with the other sports had already snuck out of the hall, and by now everyone was ready to go home, including Kevin. He gave one last appreciative wave to the room, received his trophy, and shook Lawford's hand, as each of them thanked the other for the role he had played in delivering the prize.

Kevin then stepped past the coach to be congratulated by the A.D. For a brief moment, the possibility entered his mind that Ackerman just *might* lay aside his resentment – if temporarily – for the purpose of treating an undefeated season with the unfettered appreciation it truly deserved. Kevin had, after all, brought a great deal of acclaim to Monroe High School and its athletic program. Maybe, just maybe, Ackerman would find a way to … well, the moment had come. Time to find out.

Ackerman shook Kevin's hand – perhaps more civilly than warmly, but not with any noticeable sense of physical resistance to the exchange – and said, simply, "Congratulations, Wilkerson, good work. You really earned this."

Cuuuuuute, thought Kevin. *Subtle. Pretty well done, actually. Yeah, I really EARNED this. So, obviously, there's the distinction: THIS was legitimately earned – and isn't it better this way? Huh? Don't you think so, Wilkerson? Wouldn't you rather enjoy GENUINE victories like this one, rather than that OTHER way that we both know you're trying to score one for yourself in track? Man, what a little worm. Well, you knew it all along – it was gonna happen. Let's just wrap things up here with dignity.*

Kevin had felt no inclination, over the previous month, to expend even the minimal time and energy it would have taken to inform Ackerman that, in fact, he wouldn't be attaining *any* victory in the events due for restructuring – that he had opted to keep his distance from them. He hadn't wanted to offer any gesture that could be interpreted as self-doubt, of reservations about the worthiness of his cause, because he had none. And in spite of Ackerman's token act of gamesmanship, this was the least apt setting – and time of night – to engage in private, personalized banter that would throw any sort of cloud over the triumphant tone of the evening. But just as surely, Kevin couldn't pass up the chance to let Ackerman know he was onto him. He thought quickly. Then, with a self-assured smile, he responded, "Well, I did it for all of us." If Tom Ackerman could traffic in coded language and double meanings, so could Kevin Wilkerson.

The dinner was over, and the remaining athletes and their accompanying family members, most of them half asleep, filed out into the parking lot. Mr. and Mrs. Yamasaki made a point of tracking down the Wilkersons to express their gratitude for Kevin's outreach to Mike. They had harbored concerns, naturally, over the adjustments that such a dramatic geographical and cultural shift might entail for their kids, and they credited Kevin with having played a key role in smoothing their son's transition. As Mike circled to the rear right door of his family's station wagon, Kevin caught up with him and offered a friendly, innocuous punch on the shoulder.

"One down, one to go," he said with a smile.

"Well, hopefully *more* than one, right?" came Mike's protest. "You're gonna be going out for some other event yourself, aren't you?"

"Oh, umm … yeah. Yeah, probably, I guess … I haven't really been thinking too much about that," Kevin answered in total candor.

CHAPTER 12
Variables

Over the month of November, Kevin had obtained application materials for a handful of colleges. He had deliberately put off the process of filling them out, though, until after the championship game, at which point his athletic resumé – he had correctly anticipated – would be adorned with the ultimate feather in its cap. Now he was ready, and after devoting the entire day following the banquet to relaxation and reflection, he dove into the task with a sudden sense of urgency.

As he had indicated to Coach Lawford, he was restricting his choices to candidates within Illinois and the neighboring states. Although not adverse to new experiences, he had always been something of a homebody and felt a strong urge to remain within about a half-day's drive of his roots. He had gathered the requisite paperwork from Michigan State, University of Illinois–Chicago, Northwestern, University of Wisconsin, Indiana University, and Evansville (also in Indiana), all of which boasted strong, highly regarded soccer programs. To enhance his credentials, he reserved some hours at the media center at Monroe and chipped in a few dollars to Terry Cressman, his teammate and an expert in video technology, to help him compile and edit a highlight reel from the footage taken by his parents or Jessica during various games, which he then included in each package he submitted.

With the championship a done deal, it was also time for another undertaking to begin in earnest. Kevin had actually begun some preliminary studies of the strategic particulars of the 400 prior to Mike's arrival at the school – back at the point when he first made the decision to switch his own role from contestant to trainer. He had almost immediately let that component take a back seat to his search for the right trainee, but now he was ready to resume his research.

Had Kevin been any kind of trendsetter in the area of computer science, he would have relished and seized upon the rapidly emerging technology that was suddenly allowing people to conduct wide-ranging research over their home terminals. But this early in the 1990s, the new advances in Internet design and accessibility were still only on the mental radar of a small handful of computer lab denizens among the student body. Kevin, not a part of that milieu, went about it the old-fashioned way, looking up applicable books and magazine articles at the community library and seeking out the expertise of local authorities on the subject.

His initial step in this effort was to arrange a consultation with Eric Shogren, the track coach. He wasn't at all worried that Shogren might hesitate to advise him, out of some misplaced loyalty to Ackerman. The coach, in between his fall duties with the cross-country team, had managed to attend three soccer games during October and early November. So now, upon receiving the news that the recent arrival whom he had seen zipping up and down the left sideline stood to be a new weapon in his arsenal as well, he was ready to offer any tactical points at his disposal.

Shogren remained frustratingly evasive, on the other hand, when Kevin made a marginal effort to prod an opinion out of him, some stance one way or the other, in relation to the new format. The coach kept his language in neutral, noncommittal territory: Well, this is the decision that's been made, some people feel one way and some feel another, and we'll just go with it and see how things turn out. This, it occurred to Kevin, could very well reflect an understandable reluctance to go out on a limb when the feelings of one's boss are so well known. He quickly concluded that it didn't make any difference where, if anywhere, Shogren stood on the issue. What mattered was that he and Kevin now shared an investment in seeing Mike succeed.

Shogren initially suggested referring to the records of 400-meter dash outcomes over the previous decade or so, in order to obtain a target time. He compiled a list of the winning times and presented it to Kevin three days after their initial consultation. Kevin cued in on the numbers, and tried to pay as little attention as possible to the names associated with them.

Delving into the study of technique itself – to the extent that there was much in the way of technique above and beyond "run very fast," Kevin journeyed over to the local junior college and scoured its library for guidebooks on successful coaching of one sport or another. The representative volumes for track & field were scanty, as was the specific coverage of the 400 in the couple of books he was able to locate. The totality of notes he copied for future reference ended up filling barely more than half of a single, standard 8½ x 11 sheet of paper.

One detail in particular grabbed his attention when he examined these books. Or, more accurately, it was the complete absence of a pertinent detail that grabbed his attention. At absolutely no point in any of the available texts did a single reference to lane assignment surface for discussion. As if by tacit agreement, not one of them ventured anywhere near the subject.

Helpful tips were disbursed in relation to form, posture, pacing, even what shoes or shorts to wear – but nowhere did these strategic guides see fit to alert readers to the single most surefire strategic move one could make to ensure victory: *Make sure to secure an inner lane for yourself before the race begins!* The records exhibited in the books passively confirmed the dominance enjoyed by early-namers, but their obvious implication – that being an early-namer might endow one with a formidable structural *advantage* – was unfit for print or consumption. The connection went entirely unacknowledged.

In discovering this oddity, Kevin came face-to-face, once again, with the indomitable power and influence of social convention. Here were the anointed experts in a field, going around completely oblivious – either that, or conspiring to project complete obliviousness – to the most glaring facet of that field, the ultimate elephant in the room. The thought occurred to Kevin that he might as well be reading a guide to heart surgery written by a doctor who'd never heard of anesthesia – or, better, listening to a baseball historian pondering the mystery of why black players didn't manage to hit any home runs in the Majors during the 1930s.

Still, he reasoned, that out-of-touch surgeon might know a thing or two about how to wield a scalpel, and that absent-minded historian nonetheless might have memorized who won the batting titles each year. Even the most clueless imbecile might house a valuable reserve of subject-specific knowledge. A fellow could be a "young-earth" creationist who goes through life insisting that all of existence began more recently than the domestication of animals – but he could still be the best local choice to repair your carburetor or videotape your wedding. So Kevin begrudgingly culled what he deemed worthwhile from the manuals, and formulated an outline of what to prioritize when he and Mike began their training sessions.

The senior and the junior met just before school let out for the holidays to map out their plan once it resumed. Kevin informed Mike that he stood to inherit the older of his father's two trucks on January 5th, when he would be turning eighteen. Transportation would be readily available at that point, and they made a plan whereby, starting on the 9th, Kevin would arrive at the Yamasakis' house on Saturdays at 1:00, pick up both Mike and his sister Julie, and drop Julie off at her music teacher's house, conveniently located within two blocks of the Monroe campus. He and Mike would then train for about a 45-minute stretch, finishing in time to retrieve the budding concert pianist and drop the siblings back off at home.

Kevin's initial intent was to mark off an approximation of where the advanced starting block would likely be in the outermost lane and work within the resulting path, but Mike petitioned against it, arguing that he should start by running an *entire* lap around the outer path in order to maximize his endurance and pacing instincts. As they moved further along in their training, he told Kevin, they could inch the starting point progressively forward until it lay in the vicinity of where they could expect it to be marked in the March tryouts. "If I can keep my strength up for a little *more* than 400," he explained, "it'll feel that much easier once we actually get down to the real distance. Y'know, like the guy in the warm-up circle swinging the bat with the doughnut weight on it, so when he drops it off and goes to the plate, the bat feels lighter." Kevin couldn't argue with that logic, although it would force them to delay the incorporation of the targeted running times into the mix. Because those winning times were achieved exclusively within the shortest couple of lanes, they would only become relevant once Mike was testing himself over a comparable distance.

They would ultimately be aiming for a time of a little over one minute. Pacing was the central imperative of every guide; right across the board, the admonition was to avoid going for too much too soon. The last thing you want to do, the manuals all warned, is approach the quarter-mile like a quick sprint and burn as fast as you can at the onset. You'll just wear yourself out by the halfway point in the race. Accordingly, Kevin coached Mike to settle into a velocity that he could hope to maintain for the entire lap – or, in the ideal scenario, one that he could even accelerate slightly as the race matured.

They knew, of course, that any strategy that related specifically to the staggered starting block arrangement would have to be formulated solely by the two of them, with only their intuition to guide them. Given that there's not much return on writing how-to books about undertakings that have no precedent, there existed no resources for them to consult. No authority was going to fill them in on how big a lead Mike should have coming out of curve #1, or how he might monitor the proximity of the other runners approaching on his left flank.

Kevin counseled him not to put momentary concerns over a far-sighted approach. "If you feel someone getting close to you, don't think you've gotta pick up your pace right then and there – I mean, unless we're talking about the final stretch, of course. The other guys in the race, the ones I know about, they're good, fast runners, but they're not in some different league than you. If someone in a lane near yours catches up or passes you, just know that he's expended more energy than you in getting to that point, and he won't have quite as much left in him. You can take the lead back once he starts fading. On the other hand, if Simon, or Billy Lloyd, or someone else on an inner lane catches up before the second curve, *then* we're in trouble, 'cause they'll have a way shorter path once you're on that part. You've gotta keep a big lead over them."

Once they had boosted the outer-lane block to a good estimate of its proper new spot, Kevin began assuming the role of one or another of the competing runners. On one trip around the track, he would be Simon Addison, starting from significantly behind on the innermost lane and taking a longer time to come within reach of the leader. On another go, he would pose as Tristan Downing or Vinnie Cancelliere, beginning from an intermediate point in the fourth or fifth lane and catching up more quickly. With his slightly superior speed and reliable gait, Kevin could strategize as far as the exact point along the course at which he would kick his pace up a notch, pose a sudden challenge to Mike's position, and see how Mike would respond to it.

Mike devised a component of the training where Kevin would station himself about fifteen feet before the onset of the second curve, and wait for Mike to reach a predetermined point along the arc before starting to run and seeing if, with the advantage conferred by the inner lane over that stretch, he could catch up with Mike before they reached the finish line. That, Mike pointed out, would help them ascertain exactly how much of a lead he would need to have when Simon, Billy Lloyd, and the others began the final turn – for if he could maintain his edge from a given distance ahead of Kevin, then that distance should likewise be sufficient versus a runner (a) whose speed didn't quite equal Kevin's, and (b) who would have already expended much of his energy over the previous 70 percent of the course.

They stayed faithful to their schedule throughout most of January and February. Although it snowed a fair amount of the time, a snowplow was commissioned by the city to clear the track on Saturday mornings. On the side, Kevin put in some perfunctory training of his own in the long jump and the 100-meter dash, but he was beginning to harbor some nagging doubts as to whether his heart was really in it. It occurred to him that the vicarious charge of envisioning Mike breaking the ribbon in the 400 was occupying his mind with far more frequency and authority than any projection of his own triumph in some other event. In the aftermath of the soccer title, the prospect of out-jumping a handful of other track athletes couldn't help but feel a bit anti-climactic. Before long, he had dropped the long jump from his agenda and hitched his plough strictly to the 100 meters. He still took pride in his foot speed, and still harbored the urge to test it against the best competition, but with his college applications long since mailed out, it wasn't as if anything of practical consequence hung in the balance.

During some of their breaks from the physical component of their preparation, Kevin and Mike would turn their attention to the other task that lay ahead: being ready to counter the inevitable challenges to the new arrangement, and to the legitimacy of Mike's victory – assuming the latter would, in fact, be achieved. Kevin catalogued the unclear-on-the-concept statements he could recall hearing from Mr. Ackerman, Mr. Paige, and Simon, and worked with Mike to map out the appropriate comebacks should those same implications surface on tryout day. Beyond a certain point, though, their planning, their hypothesizing as to the likely questions, their "if asked x, respond with y," began to feel redundant. Mike had stated the obvious, all that really needed to be said, back at Swirlies: He would be running 400 meters, and so would every other runner on the track. If any observers were too steeped in faulty tradition to see the validity in that, logic and reason wouldn't be too likely to bring them around.

They met only once, as it turned out, for a three-way brainstorming session with Billy Lloyd; any more ruminating than that seemed like overkill. The agenda of the meeting, of course, was limited to media strategy and not racing tactics. Billy Lloyd wasn't on board to counsel his competitors on how to maximize their chances of beating him – not that Kevin would have had the poor judgment to make such a request to begin with.

Meanwhile, as a gesture of solidarity, Kevin made more of an effort to attend Monroe basketball games, to cheer his ally on. The varsity season wasn't going very well, in spite of Billy Lloyd's individual dominance. Now standing nearly 6'7" after an additional growth spurt, he was quite capable of dunking the ball in a regulation basket.

Unfortunately, despite having enlisted a private trainer to work with him, he struggled from the free-throw line. So opposing teams that had done the requisite scouting began employing what would soon be termed the

"Hack-a-Shaq" strategy, deliberately fouling him before he could gain easy access to the hoop. Back during the 1992 season, when Billy Lloyd's inside presence was complimented by the strong outside shooting of guards Avery Patterson and Sam Newhouse, teams would have paid a steep price for focusing their defensive effort too heavily on the center. But Avery and Sam had both graduated the previous spring, and now the backcourt consisted of the turnover-prone Bobby Whitlock and the poor-shooting Lenny Darby. This allowed opponents to slack off on defending them and key in more emphatically on Billy Lloyd. He nonetheless amassed his points, rebounds, and blocked shots at higher rates than the previous year – but wins were harder to come by.

Sign-ups for the various track & field events opened on February 15th, eighteen days prior to the tryouts. Within three days, a majority of the available slots across the whole range of options had been filled, including seven of the eight entries on the 400. Two days later, the eighth name showed up. So it was now possible for Kevin and Mike to scope out the competition – again, not related to the afterthought that Kevin's participation entailed but strictly regarding the 400.

By pure coincidence, the grade distribution matched that of the previous year, with three seniors, four juniors, and one sophomore in the mix. The seniors were, of course, Billy Lloyd, Simon, and Tristan. In addition to Mike and Vinnie Cancelliere, the juniors in the line-up were named Peter Landreth and Brody Johnson. The one sophomore, Doug Andrews, was the late entrant, having become eligible to sign up for a varsity heat after the eighth spot had gone unclaimed by the upperclassmen for five days.

Kevin knew something of Peter Landreth's abilities; as it happened, Peter had been on the J.V. relay team with Kevin two years prior, during their respective first and second years at the school. Kevin, in third pole position, had received the baton directly from Peter, who had previously grabbed it from lead runner Craig Barnes. The two hadn't had any on-the-field interaction since then, however, so Kevin had no way to gauge Peter's current state of fitness or skill.

He knew nothing at all of Brody Johnson, but Mike, who shared his P.E. period with him, confirmed that he could be someone to worry about, up to a point. "Brody's got some serious speed when he needs it," Mike said, "but it's usually there in, like, spur-of-the-moment situations – like if he needs to catch up with a receiver in flag football or something. He'd probably have it over me if we were running in the hundred. But this could be different. I got a feeling he might not know how to pace himself for the whole distance. But hey, they both got the memo, didn't they?"

"Memo? Which – who – what're you talking about?" Kevin asked in sincere befuddlement.

"Dude, you didn't even *notice*?!" responded Mike, affecting an exasperated and castigating expression. "Landreth! Johnson! They're both around the middle of the alphabet, not the beginning! You don't think they would've even bothered to try out for the quarter-mile a year ago, right?"

Once again, Mike's astuteness had one-upped Kevin's in his own arena. "Oh, man – I can't *believe* I missed that!" he said. "That *totally* got by me. I guess I was just focusing on the whole late-name thing, and I wasn't tripping on anything in between. But you're right! That's – it – I mean, that proves that we're already having an effect! We're making these guys feel like they have a chance, too – for the first time!"

Mike nodded, and added, "And if one of them ends up winning – I mean, worst-case scenario – it'll help make the point, too. At least it'll be a step in the right direction."

"Yeah, umm … let's not go there," suggested Kevin.

Where they did go, after a little more discussion, was back into the gym to check the names on the other mid-range events, to see if there had been a widening of the contestant pool on any of them as well. Looking over the sign-up sheets for the 200-meter dash and the 250-meter hurdles, they were gratified to notice at least a moderate expansion from the previous boundaries. They discovered a decent number of names in the J-to-O range – a George Mintz, a Redmond O'Shaughnessy, a Nancy Lane, a Bryce Kemperman – all runners who, as Mike had indicated, probably wouldn't have considered it worth their while the previous year. But Yamasaki was still the only name from the final third of the alphabet on a mid-distance event. "It'll take a while," Kevin predicted, recalling another of Jessica's observations. "People don't always want to go out on a limb, be the first to try something. They've gotta get used to the door being open."

One week before the tryouts, Kevin heard his mother calling him to the phone to speak to "some reporter." John McNear of the Richardson Park Record was on the line, wondering if he could ask Kevin some questions. The timing was awkward; Kevin was scheduled to meet Jessica at the Plaza Cinemark to catch the new Michael Douglas film, *Falling Down*. But bearing in mind Commissioner Markbreit's request that he maximize his accessibility to the press, Kevin asked McNear to hold for a moment, managed to reach Jessica on his mother's home business line, and arranged to meet her at a later showing of *Groundhog Day,* the movie everyone had been talking about during the previous week. Relieved that she was agreeable to the switch, he returned to the phone in a relaxed and receptive state of mind. "Hi, I'm here," he told the journalist. "What can I help you with? What would you like to know?"

"Well, we'd just like to get some more information about this new arrangement, and we understand you played a key role in bringing it about," said McNear. "I'd just like to hear directly from you about the reasoning, the motive behind this concept. I'm gathering that it's along the same lines as the NFL or NBA draft. Would that be a good comparison?"

"Uh – how do you mean?" asked Kevin, already feeling a slight uneasiness creeping into his nerves.

"Well, I'm sure you know how the drafts work. They want to have a more even playing field, so they give the worst teams the top picks, the first choice among the new pool of players coming out of college, so those teams can improve their chances and create better competition throughout the league. Doesn't that sort of parallel what you're proposing here?"

"Uh, no," said Kevin, "I actually don't think that's a good comparison at all."

"Oh …" said McNear, in a tone that called to mind a deflating balloon. "Well, then … could, uh … could you explain the difference to me, in your own words?"

"Well, now, it's true," Kevin allowed, "that it would have the same kind of effect – I mean, it *would* help create more balance, and more drama in terms of how many people have a legitimate shot at winning. But that's kind of a side benefit. I think you're missing the main point."

"And that is … ?" prodded McNear.

"Well, the problem is, you said 'worst teams,' " pointed out Kevin. "That's where the comparison breaks down. Those teams that get the first pick, they actually *were* the worst teams the season before. But you see, they were given the same chance as everyone else. They went by the same rules. They played on the same field. They didn't have to go a longer distance to score a touchdown, or … or kick a field goal between thinner goalposts than the other teams. I mean, they might've gotten some bad *luck,* with injuries or bad calls by the refs or something, but nobody set them up to fail. That's the difference – the runners with late-ranking last names are in a *situation* that's uneven. You can't call them the 'worst' runners."

"Well, okay … okay, I see your point," McNear assured him. "I suppose it does sound judgmental when you assign it to the track setting, and to individuals. Could we say, then, 'least successful?' Would that be a more fair way to put it?"

Kevin had to pull away from the phone to conceal his audible gasp of disdain. With a dazed expression delivered to an audience of nobody, he responded, "No, sir, that's really not any better. It's still putting it on *them*, on the individual – it's painting it like we're just trying to do a favor, give some charity or something, to people who couldn't cut it on their own. That doesn't fit the facts. I mean, I can use myself as an example: When I tried out, a year ago, for the 400 meters – and, of course, I was in the outer lane, because of my name – I finished a mile behind these other runners, these guys who I know, from all kinds of other experience, aren't actually as fast as me. That's what tipped me off to begin with – part of what did, anyway. We aren't 'worse runners,' or less successful – well, I mean, any less *capable* of succeeding. That's the whole myth that everyone's been holding onto, 'cause they don't want to look at the set-up, and how it's rigged in certain people's favor."

"Well, but there have been quite a few studies showing that there are certain psychological barriers–" the reporter began. But Kevin cut him off, suddenly on guard against losing his cool.

"Sir, sir! Mr. McNear, sir – I'm sorry to interrupt, but those studies are bullshit. Sorry." *Oh, that's great,* thought Kevin, as he quickly lowered the receiver. *Cursing at the first reporter you talk to, that'll really score some points with Markbreit. THINK, Kevin. Don't dig yourself into a hole with this moron.*

Returning to the line, and mustering up as calm a delivery as he could under the circumstances, he said to the reporter, "Okay, let's, uh – first of all, sorry about my language. But let me ask you if you could try something for me. I assume you must have a pen in your hand and paper in front of you, right?"

"Yes, of course," replied McNear, openly curious as to where this was leading.

"If you wouldn't mind," instructed Kevin, "draw on a blank sheet of paper, draw an oval, a kind of small one – like, about … say, one-and-a-half by three inches."

"Done," responded the reporter, already engaged.

"Good. Okay, now draw five or six more ovals around it – concentric ones, the same shape, each one a little bigger."

"Okay, gimme a minute." McNear dutifully completed the track approximation, and returned to the phone to hear the next step in the process.

"Now put – wait. Are your ovals vertical or horizontal, the way you've drawn them?"

"I've got them horizontal," came the reply. "Should I rotate the paper?"

"No, no, it's cool. So now, make a vertical row of, say, x's on the lower, longer side of each stripe – like, where we'd see the starting positions set up for a race."

"Okay, so now I've got a column of x's, one in each little section. Is that right?"

"Uh, yeah," confirmed Kevin, after taking a second to visualize the diagram. "Now do the same thing on the top – where the finish line for something like a 200-meter dash would be. Got that?"

"Should they also be x's, or something else?"

"Doesn't matter. Now, this part … do you have any string– no, hold on. Okay, uh … okay, I think this'll work: Can you take a separate sheet of paper and tear a couple of strips from it – like, from top to bottom or side to side? Two thin little strips?"

"Uh … okay." Kevin heard the ripping sound as McNear set the receiver down momentarily to free up his hands. "Got 'em; what should I do with 'em?"

"Okay, so take the curved section – the lane – that connects the lowest x on the bottom and the highest x, or whatever letter you used, on the top. See if you can hold one of those strips perpendicular to the diagram and curve it around the right side of the oval from the top letter to the bottom one, but keeping it all between those two lines, like a runner staying in his lane. And once you've got it situated there, tear off the ends, so the strip goes exactly from x to the other."

"Okay … so it's like a semicircle, but a little more oblong," reported the reporter.

"Perfect – and you've torn off the parts that stretch beyond the letters?"

"Doin' it right now – okay, got it."

"Okay, so bear with me, here. Set that piece aside for a sec, and do the same thing for the lane on the inside, the one you got with the first two ovals you drew. Go from the highest x on the bottom half to the lowest one on the upper part."

"And do the same thing – tear off the excess parts?"

"Uh-huh." After hearing another pair of ripping sounds, Kevin lowered the boom. "Now, that first piece you tore off, that represents the distance *I'd* have to go between the starting line and the finish line, any time before now. The second strip represents the distance that a guy whose name starts with 'A' would have to go to win the same race. Now uncurl the second one, and set them next to each other. Notice anything?"

There followed about four seconds of dead silence on the line. Then Kevin heard the phrase, in a quiet register indicating a fair distance between the speaker and the phone receiver.

"Holy shit ..."

McNear returned to the line. "I'm – I'm going to need to, uh, to get back to you on this," he stammered. "I'll just, uh – well, I just need to take a fresh look at this, and – and I'll be back in touch. Thanks for your time." Kevin heard the terminating click of the line before he could tell the man goodbye.

He scrambled to change his shirt, grabbed his wallet, and dashed out to his truck to make it to the theater, where Jessica was waiting in front of the entrance to the ticket booth. "So how'd it go with the reporter?" she immediately asked.

Kevin sighed heavily. "Goddamn, this is gonna be rough," he mumbled.

Tryouts 1993: Kevin's Run

March 5th arrived. The track team aspirants had received their customary early release from class, and the two playing fields were swarming with the usual throng of athletes, coaches, and parent volunteers. The bleachers teemed with spectators.

But now there was an additional element. Along the front railing of the stands, a lengthy row of television cameras, microphones, and print journalists furiously scribbling notes testified to a profoundly important new development in the works. Kevin, hopeful that he could manage to postpone his P.R. obligations until after the 100-meter dash at 2:40, peered over toward the media contingent and saw a few interviews already taking place – mostly with what appeared to be random, plucked-from-the-crowd subjects.

As he stood there, marveling at the spectacle and beginning to wonder why he hadn't seen Mike yet, he was approached from behind by Billy Lloyd, who had a bit more time to kill before the 400, scheduled to take place at 3:30. They hadn't seen much of each other over the preceding three weeks or so, and each took a few seconds to respectfully regard his ally in the struggle, and to recognize the attention and intrigue their joint effort had clearly generated.

"Looks like we're gonna have our work cut out for us, huh?" said Billy Lloyd, gesturing toward the stands.

"Yeah, but we can handle it," responded Kevin confidently. "I'm not worried. I know what to say. I actually made it through one phone interview alread– oh, hey! Has anyone talked to you? I mean, you get any calls from the papers or anything?"

"Uh-huh. I did three interviews over the last, like, ten days."

"*Three!*" Kevin felt a sudden twinge of jealousy – a totally irrational one, given how much of a hair-pulling ordeal his one exchange had in fact been. "Damn, man! Why'd they all come to you? What is it; they all know your dad or something?"

"Probably they just went by alphabetizing," proposed Billy Lloyd with an unconcerned shrug. "You know, Beech before Wilkerson."

"Shit, you guys got the system wrapped up in your pocket everywhere we turn," remarked Kevin, already beginning to lighten back up and see the irony in his complaint.

"Whoa, whoa, hold on there," intercut Billy Lloyd. "Trust me, *this* wasn't a privilege. *You* got lucky on this one. Well, I mean, two of the reporters were okay, I guess, but one of them – man, I felt like I was tryin' to teach the facts of life to someone who still thought babies were brought by storks. The whole concept, why it all makes sense – he just could not get his mind around it. It was always back to square one."

"Wait – was the guy's name John McNear?" asked Kevin, furling his brow.

"No, it was Benton – Somethin' like Kirk, or Curt Benton. I didn't keep track of which paper he worked for. It's not like I'd wanna read what he wrote anyway. Listen, I gotta run and use the can. I'll catch up with you in a little bit."

"Yeah, we'll touch base later. You shouldn't be that hard to track down!" Kevin rounded his hands into a makeshift megaphone and spoke upward in a slightly raised voice, the way one might humorously address Kareem Abdul-Jabbar. Billy Lloyd gave his chest-high friend a kind of "yeah, yeah, very funny" look, turned, and jogged off toward the locker room.

Kevin, standing alone again, turned his focus back toward the broadcasters and journalists. Scanning from right to left, as far over as the portion of the stands immediately beneath the announcers' booth and the three V.I.P. boxes, he suddenly caught sight of a decidedly non-random party: the head of school, Allen Paige, responding to a reporter's questions while a cameraman filmed the exchange from a couple of feet away.

Kevin's meeting with Mr. Paige almost a year earlier had been jarring enough that he had avoided any follow-up contact in the aftermath. Then, once he and Billy Lloyd found a receptive and supportive authority figure in Markbreit, Mr. Paige's opinion on an inter-league sports matter became largely moot. It was true that Kevin had felt no real compulsion to reach out in a diplomatic effort to bring the principal "into the tent," so to speak, but this didn't reflect resentment so much as a general conclusion on Kevin's part that Paige was never meant to be a key player in this issue.

Kevin had already acknowledged to himself that, beyond the cold shoulder that had come to characterize Tom Ackerman's demeanor toward him, he had suffered no actual sanction for pursuing a course of action discouraged by his school authorities. No one had come for him, the way they came for Galileo or Thoreau. Had someone asked him to take his best guess as to Paige's thinking (or evolution) on the question, Kevin would have surmised that the principal most likely hadn't given it any additional thought at all.

Kevin glanced in a different direction for a second, and now, as he looked back, he saw that Mr. Paige was beckoning to him – not with an expression of "Hey, you, get over here," but with more of a gentle "Hey, could you spare a moment?" demeanor. Kevin, suddenly filled with intrigue, approached the bleachers. "Yes, sir?" he asked upon arriving.

Mr. Paige faced Kevin for a moment, evidently intending to address him directly, but he appeared to find himself stuck for the right words. Following a few seconds of paralysis, he turned back to face the reporter, and gestured respectfully toward his student. "This, uh … this is Kevin Wilkerson, one of the two boys who petitioned the sports commissioner for this new arrangement. Also, he's the one who just recently led our soccer team to the first undefeated season in its entire history." The attractive young woman holding the microphone nodded admiringly toward Kevin as Mr. Paige continued, "He could probably explain the idea better than I could – Kevin, would you be willing to talk to Martha, here? Do you have a second?"

"Uh … yeah, sure – I'd be happy to," responded Kevin. "I'm running in a race in about a half an hour, but I can talk for a little bit." As he prepared to field the first question, two thoughts simultaneously occupied his mind. The first was the purely practical hope that he wouldn't be subjected to a replay, or even a semblance, of his interview with the oblivious McNear the previous week. *Let this Martha come in with a clue, at least,* he privately pleaded with whatever force in the universe was in charge of disbursing clues.

The second thought was the dominant one, as well as the more encouraging. Who, or what, had brought Mr. Paige around? The very same administrator who had so thoroughly belittled and stonewalled Kevin's concerns the last time they interacted was now facilitating this media exchange with no undercurrent of bitterness or competition. Paige's tone suggested no motive of entrapment, of trying to put Kevin on the spot. What was behind this dramatic – and welcome – change?

He was about to table this train of thought to focus on the interview, but just as the reporter turned toward the camera in preparation for her first question, the voice of the announcer in the booth directly behind her came over the P.A., announcing the winners of the boys' high jump, the first event to reach completion. So she and Kevin nodded in tacit agreement to wait out the competing noise, and Kevin consequently had another minute or so to ponder the sudden transformation in Mr. Paige's manner.

He recalled that in his and Billy Lloyd's initial pitch to Markbreit, he had briefly alluded to his unsuccessful go-arounds with both Ackerman and Paige. Had Markbreit, subsequent to the commission's decision to revise the set-up, initiated some sort of a heart-to-heart with the principal, to caution him against undermining the move? Or could it have been Greg Beech, who would have had a more direct connection via the school board?

Then again, maybe it hadn't taken any outside intervention at all. Maybe the prestige brought to the school by the soccer championship, which Paige had just made it a point to highlight, had earned Kevin a return to "favored" status.

There was also the slightly more remote possibility that Mr. Paige was fishing for any newsworthy item that could deflect attention – including his own – from an incident earlier in the week that had the school community in turmoil. The previous Monday, during lunch hour, the cops had caught three seniors with drugs and alcohol in their car. One of the three was the son of a school board member, adding an extra layer to the chagrin that engulfed the campus. The disciplinary hearings were set for the following Tuesday. Maybe Paige saw this reform in the sports world, for better or for worse, as the most accessible decoy to distract focus from the embarrassing news on the police blotter.

Or could Kevin be fishing for an angle that wasn't there to begin with? Maybe, once the verdict had been delivered back in July or August, the principal had simply taken a fresh, sober look at the situation and reached a sound conclusion as to which take on the matter would ultimately stand as the proverbial right side of history.

An amusing visual suddenly popped into Kevin's head. The previous October, as part of the "Literature of Stage and Screen" course he had chosen as his fall-semester senior elective in English, he had taken a field trip with the class to a local theater production of *Fiddler on the Roof*. It had been his first exposure to the story in any form, and he was drawn in by the parallels to his own ordeal – most vividly, the play's depiction of the great reluctance in certain individuals to break from their old ways. When Tevye admonished his third daughter that "some things will never change for us," Kevin snickered to himself, *Dude's still in for some more surprises.*

Now, in Kevin's updated version of the protagonist's internal struggle, it was not Tevye the dairy farmer but Allen Paige the school principal raising his fists and passionately wailing "TRA–DI–TION!!!" to the heavens – and then lowering his arms and shrugging meekly, as if to say, *Well, uh ... guess that didn't work ... it looks like the future's coming anyway, with or without my approval. Maybe it's a better idea for me to try to make my peace with it.*

As the announcement concluded, Kevin quickly tried to redirect his thought balloon to avoid cracking up at the hilarious image – made all the funnier by Paige's lack of the signature hat, beard, and prayer shawl. He put his hand to his mouth to stifle a laugh, and said, nervously, "Sorry – just thought about something else. So what can I, uh ... oh, are we – are we actually on camera?" Kevin came to the instantaneous realization that the scope of his role as "front man," as Markbreit had put it, would be extending well beyond the confines of the individual media rep. This was going to be a bigger deal than he'd thought.

"Yes, but this isn't live, right now," Martha assured him. "It'll be edited later. Are you ready?"

"Okay, sure – go ahead," responded Kevin, still feeling like he was standing on eggshells.

Confirming with the cameraman that the equipment was rolling, the reporter began: "This is Martha Donnegan with the Channel Four Final Score, and we're talking with Kevin Wilkerson, the high school athlete who made the case – and apparently a convincing one – to revise what he saw as an unfair configuration in certain track and field events. As we understand it, the starting positions for the runners, rather than being arranged in the usual straight line, are now going to be varied so that the outer lanes, the ones with the wider arcs going around the curves, will feature advanced starting blocks, as a way to compensate for that extra distance the runners have to go on those curves. First of all, Kevin, this is very new, so – did I get that right?"

"Uh-huh," said Kevin, "you pretty much summed it up perfectly." He thought to himself, but didn't verbalize, *and I love you for it!*

"So that set-up is making its debut here at the track tryouts at Monroe High, along with the rest of the North Counties District," Miss Donnegan alerted her viewers. Turning back to Kevin, she inquired, "So, Kevin ... what was it that sparked this realization? When – or how, really – did it strike you that there was a problem that needed to be fixed?"

"Well," responded Kevin, having pretty much formulated and memorized his generic pitch, "I just kept stumbling onto things that didn't add up. There were all these outcomes, when it came to the races in the 200-to-400 meter range, that contradicted everything people knew about one runner or another." He briefly alluded to Helena Vardell, to the Greenfield meet that led to Billy Lloyd's epiphany, and to his own uncharacteristic result in the previous year's tryouts. "Anyway," he offered in summation, "it turned out that the set-up, the geometry of the track, was creating a 400-meter dash where only *one* person was actually going 400 meters! And somehow, that got past the establishment, and it just became the way it was done, year after year. And look, it's – I understand how hard this whole thing is to believe. It's gonna be hard for people to accept that something this clear could've slipped by us for so long. But, y'know, it ... wouldn't be the first time in history something like that happened."

"Hmmm. Well, you kind of beat me to my next question," said Martha, approvingly. "You talk about certain aspects being 'hard to accept.' How confident are you that people who've been used to one arrangement for so long – do you think that they'll be ready to accept this? If the changes you've proposed end up catching on, and being brought into play beyond just this school, or this district, how easy or hard do you think it'll be for the average sports fan to adjust to it?"

"It won't happen overnight," Kevin acknowledged, "but back in the fall, when some of the other students here actually came to me, or to Billy Lloyd, and got the explanation from us, most of them could recognize the point we were trying to make. They just needed it to be brought to their attention. I think it'll be like that – once folks really *get* the concept, they'll come to appreciate it. Umm ... I kinda have to start getting ready for the hundred meters. Do you have what you need? I'd be happy to come back a little later, if ..."

"No, this should be good enough," Martha responded appreciatively. "If you have just a second more, though ..." She paused to get Kevin's permission to ask one final question, which he granted with a nod. "I wanted to ask you about this rumor that you're not actually planning to participate in any of the events where this change is applicable. Is that true, first of all, and is it a deliberate choice? Can you tell me if there's a particular reason for that?"

"Sure," said Kevin. "Yeah, I made the decision because I wanted to make it clear, right from the start, that this was never about me. The motive was never to try to give *myself* a better chance of winning. I just want to see people get a fair chance, and whoever wins the race to be the one who really earned it."

"We hear you. Well, thank you for your time," said Martha, who then turned back toward the camera to conclude, "So there you have it – Kevin Wilkerson, taking to the front lines for starting lines! This is Martha Donnegan for the Channel Four Final Score. Drake, Rita – back to you." Kevin wondered for a second where this "Drake" and "Rita" were supposed to be, before realizing that the sports coverage would be edited later and inserted into the broader newscast, with Drake Somebody and Rita Whoever anchoring the studio desk.

Martha, meanwhile, gave the cameraman the fingers-across-the-throat gesture to verify that he was shutting off the equipment, and called to Kevin as he turned to head back out onto the field, "Well, good luck – today, and with this whole thing!" Kevin nodded back and offered a thumbs-up gesture in gratitude, then jogged over toward the area where the 100 meters was soon to take place. *Okay,* he thought, *so now you know how bad it can go, AND you know how good it can go.*

Seeking out some personal space to stretch and loosen up in preparation for the 100, he paused to greet the only really familiar face among the other entrants: his soccer teammate Sterling "Skylark" Larkins, who had scored that second goal in the final match, off of the assist from Kevin. He recognized only a couple of the other six runners who were readying themselves for the sprint; his focus on the 400 was such that he had done no scouting, undertaken no assessment of his own competitors' relative abilities. Maybe they'd be faster than him, maybe – probably – they wouldn't. He'd find out when the time came.

As he was about to proceed with his array of stretching exercises, an unfamiliar athlete, a well-built six-footer with a handsome, tanned complexion, approached him.

"Are you, uh … you're Wilkerson, right?" he asked.

"Yeah … ?" Kevin responded, more interrogatively than declaratively.

"Hey, man, umm … I'm Brody Johnson," volunteered the junior athlete. "I'm running against you in a few minutes, but I'm also doing the 400 in a little while … and the 200, later on."

"Oh, right – I saw your name on the list." Though uncertain of its justification, Kevin felt an influx of tension at the revelation of the name – that feeling that's always punctuated in movies by an ominous, swelling tone on the soundtrack. Here was the guy who, Mike had indicated, "might be someone to worry about" – and there was no doubt that he looked the part. But what was up? Was he just here to make small talk, as a way of releasing his own tension before the competition?

"Well, look, man, I don't wanna distract you or anything," said Brody, "but I wanted to – well, I asked Peter, y'know, Peter Landreth, to point out which one you were, 'cause I just wanted to track you down so I could thank you, man."

"Thank me?"

"Yeah, man! Shit, me and Peter both! You're the one who pushed for this change, right? Well, it's gonna give us guys in the middle of the alphabet all these options we never had before! My family moved here from Chicago about a month before school started, and I was at that orientation meeting in September, 'cause I was going out for football. And when Ackerman started talking about this new set-up, I was pretty sure I followed what he was saying, but I didn't feel like I should just walk up to you and ask. I didn't know who you were, to begin with. But Peter said you explained it to him."

"Oh, yeah, that's right," recalled Kevin. "He did ask me about it; I remember."

"Well, anyway, so we were both like, '*Finally!* Someone noticed! Somebody's gonna *do* something about this! You won't have to have an A or B name to feel like it's worth giving it a shot!' We knew right then and there we were gonna sign up for both the 400 and the 200, when the time came. I was all like, 'Man, I switched schools right at the perfect time!' "

"That's great, man, that it worked out like that," replied Kevin. His enthusiasm was a bit reserved, a tad halfhearted, given the competitive context. While Mike had described a hypothetical victory by a mid-namer as a good intermediate step, Kevin was still holding out for something more, something bigger – an outcome that could truly start to tear down the stigma that society had long attached to late-namers.

Right on cue, as if reading Kevin's mind, Brody wrapped up his tribute.

"Now, I know you've been training with Yamasaki," he said. "I know he's kinda your horse in the race, and that's cool and everything. But I'm just sayin', if I win it, or if Peter wins it, man, you deserve some of the credit for that, too. I know we're up in a minute or two, so I'll just leave it there, let you get ready." He put a little distance between himself and Kevin, and segued into his own warm-up regimen. Kevin, for the first time since he had embarked on his reformist undertaking, found himself getting a bit choked up.

Damn, he thought. *Guy feels like he's "finally getting a fair chance" – and he's thanking ME for it. I could get used to this.*

He rounded up his emotions and bottled them just in time for the line-up to be announced. Like in every other track event, alphabetization determined the lane assignments, but because the names endowed no advantage or handicap in a race with no curves, nobody paid them any mind, or bothered to formulate any sociological theories about their relationship to success in the 100 meters.

The names were announced, and Ryan Corzine, Jed Evans, Brody Johnson, Sterling Larkins, Dominic Perez, Jeff Petrovsky, Kent Smith, and Kevin Wilkerson made their way to their respective spots on the starting line. Corzine and Smith were fellow seniors. Though Kevin didn't know either of them very well, he had witnessed enough of their performance in shared P.E. classes over the years to know that neither posed much of a threat to him. He knew the same about Larkins from their soccer affiliation; Skylark was serviceably fast, but no burner. Though Kevin never would have made it public, he had done a slight double take when he first saw that his teammate had signed up for the 100. On the other hand, Evans, Perez, and Petrovsky – presumably all juniors – were absolute mysteries to him. And all he knew of Brody Johnson was Mike's scouting report.

Kevin had assumed, during the winter weeks when he was committing all of his attention to Mike's progress, that the adrenalin would automatically kick in as his own participation in the tryouts drew closer. But now, as he waited for the judges to position themselves at the finish line, it occurred to him, with some surprise, that his internal monologue was still not one of urgency, but of borderline indifference. *Whatever's gonna happen is gonna happen,* he thought. *Just run as fast as you can. If you win, that's great; if you don't – whatever.*

"Hey, man!" came a familiar and decidedly unwelcome voice from the front rail of the bleachers, about six feet to Kevin's right. He unwittingly glanced over at its source.

"You sure you're okay starting right there, with everyone else?" asked Simon Addison, dressed in his own athletic gear in preparation for later events. "You don't wanna ask them if you can, uh … ?" Holding his hand perpendicular to the ground, he moved it about ten inches to the right, to symbolize a bumping up of the starting block.

Kevin turned his gaze back to the stretch of track directly ahead of him – but, just to indicate to Simon that he, too, could use his hands to communicate ideas and concepts, he let his right middle finger descend from his loosely clenched fist. Suddenly, he felt his motivation returning to him.

The starting gun went off. Kevin pumped his arms and moved his feet furiously. He kept his eyes predominantly straight ahead, but he could tell from his peripheral vision that he wasn't creating any veritable distance between himself and his competition. This junior class had some serious speed in its ranks.

When he reached the finish line, a few seconds after this realization, Brody Johnson had already broken the tape. Dominic Perez was second, Kevin third, and Jed Evans fourth.

That, then, would be the foursome representing Monroe in the 100 over the course of the '93 track season, unless one of them were to decline the opportunity and cede his spot to the fifth-place finisher – which Kevin was already beginning to see as his likely course of action. After taking a few minutes to catch his breath, he made his way over to Brody and congratulated him. "Man, that was really something," he said. "They were right about you."

"Thanks a lot, man," responded Brody sincerely, not bothering to ask for any clarification as to who "they" were. Looking over Kevin's right shoulder, he alerted him, "Hey, there's your boy." Kevin turned around and saw Mike waving to him from the near portion of the soccer field.

In a heartbeat, the warm-up act was ancient history, and the main event front and center.

CHAPTER 14

Tryouts 1993: Mike's Run

"Well, at least you made the team," Mike offered encouragingly when Kevin went over to meet him.

"Yeah," responded Kevin, with no real sense of either triumph or defeat in his voice. "I might turn it over to someone else; I gotta think about whether I want to commit that much time. Speakin' of time, how much do we have?" His instinctive use of the collective "we," in reference to a race that didn't actually include him, reaffirmed where his emotional investment had resided all along.

"About twenty minutes, I think," replied Mike, absent any watch or venue clock to consult.

"Has anyone from the media talked to you?" asked Kevin.

"Not yet. I kinda figured they're gonna wait for the results."

"Yeah, probably. So how're you feeling?"

"I'm all set to go, anytime they're ready. Oh, and I'm pretty sure we only got six people to worry about, not seven."

"What're you talking about? Did someone back out?"

"I don't know if he backed out, but Cancelliere's got something wrong with him. I think it's a hamstring or something. I just know he's been sitting out P.E. for a couple of weeks – unless it's been something where we didn't have to move around as much, like volleyball. I'm pretty sure he's not gonna be at full strength."

"Oh ... okay ..." responded Kevin in a tone that conveyed appropriately mixed emotions. "Well, that's uh ... that's good news and bad news, I guess. But let's not assume anything; he could've just been saving himself, saving it all for today."

At that moment, the announcement of the top four finishers in the 100 commenced. Kevin's mind was on other matters, but he kept his ears alert enough to hear his own name called, so he could give a respectful wave to the crowd. As in the case of Quentin Baker in the previous year's 400, the announcer made sure to point out that Kevin was the lone senior among those who had made the cut.

As Dominic Perez and Brody Johnson were acknowledged for their second and first-place finishes, Kevin resumed what he had been pondering on the side. All the other schools in the district were adopting the new standards, as per the commission's edict, along with Monroe. Were those schools, right at this moment, besieged by a similar horde of media personnel? Or would the initial attention be centered exclusively or predominantly around Monroe, given that it stood as the wellspring of the idea? Kevin made a mental note to call Markbreit a week or so following the tryouts to find out what sort of expansion had (or hadn't) taken place in the affected events across the district, both in terms of participation and outcomes, and what sort of response the revision had spurred.

All of the attention right here was on the imminent running of the 400, and on the official genesis, the first road test, of staggered starting blocks. The other events that would similarly employ the new concept would follow in short order after the quarter-mile. The media was homing in on the starting territory as the contestants went through their individual preparatory routines. About ten minutes remained to go.

Kevin noticed Simon lingering near him and Mike. Sensing that Simon was waiting for the opportunity to get one last dig in, his desire to see the elitist get knocked from his pedestal was magnified to a new extreme. When he was finally instructed to depart for the bleachers and leave the warm-up area strictly to the participants, he snuck in his last few words, practically pleading with Mike, "We gotta break through on this; it's gotta happen. Just remember everything we went over."

"I got it, I got it," Mike assured him. Kevin headed for the stands.

The moment Kevin was away, Simon edged closer to Mike. "How it feel get beeg head start?" he inquired in a perky, Charlie Chan-style inflection.

" 'Beeg' head start?" responded Mike, feigning puzzlement. "Oh! You mean my big head start over you in learning grammar! Yeah, I'm actually pretty okay with it. Keep studying, though, and you'll come around."

"Whoa, good comeback!" applauded the relentless Simon. "Real brainy, huh?"

Mike let his shoulders and arms droop, as an indicator of complete and total disgust, as he responded, "Yeah, that's right, Addison, you got my number. Total intellectual, real articulate, always know exactly what words to use. It's cool, actually – 'cause if I ever need to say something like *how about you get outta my face before I kick your nuts right through the roof of your mouth,* it just flows right out." He stepped toward the slightly larger Simon and delivered the threatening component of the sentence with a no-nonsense tone and unblinking glare, alerting the senior to his willingness to follow through, if necessary. Simon retreated, with his hands raised in a nonconfrontational, gee-I-didn't-realize-you'd-be-so-touchy gesture.

Too far away by now to have heard the exchange, Kevin nonetheless pieced together, relying on both the cumulative body language and his knowledge of the participants, that whatever Simon had pulled had gotten under Mike's skin. Fortunately, he had a remedy all ready and waiting.

"Hey, Mike!" he called. "Don't even trip on it; he's nothing. Check out what we got here!" He tilted his head to the left twice, to indicate where to look.

Mike followed the gesture and saw, about ten feet further down along the railing, Jesse Irving, Cody Orbach, Dallas Tompkins, R.J. West, Todd Smith, and Jay Marcivius, the one whom Mike had supplanted in the starting line-up.

"Golden Gate," called out Jesse, "you can take 'em. This is all yours!" The other teammates added a combination of nods, waves, and thumbs-ups to the mix, as Sterling Larkins joined them after recuperating from his poor showing in the 100. Mike smiled and waved back at his rooting section, which also included his parents and sister – as well as Jessica, who stood next to Kevin along the railing, knowing that the upcoming endeavor meant every bit as much to her boyfriend as it did to his representative down there on the track.

The time had come. "Alright, let's get in our starting positions for the 400 meters!" called out Coach Shogren, having deemed it good protocol to preside over the groundbreaking event himself, rather than to farm it out to an assistant coach. Referring to the list in his hand, he called into his megaphone, "Lane one: Simon Addison!"

For the first time in Kevin's memory, Simon steered clear of his conventional I'm-number-one posturing and proceeded, workmanlike, to the designated starting block on the innermost lane. Kevin wondered, momentarily, whether Simon had finally caught on to the detrimental effect of excessive self-celebration on his public image – or whether, in some latent recess of his conscience, he was weighed down by the awareness that he'd actually have to *earn* this one.

"Lane two: Doug Andrews!"

The lanky, blonde sophomore made his way to the track and, having received only a precursory briefing on the new arrangement, instinctively stationed himself immediately to Simon's right. Seeing Doug search around his feet in vain for a starting block that wasn't there, the nearest assistant coach quickly intervened and escorted him forward to the advanced position, as the young runner clenched his teeth in an embarrassed grin.

It was at this point that a murmur, distinctly louder and more intense than the inevitable random conversation that had already been taking place, first began to progress through the crowd. This was, after all, the first time in anyone's experience that one runner had begun a race on a different line from another. Most of those present had been filled in on the general nature of the revision, but at least a handful had not – so the first detectable objections, the first variations on "Hey, why does he get to start up ahead of the other guy ..." were now emerging. They wouldn't qualify as dominant, however. The vast majority of the crowd was merely intrigued and expectant.

Billy Lloyd's name was the next to be called, and as he headed toward the block in lane three, he made a point of coming into eye contact with Simon. His look was stoic, almost deliberately expressionless – solely intended to signal to Simon that, yes, this was the new reality, no one was rethinking it, hiding from it, or apologizing for it, and he'd better get used to it. Simon responded with a sneer and a disapproving shake of his head, a wordless conveyance of the message, "You just *had* to do it, didn't you?"

Kevin, while not party to the exchange, wondered right at that same moment how the renovation's other prime opponent was handling the spectacle. Accordingly, he began scanning the field for some sign of Tom Ackerman, hoping that he'd be standing close enough, and at a workable angle, for Kevin to discern the look on his face. His line of vision finally tracked down the A.D., who stood on the field, twenty feet or so from the internal boundary of the track and parallel to a mark about thirty feet past the starting line. Another adult, either an assistant coach or a parent volunteer, was consulting with him on some matter that appeared to be unrelated to the business in the immediate vicinity. When the unknown party headed back toward the other field, Ackerman turned his largely passive attention back to the race, and the innovation, about to commence. He stood with his arms folded, wearing the disappointed look of someone whose favored candidate just lost an election or whose preferred sports team fell a little short in a playoff match.

Meanwhile, Vinnie Cancelliere and Tristan Downing were summoned to their respective spots, followed by Brody Johnson and Peter Landreth – both of whom, in turn, made a point of sending appreciative glances toward Kevin out in the bleachers and toward Billy Lloyd, lined up behind them and to their left. Neither had actually met Billy Lloyd, but Kevin had cited his partner's involvement in his earlier briefing with Peter, who had subsequently relayed that information to Brody. They'd heard his name announced prior to theirs and – as Kevin had lightheartedly reminded him – a 6'7" runner was pretty easy to pick out of a crowd.

By this point, the stands were rife with one-to-one dialogue or small-group conversation, with various spectators filling in others on the logic and purpose of the staggered-block concept – in many cases, to whatever limited extent the novice explainers could piece it together: "Well, you see how, over there around the curve, when you go further out, it kinda looks bigger ..."

When the name "Mike Yamasaki" was finally announced, a spontaneous "Oooooooh!" made its way through the crowd, followed by another crescendo of murmurs. The onlookers comprehended, in unison, that if this new arrangement stood to turn a runner with a Y surname into a viable contender in a mid-range race – or even to convince him that he *might* be a viable contender – then it was historically significant. There was far from a consensus as to whether this change was necessarily for the better, but there was no question in any mind present that it meant *something*.

On top of the inherent drama, there was, of course, the anomalous ethnicity of the groundbreaker within a racially monotone community, which couldn't help but add a subcomponent to the overall reaction. Various spectators, noting as a reference point that Kenyans seemed to enjoy inordinate success when it came to running marathons, began asking their neighbors whether they knew of any similar correlation between mid-range event dominance and Japanese (or, variously, "Asian," "Oriental," or "Chinese") runners.

About fifteen feet behind Simon's recessed starting position, the race officials were stationing themselves at the finish line to judge the outcome. There were four judges instead of the usual two. They had been briefed on the increased likelihood of a photo finish, and the consensus was that a few extra sets of eyes might not be a bad idea. Of course, they all had ample experience with close races, having judged the results of plenty of 100-meter and 120-meter dashes. This would be the first occasion, however, for which that additional level of scrutiny might be required for a 400-meter dash. Historically speaking, it had tended to be remarkably easy to determine the winner in this event.

Meanwhile, the reporters and general spectators were experiencing widely varying levels of success in assimilating the sight before their eyes. With all eight runners poised to begin from individuated starting lines, many viewers found the layout too visually jarring for their comfort zones. Among the uninitiated, the prevalent comments started to fall in line with a handful of prototypes:

"Well, of *course* he's going to win – look how far ahead they're letting him start!"

"Why are those guys in the middle starting way back there? Are they being punished for something? Did they do something wrong – break a rule, or something?"

"Why are those guys way out in front of the others? Do they think they're not good enough to win it fair & square?"

Some of these observers had the benefit of a more far-sighted spectator nearby who could enlighten them on the concept, while others didn't. As it stood, the stretch of silence that ordinarily preceded the starting gun took longer than normal to settle in. Finally, when it was evident to all present that the signal was merely seconds away, they hushed their dialogue, doing their part to contribute to the aura of suspense. The runners were poised in their crouched postures.

BANG!

What should have been the sole focus of the event took a momentary back seat to another spectacle, and not a welcome one. Proving Mike's forecast correct, Vinnie Cancelliere went about twenty yards before he pulled up, shook his head in the clear awareness that his injury wasn't sufficiently healed, and headed gingerly off to park himself on the nearest bench. Each onlooker in the crowd, following the obligatory grunt or moan of empathy and vicarious discomfort, debated internally as to how soon it would be appropriate, and not callous and unfeeling, to turn his or her attention back to the race. The verdicts ranged from one-and-a-half to about four seconds. Meanwhile, a trainer with a first aid kit ran immediately over to the bench to tend to Vinnie.

Re-orienting himself after this unfortunate distraction, Kevin promptly began his analysis of how the race was shaping up, as Mike emerged from the north curve still holding a sizable lead. His assessment simultaneously juggled three factors: at what pace the trailing runners were gaining on Mike, which specific lanes the runners making the most progress occupied – again, it would be more of a problem if they were on the innermost lanes – and how much energy they appeared to be expending in the process. Kevin could tell at a glance which entrants had done the requisite research on pacing. The measured strides of Mike, Billy Lloyd, Tristan, and Peter

Landreth stood in marked contrast to the more insistent running style of Simon, Brody, and the younger Doug Andrews.

Mike kept his velocity steady and disciplined. As a result, the all-out effort of Brody, just two lanes to Mike's left, served to narrow the gap to a mere three or four meters as they reached what Kevin estimated as the halfway mark of the course. Kevin began to worry; it was too early for this to happen. His only hope was that Mike's prediction regarding Brody and his likelihood of a too-much-too-soon approach would prove to be as accurate as his call on Vinnie's injury.

Simon, Doug, and Billy Lloyd still trailed by wider margins, but were gaining as well, with Billy Lloyd's stride – with a length about 140 percent that of his more compact competitors – aiding in his acceleration. Kevin also noted Tristan edging to his left as he ran, to the point where he was skirting the border between his own lane and the slightly shorter one that had been vacated by Vinnie. The suspense was building, and not just for Kevin. For the first time in history, a quarter-mile had reached its midpoint with nobody having *any* idea who was going to break the ribbon. Row by row, beginning with the front benches, the spectators began rising to their feet. The unprecedented excitement was palatable by now to converts and detractors alike.

Soon they arrived at the moment Kevin and Mike had designated as the key measuring point. The other runners were about to enter the second turn. Was Mike's advantage big enough to maintain over the disparate stretch? Kevin, looking at a roughly 35-degree angle to his left, noted with alarm that Mike had not reached the point from which he had been able to hold the lead and finish ahead of him in training.

The gap wasn't big enough to sustain until the end – or it wouldn't have been, if they were still engaged in their one-on-one exercises back in February. Kevin quickly reminded himself that these runners weren't as fast as him, before realizing with alarm that Brody Johnson had poked a major hole in that assumption about a half-hour earlier. But there was still the legitimate hope that the wear and tear of the 300 or so meters they had already run factored into the mix.

Simon, Doug, Billy Lloyd, Tristan, Brody, and Peter all began veering to their left. By the halfway point of the arc, Tristan and Billy Lloyd were both within a step or two of Mike's relative position in his lane.

Brody's energy looked to be waning, as he began to fall behind. At a certain point, as if suddenly becoming aware that he was lagging, he put on a burst of speed to catch back up – but Kevin could see, even at a great distance, that it was taking every last bit of strength he had. Meanwhile, Peter Landreth, who had trailed by what looked like an insurmountable margin coming out of the first turn, suddenly began accelerating and challenging the leaders, the longer arc of the seventh lane notwithstanding. Over the second half of the turn, the far shorter distances of their respective lanes helped Simon and Doug catch up with the rest.

As the runners emerged from the south curve and headed toward the finish line, which waited a mere forty meters ahead of them, Mike was trailing all six of his rivals, by margins varying from three to five paces.

Kevin's hopes were dashed. He launched into the dreaded process of trying to reconcile himself to the undesirable result. Lowering his head in dismay, he began pulling for the consolation prize of a victory by Landreth or Johnson, and started formulating the terms of a "well, at least we came close" speech on Mike's behalf.

All of this took place over an interval of about a second and a half, before he was interrupted by a jab in the upper arm from Jessica's elbow.

"God damn it, look!" she commanded. Kevin looked.

The other runners had, indeed, passed Mike up over the latter half of the curve. But, to a man, they had exhausted their supply of energy in doing it. Mike had preserved his. Over the final twenty-five meters, he suddenly kicked into a velocity well beyond what he had maintained throughout the race, re-assumed the lead, and broke the ribbon four steps beyond his nearest pursuer.

Kevin had never in his life experienced such an instantaneous transition from anguish to euphoria. He and Jessica embraced in triumphant excitement, while high fives and fist bumps made their way around the assemblage of soccer teammates. Kevin realized, as the two of them made their way over to join the celebration, that he had no idea who had finished second, third, and fourth in the race. After a few seconds, it occurred to him to ask if anyone knew.

"Seriously, I couldn't tell – it was too close!" volunteered R.J. "I know it wasn't Addison, or the kid who was next to him. They were further behind. Your basketball buddy was in the mix somewhere."

Amid all of the ecstatic excitement of the rooting section, and his own marginal curiosity as to the order of finish, Kevin's ears detected a sudden, noticeable reduction in the volume level of the crowd's cheering.

Initially, the response to the outcome had been a roar commensurate with the one that greeted the soccer championship. It was an instinctive, visceral reaction, befitting the most thrilling, well-contested 400-meter dash ever run. But in quick order, the provisions that had made this possible suddenly re-emerged in the minds of a sizable portion of the crowd, and they hadn't yet made their peace with it. Momentarily distracted by the undeniable enhancement of the spectacle, their internal debates now resumed: *Should* they be applauding a winner who hadn't started from the same line as the others? Was this legitimately earned, or had this Yamasaki fellow merely reaped the benefit of a systemic boost? Meanwhile, from those who had already grasped the logic – either on their own or with some assistance – the applause continued unabated.

Kevin, of course, had no hint of uncertainty intruding on his conscience. The farthest concern from his mind was the qualms of the unclear-on-the-concept sector. The wall had been smashed, and now it was only a matter, he thought excitedly, of laying the groundwork to welcome other late-namers to the Promised Land. Maybe that terminology was a little premature and overdramatic, he quickly cautioned himself – but he knew beyond any doubt that this was a historic moment.

He made his way to the nearest opening in the rail between the stands and the track, and headed out onto the field to celebrate with Mike. While making his way to where the winner was standing, hunched over and gathering his breath, Kevin also admonished himself not to ignore Billy Lloyd in the process. It wasn't reassurance he was seeking. He had no real fear of encountering any sudden buyer's remorse, any sort of me-and-my-big-mouth regret in his partner. All the same, Billy Lloyd had done something unprecedented in this micro-field, in willfully and pro-actively ceding his traditional advantage in favor of his sense of honor. A gesture like that was not something to be glossed over, by any stretch.

Mike saw Kevin approaching, and held up one hand in a wait-a-second type of gesture. "Gimme a minute," he said, regaining his breath. "I wanna go check on Vinnie."

Kevin nodded as Mike headed over toward the bench, about twenty meters beyond the starting line, where Vinnie Cancelliere still sat, his left thigh wrapped in ice and tape. Kevin saw Vinnie offer an appreciative thumbs-up in response to whatever Mike said, which he interpreted from a distance as a combined congratulations to Mike and an assurance that the injury – or re-injury – wasn't too severe. Meanwhile, Kevin made his way over to the spot on the turf where Billy Lloyd sat, resting up from the exertion.

"I know this is weird," he began, "but I really couldn't tell how everyone finished. It was just this big clump. Where'd you come in?"

"I'm not a hundred percent sure myself," Billy Lloyd replied. "Third, I think. We'll find out in a minute."

"How're you feeling?" asked Kevin – realizing, as he spoke, that the question carried a definite ambiguity.

"How do you mean?" responded Billy Lloyd, immediately confirming that realization.

"Well – does – I mean, uh – do you –"

Looking completely at peace with the planet, Billy Lloyd raised his palm to stifle Kevin's tightrope act. "Don't worry about me," he instructed Kevin. "You got that? This is for real. I know what I gotta do now. I mean, *that* was what you call a race, wasn't it? Huh? I mean, wasn't that the real thing out there? Listen, man, I'll take that over last year any day of the week."

Kevin smiled in admiration and gratitude, just as the announcer's voice came blaring from the booth. "Can we have your attention, folks – we have our results for the boys' 400 meters. We'd like to announce the top four finishers who'll make up the Monroe High team in the quarter-mile for the upcoming track season."

The crowd ceased its wave of conversation, and the reporters stood poised and ready with their note pads or microphones.

In contrast to the '92 announcer, this one opted to maximize the drama by revealing the order of finish from fourth to first. Of course, the drama was already heightened by the uncertainty of the spectators – and even the runners themselves – as to the exact order of finish, behind Mike's clear victory. This, many observers realized, was another novel experience for the 400: an announcement of the winners that contained an element of suspense, rather than one that amounted to a redundant anticlimax.

"Finishing fourth, in his junior year, we have Peter Landreth," came the report. Peter clenched his fists in a gesture of joy and relief, not having been sure until that moment whether he had made the cut.

"In third place, and our one returning member of the quarter-mile team from '92: in his senior year, Billy Lloyd Beech!"

Billy Lloyd gave his usual gentlemanly wave toward the crowd. Kevin could see the news reporters' interest perk up a bit at the mention of the name. Presumably, as Markbreit had indicated, they had been given the walk-through on who the central actors in this transition were, and now they seemed poised to charge like a herd of rhinos, in attempt to get the premier interview, the moment the announcements were done.

"Our runner-up, also a member of our senior class. Congratulations to Tristan Downing!" Tristan, who never made much of a show of things – despite the elevated stakes of athletic outcomes – simply responded to the good news with a satisfied nod toward the booth from where the announcement had come. Jessica, who was still tutoring Tristan weekly in the learning center, let out a little cheer and pointed at him in a "way to go" kind of gesture, which Tristan acknowledged with a smile. Kevin witnessed the exchange, and turned toward his girlfriend with a mildly inquisitive look. She met his curious expression with a stoic, nothing-to-trip-on-or-apologize-for-here-so-move-on countenance, and they moved on. Now came the big moment.

"And finishing in first place, in his junior year, and his first here at Monroe, Let's have a big hand for Mike Yamasaki!"

Mike, who had returned to the vicinity of the other runners around the time Billy Lloyd's name was announced, waved to his family and soccer comrades, and then gave a nod of appreciation to Kevin, who stood about seven feet away. Kevin had a handful of competing thoughts running through his mind, each of them pre-empted by another at about five-second intervals. He noted his own relief that the announcer refrained from any commentary, any auxiliary reference to the new arrangement, in relaying the results to the crowd. He listened for the crowd's response to the announcement, and caught a definite repeat of the ambiguity that had characterized the initial applause at the finish of the race. In spite of the announcer's urging, it was merely a medium-sized hand, not a big one.

Seeing the media personnel waiting anxiously for the go-ahead to mingle with the key players, he began to play out scenarios for the interviews that he knew were about to take place, whether with him or with the other VIPs. He heard the announcer's voice resume: "Attention, please! We've been asked to relay a request from the school that all interviews and news reporting be confined to the bleachers, in a manner that doesn't obstruct people's view of the playing field. We have other tryouts coming up, and we need to keep the track and the field clear of anyone who's not participating in those events. We appreciate your cooperation."

In accordance with the request, reporters began calling and beckoning to their intended interviewees. As they leaned out over the railing, their shouts overlapped in a cacophony of solicitations:

"Mr. Ackerman, can we get a word?"

"Mike? Hey, Yamasaki, do you have a minute?"

"Excuse me, can we ask you a few questions?"

Mike glanced over at Kevin, and arched his eyebrows slightly. "Well, here comes the fun part," he muttered.

"Just be prepared for the whole range," counseled Kevin. "Some of them'll have the concept down, and some won't. Just don't let anything shock you."

Mike assured him, "I got it under control," and headed confidently toward the stands. Kevin followed, at a casual pace. Although he had yet to hear his own name called out, he made the decision simply to remain present and accessible – and to eavesdrop on the other interviews whenever the opportunity might present itself.

The reporters consulted Simon, who took what he viewed as the diplomatic approach – concluding, loftily, "Well, I've won a lot of these races in the past, and it seems like they just kinda decided it was time to let someone else experience that feeling."

They talked to Billy Lloyd. "Now, as we understand it, you were one of the strongest backers of this new set-up. Is that correct, Billy?" asked a spot reporter.

"That's right," he affirmed in a resolute tone. "It's Billy Lloyd, by the way, not Billy. I go by the double name."

"Okay, my apologies. Billy Lloyd. So, umm … any second thoughts?"

"Well, it takes a little longer to write, but other than that …" responded Billy Lloyd in a deadpan manner, pantomiming signing his name on an imaginary sheet of paper.

"No, I mean –" began the reporter, before Billy Lloyd quickly raised a hand to indicate that he had, in fact, understood the question.

"I knew what you meant. It's just that – well, I really don't get *why* you're asking me that," he said. "Why would you assume I'd have second thoughts about it?"

"Well, we looked at the records: Last year, you were the first-place finisher in the tryout for the 400 meters, and just now, you came in third. So with the new starting arrangement having cost you the race, it seems like an obvious thing to ask," suggested the reporter.

"Please try to get this straight, okay?" said Billy Lloyd, letting a minor fraction of his annoyance reveal itself. "Let's get our terms right, so people can get an accurate picture of what's going on here. The two guys who finished ahead of me ran the same distance I ran. The starting arrangement didn't cost me the race. I didn't run fast enough – *that's* what cost me the race. Are we clear on this?"

Kevin took precautions to remain out of Mr. Ackerman's line of sight as he listened in on the A.D. fielding questions from a print journalist. The reporter – obviously having been briefed on Ackerman's adversarial stance on the issue – tried in a gentle manner to play devil's advocate, imploring him, "Well, I think anyone would have to agree that this added a real level of excitement to this event, which hadn't quite been there in the past. Wouldn't you say so?"

"Well, about a month ago, I saw a football game that wasn't all that exciting or suspenseful," responded Ackerman, referring to the 52-17 rout by the Dallas Cowboys over the Buffalo Bills in Super Bowl XXVII. "Now, I'm sure *that* game would have been a lot more exciting, down the stretch, if they'd spotted Buffalo a four-touchdown lead, or something like that. But that's not the way we do things here. In my book, you *earn* your victories. You push yourself harder if you want to come out on top. It's one of the oldest cliches in the book, but it's there for a reason: If at first you don't succeed, try; try again. But I have to say, I think we're headed down a kind of slippery slope here, where if you don't succeed, you try to get the *rules* changed to give yourself a better chance. In my day, we started at the same line, and we finished at the same line, and we didn't complain if the results didn't go in our favor. This finagling, here – yeah, it made the race closer, but I don't know that manipulating things like this is in anyone's best interests, in the long run."

Right, thought Kevin. *He's got us all figured out. "To give yourself a better chance." This after one of us pulled himself out of the competition, and the other set it up so five more guys would suddenly be starting AHEAD of him. C'mon, man – you're a reporter! Ask him about THAT shit! At least about Billy Lloyd ...*

But the writer moved on to another subtopic, and the obvious challenge was left unissued. Kevin, still not on the radar of any of the media reps for the moment, scanned the area to determine where Mike was engaged. Seeing him about twenty feet away, fielding questions from a group of about three reporters (one with an accompanying cameraman), he edged over to the nearest bench to lend support, if needed.

As he arrived and sat down, he saw the TV reporter anxiously waiting to field the next question, as Mike responded to whatever had been asked before Kevin arrived on the scene. Kevin's warning about the "whole range" promptly proved well-founded, as the reporter began, "So, Mr. Yamasaki – you're officially the first person to win a 400-meter dash with the special head start given to people with late-ranking last names ..."

The loaded phrasing of the intro immediately sparked Kevin's ire, and he instinctively began to rise from the bench in protest, but Mike, seeing this, shot a deflecting hand out to let him know, *I've GOT this.* Kevin acknowledged the gesture and obligingly just sat there, fidgeting nervously, like an over-exuberant student who's been informed by the teacher in no uncertain terms that it's time to let someone *else* answer the question. "Hold it a sec," said Mike, turning back to face the reporter. "How about, 'the first person to win a 400-meter dash where everyone actually ran 400 meters?' Does the story work if you put it that way?"

"Sure, we can put it that way, if you'd like," agreed the reporter, but in a tone that was clearly more dismissive than receptive. "Now, we saw from this race that you have some serious ability as a runner ..."

"Thank you," responded Mike, a bit uneasily, as he and Kevin both waited for the other shoe to drop.

"But clearly, this win *was* aided by the new arrangement, if you compare the margin of victory to the distance between the starting lines. So ... does it feel okay, knowing that your name helped you win?"

"What're you talking about?" asked Mike, as he glanced at the other two journalists in his presence as if to say, *Please tell me you two have more sense than this guy.* "You just agreed with me when I pointed out that that we all ran the same distance. What you're asking doesn't make any sense."

"Well, hold on a minute," the reporter went on. "In the normal, traditional form of these races, the person in the eighth lane never won. Now, this special, preferential set-up's been put in place, and the very first result is that the person in lane eight wins. And you were *in* that lane because your name ranked last alphabetically. So I'll ask again: Does it feel okay to know that your name helped you win?"

Kevin sat grinding his teeth, itching to put the reporter in his place – but confident that Mike could handle his own heavy lifting. Mike, recognizing a lost cause when he saw one, repeated the query. "Does it feel okay that my name helped me win?" he asked, as he looked off into space, as if pondering the matter from every conceivable angle. "Well, I'll tell ya," he said as he resumed eye contact with the questioner, "it feels a whole hell of a lot better than my name guaranteeing that I *wouldn't* win."

Breakthrough at Burbank

Simon Addison did make the track team, as was all but inevitable. He had been the team's most adept hurdler throughout his years at Monroe, and he placed first in the 250-meter hurdles even with the installation of the newfangled "A-name handicap," as he quickly took to calling it.

That served as the final straw in pushing Kevin to a verdict that had already stood about ninety percent certain, the decision that he would, in fact, pass on participating in track & field during the '93 season. Even though he had the option of driving himself to meets rather than taking the team bus, there would be ample on-the-field and locker-room interaction, and hearing Simon harangue any available listener on how "*some* of us don't get special treatment; we have to *earn* our victories" fit Kevin's definition of medieval torture. Well, maybe not quite medieval torture, but definitely late 20th Century Illinois torture.

That was far from the only factor. His college applications had long been submitted, and he knew the responses should be arriving imminently, so adding another letter to his athletic resumé provided no practical advantage in that department. He felt that his after-school hours would be put to better use with a part-time job than at endless practices and meets where he would only be competing for about a half a minute.

Also, he wanted to maximize his available time to spend with Jessica. Lingering in the back of his mind was the awareness that they were inching closer to the inevitable point in time when their respective journeys would diverge. For just as surely as Kevin's college prospects reflected an attachment to his geographical roots, Jessica chose hers in accordance with a burning desire to expand her boundaries and explore new horizons. Her applications were mostly to universities in California and Oregon, along with a few Ivy League schools, and she had made clear on numerous occasions her intent to settle in a new and distant region in the long run.

Bearing all this in mind, Kevin approached Coach Shogren four days after the tryouts and ceded his position on the 100-meter dash roster to Ryan Corzine, who had finished fifth in the tryouts and would now supplant Kevin as the lone senior in that event.

The downside of this decision was that it would deprive him of the chance to investigate, first-hand, the effect and scope of his reform across the other schools in the district, but he concluded that he could live with that. He had rethought his initial plan to call the commissioner for some kind of blow-by-blow report on the respective unveilings and reactions; having become acutely aware of Markbreit's busy schedule, he was reluctant to risk wearing out his welcome with any potentially burdensome requests.

Part of what aided this lack of urgency was the realization that he had his own ready-made data collection team, courtesy of the allies who would be participating – a group now up to four, with the inclusion of Brody Johnson and Peter Landreth. In addition to Mike, Billy Lloyd, and Peter all making the roster for the 400, Peter and Brody would both be running in the similarly adjusted 200-meter dash. (After falling short in the quarter-mile, Brody had rested up and then easily reclaimed the winner's spot in the 200.) Following his decision to step down, Kevin initiated brief conferences with all four of the team members and asked each of them – to whatever extent it wouldn't interfere with their competitive focus – to take notes at the upcoming meets, so he could assess the level of participant expansion that the revision had stimulated at the other schools.

Of course, he wasn't inciting them to sneak off with copies of opposing squads' rosters, or anything as elaborate as that. They could simply keep their ears open when line-ups were announced for the relevant events, staying alert for names from the middle and late portions of the alphabet. Furthermore, Brody and Peter could observe how many opposing runners in a given race were stationed in lanes further out than their own.

Within a couple of weeks, the reports began to come in. Based on the first four meets of the season, the impact appeared to mirror what had taken place at Monroe. There was no question that the pool had expanded, but only within a moderate range. The names relayed back to Kevin all represented the middle of the alphabet – still no Tylers, no Warners, no Youngs. Peter Landreth brought him an accounting of some of the runners he and the others had faced to that point; the list included a Mackinich, a Newell, a Jaeger, a Morrison, a Paranelli, and an Orman. In the meet versus Poly Tech High, Brody and Peter ran against a Jared Karsten in the 200; they concluded from the fact that the opponent was stationed between the two of them that it had to be Karsten with a K, not a C.

Billy Lloyd conveyed the gratifying news that among the mid-namers who had joined the fold at the opposing schools, several had sought him out in order to express their appreciation, in the same manner that Brody had first approached Kevin. Having heard through the grapevine that the new policy that had opened the doors to them had been initiated by two Monroe athletes, they had asked around in anticipation of their meet with Monroe, and now Billy Lloyd found himself receiving a hero's welcome of sorts. (*Not*, he and Kevin were quick to reaffirm to each other, that that was ever their underlying motive.) He also found himself, from time to time, enduring dagger-eyed looks from various competitors – who never disappointed his prediction that he'd find them on the innermost lanes when the time came.

Mike finished first in two of the 400-meter races over those first four track meets, Billy Lloyd broke the ribbon in one, and a Hillside runner named Ricky Polian edged the rest of the field to take the prize in another. Spectators and school officials were still far from unanimous in their acceptance of the new arrangement. The crowds' applause following the declaration of Mike (or Ricky Polian) as the winner still had that tepid and tentative feel, that uncertainty as to whether the victor truly deserved it. But the transformation of the mid-range events from preordained conclusions to hair-raising crowd thrillers was readily apparent to even the most resistant traditionalist. All four finishes were down to the wire, with the outcome entirely up in the air until the moment the finish line was crossed.

A couple of days after the fourth meet of the season, Kevin received a call from Commissioner Markbreit.

"How's it going, sir?" he asked – leaving it up to Markbreit to interpret the question in a general vein or a specific one.

"Reasonably well, I'd say," responded Markbreit. "There's still the whole range of reactions. Some people get it and some don't, some are better at adjusting than others. Overall, the departments are handling it alright. I mean, nobody's threatening to boycott the rest of the track season. I've got a little request, though, which I think you'll be glad if you can manage to fill."

"Sure, anything you want," said Kevin without hesitation. "What's up?"

"Well, Billy Lloyd let me know that you didn't end up joining the team at all for this season."

"Yeah, I just … I mean, I made the squad for the hundred, but I kind of needed to start looking for a job, helping my folks out a little more."

"Well, that's certainly understandable. But you realize that's shifting a disproportionate amount of the P.R. responsibilities onto him."

"Wait – are there still reporters showing up at the meets? I didn't know

– I mean, I thought they were just gonna be there on tryout day. I guess I should've thought of that. We've been talking, though; he's been keeping me up to date, and he didn't mention anything, or say anything was bothering him."

"Oh, it's not that big– I mean, it's nothing he can't handle. But if you're available, I'd really appreciate it if you would accompany the track team to their meet at Burbank High tomorrow. If you need to get out of seventh period or hitch a ride on the team bus, I can call in the morning to arrange that for you."

"Oh, no, that's cool – I can drive there myself. I mean, yeah, that's no problem. But is there something specific about Burbank?"

"I have a feeling you'll see your efforts coming into a little more fruition there," responded Markbreit.

"Why's that– *OH!!* Wait a minute!" Kevin literally jumped out of his chair in his excitement. "Is this one of the – okay, when we talked back in November, you mentioned two A.D.'s who you said were, like, real pro on the idea. And I remember the names. You said Wohlford and Turlock. But I didn't keep track of which schools they were from. Is this – is one of them with Burbank?"

"That's right," confirmed Markbreit. "Stephanie Turlock. She'd like to meet you, first of all, and there'll almost certainly be some more media presence, which you could help accommodate. This is a good story. Think about it! The school where the idea was conceived versus the one that's done the most to put it into play."

"I'm there," said Kevin. "Should I ask around for her, or will she track me down? I don't wanna get in the way of the action."

"Just let Billy Lloyd know where you'll be – like, what section of the bleachers. He'll make the initial contact with the director, and facilitate an introduction when the time's workable for her."

"Got it," said Kevin, already overwhelmed with eagerness to see his efforts "coming into a little more fruition." He was pretty sure his guess as to what the phrase meant was accurate.

He estimated that he could make the trip from Monroe to Burbank within the fifty or so minutes between when his economics class ended and when the meet could be expected to start. The class ended at 3:10, and by 3:15 he was pulling out of the school lot and heading toward the freeway. As he drove eastward, he involuntarily began formulating dramatically varied images of what Stephanie Turlock might look like. It crossed his mind that he had never encountered a woman in the position of athletic director before, and he soon found himself wondering whether her gender might not have had a little something to do with her receptivity to the new, inclusive policy. He had previously assumed that it all boiled down to the T that began her last name. But now it occurred to him that, as a woman in a position customarily and historically filled by men, she might have more of an instinctive empathy for other people seeking to break down barriers.

He also reflected on the fact that Ackerman, naturally, had been his only example, his prototype, of an A.D. informing student athletes of the new policy. And he remembered full well the spiritless tone and body language of that presentation. Now, suddenly, he was transporting himself to an alternate reality where he sat in a comparable assembly at Burbank and listened as Miss Turlock, or Coach Turlock, or whatever they called her, relayed the news to her own prospective track team. How would she have put it to them initially, and what kind of follow-up strategy would she have employed? Maybe he'd get the chance to ask her.

He ran into a slight stretch of early rush-hour traffic as he approached Whitfield, the center of a handful of neighboring towns that Burbank High served. When he pulled into the parking lot of the school, his dashboard clock read 4:15. He knew that the team had long since arrived, and anticipated that the first events of the meet would already be in process by the time he reached the stands. Heading from his truck to the field's entrance, he didn't run, but walked at an accelerated pace.

He went through the gate, which was situated behind the bleachers, and made his way around their left side to a point where he could first see the action on the field. A hurdling event had already begun, and although Kevin carried a slight morbid curiosity as to how Simon was performing, the runners were too distant, and too clumped within the same line of sight, for him to pick his nemesis out of the mass.

He edged along the front railing of the stands, scanning the field for Billy Lloyd. Within about ten seconds, he saw him seated near the middle of the field, stretching to stay loose as he waited for the 400 to take place. Rather than waving or calling out, he simply waited for Billy Lloyd to come into eye contact.

When Billy Lloyd saw him, he acknowledged his presence with a slight wave, and mouthed the words, "That's her," as he pointed toward a slender, 35-ish woman standing about sixty feet to his right, wearing a sweat suit and sun visor in the evergreen color of the Burbank Rangers. He then pointed to the spot on his wrist where a watch would be if he were wearing one, held up six fingers, and then wobbled them in a kind of "more or less" gesture, to indicate that proper introductions would be made somewhere in the vicinity of six o'clock. Kevin nodded.

Having a little over ninety minutes to wait, and not seeing more than a couple of TV cameras along the front barrier of the stands, he settled back to watch the action – and to learn, up close and first hand, what sort of increase in name diversity had taken place. Seeing the blocks being installed in the new, staggered form for what looked like the 200 meters, he listened intently for the announcement of the line-up. This was strictly an on-the-field matter of business. The announcers' booth only came into play when it came to acknowledging the winners. So the coach calling out the respective runners' names through his electronic megaphone was directing the information to the athletes themselves and not the fans in the bleachers. Kevin hoped that the names would be audible where he was sitting, and not drowned out by competing noise.

He was relieved when the coach's voice came through in a clear and decipherable delivery. Now was the moment to learn the real impact of his effort, put into unrestrained play. The names were called, beginning with Travis Breeland and Jed Evans from Monroe. The next name called, and the first from the Burbank side, was Benji Hickman.

Kevin found himself trembling with triumphant excitement. In any track season prior to this one, an H-headed surname would have relegated its owner to the forget-it, not-worth-the-trouble, no-one-like-you-ever-wins-these-things demographic. Now, all of a sudden, the *earliest*-ranked name on a team's 200-meters roster began with an H. Three names into the list, the payoff was already evident. Would it get even better?

He heard his comrades' names called: Brody Johnson in lane four, Peter Landreth in lane five. Kevin was now anticipating the remaining three Burbank runners' names with the enthralled intensity of someone waiting to learn what his windfall from a sweepstakes was to be.

"Lane six: Joe Servino! In lane seven, Jake Summers! Lane eight: Troy Welch!"

Screw the Hokey Pokey, thought Kevin. *THIS is what it's all about.*

As the runners positioned themselves for take-off, Kevin contemplated the realization that he genuinely didn't care who came in first. If Summers or Welch broke the ribbon, it would stand as another welcome stab at the status quo, another brick falling from the wall. But if Breeland or Evans won – hey, at least their win would be legitimate.

Both alphabetical extremes were soon rendered a moot point, as the gun went off and Brody rocketed around the curve, easily bypassing the four runners to his right and leaving all seven competitors in his wake. Jake Summers and Joe Servino edged out the rest of the pack for second and third place, respectively. *What an athlete,* marveled Kevin, and he wasn't alone; even the partisan home team fans couldn't help applauding the Monroe star's excellence on the track.

Kevin's train of thought built on itself. *And Brody winning is perfect, actually. He's breaking the barrier, showing that it's not just the A's and B's who have a chance anymore. But he's also proving that the new deal doesn't just hand the prize to whoever's LAST in the alphabet, either. ANYONE has a chance! It's all about your ability now. They'll all know they can win the race if they run fast enough.* He let out an audible laugh as he pondered the fact that the sentence he had just uttered internally – *they can win the race if they run fast enough* – should rightfully have stood as the most obvious, second-nature truism. Instead, given the history involved, it could legitimately be modeled into the slogan for a sort of revolution.

Kevin was happy. He sat through a handful of field events, awaiting the 400 meters with eagerness, but no anxiety. Of course, his school loyalty and his closer ties to Mike and Billy Lloyd carried some weight, and he would certainly be pulling for them, but he was also pulling for – well, for the *event,* itself, to whatever extent that made sense.

As the 400 neared its place in the schedule, Kevin saw a red-haired Burbank athlete approach Billy Lloyd in the warm-up area. Standing about six-foot-four himself, the redhead didn't need to crane his neck nearly as much as the average person when addressing Billy Lloyd. Though he was too far away to hear anything, Kevin saw Billy Lloyd nod in response to an apparent question. A friendly dialogue ensued, which culminated in a solid handshake, followed by Billy Lloyd escorting the Burbank runner a few yards over and introducing him to Mike. *Another one,* thought Kevin with satisfaction. *One more late-namer – or maybe a mid-namer – thankful for getting his first legitimate chance.*

A few minutes later, the delegated assistant coach called out the line-up for the 400, beginning with a Burbank runner: "Lane one – Patrick Aberdeen!"

Kevin could barely assimilate the sight that followed. The tall redhead in the green uniform proudly and unhesitatingly made his way to the inner lane and positioned himself on the most recessed of the eight starting blocks. This guy was no Williams, no Thompson, no Zane – he was *Aberdeen*. He was Burbank High's alphabetical equivalent of Simon Addison, the one who would have reaped the greatest benefit from things remaining as they were. And yet he seemed, from all appearances, to be as comfortable with the revision as Mike Yamasaki or Brody Johnson – or, more aptly, as Billy Lloyd Beech.

Kevin made eye contact with Billy Lloyd and pointed toward Aberdeen with a look on his face that asked, *Is this really happening? This guy's on board?* Just prior to his own name being called, Billy Lloyd nodded at him in confident affirmation, as if to say, *Yep, we got another one right here – another early-namer who gets the concept.*

Kevin heard Billy Lloyd and Tristan summoned to their lanes, followed by Clark Harrison of Burbank, and then Peter Landreth. More of the "fruition" forecast by Markbreit became evident as an Alex Tarkington and a Jayson Valencia rounded out the Burbank squad, before Mike assumed his usual spot in the outermost lane.

The gossip murmur that had made the rounds in the bleachers following the announcement of "Yamasaki" at the Monroe tryouts was conspicuously absent here. Nobody in the Burbank stands, at least by the sound of things, appeared thrown for a major loop at a "Y" name being in the mix for the 400. They just seemed poised to take in the excitement of a well-contested footrace. Kevin reasoned that Stephanie Turlock must have – well, how *did* she get the point across to the Burbank community? Had a memo been sent home to parents, alerting them to the change and explaining the logic behind it? Again, he hoped he'd get a chance to ask her in about a half an hour.

The gun went off, and the runners proceeded to round the track in their measured gaits. As Kevin watched, he noted that Mike seemed a little off from his normal performance, unable to maintain the early lead as Kevin had stressed during their winter training period. By the time he reached the second curve, several runners had caught up to him, throwing the advantage in their favor. They exited the curve and hit the home stretch, with Jayson Valencia of Burbank breaking the tape, followed by Billy Lloyd in second and Peter Landreth in third. Alex Tarkington came in right behind them. By Kevin's estimation, Mike in the outermost lane and Patrick Aberdeen in the innermost appeared to finish dead even with each other, tying for fifth place. Tristan was right on their heels, and Clark Harrison finished eighth – a mere four seconds after Valencia, the winner, crossed the line.

The Burbank fans – again, in sharp contrast to the ambiguous early reactions of the crowd back at Monroe – roared in unanimous approval of Valencia's triumph. Kevin, while not overtly rooting for an opposing team's runner, was largely with them in spirit. In fact, the more he thought about it, the more he realized that a victory for a home-team runner like Valencia was really preferable, in terms of aiding the cause. It drove home the upside of inclusiveness in a more personal, identifiable sense. Everything seemed to be going as it should.

Within another 45 minutes, the last events of the meet were concluding, the final winners were acknowledged, and the crowd began to dissipate. Burbank parents, along with a few from Monroe, were waiting for their sons or daughters to finish their obligations on the field and meet up with them in or near the bleachers to catch their rides home. As Kevin waited for Billy Lloyd to summon him onto the field to meet Stephanie Turlock, a man, evidently the father of two Burbank team members who stood nearby, approached him and introduced himself as Stuart Volk.

He presented his son Kirby and his daughter Julie, whom Kevin had seen winning the girls' 200 a little while earlier. Not having heard the name "Kirby Volk" announced that afternoon, Kevin concluded that the brother must have competed in his events early on, while he was still making his way through traffic. Mr. Volk also mentioned that his younger son Riley was running the 400 and the hurdles for the JV team, which would probably be getting ready to head home from the Monroe campus at about that same time. (JV and varsity sports events between any two schools always took place simultaneously, one at each site.)

Mr. Volk then informed Kevin that on the day of the tryouts – March 5th, just like at Monroe – his family had seen Kevin's Channel Four interview with Martha Donnegan on that night's newscast. He had called Coach Turlock the very next day and requested an audience with Kevin when the time came for Monroe to visit Burbank. Turlock initially contacted Tom Ackerman, who informed her brusquely that Kevin wasn't running track for the '93 season. Determining that her counterpart wasn't going to be much help, she then followed up by making the personal invitation through Commissioner Markbreit.

"My kids, here, are going to have opportunities to prove themselves that wouldn't have been conceivable if you and your friend Billy hadn't stepped forward," Mr. Volk told Kevin, "and I wanted to make contact with you to let you know that this can't stop here. A number of us were already on board after seeing it in play the first time. Myself and some other parents – Melina Rivera over there, Chris Tarkington – as soon as we can get the time, we're going to be pooling our connections and resources, pulling whatever strings we can, and getting word out to other districts, letting them know how important it is for them to adopt the changes you've got going here. Your system needs to become the new norm. It needs to get to a point – and it'll take some time, of course; there'll be some resistance – but it needs to reach a point where people look at the *old* arrangement like, 'What the hell could we have been thinking?' "

"Wow …" sighed Kevin, feeling simultaneously appreciative and a bit daunted. "I'm, uh … not sure what to say. I mean, that's great to hear …"

"I don't mean to overwhelm you," Mr. Volk assured him, reading Kevin's body language. "In fact, one of the main reasons I wanted to talk to you up front was to ask you – and this isn't something you need to have an answer for right this minute. There's time to think about it. The question is, when we start pushing this toward wider adoption, how much – or how little – do you guys want your names to be part of the picture? See, because I don't want to see someone else try to claim credit for what you formulated. But then, another part of me thinks, these boys are busy finishing high school, probably getting themselves ready for college … it might not be a time when you need any big distractions. You see what I'm saying? I want to be respectful to you and the Beech boy–" He and Kevin both caught the humor in his inadvertent pun. "That was totally unintended, I promise," he said with a laugh. "But do you have any sense of – of how involved you want to be when this moves forward?"

"Man, it's cool of you to ask that," responded Kevin. "I guess I do need to give that a little thought. This is kinda hitting me all at once, you know? I mean, I thought I'd reached the goal when the commissioner told us they were looking at putting it into play. You think other districts, other organizations, they'll be open to trying it too?"

"Let's just say, they will be when we get through with them," responded Mr. Volk confidently.

Kevin couldn't believe what he was hearing, this early on in the game. Every piece of the equation seemed to be falling into place. Jessica had figured out why the door wouldn't open. Kevin had found the key. Billy Lloyd had convinced them to change the locks to fit it. Mike had used the key to unlock the door. And now everyone from Brody Johnson to Jayson

Valencia to Julie Volk was walking – running, actually – through that door.

And at the same time, a recurring thought kept gnawing at the back of his mind: *If so many people can see how much sense this makes, why did they all wait for ME to bring it up?!* Knowing better than to look a gift horse in the mouth, though, he kept the question to himself. Instead, he did his best to reply to Mr. Volk's question.

"I guess you can just – I mean, I'm not hiding from it or anything; I'll answer any questions anyone might come up with. But it's not about getting credit as much as, just … uh … yeah, I guess it can pretty much be like, 'two high school athletes' came up with it, or something like that."

Mr. Volk nodded and reached out to shake Kevin's hand before leaving. "Your friend's over there waiting for you," he said, gesturing toward Billy Lloyd out on the field. "We'll be in touch. We'll keep you up to date on whatever materializes. Again, just … thank you." Kirby and Julie both echoed their father's appreciative words as they left.

Kevin stood leaning on the rail for about six additional seconds. Then, with the cool confidence of a player who's already dribbled past the defense and faked out the goalie, and can now simply tap the ball across the goal line rather than clobbering it into the back of the net, he made his way out onto the field. Its population had thinned out during his exchange with Mr. Volk. Just about thirty people now remained out of the 150 or so who had been there in one capacity or another a half an hour earlier. Billy Lloyd ushered him in the direction of Coach Turlock – stopping along the way to introduce him to Patrick Aberdeen, who thanked Kevin sincerely for "finally giving me some decent competition."

When Kevin finally got to meet Stephanie Turlock, the athletic director began by expressing her great appreciation, and telling Kevin how she wished someone like him had been there when she was running track in Cleveland twenty years earlier. The question once again ran through his mind, but remained his own private thought: *Okay, thanks and everything, but why ME, and nobody else in the damn universe?*

He asked her, instead, how she had managed to get everyone, or at least a majority, on board, and her response was more or less in line with what he had envisioned. She had created diagrams of both the traditional and revised alignments, and used varied-length pieces of rope to illustrate the problem and the solution. She outlined the concept initially for the likely track athletes at an orientation assembly in February, and subsequently in a memo that was sent home to their parents. She followed that up by making direct pitches to those students who she figured could best capitalize on the new opportunity – Jayson Valencia, Alex Tarkington, Jake Summers, the Volks – and stressed to them the importance of their carrying the banner, just as Kevin had made his request of Mike.

"Anyone give you any flack?" asked Kevin.

"I had to answer a handful of 'concerned' inquiries, yeah," responded Turlock. "I'm not going to say I was able to bring *every*body around, but most people seemed to get the idea, what we were trying to do. A big key was that guy over there – see the tall one with the red hair? That's Patrick Aberdeen." Of course, Kevin knew this by now, but Turlock didn't know he knew.

"He's kind of a 'Big Man on Campus,' if you know the expression," she went on. "He's big in both football and basketball, and people look to him as a leader. I knew, just from experience, that he would understand the whole point of it – even though, with his name, the change would hit him the hardest of all. I met with him one-on-one before I broke the news to the rest of the athletes, and he committed himself, said he'd go to bat for the new arrangement, and help explain to the others – you know, the ones early in the alphabet – why they should be okay with it."

"That's fantastic," said Kevin appreciatively, as it now occurred to him that Patrick and Billy Lloyd were not, in fact, meeting for the first time that afternoon, but would be well acquainted through sharing the basketball court over several years. "I guess that's what it takes – people who are ready to do what … what's right, even if they don't end up getting the advantage from it."

"There's a life lesson for us all," affirmed Coach Turlock, before shifting gears. "I see that you also got the, uh … the 'Stuart Volk experience.' I hope he didn't come on too strong."

"Nah, he was cool," Kevin assured her. "Actually, he was making sure to … I mean, he was trying to be sensitive about things. But yeah, he does sound pretty determined to take this to the next level."

"Well, I wouldn't put it past him," said Turlock. "There's also Mrs. Rivera, a mother of two students here, who's really good at getting the wheels turning when it comes to things like this. I'll help where and when I can, too. If we need to reach you, we can go through Commissioner Markbreit. Would that be the way?"

"Sure," said Kevin. "And hey, I just wanna say, thanks for the support, for doing what you could to work this in smoothly. We didn't get anything like this back at Monroe."

"I know. We've all been briefed," responded Coach Turlock with an empathetic nod. "Don't worry about Ackerman. One turkey don't stop no show."

The unfamiliar and grammatically casual colloquialism caught Kevin off guard.

"Never heard that one," he mused.

"I picked it up back home in Cleveland," the A.D. explained.

Kevin walked at an unhurried pace toward the parking lot. Although he had been a mere spectator and not a participant in the day's activities, the excitement, drama, and novelty of the whole afternoon had him feeling as though he had just finished running a marathon. Earlier, he had toyed with inviting Mike, or maybe Brody or Peter, to hitch a ride back to Richardson Park with him, just for some company on the long drive. But by the time he made it to the lot, the third and final bus bound for Monroe was already pulling out. Kevin stopped walking for a moment, and watched it exit onto Kensington Avenue, which led back to the freeway. A few straggling individuals or families were still climbing into their cars in the far reaches of the lot, and yet Kevin felt, somehow, as if he stood completely alone on the entire Burbank campus. A serene silence seemed to pervade the whole area.

He turned and took one last look in the direction of the athletic field, affecting the air of an architect contemplating the magnificent end product of his own blueprint. He then spun around again and proceeded to his truck, suddenly remembering with alarm that he still had about ninety minutes of homework to complete before bed.

He got in, started the engine, and shifted into drive. As he was about to lift his foot off the brake, he noticed a very stern-looking, fiftyish man in an olive green sweater swiftly approaching him. A teenager, presumably a Burbank student and the man's son, lingered at the far end of the lot. Kevin shifted back into park.

"Is your name Wilkerson?" asked the man.

"Y– yeah … ?" responded Kevin in an uncertain tone.

"Good; I'm glad I was able to find you," said the man, his choice of words momentarily abating Kevin's uneasiness.

"Is there … something I can help you with?" Kevin asked, not meaning to be rude but trying to convey through visual cues that he was anxious to hit the road.

"I just needed to ask you, face to face," said the man, "if you ever really, fully understood what it is you've done here."

"I think so – I mean, I …" Kevin stammered.

"Well, I just needed to say that I don't think this is how you handle defeat," declared the stranger. "If you're jealous of other people's success, the answer shouldn't be to try to punish them for doing what you couldn't do."

"Sir, that's not what this–" began Kevin, but the man quickly extended a palm in his direction to intercept the words.

"No, *NO!* I don't want to get into it with you!" he blared preemptively. "I just had to let you know – real people are affected by these things. You may be a little too young to understand that. Now, you and your whining might end up costing my son his scholarship to college. I just thought you needed to hear that."

Kevin took a couple of seconds to formulate the proper response. A couple of seconds, however, was too long. The man was already gone.

CHAPTER 16
The Bon Fire Influence

In early May, Kevin received his acceptance notifications from the various colleges to which he'd applied, weighed the various scholarship offers, and opted for Evansville University in Indiana. Wisconsin was a close second. Had he been in possession of a crystal ball, he would have foreseen that his likely first year on the varsity would coincide with the Badgers' 1995 national championship in NCAA soccer. But financial considerations took precedence – Evansville had offered virtually a wholesale scholarship, along with the greater likelihood of significant playing time as a freshman.

Beyond finalizing his plans for the fall, he had secured a coveted summer job as a junior coach at a prestigious local soccer camp. Things looked promising, for the time being.

As the track season neared its final couple of weeks, he still relied mainly on reports from Mike, Billy Lloyd, Brody, and Peter to monitor the impact of the new policy. He did, however, make a point of attending the meet when Monroe hosted Marshall High, the other school whose athletic director was solidly behind the change. Although Jack Wohlford didn't accompany his Marshall athletes to that particular competition, the effect of his systemic encouragement was readily apparent. Mirroring the transformation at Burbank, Kevin heard an entire alphabet's worth of names across the Marshall line-ups.

He didn't hear any updates from Commissioner Markbreit, Stephanie Turlock, or Stuart Volk on the prospects for expansion, so his progress assessment remained a local matter, strictly within the context of the North Counties District – until he received a letter from his cousin Derek in New Berlin, Wisconsin.

The envelope contained a folded-up clipping from the Milwaukee Journal Sentinel. Stapled to it was a note that read, *Assuming this is you. What's this all about?*

Kevin quickly unfolded the newspaper clipping and came face to face with the headline of an op-ed piece: *Equal Footing – or a Kick-Start?* He read the editorial, which alerted the readership that two high school athletic associations in and around Milwaukee were toying with following the lead of this district in Northern Illinois, which had instituted a special new arrangement to give late-namers a more tangible opportunity to compete in the events from which they'd been historically excluded. He saw his name, along with Billy Lloyd's, mentioned in reference to the initiation of the procedure.

Kevin wondered, as he read, whether this awareness and consideration of his idea stemmed from the efforts of the Burbank parents, or the media exposure it had received to that point, or some other anonymous word-of-mouth referral. He figured it probably wasn't Stuart Volk's group, given that Volk had implied they might need some time, and had emphasized his commitment to keep things discrete if Kevin preferred it that way. He quickly realized it made no real difference how word had gotten out; here was Kevin Wilkerson's prescription, out there for the world – or Milwaukee, at least – to see.

The writer seemed to be taking pains to present an even-handed, objective portrayal of the staggered-line concept, avoiding the injection of any personal editorializing. Yet the terminology consistently presented the measure not as a moral imperative, not as a necessary move toward fairness, but rather as a gesture of charity. True, the concern was acknowledged to center around "giving certain people a chance." But little or nothing in the article spelled out the actual nature of the *denial* of that chance. Nowhere was it explained that the success gap was a condition imposed by the system, and not just an outcome of random chance or destiny. Along the lines of John McNear's analogy to the NFL draft, a reader would assume that the general message of staggered starting lines was, "These people never get to win. Wouldn't we all feel better, and wouldn't it look better, if sometimes they did?"

In contrast to the blurred conveying of the "pro" message, the "con" part of the analysis was dismayingly clear and coherent. The writer, while giving lip service to the benefits of the new arrangement, alerted readers that "many people" had concerns about it. (Kevin wondered who, exactly, these "many people" were supposed to be, so soon after the unveiling.) The concerns involved such potential costs as "stifling the motivation" of early-namers, "hampering the work ethic" of late-namers, and sparking a wider trend of "reverse namism." The writer worked in one quote from a supporter of the change, and counterbalanced it with four quotes from opposing voices.

Kevin got on the phone to his cousin and gave him the rundown. Derek Wilkerson, already in college, and not involved in any sport other than sailing, was nonetheless intrigued. "So this might get to a point where I'll be able to say, 'My cousin invented that whole thing,' huh?" he speculated, half humorously.

Kevin suddenly came face to face with that very possibility – along with some ramifications that hadn't occurred to Derek.

"I don't know if I'd go around advertising it right away," he cautioned. "It'll impress some people, but it could make you some enemies, too. Just, uh … well, whoever you're talking to, make sure you know their last name before you bring it up."

The moment he got off the phone with his cousin, Kevin called Billy Lloyd, told him about the article, and read it to him in its entirety. As he did, he repeatedly found himself wishing he could have intercepted the print on the way to the press and altered it to state the case as he knew it deserved to be stated. He had no doubt that Billy Lloyd was thinking the same thing; he heard occasional R-rated mutterings over the line in reaction to one misconception or another. When he finished, he simply waited for a response, without adding any commentary or questions.

"Alright," said Billy Lloyd, "now you listen, and listen good. From here on out, ANY request for an interview, any public discussion, any chance you get to set the shit straight, you jump on it. Got that? Doesn't matter what else is goin' on – studying for finals, whatever – if the press, the TV people, they wanna talk to you, you say yes to *everything*. I'm gonna do the same. And I'll talk to Mike tomorrow at practice, and let him know to be ready to answer questions, too, if they track him down. This has our names on it now; there's no going back. So that means if we're the only ones – so far – who know how to explain it the right way, we gotta do that *any chance we get*. We can't leave all the talking to people who don't get the concept themselves."

"I'm there; I'm on," Kevin assured him. "I'm even wondering if we should reach out to these papers or reporters, saying we wanna tell our side of the story …"

"Let's play it by ear, just at the very beginning," advised Billy Lloyd. "See what the vibe is with the first few people that talk about it. If too much bullshit starts goin' around, then yeah, we'll hafta step in. But we won't be alone. Turlock got it, Aberdeen got it … there'll be others out there, before too long. But you and me, we gotta be okay with carrying the load until they're ready."

"… and getting the hate mail," Kevin added – knowing full well that a disproportionate amount of the backlash would be descending on the W name and not the B name.

"Hey, man – who did you mention to me, the first time we talked about this?" responded Billy Lloyd, a sudden fiery intensity in his voice. "Martin Luther King, Susan B. Anthony, Galileo? Well, they had to worry about things a lot worse than a few 'up yours' letters, know what I mean? Either we let it beat us, or we don't let it beat us! If Simon Addison or some asshole parent has a problem with it, they can stick it up their ass! Are you ready for this, or what?!"

"Man, how'd that basketball team ever lose a game?" remarked Kevin in admiration of his friend's motivational speaking skills.

The mail did start coming, divided almost into perfect thirds between the hate letters, the appreciative letters, and the I-need-you-to-explain-this-to-me letters. Kevin made sure to respond immediately to those who requested it, either by phone or in writing depending on the submitter's preference. In his two-way dialogues, he managed to usher nearly all of the undecideds into the "pro" camp. By the time graduation was in sight, several other communities had evidently gotten word of this new concept and were now engaged in their own debates. Of course, Kevin didn't have cousins in all of these districts, but people sent their letters to the Monroe office, marked for Kevin's and/or Billy Lloyd's attention.

While the supportive letters featured a fairly wide range of styles, terms, and personal testimonies, Kevin began to notice definite patterns that characterized the hostile commentaries. He found repeated stock phrases, counterarguments delivered in almost identical wording, and lockstep accusations or speculations as to the underlying motives behind the reform.

A common complaint revolved around the observation that, even allowing that the traditional alignment *was* imbalanced (which a few writers insisted had bothered them all along as well), the beneficiaries of that disparity were early-namers who had *already* run in track and field competitions. But the ones who would shoulder the burden of backed-up starting blocks, if this change went into wider effect, were early-namers of the *present* and the *future*. How, they asked, did it make sense that some 5th-grader who wouldn't be running in a 400 for another several years should be forced to suffer the consequences for someone *else's* unfair advantage? Why should they pay the price for a perk that *they* hadn't enjoyed?

Even the most esoteric, "out there" letters were subject to inexplicable duplication. No fewer than three different letters informed Kevin that in certain regions of Africa and India, most schools and communities were so poor that their track & field programs could only afford tracks of four or five lanes, not eight – and so, if he gave it some real thought, he should thank his lucky stars that he lived in a country that even *had* an eighth lane to accommodate people like him.

Five letters raised the point that there were many possible factors besides name-based lane assignment that could affect a runner's chances. Why, they asked, should a late name be the *only* hindrance that called for an official countermeasure? What if a participant was just recovering from a cold, or was nursing a tender ankle, or had missed a week of practice because of some scheduling conflict? (All five letters contained the same three examples.) Shouldn't they, likewise, be allowed to demand a bump forward in their starting block to compensate for the disadvantage? How was it fair to reward one adverse circumstance and not the others?

Kevin brought a handful of the letters to show Jessica, and called her attention to their eerie similarity. "Isn't it weird how the same whacked-out ideas occur to so many different people?" he marveled.

"Nothing 'occurred' to them, babe!" she responded, rolling her eyes. "Isn't it obvious what's happening here?"

Kevin, by now well accustomed to concepts being obvious to his girlfriend but not to him, simply sat expressionless and muttered, "Tell me."

"They're all listening to the same person," she said, as if nothing could be more, well, obvious. "One of those radio shows, like Rush Limbaugh, or some local TV guy somewhere. Somebody's telling them what to think, how to feel about it, and they're just echoing whatever he says."

Kevin wore a dubious expression. "Wouldn't they worry about, like … looking kinda dumb, when people figure out that they're just putting out a pre-recorded message, and they're saying it like it was their idea?"

For his effort, Kevin received another did-I-really-hear-you-ask-that look from Jessica, as she asked, "Would somebody who'd fall for arguments like the ones in these letters be smart? Or dumb?"

"Gotcha," said Kevin hastily. "But how do we find out who the person is – I mean, who they're getting it from? And … well, I mean, I guess there's not a whole lot we can do about it even if we do find out."

"Start saving the envelopes," Jessica advised him. "See how many of the same arguments come from one place. Like, if a bunch of people from Minneapolis all say the same thing, you know that's where to look, to see who the popular radio or TV guys are."

Kevin, accordingly, began collating the letters in relation to specific content and tabulating the return addresses, but no distinct geographical pattern emerged. He turned out not to need one, thanks to his soccer teammate Cody Orbach, who called him two weeks prior to graduation.

"What's up, Bounce?" greeted Kevin. "You all ready for the big day?"

"Yeah," said Cody, in a hurry to get to the point. "Hey, Wilks, you get all the cable channels at your house?"

"Just HBO and Showtime, I think. Why, what – there's something I'm supposed to see?"

"I got a blank tape – I'll record this segment for you," said Cody. "It's Garland Bonham, and he's talkin' shit about you."

"About *me?* What's he – wait, first of all, what – who the hell's Garland Bonham?"

"He has one of those cable news shows – y'know, 'The Bon Fire?' You never heard of it? Hold on, it's coming back from the commercial. Lemme get this tape going."

Kevin waited anxiously for Cody to return to the line. When he heard his presence on the other end again, he asked, "So whaddya mean, he's talkin' shit? What's he saying?"

"Well, he gave a little teaser before they went to commercials – something like, 'When we come back, we'll pick up on our story of the Illinois high schooler who got them to change the rules so he could win in a track meet.' I think–"

" 'So he could *WIN?!*' " blurted Kevin. For a brief moment, all of his internal buildups, his you-know-it's-going-to-happen-so-just-be-ready-to-handle-it speeches to himself, fell by the wayside, as he stammered, "What the– Doesn't he know– Who is this son of a bitch?!" (He had the urge to add, but didn't, *and why would you be watching him?*)

"He's always looking for someone he can talk about, say they're tryin' to get over," explained Cody. "He'll pick up a story about some dude who's skimming a few extra bucks off welfare payments or food stamps, and he'll play it up for a whole week. I just watch him 'cause he's entertaining; I don't agree with everything he says. Look, lemme see what's goin' on here, and I'll connect with you in Sherman just before 3rd and give you the tape."

"Okay, uh … cool. Thanks, Bounce," responded Kevin, already knowing he wasn't likely to sleep too well that night.

As planned, they met in Sherman Hall, just prior to Kevin's American studies class and Cody's calculus class, to exchange the videocassette. "It's pretty ugly," Cody warned him. "Don't have a glass or anything like that in your hand when you watch it."

Kevin nodded, and then spent the remainder of the school day gravitating toward any available distraction to blunt his frazzled nerves. Not happening to cross paths with Billy Lloyd, he made a mental note to call him that night to discuss possible responses – both in word and action – to whatever would turn out to be on the video. When school ended, he rushed straight home and threw the tape in the VCR.

"We're returning to last week's fascinating story," began the stocky, brown-haired Garland Bonham, "of the high school runner in Richardson Park, Illinois, for whom 'you win some, you lose some' apparently wasn't enough. After failing to make his school's track team in the 400-meter run, Kevin Wilkerson could have learned the lessons of history. He could have respected what every statistic has taught us about people of his alphabetical range and their struggles in that event. He could have taken satisfaction from his apparent success in other sports. But no – he went to his school officials and moaned and groaned that he wanted 'the same chance to win as everyone else.' " Bonham made air quotes around the last phrase and adopted a mockingly effeminate tone of voice, akin to the Church Lady from *Saturday Night Live*.

"And somehow, he convinced these enablers to give him, and other people like him, a special handicap, an actual boost in their starting positions. Nobody thought to tell him, 'How about you just *try* harder? Did you ever think of working on your *own* performance, rather than throwing all the blame on the system, and on the ones who've done better than you?' Nobody wanted to hurt this poor kid's feelings, or teach him the value of a good, honest effort. Let me show you what they did instead – what they forced on his whole district."

As thankfully unfamiliar as he was with Bonham, Kevin had gone into the viewing fully prepared for the TV commentator, just like Ackerman, to treat Billy Lloyd's role in the reform as nonexistent, and play the whole thing as Kevin's desire to rig the system in late-namers' favor. In a very short time, he had already grown accustomed to that correlation. For anyone weighing in against the new approach, there officially *was* no Billy Lloyd Beech. It was all about Kevin Wilkerson, the poor sport with the inflated sense of entitlement.

Kevin had no forewarning, on the other hand, about Bonham's determination to overlook his withdrawal from the competition – to steer the Bon Fire viewers headlong into the assumption that Kevin had launched a purely self-concerned protest and then reaped the benefit of it.

Now it was time to take the deception to the next level. Bonham strolled over to a whiteboard, and invited the camera to pan in on two diagrams, showing the contrasting starting-block options. But unlike the visual aids Kevin had carried around with him in the fall, no oval-shaped track was to be seen. Bonham's illustration merely depicted two short, completely straight segments of track – as if the event in question were a linear dash of about ten yards, not a curving run of 400 yards.

Bonham pointed toward the drawing where the x's indicated a traditional, parallel starting arrangement, and marveled to his viewers, "Again, for those of you who missed it last week, this – *this* arrangement, with all runners starting *even* with each other, at the *same place,* was what 'Whining Wilkerson' found to be such a grievous offense to his sense of fairness, his expectation that he should get to win a race even if someone else shows better speed. *This* was his idea of a balanced race,*"* he said in a shocked tone, as he switched the focus to the staggered-line representation, "where *he* gets to begin way up here, and his peers, who never did anything to keep him from running faster, are forced to start all the way back here!"

Bonham, Kevin realized, was using his monopoly control of the discussion to strip away every last shred of context that could give the viewer a clue as to what had actually taken place in the North Counties District. His fan base was given none of the biographical background or anecdotal evidence that tipped Kevin off to the problem. They received no updates on Kevin's later course of action – or inaction, technically – which would have certified his pure motives. They weren't even offered the *visual* context of a full diagram, on which a few of them might notice the *other* troubling factor that the staggered lines were designed to offset. Absent any of the relevant details, this amounted to a story about a kid approaching his athletic association and asking them to hand him a win.

Then Bonham capped it off with his idea of a real zinger: "We've heard reports, albeit unconfirmed, that Mr. Wilkerson also put in a request for an on-hand assistant to carry him part of the way if he should get tired."

Kevin had to summon every ounce of self-restraint within him to keep from throwing some heavy metallic object at the TV screen. He did his best to distract himself from his own anger by trying to recall whether any of what he'd just heard could have served as the original, the "master" version, of the recurring themes in the letters. Nothing specific jumped out, but he had no doubt that the repeated talking points – the one about the depleted tracks in the third world, the one asking why the "innocent" should be made to atone for the "guilty" – had been supplied by Bonham on the previous week's show. Or could there already be *other* TV or radio personalities of similar stripes who were pouncing on the same story?

Kevin was shocked to find Billy Lloyd responding in an unemotional, resolute tone when he passed the news on to him. "Don't we need to put together some kind of comeback to this asshole?" Kevin prodded.

"What'd be the point? He'd just toss it in the garbage," said Billy Lloyd. "Kev, this isn't where the fight is. Bonham's a dickhead, and so are the people who get their info from him. They're not the type you're gonna be able to reach."

Jarred by his partner's choice of a singular pronoun, Kevin persisted, "We can't just let him spout this shit and not let people know what the facts are!"

"What – like we got 'the facts' to Simon?" countered Billy Lloyd. "Like that guy who approached you at Burbank was ready to hear some 'facts?' Dude, you can't fix stupid! You can fix uninformed, you can fix confused, but you can't teach a lesson to people who've already decided they're not lookin' to learn anything. That's why we haven't wasted any of our time trying to reach Simon, or Ackerman. When I said we should take every chance to give our side of things, I'm talking about stuff like that Milwaukee paper – situations where people are gonna *hear* what we have to say. This would just be a waste of energy."

Easy for him to say, thought Kevin. *He's not the one who just got called out, and lied about, in front of forty thousand –*

His thought was interrupted by a knock on the window of his living room, which overlooked the walkway alongside the front of the house. He spun around to the unexpected but welcome sight of Jessica outside on the path, waving at him. He held up the receiver to indicate that he was on the phone, and gestured for her to let herself in, which she did.

"Okay, I see your point, yeah …" he told Billy Lloyd halfheartedly. "Look, Jessica just got here. Lemme check in with you later."

"Sure, man," responded Billy Lloyd. "And don't get all freaked out – we *will* get our chance. We've already convinced people, people who matter."

Kevin hung up in time to receive a hug and kiss from Jessica, who explained the business of the visit: "I just thought you might need a little support."

"You know about the TV thing?" Kevin asked, not altogether surprised. "How'd you find out?"

"Cody told me. We have advanced bio together, 5ᵗʰ period. How bad was it?"

"I didn't know it could *get* that bad," admitted Kevin, suddenly feeling like he was fighting off tears. "I mean, a guy with a camera on him, just making shit up off the top of his head about somebody ... it feels like you shouldn't be allowed to do that."

"You look like you just got mugged," observed Jessica.

"Well, you told me a year ago, just 'cause something's the right choice doesn't mean people are gonna make that choice," recalled Kevin. "I should've listened."

"And then what?" reprimanded Jessica. "Just decide to let it keep going, forever? Make your peace with something that you know isn't right? Didn't we talk a little about *that*, too?"

Kevin had no answer. He sat down on the couch, and leaned against the corner of the back and the armrest, the way one plops down after a grueling day at work. Jessica sat down and curled up to him.

"Hey," she said, "you know how we celebrate Martin Luther King's birthday every year?"

"Yeah," muttered Kevin. *Again with Dr. King,* he thought, before it quickly occurred to him that it wasn't exactly a negative thing to have people continually invoking a name like that in reference to one's own agenda.

"And you hear every politician talking about, y'know, 'He showed us how to live up to the ideas our country's supposed to stand for, how to be the best we could be,' and all that stuff?"

"Right," said Kevin, his hand gestures urging her to get to the point.

"Well, you think they did any of that while he was still alive?" She paused a second for Kevin to arrive internally at the answer, then continued, "Babe, they *hated* him – I mean, the ones who had a stake in the system the way it was. They called him a communist, said he hated America. The FBI followed him everywhere, bugged his hotel rooms, trying to get any sort of dirt on him that they could. They said *he* was the one causing all the violence in the South. Even the ones who kinda sorta claimed to support him still said he was rushing things, that he needed to be more patient and just let the problem take care of itself."

"You left out the part about them killing him," Kevin reminded her in a monotonic mumble.

Bypassing any discussion of why Kevin brought up that detail, she segued toward her conclusion: "I'm just saying, he wasn't 'Mr. Popular' back then, babe. Nobody is, when they show people the things that they don't want to see. People get used to being on top of the ladder. They get addicted to that feeling, and they tell themselves it's *gotta* be because they deserve it – that, y'know, anyone else could've gotten to this point if they just had their shit together, like I do!" She affected a lofty expression while saying "like I do," to verify that she was play-acting as the prototype who would rely on that cliché.

"And I know it's a whole different level – winning a race isn't the same as getting to vote, or being able to sit where you want on a bus. But really, you *are* saying the same thing as him. You're telling these people, 'No, damn it, you *didn't* get where you are just by being the best! You got there by setting things up, or having them set up for you, so people who *could've* given you a challenge never got the chance.' And they don't want to be told that. Their egos are too tied up in … in how things turned out for them. I mean, a year from now, if Steffi Graf wins all the big tournaments, you think the Germans are gonna want anyone to remind them what the real reason was?"

Jessica was alluding to an act of violence that had shocked the world of women's tennis only three weeks earlier. Gunter Parche, an obsessive fan of fellow German Steffi Graf, had snuck down from the stands during a tournament and thrust a knife into the back of Monica Seles, the Serbian star who had supplanted Graf as the top-ranked player in the world. Seles would require two years to recover, physically and emotionally, during which Graf easily reclaimed her #1 ranking.

"Can we steer this away from people getting shot and stabbed?" pleaded Kevin, near the end of his rope.

Jessica gave him a empathetic smile. "Be strong, babe, and think of the bigger picture, that's all I'm saying," she counseled him. "You're taking some crap, yeah, but you're also being treated like a hero by a lot of people. Just keep reminding yourself that they're out there, too – and there's more of *them*, actually. Now let's go out and do something. Let's get your mind off of this."

They settled on an outing at the miniature golf course. Jessica chained her bike to the inside of the Wilkersons' gate and climbed into the passenger seat of Kevin's truck. "Now remember," she said in a serious tone, once they got moving, "we both start the *same distance* from the hole."

Kevin spun his head abruptly to face her, wearing a perturbed expression.

"You gotta lighten up, babe," she advised him.

CHAPTER 17
Windows and Doors

Kevin's backyard was adjacent to a small community park that featured playground equipment, picnic tables and barbecue pits, and a small basketball court. The park occupied a triangular landscape, with access to the nearby streets on the northeast and southeast corners, and a walkway that connected the west end to the Wilkersons' street. Kevin's room and the kitchen were closest to the fence that separated their property from the footpath.

Five days after he had watched the Garland Bonham video, Kevin was sitting at his desk, studying his chemistry notes. Seniors received no concrete homework assignments over the last three weeks of the semester, allowing them to focus strictly on preparation for final exams and commencement.

Mr. Wilkerson was in the living room watching the Bulls play the Knicks, and Mrs. Wilkerson was out at her Tuesday night Women's Writing Circle. Kevin felt a sudden urge to make a chicken sandwich for dinner, and he grasped the armrests to hoist himself from his chair.

Suddenly there was an ear-shattering crash, and glass was everywhere. Kevin shot up from the chair in a panic, and pinned himself against the closet door, at the farthest available point from the window – or from what used to be the window. Breathing at a near hysterical pace, he scanned the carpet of his room until he saw the brick that had flown through the pane.

By the time he collected himself enough to listen for footsteps, everything outside was quiet. He figured it would be futile to try to pursue the culprit. By the time he went out his front door, down the long driveway, through the gate, and around to the path, the vandal would have long since escaped via one of the east-side exits.

Right on cue, he heard a distant sound of a car motor starting up and revving dramatically. He crouched down to grab his soccer cleats from the closet, slipped his bare feet into them, and dashed out the front door, almost colliding with his father, who had heard the crash and was rushing toward Kevin's room to check on him.

"I heard a car!" Kevin said. "Lemme see if I can catch it!" He realized as he spoke the words that "catch it" could be interpreted as the intent to take off on a vehicular chase through the residential neighborhood, and he quickly assured his father that that he wasn't thinking alone those lines.

"I mean, like, just – see what kinda car it is."

He ran out to the curb, and did catch a glimpse of a car making a sharp turn two blocks down to the left, at the intersection of his street and the one that circled around to the southeast side of the park. But from such a distance, and in the fading light of the evening, he couldn't ascertain the make of the car, let alone read its license plate. All he could see was that it was mid-size and gray.

Still trying to breathe at a normal pace, Kevin headed back inside and met up in his room with his father, who had put on his work boots and was already sweeping the shattered glass into a pile. Mr. Wilkerson paused to regard Kevin as he came in. He didn't look angry, merely concerned. "This is serious stuff," he said, stating the obvious. "Somebody's gotta be pretty upset to pull something like this. First of all, are you okay?"

"Yeah, I'm – I mean, I didn't get hit by anything, or … anything," Kevin assured him. "What should we do? Geez, I didn't know anything like this was gonna … do you think I should stop?"

"Well … stop what?" asked his father. "I mean, what have you really been *doing*, lately? I know you got the ball rolling to begin with, and you talked to some reporters, but … this thing looks like it's got its own momentum now, with or without you. I don't think there'd be a way to … to … to divorce yourself from it, even if you wanted to. You think someone might've gone after Billy Lloyd's house, too?"

"Oh, shit – I better call!" responded Kevin.

"Go use mom's office line," his father instructed him. "I've gotta call the cops. Keep the door open, 'cause I might need you to fill in some details, depending on what they ask me." Kevin obligingly went into his mother's office and phoned Billy Lloyd.

"Hello?"

"Hey, man, is – did anyone try to mess with you? Like, do something to your house?"

"No. What're you talkin' about?"

"I just got a brick through my window."

"What the fuck?!" yelled Billy Lloyd. "When?"

"Just like ten minutes ago."

Kevin overheard Greg Beech in the background, urgently asking, "What? What?!" Billy Lloyd pulled away from the phone to tell his father, then returned to the line.

"Was there a note attached to it or anything?" he asked Kevin.

"No," responded Kevin. It occurred to him that he hadn't actually checked the underside of the brick, but he figured it was highly unlikely that a taped-on piece of paper would have survived the tumultuous entry undisturbed.

"Chickenshit bastards," muttered Billy Lloyd. "You didn't see anyone? Hear anything?"

"I saw the car of – well, of who I think did it, but it was two blocks away. It was gray, but I couldn't see what model or anything like that."

"Okay, look," said Billy Lloyd, resolutely. "First of all, don't worry about the cost. We'll pay to get the window fixed."

Kevin instinctively protested, "No, uh-uh – c'mon …"

"Look, man, don't be stupid!" his partner commanded. "My dad's standing right here in the room with me, okay? This could've happened to you *or* me, but it happened to you – and you might not've even pushed this whole deal if I hadn't gotten involved. We're both in this. One of us shouldn't hafta pay the whole price. And let's be real; the cost to fix a window is not a big– I mean, it's pocket change for my dad. That's just the reality. C'mon, you got into this to solve a problem, not to make yourself a martyr. Look, my dad wants to talk to your dad – is he home?"

"Yeah, he's in the other room."

"Okay, put him on. But look – after they get off, call and check on Mike. They could be coming after him, too. My dad'll call Mr. Paige, at home."

"Pai– wait – you think someone from *here* did it? You don't think it might've been that guy from Burbank, or something?"

Billy Lloyd took a few seconds to consider the question, then responded, "I dunno … well … nah, I don't think so, really. I mean, track & field's mostly an individual sport, y'know? We could have someone on our own team just as pissed off as someone from another school. And it'd be easier for a Monroe person to track down where you live. But shit, it could be anybody. It could be some Garland Bonham nutcase who's got nothing to do with sports … it could … I don't know what to tell you. But do what you gotta do with your house, and let me know. If your insurance doesn't cover the whole thing, don't go digging in your own pockets."

Still uncomfortable with the feeling that he was accepting charity, Kevin mumbled, "Okay, umm … well, here's my dad."

Kevin handed the phone to his father, who had just entered the room after talking to the police. He got on the line and introduced himself: "Mr. Beech? Hi, this is Gordon Wilkerson."

Intuitively, Kevin could piece together most of what his father was hearing, based on his end of the dialogue: "Well, I can repair the window myself, and put up some – uh-huh ... sure, no, I really appreciate that. It probably won't be too ... right, no, I took care of that already. They're on it. I'll call our insurance rep in the morning. Our deductible is ... right, right, of course. Is there any particular ... uh-huh ... so you'll talk to them? Okay ..."

Kevin's mother came in the door about 25 minutes later, just as Kevin hung up the phone after checking to see if the Yamasakis' home had been vandalized. (It hadn't.) As well thought-out as Mr. Wilkerson's delivery of the news was, it took some time and concerted effort to calm her down. Kevin's reminder that the brick missed him didn't exactly placate her, either.

"And they *knew* that?!" she asked, reasonably. "They *checked* first, to make sure you wouldn't be standing near the window when they shattered it?"

"Mom, I'm okay," he reassured her. "We gotta ... I mean, we got no choice but to ... to just ... deal with it. I mean, you saw the letter from Derek. This is already catching on in Wisconsin, and it's gonna catch on in other places too, whether I say another word about it or not. There's no way I can, uh ... divorce myself from it, even if I wanted to." He shot an appreciative glance at his father for having provided the right words to use, and then returned to the key issue.

"But I can handle it, mom. I can take care of myself. It's not gonna get – I mean, no one's gonna risk going to jail 'cause they're upset about a ... a sports rule." He stumbled over the end of the sentence as it occurred to him that someone *had* just done precisely that.

Mr. Wilkerson prudently steered the conversation toward the subject of preventative measures, to drive the point home to his wife that they had the wherewithal to guard against a recurrence of the attack.

"I'll have to put some sort of grate over that window, and the kitchen too," he said. "It'll cut down a little on the light in the room, but you get most of your light from the back window, anyway. We're lucky – I mean, we're lucky that those are the only two windows that are vulnerable from the path." The Wilkersons had a sizable front lawn and a long driveway that put ample distance between their house and the front fence. Any object that could damage a front window would be far too heavy to heave from out on the sidewalk, and the height of the fence would obstruct any attempt to throw a line drive with a rock.

"We'll need to get a lock for the gate, and we'll have to pull all three cars into the driveway – no matter how tired we are when we get home, how much we'd like to just park out on the street, we can't take that chance. Got that, Kevin? You get out of the truck, you unlock the gate, you pull in as far up as you can go, and you lock it behind you. We can have an extra key made for Jessica, if you want." Kevin nodded.

His father concluded, "We'll have to be a little careful – there's no getting around it. But let's not panic. It won't do any of us any good, won't prevent anything from happening. Look, I'm gonna … I'm gonna leave a message for Randall at Farmers, and follow up in the morning to file a claim."

Luckily for Kevin, the night breeze that circulated freely through the gaping hole in his room had a gentle warmth befitting the late spring. He lay awake and wondered to what extent the reassuring words he had spoken to his mother were actually intended to quell his own uneasiness. He thought back to Billy Lloyd's ominous observation, at the meeting where they first determined to pursue the mission together, that reformers are often subject to harsh treatment. Now he had been the victim of two vicious assaults – one verbal, one physical – in less than a week. Billy Lloyd was also correct earlier that evening when he reminded Kevin that martyrdom was never the goal. Was that where things were headed? Would these attacks continue – or worsen, even?

He steered his train of thought back to the point that his father had made, which he had subsequently reiterated to his mother. It was largely out of his hands now. He couldn't stuff the bird back into its cage, and he couldn't bar any commentator from citing him as the originator of the idea, however they chose to portray it.

To his surprise, this powerlessness imbued him with a sense of liberation. *If this is as bad as it gets, you can take it,* he told himself. *And if it gets worse … well, what's somebody gonna do that'll top this, or top Bonham's crap? And remember, more people are gonna sign on. The wider this thing spreads, the harder it'll be for the holdouts to trace it back to you. They'll blame their own A.D.'s, their own sports commissioners. This is not what your life's all about. You graduate in ten days, you're gonna do a great job coaching for Lakis and Murphy this summer, and you're going to college in the fall on a full scholarship. Now go to sleep.*

I said, go to sleep.

The next morning around 9:50, Kevin was in chemistry class when he heard the voice of Kay Holland, the Vice Principal, coming through the intercom. "Attention, all students, faculty, and staff: We have a very important announcement. We need everyone to stop whatever you're doing, and give us your undivided attention."

The firm tone of the V.P.'s delivery yielded immediate compliance across all classrooms and campus facilities. To the silent listeners, she announced, "The home of a Monroe student was vandalized last night, in a very violent and dangerous manner. We don't know who did it, we don't have any specific evidence tying this criminal behavior to anyone in the Monroe community – but we *are* convinced that this was a targeted act, not a random one. We believe that this was someone's twisted and cowardly manner of staging a protest."

Miss Holland paused to let the student body process the information she'd just delivered, and then resumed. "As you heard, we don't have evidence of any particular perpetrator – yet – but two things are crucial for all of you to understand. If this crime *is* determined to be the work of any student at our school, the penalty will be extremely severe. There is no possibility that someone who would carry out such an act would be allowed to return to Monroe. That would hold true for a senior five days, or *two* days, from graduation. And secondly, if anyone has *knowledge* related to the crime and who committed it, they are absolutely required to come forth with it. If anyone is found to have concealed information about such inexcusable conduct, that individual could very well end up implicated as a party to the crime. The safety of our students is the foremost of our concerns, and that obligation does not drop off the map the moment you go home for the day. We will continue to work with law enforcement to track down the guilty party – a party we hope, with all our being, is not on this campus. Thank you for listening. Please resume your activities."

The moment the nature of the announcement became clear, Kevin instinctively began to take intermittent, undetectable glances at Simon, who sat in the same row as him, four desks over. He hadn't suspected Simon as the culprit, knowing that his tormentor valued his standing and his aspirations too highly to risk them over a stunt that could saddle him with a criminal record. He also knew that Simon drove a maroon car, not a gray one. Still, if Simon should happen to send some sort of "not guilty" gesture in his direction – or even if he were to turn to face Kevin as an involuntary reaction to the news – the logical follow-up question would be, "How did you know it was my house that got hit?"

Simon, however, just stared straight ahead, and widened his mouth in vicarious discomfort, the way a commuter might in observing the carnage of an accident. Kevin trusted that it wasn't an act. Plus, having tasted the ugly sensation of Garland Bonham's libel, the last thing he wanted to do was level unfounded accusations against anyone else.

By fourth period, everybody in the upper grades knew that Kevin had been the target of the attack. Kevin had no idea how or with whom the grapevine originated, but he spent his entire lunch hour fielding questions and expressions of sympathy and support. Most vociferous of the concerned parties was Brody Johnson, who told Kevin, "Man, if I find out who pulled this, their ass is *mine.*" Kevin thanked him for the loyal sentiment but urged him not to turn vigilante, and risk getting into trouble, on his behalf.

The perpetrator was never caught.

Nine days later, on a giant stage set up in the middle of the soccer field, Kevin Wilkerson, Jessica Mather, Billy Lloyd Beech, Simon Addison, Tristan Downing, Dallas Tompkins, Cody Orbach, Seth Langdon, Jesse Irving, Terry Cressman, and 173 others sat in their caps and gowns as the commencement exercises ran their course. Over a thousand relatives and friends sat in the rows of chairs facing the stage. Kevin's rooting section consisted of his parents, a few additional relatives, and all four members of the Yamasaki family. Mike had ended up finishing second in the district-wide championships in the 400.

Mr. Paige, Vice Principal Holland and Superintendent Don Garthwaite each offered a brief outgoing message to the graduates. Student Body President Marlon Rhodes gave a largely comedic sendoff to his fellow seniors, and Hailey Corringer, the Class of 1993's vocal prodigy, performed a soaring rendition of "Greatest Love of All."

A handful of academic and special-achievement awards were handed out, in a sequence that climaxed with the honoring of the class salutatorian, Annabel Shray, and the valedictorian, Danny Hattenberg. This acknowledgment happened to involve a personal tie-in for Kevin: He and Danny had been lab and study partners in physics and biology over their freshman and sophomore years, before Danny had accelerated beyond the customary science placement options for juniors and disappeared from Kevin's landscape altogether.

As Danny thanked the academic advisors who had facilitated his advanced study opportunities, Kevin felt a slight pride of association surging inside him. He had never socialized with Danny outside of class – actually, no one did – but he had always harbored a strong admiration for him, and for the whole range of his academic skills: his intuition, his diligence, his determination not only to arrive at the right answer but to know exactly *how* the journey was made. By about a month into freshman year, the two were seeking each other out as lab partners. Danny saw in Kevin a collaborator who wouldn't just abdicate responsibility and let his genius partner do all the work. Kevin was drawn to Danny because, in the event that he might at some point feel the *need* to abdicate responsibility and let his genius partner do all the work, he at least wanted the "genius" part covered.

And then Kevin heard it, from voices dotting the sea of graduates – the spate of under-the-breath mutterings of "I *know* you are, but what am *I*? I *know* you are, but what am *I*?" It was one of the signature lines from *Pee Wee's Big Adventure*, invoked to play up the honoree's slight resemblance to the star (when Danny's glasses weren't on), and to ride him for general nerdiness, as these classmates perceived it.

Listen to that shit, thought Kevin in disgust. *So many damn people can't feel like they're alive unless they're stepping on someone! If it's not Simon or Ackerman thinking they're better than the rest of us, it's these assholes thinking they're so much cooler than someone, just 'cause the guy's not into the same meaningless shit they're into. Yeah, we'll see how cool everyone is ten years from now.*

He discovered, almost in spite of himself, that the instinct to stand up for what was right had become a core component of his psyche, prompting him to open his mouth and command the discourteous students within the immediate vicinity and earshot of his seat, "*Hey!* Knock it off!"

The local hecklers, though mostly unsure of where the order had originated, heard the intense authority in its tone and adhered to it. As V.P. Holland wrapped up the acknowledgments and segued into the introduction of the faculty speaker, Kevin contemplated his impulsive quickness to take a stand – and the somewhat profound realization that he felt completely comfortable with himself having done so. *This is who you are now,* he told himself. *When no one else speaks up, it's gonna fall on you. And if someone's gonna give you any shit, screw 'em. What're they gonna do, throw a brick through your window? Hell, been there, done that.*

Then up to the podium stepped Charles Bowerman, the history teacher who had been elected by the seniors as the faculty speaker for their graduation. As someone who primarily taught underclassmen, he hadn't been in day-to-day touch with most of the graduates in about two years, but enough of them appreciated his classroom style, his innovative methods, and his having opened up new avenues of thought to them that they reached back into their past to request him.

He began with a few entertaining anecdotes from those early years, all meant to convey the idea, "Remember where you were at one point, and now look at you." He urged the graduates to prepare themselves for the dramatic changes that lay ahead, citing some of the elements of college life that had caught him off-guard back in his youth.

Then he fished around in his shirt pocket for something, but came up empty, presumably by design. "I wanted to read you this little comic strip I had saved, but it kind of got lost among heaps of term papers and grade reports," he confessed, "so I'll to have to cite it from memory. It's by Dave Berg, from Mad Magazine. What it depicts is a successful man – like, an executive type – sitting behind his desk and talking to another man, obviously someone beneath him in the company, who's standing on the carpet in front of him. The executive is lecturing the underling, saying, 'You know what your problem is, Jones? You have no ambition, no drive! We've been here the same amount of time, but I've risen to become Vice President in charge of accounts, and you're still barely out of the mailroom! In all this time, you'd think a guy would at least … say, how long *has* it been, anyway?' And the employee responds, 'Well, let's see – I think we both started working for YOUR FATHER'S company back in '68 …' "

The attendees laughed as expected at the punchline. Then Mr. Bowerman got serious.

"You have just accomplished something, every one of you, of which you should be extremely proud," he told the graduates. "Some had an easier journey than others, but it was never an automatic, a rubber-stamp guarantee, for any of you. It took hard work. It took determination. It took thoughtfulness. You brought those key elements with you, and you're reaping the reward today. Every door you've passed through along the way represents a triumph for you, a feather in your cap …"

"But every door that you've passed through also represents something else," he said. "It represents an opportunity that was *there* for the taking. It's to your full credit that you did make the most of it, and nobody can take that away from you. But I'm asking, with all my heart, that you remind yourself what the guy in that comic managed to forget: that those same doors *are not open for everyone.* It doesn't cancel out your accomplishments, it doesn't throw any sort of pall over them, to be aware that not everybody has the same resources, the same support, the same promises made to them."

"So for every door you've passed through," he instructed them, "recognize that you've done so – and be proud. But at the same time, step outside the walls of your own experience, learn that those doors were not there for everyone you may run into along the journey – and bearing that in mind, be humble. Call that knowledge up anytime you find yourself about to form a judgment about another person. Finally, and this is the big one: Try to gain the experience, at least once in your life, of opening a door *for someone else* – someone who hasn't had the chances that you enjoyed."

"This is not some abstract, head-in-the-clouds thing I'm talking about," he continued. "In fact, over the past year, we saw someone right here within this Class of '93 who discovered the value of opening doors for others. He was already inside the building, within a particular arena, enjoying all the perks that come with being there. But someone … someone very insightful and courageous, who's also graduating today, brought it to his attention that something was not right about that entryway, that certain people were being denied their access to the other side, through no fault of their own."

"Well, it would have been the easiest thing – maybe even the natural thing – to say, 'Hey, that doesn't affect me; it's not my problem.' But something in this young man's conscience wouldn't allow him to settle for that. He knew that if he truly wanted to stand tall, he, uh–" At this point, Mr. Bowerman froze in midsentence and turned to look directly at the 6'8" figure towering over his fellow graduates. As the crowd, in shifts, began to get the joke, Bowerman continued, with deliberate awkwardness, "Okay, well, I mean, he was *already* standing tall, but it – if he – well, you know how I mean that …"

The audience was still enjoying the humor of the moment. Of course, some grandparents or distant relatives needed the reference to Billy Lloyd explained to them, and other audience members found themselves at odds with Bowerman's stance on the issue. But the teacher forged ahead. "He knew that he had to answer the call, and do what he could to open that door for them – even if it meant that the space inside would be more crowded, and might afford less room for him. He reached back, and helped pry that door open – and many people are already feeling, for the first time, what it's like to be inside. That, folks, is an experience I wish on all of you, at least once in your years to come."

Billy Lloyd, from the moment it had become clear that the accolade was directed toward him, was shooting concerned, uneasy looks over his left shoulder in Kevin's direction, and making intermittent, subtle gestures toward the speaker, as if to say, *It's not supposed to be like this, with me getting all the recognition. If he's gonna bring this up, he should be talking more about you ...*

But Kevin simply smiled back at him and signaled, in every way he could devise, for Billy Lloyd to take it in, relish it, and not worry about him. His reaction was a sincere one. Jealousy or territoriality had no place in his thoughts. He'd been slandered on television and had his window shattered, and now his partner was getting the accolades – and he couldn't have been more content. It had been about the cause all along, and by praising Billy Lloyd in this public forum, Mr. Bowerman had officially vindicated the cause – and vindicated Kevin along with it.

Finally the time came for the handing out of diplomas. As they had rehearsed it, one row after another of the students proceeded to the dais to receive their certificate of graduation from Vice Principal Holland and a congratulatory handshake from Principal Paige. Cheers and applause of varying origins and volumes sounded out in response to each name that was announced.

As Kevin approached his turn in the sequence, he heard the principal's perfunctory words to the four graduates immediately ahead of him: "Good job, Watters." "Congratulations, Phil." "You did it, Wenstrom." "Good work, Karen." Expecting nothing out of the ordinary, Kevin was handed his diploma, thanked the vice principal, and stepped forward to shake Mr. Paige's hand.

As he did, the principal hastily muttered under his breath, "It did occur to me that I never gave you the apology I owed you ..."

Kevin took a quick glance at the thirteen or so students still waiting in line behind him – Susan Winter's name had already been announced – and gave Mr. Paige a subtle, waist-high wave of his hand. "It's all cool," he whispered back, calmly.

Mr. Paige gave Kevin the obligatory handshake. In the same gesture, he reached his left hand forward to give the clenched hand of his graduate an extra little pat. "Congratulations, Wilkerson," he said. Lowering his voice again to a nearly inaudible whisper, he added, *"and thank you."*

CHAPTER 18
The Counterpunch

The culture shock associated with college life was miles beyond what Mr. Bowerman had alluded to in his briefing. Kevin had to get used to total autonomy, with nobody to remind you to do your homework, to make sure you ate a healthy dinner (not that he needed reinforcement in that department), or to wake you up in time to get to class. It was all on him now. That was the first realization that sunk in.

He also hadn't been mentally prepared – not that it carried any practical implications – for the vast expansion of his new peer group's age range. He had always taken it as a given that his classmates would be of or near the same age as him, and he found it an amusing oddity to find himself seated in lecture halls next to a 50 year-old re-entry student, or to hear a member of his study team say she had to leave to go pick up her kids. All of it served to drive home the reality that, though only eighteen, he was now in an adult setting, and was expected to navigate it in something approaching an adult manner.

One factor that aided in the comfort of the transition was the quick rapport he managed to develop with his assigned roommate, an aspiring communications major from Indianapolis named Blake Zamora. Talkative, inquisitive, and passionately up-to-date on current events, Blake clearly took vicarious excitement in the dramatic details of Kevin's adventure in sports-arena politics.

Between his academic responsibilities and his obligation to Evansville's JV soccer team, it wasn't as if Kevin could afford to let too many competing interests distract his focus. He told himself that the development of a social life could not rank as a high priority for the time being. Not that he isolated himself from human contact altogether. Over the first three months of college, he did go out on a few dates with a pre-law student and later hung out for a brief stretch with a philosophy major, but both seemed a bit shallow, and not nearly stimulating enough, compared to Jessica.

Jessica, of course, was far away now, expanding her geographical and cultural horizons as planned at Cal Berkeley. They had left things open-ended when they parted at the end of the summer, but the unspoken truth was that their lives, if not their feelings for each other, were heading in different directions. Still, he would think about her, and reflect on how much he felt he had gained, in areas beyond just companionship, through their connection.

Other thoughts occupied his mind in shifts. He thought about the soccer team he had left behind at Monroe, and wondered how Mike, R.J., Skylark, Jay Marcivius, and the others were faring in what inevitably stood to be a rebuilding year. The Mustangs faced the onus of replacing their most potent offensive weapon, their strongest defender, their goalkeeper, and their entire starting midfield. Still, between Mike's talent on offense and R.J.'s leadership on defense, he was confident that they would remain competitive, week in and week out. He intended to call Mike at some point in October to ask how the season was progressing, but he found himself procrastinating.

He thought ahead to his home district's upcoming track & field season, and wondered how many additional Yamasakis and Volks, and how many more Brody Johnsons and Peter Landreths, would decide they were ready to strive for the prize that was finally accessible to them. Would the full-alphabet expansion still be limited mainly to Burbank and Marshall, where the athletic departments were solidly behind the change? Or would other schools catch on that the new system stood to increase their own talent pool and, in that light, was something to embrace?

He wondered how Billy Lloyd, Dallas, Jesse, Seth, Cody, Terry, Tristan, and even Simon were handling their respective versions of the same transition he was experiencing. He and Billy Lloyd, of course, needed to stay in contact to exchange updates and talk strategy, but email was not quite yet the universal convenience it would soon become, and Kevin was still at least two months away from opening his first account. Given the high cost of long-distance calls between Evansville and the University of Colorado, it was imperative to keep small talk and personal-life bulletins to a minimum.

Reflecting on everyone's achievements back at Monroe, Kevin found himself wondering how large or small a role their proclivities in the sports arena might now be playing in their lives. For some, like Dallas and Tristan, athletic pursuits figured to be the centerpiece of their early adulthood. Others, such as Cody, Simon, Billy Lloyd, and Kevin himself, had used sports primarily as their ticket to the wider benefits that a college education offered. For still others, like Jesse and Terry, the soccer championship would likely stand as the one major triumph of their athletic careers. Their lives would go in other directions, into new endeavors.

Of course, none of them, not even Billy Lloyd, had to balance their agendas with the burden of serving as the figurehead for an entire social transformation (to the extent that such an optimistic term could be used at such an early point). Kevin realized very quickly that the obligations of his own drum major instinct were destined to increase exponentially, not to lessen.

The vast majority of high schools across the country based their track & field programs in the spring semester, when they wouldn't force the best athletes to choose between track and either football or soccer. Still, there were a handful of leagues, mostly consisting of smaller private schools that lacked the numbers to field football teams, which held their track seasons in the fall. Those seasons were in process right at this time, and a small handful of those districts had heard about this new model and deemed it a sensible one to follow. That meant more people having the innovation thrust upon their landscapes, and forming and sharing their reactions to it.

One way or another, an ever-expanding pool of responses found a route to the mailbox in the lobby of Kevin's dorm. Mindful of the need to promulgate his side of the issue at every chance, he had requested of both the Monroe administration and his parents that they forward any letters to Evansville. By the third week of the fall semester, he found himself having to allot a ninety-minute stretch every other day to review his fan mail and his "detractor mail," and to respond to as much of it as he feasibly could, prioritizing the correspondents who he suspected might be amenable to reason.

He noted a continuation of the earlier pattern in which positive feedback was varied and nuanced, while the negative commentaries came in as virtual dittos of each other. Predictably, some of the latter were from resentful early-namers – or, more often, their parents – ranting about being "punished" or "forced to pay the price" for something that they played no part in creating.

A Mrs. Colton from Peoria recounted how her son Nathan, after running in the 200 meters his first three years in high school, lost his spot to a Sebastian Van Tassel in the September tryouts, with the new configuration in play. But Van Tassel, she went on to report, hadn't finished first in any of the track meets once the actual season had started. So Kevin's system had cost the school the victories they *would* have attained if only the "most qualified" runner – that obviously being Nathan Colton – had been awarded his rightful spot on the team.

In far greater numbers than these descriptions of personal travails, though, Kevin could recognize when correspondents were acting as voluntary mouthpieces for Garland Bonham or some other puppet master in the media. The uniformity of their talking points was too blatant to be purely coincidental. It got to a point where, by the end of a letter's first sentence, Kevin could tell by a few choice words whether the writer was coming out for him or against him.

At least twenty-two letters contained minor variations on the generic plea: "Why couldn't we just stick with the old system? Why does everything have to be all about *names,* all of a sudden?" Kevin, when he had the time to respond, gently reminded them that the old system, being alphabetically based, already *was* all about names.

One writer went as far as to submit a second letter, a response to Kevin's response, granting that the previous format may indeed have been name-based, but adding, "It was a whole different kind of feeling, though – people weren't all *obsessed* with names like they are now."

Several other critics clung to the conviction, just as Mr. Paige had initially insisted, that the disparity in lane lengths was strictly an illusion, a trick that the layout played on one's eyesight. After all (they pointed out in unanimous agreement), if a smaller arc brought about an artificial enhancement of speed, it would logically follow that the innermost tracks of a phonograph record would sound faster than the outer ones.

On the other hand, one recourceful contributor acknowledged that, technically, the runners in the traditional 400-meter dash may not all have been running *exactly* 400 meters, but cautioned Kevin at the same time not to interpret sports terms "from an overly literal mindset." To bolster the argument, the writer reminded him that American "football" is played primarily with the arms, that in "soccer," only one player is actually allowed to "sock" the ball, and that in "shuffleboard," the board in fact remains stationary.

Of course, a supplementary theme that ran throughout the vast majority of these letters was the presumption that self-centered motives, a quest for a free ride, had fueled Kevin's advocacy. One letter after another urged him to examine his conscience and wake up to the value of good, hard work, rather than "playing the name card," as the proper way to triumph over adversity.

The runner-up in terms of frequency was the question of why Kevin felt the need to "punish" those who, through no manipulation or malicious motives of their own, had been the incidental beneficiaries of the traditional format. Time and again he was asked what they ever did to him that could have sparked such hostility and reverse namism.

A recognizable phrase here, or a drop of a name there, would alert Kevin to the sinister presence of Garland Bonham operating the gears in the correspondent's brain. The bombastic TV host had tabled his rhetorical assault on Kevin during the summer, when athletic leagues were on hiatus. Now he was back in full force, gleefully making sport, so to speak, of Kevin's quest for fairness.

One expansive, detailed letter called Kevin's attention to data that supposedly showed that late-namers actually enjoyed a slight historical edge when it came to the running events *outside* the 200-500 range. Bonham, evidently, had displayed a chart that showed the statistics for the 100, 120, and 2000 meters over the previous twenty years of NCAA competition. The writer expounded on this oddity:

> If you could pull yourself away, for just a moment, from this obsession over the events where you're so sure you're being cheated, you might discover that you don't have it that bad, actually. You'd find that if you look at results for the short sprints and long-distance runs, people with names starting in the second half of the alphabet win *more* than half the time.
>
> *And,* if you expand that by just six letters, and consider the range from H to Z – so we're talking about the same group that you're always saying can't catch a break in the mid-distance events – your first-place finishes in the short and long runs climb to 73 percent. That's almost three out of every four races! Do you hear any of us complaining about that?

Seeing the pronoun "us," Kevin instinctively glanced down at the signature that concluded the letter, which read "Lance Aldman."

Scanning back up to resume reading where he'd left off, Kevin promptly entered into the world of Aldman's – and, undoubtedly, Garland Bonham's – conspiracy theory. "It's not hard to see what's happening here," Aldman declared.

> When you have events where you do just fine, where you win *more* than your share, you want to keep

everything the way it is. But with the events that you don't dominate, *those* are the ones where you moan and groan that everything's unfair and that we need to change the rules to let you win. What would that suggest, to any reasonable person? Obviously, you're pushing for a complete stranglehold on the track & field prizes, a system that's all about serving late-namers. You people get your way, and pretty soon they'll be telling the Andersons and Chandlers to not even bother showing up. They'll say, "Sorry, we're all about making sure the V's, W's, and Y's win."

Kevin tossed Aldman's letter in the "Don't waste your time on this bozo" pile.

As reckless and deliberately misleading as Bonham's running diatribe was, it had one upside: It attracted attention. And while the majority of the early attention, naturally, germinated among his own fan base, it also extended, inevitably, to people who did grasp the concept – and, in a few instances, who happened to have amplified voices of their own.

Kevin was studying in his dorm room one evening in late October when the phone rang. Blake, his roommate, was on the line. "Hey, Kev!" he practically shouted into his cell phone, as Kevin could hear the car radio in the background. "Turn on the boom box and go to 870 AM, right now. You know that Rhonda Mulcahy that I listen to sometimes? She's about to talk about *you*, man, you and your buddy from school. I think she might be gettin' ready to call out Bonham. She always knows how to nail him on his bullshit. Hey, you need anything from the store? I'll be back in about a half an hour."

"Nah, I'm cool," responded Kevin. "Hey, thanks, man. I'll see you in a little bit."

Kevin turned the portable stereo to the station Blake had indicated. Beginning about ninety seconds later, he was treated to the exact illumination of the subject that he would have orchestrated, had he been the supervisor of the show in question. Over fifteen minutes, Rhonda Mulcahy alerted her listeners to Kevin's background, to the incongruities of the traditional set-up, and to the role of Billy Lloyd Beech the early-namer.

Because it had been completely omitted from the narrative to that point, she placed special emphasis on Kevin's voluntary passing of the torch once the revision was in place: "The moment this boy, Kevin Wilkerson, was told that his proposal had been adopted by the league, he made the decision to remove himself from any of the events where it would come into play – *that's* how determined he was to avoid any conflict of interest. He became a voluntary trainer for other runners, and let *them* enjoy the victories that had always been placed out of their reach! Somehow, Mr. Bonham didn't consider that little detail worth mentioning."

She then proceeded to dismantle a couple of Bonham's most prized talking points, taking aim at the statistics he had recently trotted out to fuel the "late-name takeover" theory that Lance Aldman had parroted in his letter.

She started by pointing out that it shouldn't be too surprising or controversial, actually, if people with H thru Z names won 73 percent of *any* sort of competition, given that H thru Z happened to represent 73 percent of the letters in the alphabet. For comparison, she offered, "That'd be sort of like announcing the 'shocking discovery' that in a thousand rolls of a die, a 1, 2, 3, 4, or 5 came up 5/6 of the time!"

She granted Bonham's revelation that the second half of the alphabet did enjoy slightly more than a perfectly proportional 50 percent of the victories in the short and long runs – their advantage was, in fact, about 53 percent to 47 percent.

However, instead of leaving it at that, she took the sociological study a step further by actually examining *why* that might be the case.

"Suppose you're an athlete, a good runner," she said, "and you're looking for an event that could yield some success for you. Prior to this new system being installed, in the few settings where they have adopted it, what were your choices? Well, if your name was Anderson or Benson or something like that, you had *all* the options open to you. You could run a quick sprint, like the 100-meter dash. You could try something in the middle range, like 250 or 400 meters. Or you could do a longer, more endurance-based run, like 2000 meters. The only factor governing your decision was which event best suited your talents, your strengths."

"But if your name was Taylor or Wilson – in fact, even if it was Nelson or Jackson – you knew that, realistically, you only had *two* of those three options. It would have been made crystal clear to you, either verbally or from direct experience or observation, that you had no chance in the 200 or the 400. Maybe you sensed that there was some sort of inequity built into the system, or maybe you bought into the conventional wisdom that you simply weren't good enough."

"The point is, wouldn't you gravitate toward the events where you *did* have a chance? And of course, those would be the alternatives to the middle distances. Doesn't it stand to reason that if certain doors are slammed in a particular sector's faces, then we'll end up with a bigger talent pool from that sector in the areas where the doors *are* open to them? Couldn't *that* explain how you might end up with just a slight skewing of the numbers in their favor across those areas?"

"While I'm at it," she continued after a brief pause, "is it me, or does it strike anyone else out there as just a little … I dunno … insensitive, a little disingenuous, to bring up a 53-to-47 percent advantage as a counterargument to a 100-to-*zero* percent disadvantage?"

She concluded by turning Bonham's own claim to alphabetical victimhood against him, proposing that "if Mr. Bonham is so concerned about the Andersons and Bensons falling shy of their rightful share of wins in the short and long distances, he might want to look at this innovation from a whole different angle, as a step that might spread out the competition a little more broadly, which could finally open up that room for the A's and B's that he seems to feel has been tragically lacking. Maybe this'll be their chance, after all those years, to finally close that three-point gap!"

Kevin sat enthralled through every word Mulcahy spoke, and occupied a state of pure exhilaration at the conclusion of her piece.

Against all of his normal inclinations, he looked up the time and station, and tuned in to Garland Bonham's radio hour the following evening. He figured it was a near certainty that Bonham, facing the first challenge to his stranglehold on the subject, would be quick to respond to Mulcahy's arguments. His instincts proved correct. Bonham opened the show with a prolonged verbal assault on some recent statement or other by First Lady Hillary Clinton, during which Kevin promptly tuned out but kept his ears on alert for familiar terms or names.

Following the first commercial break, it was all about this special privilege for late-namers, and Rhonda Mulcahy's "totally dishonest" response to Bonham's ruminations on the subject. He started by denouncing the notion that the original configuration knocked late-namers out of the running, referring to the idea as "specious, inaccurate, and self-defeating."

As his evidence, he cited some applied research that he claimed to have conducted himself. He had enlisted eight staff members from his TV show, all with reputations for being solidly athletic. He had accompanied them to the nearest high school's running track and instructed them to arrange themselves in the traditional format – side by side, alphabetically from inner lane to outer lane – and had them compete in a 400-meter race.

"So who won?" he asked on behalf of his listeners. "Who finished in first place, against seven strong runners, in the format that we were told made it impossible for late-ranking names to win? I'll tell you who. It was a camera operator whose name is Donovan Tobin. Yeah, you heard me right – not an Adams, not a Baker, not a Carlson, but Tobin, with a T. Twentieth letter of the alphabet, seventh from the end, last time I checked. When I asked him to participate in this competition, did he play the victim? Did he whine and say, 'I'm not gonna get a fair chance,' or 'Shouldn't I get to start further ahead because of my name?' Did he quit before the race even started because he thought he had no shot at winning? No, he hung in there, he gave it his best effort, and he won – just like anyone should be able to do if they want it bad enough."

Kevin was taking bets against himself, for the pure entertainment value of it, as to what percentage of Bonham's loyal following was actually buying the story. His answer arrived promptly, as the on-air calls started coming in, beginning with three callers who praised this Donovan Tobin for relying on his own ability, and not some preferential treatment, to take the gold at the Bonham & Company Olympics.

Then a fourth caller, a Paul Somebody who had somehow made it past Bonham's screener, said to the host, "Well, I'm happy for this guy Tobin, and I'm sure he's a good runner, being able to finish first with a name that late in the alphabet. I was curious, though, 'cause I don't think you mentioned … well, umm … any chance you could tell us what the names of the *other* seven staff members were?"

Bonham responded, "I'm curious about something else, Paul. Any chance you could take your trick questions and stick 'em where the sun don't shine? And while you're at it, go tell your boss, Mulcahy, that if she has a problem with my presentation of the facts, she can bring it directly to me, instead of assigning some flunky to do her work for her!"

"Actually, didn't Rhonda invite you onto her–" began Paul, before Bonham hung up on him.

CHAPTER 19

A National Forum

It was official: The debate had gone public.

Lower-profile talk-show hosts and their callers began weighing in, and Kevin's mail doubled in very short order, to the point that it was attracting the attention of his dormmates. A few considered the overflowing mailbox an amusing oddity, and a few others found it a slight annoyance. But Blake, along with Steve Rockland and Chip Tolliver down the hall, found it exciting and galvanizing to have this upheaval play out within their own confines. The three fellow freshmen soon volunteered variable blocks of time in the evenings to help Kevin sort through the letters, applying their best judgment to assess which ones would be suitable for a response (and eventually helping to formulate some of those responses), versus the gutter-level "go to hell" or "go to Cuba" rants that could be discarded without anyone missing them.

Billy Lloyd likewise reported a significant increase in his own mail at Colorado following Rhonda Mulcahy's illumination of his role, though it still came nowhere near the volume of Kevin's. Because their respective names made his participation appear more inherently altruistic and self-sacrificing than Kevin's, a larger percentage of the letters to him offered words of appreciation and admiration. Yet he faced his share of detractors as well. Only two letters went as far as to call him a "name-traitor" – a designation in which he took great pride – but many self-styled analysts concluded that his embrace of the Wilkerson model probably stemmed from feelings of "early-name guilt."

Meanwhile, the concept, though still subject to widespread confusion and susceptible to misrepresentation, had intruded enough into the public consciousness that the first surveys on the matter were being conducted. Interestingly, the political leanings of respondents proved a more reliable indicator of where they would come down on the issue than their initials. People who generally gravitated toward conservative views, even if their surnames happened to be Williams or Vincent, tended to oppose the revision, while more liberal and progressive types, even those named Albertson or Banks, were more likely to support it.

Of course, how a polling organization chose to phrase the question could have a profound impact on how people responded. The difference between "Do you think runners with later alphabetical names should be given a special head start so they can win more races?" and "Would you favor adjusting the starting blocks for runners in the outer lanes to counterbalance the longer distance they have to go on the curves in the track?" could affect as much as a 25-point swing in the data across a given demographic.

The spectrum of prominent voices demanding to be heard continued to widen, soon encompassing political figures, social activists, and even the clergy. Televangelist Wilfred Ennis assured his audience that if God had intended for there to be staggered starting positions, "they would've been drawn that way."

Megachurch pastor John Granbolt found it prudent to remind his parishioners that "when our Lord and Savior Jesus Christ made His journey up the hill to Calvary, He didn't ask for a 20-yard head start."

On the other hand, an Episcopalian priest named Debra Southerly referred her followers to the admonition in Matthew 19:30 that "many who are first shall be last, and many who are last shall be first."

"That's one of the most oft-quoted passages in the Bible," Reverend Southerly observed, "and I don't think I've ever read it, or heard it read, without hearing at least a handful of 'amens' from the congregation. Are you telling me that now we're actually going to turn our backs on the perfect opportunity to put this principle into play?"

Kevin did well to maintain a B average over his first semester, as he braced himself for even greater demands on his time in the spring, when track & field seasons would be in full force. He took solace in the awareness that it would be the off-season for soccer, which would free up many additional hours for him.

Blake finally prevailed on Kevin to allow him to design and maintain a website based around the issue, through which people could learn about the concept and submit their questions and comments. Although an Internet novice for whom the term "website" still needed a bit of explanation, Kevin was quite capable of following step-by-step instructions, and by late January he was relying on Startinglines.com to field the majority of the correspondence.

Blake set up a graphic demo featuring diagrams of the "before" and "after" alignments, with bright red lines marking the curved paths from start to finish in each lane. After about four seconds, these lines would suddenly un-curl themselves and emerge as parallel, straight segments. Viewers could clearly see, then, how the traditional arrangement yielded uneven distances from start to finish, while the revised setup produced uniform distances. Of course, some holdouts would insist that the computer graphics were manipulated to falsify the actual dimensions.

As per Billy Lloyd's instructions, Kevin responded affirmatively to every legitimate request for an interview. By the beginning of 1994, he had participated in five phone conversations with radio hosts and another four interviews with print journalists. He went into these exchanges prepared for an ideological battle, but found nearly all of his solicitors to be respectful and generally supportive of his side of the issue. This surprised him at first, but it eventually began to make sense that those who sought him out would be the ones who placed some value on his opinion. Relying on Garland Bonham as his prototype, it hit home that the more hostile pundits would sooner put words in his mouth – and motives in his brain – than let him speak for himself.

On March 19th, Kevin received a phone call in his dorm.

"Hi, this is Kevin."

"Kevin Wilkerson? That's you?"

"Yeah, I'm – it's me. Who's this?"

"Kevin, my name is Logan Hewer, and I'm a program director for Sports Nation. Are you familiar with us, with our channel?"

"Uh … yeah, I think – you guys do, like, player profiles and stuff like that, right? Off-the-field stuff, like their work in the community – those kind of stories, right?"

"Yes, that's part of our programming. But we also look into social issues that involve sports – how they fit into society, things like that."

"Okay, right, uh-huh. I'm not sure … I've probably caught a few of those."

"Well anyway, I'm calling because I have an invitation for you. The debate over your model for track events has kind of caught fire over the past few months; the dialogue has expanded into some pretty prominent and far-reaching circles – I'm sure you're well aware of this …"

"Yeah … my dorm monitor's ready to strangle me, with all the mail he has to sort through. But, uh … yeah, so what do you have in mind?"

"Well, what's happening is, we're planning to hold a panel discussion on the whole question, which would consist of two people supporting the change and two others opposing it. We already have one outstanding advocate on the 'pro' side, and there were some solid options for the second – for, y'know, whoever would partner with him. But then, one of our staff said, basically, 'What if we were to go out on a limb and ask the kid who started the whole thing? If he got his whole district to go for it, there's a pretty good chance *he* knows how to argue the case.' Now, this might be the furthest thing from anything you can worry about right now. We didn't know whether you'd be comfortable with such wide exposure, or whether you'd have the available time, with college and everything. But we were able to track down recordings of a couple of your radio appearances, and based on what we heard, we're pretty confident that you could hold your own in the discussion, if you think it'd be something you'd be … interested in …"

Kevin's mind was in a whirlwind over the prospect, and it took all his focus to keep his follow-up questions coherent.

"So, you're … you're talking about something that would be aired nationally? Like, everywhere?"

"That's right, we're a national station. Like I said, if it feels like too big a step right now …"

"Well, no, it's just … well, where would I have to go, first of all?"

"Our studios are in New York, but of course you wouldn't – I mean, we would handle everything. We'd arrange your flight, have someone meet you at the airport, and put you up in a hotel. And, obviously, you'd be paid something for your appearance on the show."

"Wait – I would?" Once again, what was "obvious" in someone else's book had failed to even cross Kevin's mind.

"Absolutely. It would be something around seven or eight hundred dollars. I hope that's acceptable."

Kevin couldn't believe what he was hearing. *Seven or eight HUNDRED DOLLARS for going and making an argument that I've been jumping at every chance to make for free. Man, like you saw THIS coming a mile down the road …*

"Umm, yeah, that, uh … that'd be fine. Uh, but is it already … like, when is this supposed to happen? Is a date already set?"

"No, we haven't finalized the exact date just yet, not until we've secured all the participants. But you have a spring break coming up in two weeks, don't you? We shouldn't have too much trouble fitting it in there."

"Oh, that's right …" Kevin was asking these questions not so much to gain the answers as to stall for time before making a commitment one way or the other. Suddenly, *he* was the one re-enacting scenes from *Fiddler on the Roof,* as he weighed the pros and cons in his head while the person waiting for his answer sat frozen in time.

Okay, alright, so, like … we're talkin' NATIONAL, dude, and it'd be YOUR FACE up there. No more privacy after this; everyone would know who you are – and that includes all the Addisons and Ackermans, all the Bonham fans out there.

But on the other hand, it's not like your name isn't ALREADY out there, already totally connected to this. And this won't be someone else spouting a bunch of crap about what was driving you. You'd get to make your own case, and you know you can handle that.

But on the other hand … who are they gonna get to go up against you? These guys might be sports lawyers, or beat writers who've covered track for years. What if they ask you something you can't answer, or come up with a challenge you don't have a comeback for?

But on the other hand, man, if these last two years have taught you anything, it's that big-time credentials aren't any guarantee of common sense. Your girlfriend was seventeen, for Christ's sake, and she was smarter than anyone else in your life. You can't let yourself be intimidated; you KNOW you're right about this, and plus, you'll have … wait, who WILL you have working with you? You forgot to ask.

"Wow, this is … I really appreciate the invite, and I'd like to do it, I think. Can you tell me who the other people are? Do you have the, uh … I mean, the people who'd be on the other side of the issue, are they already lined up? And who'd be working with me? Anyb– like, would I have heard of 'em?"

"The other three spots, yes, they've been filled. You would be teamed with Dr. Wesley Herndon. He's a psychology professor at Princeton who also works as a consultant to a few different pro sports teams."

"Not too shabby …"

"Oh, he's very sharp, very insightful. He's the kind of guy that you'll be glad is on your side of the issue. And then, for the 'anti' side, we've got Emmett Brantley, the former NFL quarterback who's now a state senator from Kentucky …"

O-kayyyyy, thought Kevin, *an Ivy League professor, a state senator, and little ol' me. This is REALLY getting interesting. Wait – who the hell was "Brantley" in the NFL?*

"He was a quarterback? Who'd he play for?"

"About three different teams during the 1950s, up until about '62. He was a backup, never a starter."

"Oh, okay, before my time – yeah, I couldn't place his name. And then, you got the fourth person, too?"

"Yes, we do. We have Jordan Elgin, a sportswriter from–"

Kevin, with his pulse suddenly racing a mile a minute, cut in: "Detroit Free Press, right?"

Jordan Elgin – the apologist for the old, exclusionary system. The one who wrote all those smug, clueless articles trotting out every theory under the sun about why Helena Antonelli suddenly couldn't compete in the 200 after she got married and took on the name Vardell.

"That's right," said Mr. Hewer. "You've read some of his writing?"

"A little. But anyway, look, uh … you can count me in. I'll do it. Just lemme know when the date is, and I'll be good to go."

Alone in his room after getting off the line, Kevin sat in silent contemplation for about four minutes.

Then he picked the receiver back up and began to dial – not to consult with Billy Lloyd in Colorado, not to talk it over with Jessica out in California, but to reveal the news to his parents, back home in Richardson Park.

"Mom?" he said when his mother answered the call. "I gotta tell you about something pretty big that's happening."

"Is everything okay?" she asked instinctively.

"Yeah, things are good. I just, uh … I just got invited onto this big-time sports talk show, to be part of a panel discussion with three other guys. I'm talkin' about, like, a national show, mom, one that airs all over America."

"Are you asking me what you should tell them, or did you already accept the invite?"

"I already did, yeah …" In the same manner that one tenses up in anticipation of an opponent's throw in a dodgeball game, he got himself mentally ready for a lecture about overreaching and picking unwinnable battles.

"Well … do a great job, hon," his mother said.

"You don't think it's biting off too much, setting myself up for …" he trailed off, tacitly inviting his mother to complete the sentence for him.

"There's not too much I would put past you right now," she said. "After everything you fought through this past year, I'm pretty confident you can make it through this next step, too."

"You think I can do it …" Kevin verbalized her response to himself, just to verify that she had, in fact, said what he heard.

"Thanks, mom. That's great to hear. And I do feel like I can pull this off.

But I'm just sayin', I know you're getting some letters at home, too, and that'll pick up even higher after this."

"Well, we were already planning to talk to the post office about getting them all forwarded to your dorm. We just hadn't gotten around to it. If it goes to a whole new level ... well, I guess this'll be the little kick in the butt that gets us to follow through on that."

"Okay, cool – yeah, if they'll do that for you, that'd be great. Well, uh ... got any parental tips? Anything I should keep in mind?"

"Hmmm ..." Mrs. Wilkerson gave herself a moment to consider the question. "Well, you only have a limited time up there, so make everything count. Don't overstay your welcome on any one issue, or get too sidetracked. Whatever you *do* say, make sure it's something that'll score points for you."

"I hear you ... will do. Love you, mom. Let dad know about it, okay?"

"Wait! You didn't say when the show was going to be on."

"Oh, right. Well, that's 'cause I don't know yet. They haven't finalized the date, but it'll be sometime in, like, early April. I'll let you know as soon as I find out."

"Do you want us to tell our friends? Or would you rather we tape it first, and then let you decide whether you feel good about people seeing it?"

"No – well, I ... nah, I'm cool. I mean, if I'm gonna be heard by everyone in the country who tunes into the show, I better not be approaching it like I'm afraid I'm gonna look bad."

"For what it's worth, I'm not worried about that either, Kevin."

"Thanks, mom."

For no definitive reason other than to give his mind a rest, Kevin waited a full day before relaying the news to Billy Lloyd. He called him at about 7:00, Central Time, and filled him in on all the details.

"I knew what I was talkin' about when I told you we'd get our chance, didn't I?" said Billy Lloyd, with a triumphant laugh. "You aren't nervous, are you?"

"Yeah, a little," admitted Kevin. "I mean ..."

"Yeah, no shit, it's big, it's serious," acknowledged Billy Lloyd. "But that's only a problem if you don't know what you're doing. And look, I did three interviews with the media this fall, so that means you must've had a lot more than that, right? How many, would you say?"

"Eight or nine," estimated Kevin.

"And was there any point, in any of them, when you felt stupid? Where you came away like, 'Shit! Why'd I hafta go and say that?' "

Kevin thought back. "No, you know what? I, umm … I don't think I have. I mean, there've been times where I thought of something later on that I wished I'd said during the–"

"Yeah, but when's that not gonna be the case?" cut in Billy Lloyd. "The point is, you've never done actual damage to the cause. You've never sounded out of your league, even if the person you're talking to was older, and had more experience with these things."

"Yeah, but the ones I've talked to haven't been that confrontational."

"Right – but you also didn't have a guy with a PhD from Princeton sitting there with you and helping you make your case!"

"Well, yeah, there is that, I guess …"

"Stop trippin', man. Just go out in front of those cameras and kick ass. And don't, y'know, don't wave 'hi' to me, or your folks, or anything like that – act like you've been arguing this on TV for years. They're paying you, right? I mean, you're gonna get something for going on, I hope?"

"Yeah," affirmed Kevin, as he quickly realized that his initial instinct to bypass the matter of compensation made no sense, given the Beech family's wealth. "The guy said somp'm like seven hundred."

Billy Lloyd laughed in amusement once again. "Dude, you're on your way. I mean, look: They respect your opinion enough to pay you damn near a grand to hear you say it. Keep thinkin' about that, if you need – y'know, if your confidence needs a little pick-up. Hey, I gotta go, man. Call me and let me know as soon as the date's all set."

Whether in his dorm, in class, in the cafeteria, or in the student lounge, there were very few half-hour stretches over the next twelve days in which Kevin did not devote at least fifteen minutes to the upcoming climactic point of his brief career as an advocate. He ran an endless string of scenarios through his mind, day and night. He pondered what Dr. Herndon might contribute to the mix, how solid-sounding or inane the arguments from Jordan Elgin and Senator Brantley might be, and how he might best respond to every hypothetical question or counterargument.

Over the course of two follow-up calls from the producers, he had been briefed on a few details. To keep the conversation genuine and the terms equitable, the respective "teammates" would not have more than a few minutes of preparatory time together. However, as a courtesy to Kevin's status as a novice commentator amidst three veterans of debates and panel discussions, they would award him the first speaking segment; he could prepare his introduction to the topic without fear of the other participants already having painted it one way or another.

He conferred with Blake regarding what to wear. His P.R.-minded roommate suggested a nice blue shirt and a tie, but no suit jacket or overly formal accessories. "Don't go there looking like you're trying to make up for being younger or newer at it by overdressing," Blake counseled him. "But look like you at least gave it some thought."

On the morning of Tuesday, April 5th, Kevin drove himself to EVV Airport to catch his flight to New York.

He would participate in the show that evening, stay overnight in the provided hotel room, fly back to Evansville on Wednesday morning, and then drive from the airport straight home to Richardson Park for the remainder of the vacation week.

Kevin had flown only once before in his life. He had stayed in a couple of hotel rooms when traveling long distances for two-day soccer tournaments, but they were always shared with two or three teammates. He was in a bit of a daze throughout the flight, a condition exacerbated by getting a grand total of ninety minutes of sleep the previous night. It was only when he came out of the tunnel into the terminal and saw the driver holding the "Kevin Wilkerson" sign that it truly sank in that this was for real.

The schedule granted him about two hours of rest in his room before a production assistant knocked on the door to summon him to the car that would take him to the TV studio. Everything in New York looked artificially huge, even managing to drawf the image he had formed from photos and movies. It had a daunting effect on the young, semi-rural Illinoisan; Kevin found himself half expecting either King Kong or the Giant Marshmallow Man from *Ghostbusters* to emerge from behind one skyscraper or another.

And then he found himself in the Sports Nation building, going through the make-up procedure, being briefed on the dynamics of the clip-on microphone, and finally being introduced to his partner.

Dr. Herndon was a sixtyish, erudite-looking African American man, who congratulated Kevin on his success to that point. Kevin asked if the professor had any special words of advice, and Dr. Herndon responded, "Just remind yourself that you're on the right side of history on this one. Let's make eye contact when it feels like our turn to talk, so we don't step on each other's sentences. It'll be alright. Just be prepared for some of their arguments to be too ridiculous to *know* how to respond."

"I've gotten a taste of that, these past couple of years," Kevin responded.

"If you're not sure what to say, I'll cover it," Dr. Herndon counseled. "If you *are* sure what to say, don't hold back."

Before he knew it, he was on the set, seated farthest to the left from the camera's perspective, with Dr. Herndon next to him behind a curved table. Opposite them, along a widely obtuse angle, sat Jordan Elgin, in his mid-fifties, with thinning hair, a reasonably handsome face, and a style of dress that mirrored Kevin's. Finally, on the far side of the table sat Emmett Brantley, who had that Charles Durning look that matched Kevin's intuitive picture of a Southern Republican politician: in his mid-sixties, a tad oversized, with white hair and a square jaw.

Between Dr. Herndon and Jordan Elgin, in what would be the center of the camera shot, sat Jim Newkirk, the host and mediator. Upon being introduced to Newkirk about an hour earlier, Kevin realized that he had, in fact, seen a handful of topical round-tables on the network.

The cameras rolled, Newkirk introduced the topic and the panelists, and Kevin was on.

"Well, I stepped forward," he explained to his co-panelists and the viewing audience, "because I kept running into outcomes that didn't make any sense. I mean, there's no other example, anywhere in sports, where someone's *name* determines whether they win or lose. Right now, in football, we've got Troy Aikman, but we've also got Steve Young. Baseball had Dimaggio and Cobb, but it also had Babe Ruth and Ted Williams. Y'know, for every Muhammad Ali, there's a Mike Tyson, a Sugar Ray Robinson. But when I checked my own school's records, there was *one* winner of the 400 meters who shared my– whose name started with a W. One, in seventy years."

"And when I looked into it a little further, I found out the exact same year that this guy won, there was damage from an earthquake that made it impossible to use the track. So they had to set up some other deal where they ran on a straight, linear path. So the *one time* the race doesn't take place on an oval track is also the one time a late-ranking name breaks through? That had to be more than just a coincidence. So I took some measurements, verified what the problem was, and came up with a way to fix it."

"But everyone kept insisting that the difference in results was a *natural* thing. I kept getting reminded that tall people have an advantage over short people in basketball. People actually thought that was a good comeback. But the comparison never made any sense. Your name's not a physical characteristic. If it were, then it would show up somewhere else, too. It would affect people's performance in some other sports setting, not just this one, isolated situation. The problem was with the set-up, all along – but that turned out to be something a lot of people just weren't ready to hear."

"So … how do we respond to that?" the host asked Elgin and Brantley collectively, giving either one permission to lead off the counterargument.

"Well," began Senator Brantley, after getting the go-ahead nod from his partner, "First of all, I just want to commend this young man for taking action when he saw what he perceived to be an injustice. That's an important quality, to be willing to put it out on the line when you're sure something needs to be revised or brought up to date …"

Not having engaged in any dialogue with his opponents prior to the cameras rolling, Kevin found himself momentarily surprised not to hear any veritable Southern accent from Brantley. His autopilot had been entirely prepared for "Wayell, ah jus' wowna commayend this yung mayen …"

The senator segued into his critique: "But I think what a lot of people have concerns about is the *way* he went about trying to fix the problem … to fix what we all realize *was* a problem …"

Don't scoff or roll your eyes, Kevin quickly instructed himself.

"See, when you have everybody running a race from separate starting lines, the effect of that is, it emphasizes our *differences*. It announces to everybody watching that there are different conditions, different expectations, for each contestant. On the other hand, when runners start off together, side by side, that emphasizes their commonality – their shared path from start to finish, their shared ambition to come out on top. It *unites* them, which is always a goal worth striving for. There's a reason we worked the word 'united' into our country's name …"

"If I can cut in here," interjected Dr. Herndon, "I think we would do well to remind the good senator that there's a big difference between being *in close proximity* and actually being 'united.' The owner of a supermarket chain can spend an afternoon in one of his stores, and hang out with the folks who earn minimum wage working for him. That doesn't make him 'united' with them in any meaningful sense of the word. It doesn't create any sort of 'commonality,' as you put it, between his experience and theirs

– as much as his P.R. materials might try to convince us that it does."

"So, the point to that is … ?" prodded Jordan Elgin, speaking for the first time.

Dr. Herndon responded, "The point is, let's look at content here, not appearances. It's substance that matters, not style. This boy's new alignment might not *look* as aesthetically pleasing to your eyes as the traditional set-up; that doesn't negate or override the fact that it might be necessary."

"Well, again, I don't think anyone is trying to deny that *some* sort of steps were called for to create more opportunities for late-ranking names to compete," asserted Elgin. "But many are saying that this special boost in starting blocks was adopted too, umm … hastily, without the discussion it deserved, or the consideration of how people would be affected. There were other possibilities that had been proposed, other ways to address the issue of too much domination. But they were never given a fair chance to–"

Kevin raised a hand, as if in a classroom. "Yes?" Elgin asked in response.

"Sorry to interrupt," said Kevin, "but 'other possibilities?' I'm just curious, 'cause I *never* heard any other ideas put out there. I mean, you'd think someone would've filled me in at some point, let me know that … that things were already in the works. Can you tell me what a couple of these 'other possibilities' are?"

The opposing side faced its first awkward moment of silence, as Elgin and Brantley each seemed hopeful that the other would take the ball and run with it. Elgin finally took the initiative: "Well, for starters, schools and … and track & field organizations could set up special training programs to help certain runners improve their performance."

Dr. Herndon attempted to clarify, "And these programs would be exclusively for late names?"

"Well-l-l-l … you wouldn't want to single people out, I think," answered Elgin. "But coaches could encourage certain athletes to take advantage of the opportunities. We could also institute sort of a lottery system, where names from, say, N thru Z could have some kind of drawing for a chance to run– uh, to–"

He stopped just short of finishing the sentence with "on an inner lane," as it occurred to him that his side's whole premise was supposed to revolve around the denial that the inner lanes conferred any unfair advantage to begin with. Awkwardly, he forged down a different path: "Or … or you could offer special incentives, bonus points of a sort, that would give some extra motivation to the runners in the– in, uh, underperforming groups."

"Yeah, that, uh … that'd work wonders," muttered Kevin. "Maybe I've been looking at this whole thing the wrong way, for the two years I've been going at this. Maybe the whole problem was I just wasn't motivated enough." He looked directly at Elgin after finishing the sentence, to assess whether the irony was sinking in.

"So … let me just make sure I have this straight," Dr. Herndon followed up. "These, uh, 'alternate proposals' that you're suggesting, what they all seem to have in common is that they would leave the alphabetized line-up and adjacent starting blocks unchanged." He mapped out a straight line in the air with his finger as he spoke.

"Well … at first, maybe," responded Senator Brantley. "We just want to find a solution that's fair to everybody."

"So what I'm getting here," continued the professor, without missing a beat, "is that you're committed to an arrangement of complete and total fairness, provided that it in no way requires you to give up your own unfair advantage?"

"Now, that's not fair– I mean–" Brantley paused to collect himself. "You're trying to paint this as a deliberate attempt to rig a contest, or to set people up for failure, and it's not right to make that accusation against an entire stretch of the alphabet. Look, I don't have anything against late-namers; I voted for Ronald Reagan twice. Nobody's trying to hurt anybody, we're just trying to come up with a solution that works for everyone. But the narrative on this matter has gone, I think, in a very counterproductive direction, with all this talk about punishing people for the disparities that they didn't create to begin with!"

Kevin edged back into the exchange: "That *is* where it's gone, sir. You're right about that." Jabbing himself in the chest with his left hand, he clarified, "But *we're* not the ones who took it there. All the talk about 'punishment' has come from your side of this issue. A hundred percent of it. Because nobody's taken the time to really understand the whole point."

"Well, but the system wasn't *given* any time to understand, any time to adjust," argued Brantley. "You have to be prepared for a reaction like this when you take what's been the basic understanding for centuries and turn it on its head. Folks are just naturally gonna get upset when you mess with what they're accustomed to."

"Custom will reconcile people to any atrocity …" orated Dr. Herndon to the air in the studio.

As the moderator, the journalist, and the politician froze in silent uncertainty, Kevin saw an opportunity to score a point for humor. "That's *exactly* what I was gonna say!" he said emphatically to the opposing side. Then swiveling his head to face his senior partner, he asked, innocently, "What does it mean?"

Everybody responded positively to his comedic timing. Then Dr. Herndon explained: "The quote's from George Bernard Shaw. It means, basically, that when policies, or patterns of behavior, are served up to the public as 'normal,' as 'just the way things are,' then people have a really strong tendency to make their peace with them, to cohabitate pretty comfortably with them – even when those policies or behaviors are very clearly wrong, when they'd be unacceptable by any objective standard."

As the professor paused for a breath, Kevin related, "That's just what my girlfriend back in high school said. She brought up how a lot of things that are, like, 'obvious to everyone' today, they actually took a long time before people got on board with them."

Dr. Herndon nodded in support, then resumed his point. "But embracing those routines and patterns is going to be a hell of a lot easier when *you're* not the one, or a part of the group, that's feeling the harsh end of the stick. You don't know how many times in my experience I've brought up one injustice or another, one inequity or another, only to be told, 'but that's how it's always been,' just as you're saying to Kevin here, as if that justifies leaving a problem unaddressed. And of course, that rationale pretty much always comes from someone who doesn't *have* to see it – whatever the ordeal happens to be – from my angle. When they've warned me that 'people might get upset,' I've noticed how consistently the word 'people,' in their vocabulary, seems to refer to a group of which I'm not a member. Why is *their* comfort the only criterion we're supposed to worry about?"

"But you're missing the point, which is that we *are* trying to look at this from the other angle," protested Elgin. "This is not about us just trying to protect early-namers from discrimination. We're just as concerned for the impact on late-namers themselves. When Kevin, here, and people in his alphabetical range win races under this new format, there's absolutely *no way* those wins will receive the same credit that they would under the normal system."

Aiming the remainder of his address directly at Kevin, he continued, "It's important to think about the bigger picture. Not everybody out there is going to understand the purpose of this, the way we do. They'll say that your victories were handed to you, instead of being legitimately earned. We don't want to see you end up stigmatized like that!"

Being addressed in this patronizing manner made Kevin angry. He made a conscious decision not to sidestep it. Responding to Elgin, he kept his voice at low volume, but let every physical tool at his disposal indicate that he'd been pushed past his limit.

"Alright, okay, uh … I'm gonna let you in on a little secret here," he told the sportswriter, "the little piece of all this that somehow got past you. See – we were *already* stigmatized. We already had to hear, from everybody, everywhere we turned, that we didn't measure up, that we just didn't have the ability, the tools to compete in this field. And when the evidence on the physical side of things made those arguments sound as crazy and … and full of contradictions as they were, *then* we had to hear that we were, like … playing mind trips on ourselves, psyching ourselves out of any chance to win. And there was never any way we could prove that it was wrong, with the set-up the way it was. I mean, unless we could pit some Jesse Owens type against seven guys with bad ankles. And – *and*, if we *did* ever pull that off, you would've turned that against us too. You would've said, 'See? If he can do it, what's wrong with the rest of you?' "

"Why do you keep personalizing this, saying 'you' all the time?" protested Elgin.

"Because you actually, I mean *you* – you *did* play a part in it," Kevin insisted, "with all that stuff you wrote about Helena Vardell at Michigan State!"

Elgin, with a caught-in-the-cookie-jar look on his face, asked, "How do you know ab– what– were you even born yet?"

"Just barely," answered Kevin, "but I did my research. I'm lookin' at sports journalism as something I might wanna go into myself, so I wanted to see how different people went at it."

At the mention of this possible career option, Dr. Herndon, outside of Kevin's line of vision, widened his eyes dramatically and gave an understated nod as if to say, *Yes … please, yes!*

Jim Newkirk intervened, requesting of either of the knowledgeable parties, "For those of us who *haven't* done the research, could you tell us who this is we're talking about?"

Kevin pounced. "Sure. There was this girl – well, she'd be in her 30s now, but in the late '70s, she dominated track & field, and basketball, in my area of Illinois. Then she went to Michigan State, and kept it goin' there;

nobody could touch her. But when she got married, her last name changed from Antonelli to Vardell. Well, after that, she *still* dominated in everything, except the 200 meters. That was the *one event* where she suddenly, like, 'didn't have it' anymore. And Mr. Elgin, here, pulled out every argument he could think of to explain it, except the one that actually *did* explain it! When she came back as Helena Vardell, she couldn't win the 200 meters anymore because she wasn't *running* 200 meters! In the outer lanes, she was running 225, 230 meters!"

He looked and gestured directly at Elgin as he concluded: "But see, you couldn't let that sneak into the picture, because you just had to have a way that you could lay it all on *her*, say it was something, some way that *she* was coming up short. You didn't seem to give a damn how she might've felt about being called a loser, when she was probably the best athlete on campus, besides Magic Johnson. So now you're gonna try to tell me that your *real* worry is that, if we finally get the chance we've deserved all along, and we make it pay off, that we'll have to deal with some second-guessing from the same people who were *already* convinced we didn't have what it takes? I'm gonna go out on a limb here, and say that's a sacrifice most of us'll be willing to make. But look, we appreciate the concern."

The debate still had about eight minutes to go, but it was effectively over at that moment.

Kevin slept well in his hotel room that night, caught his plane the next morning, landed at EVV Airport, and then drove northwest, at unhurried speed, from the Illinois-Indiana border to Richardson Park. He spent most of Thursday, Friday, and Saturday taking a well-earned break at home with his parents, although he did get together with Mike and Brody for lunch on Saturday, to check in on how the '94 track season, and their senior year in general, were going.

From the restaurant, he drove to the library, to get on a computer and see what sort of commentary had surfaced on his website.

He went to his site, entered the password to enable administration, and then clicked on the correspondence page. He had privately predicted something in the range of 350 comments, and was a bit thrown when the page indicated a tally of over 1,100. Knowing that it would take many hours to pick through the entire feedback reel, he merely scrolled down the thread at a leisurely pace, to see if any key words or phrases jumped out at him and spurred an instinctive response. He thought of solid, economical replies to two early challenges and fired them off to the submitters. He browsed a little further and was about to log off when he saw a recognizable name flash past.

Scrolling back up to it, he found the following message:

> Hello, Kevin, I'm reaching out to you because I suspect, based on your thorough knowledge of the Helena Vardell story, that you may have read some of my father's old columns. His name was Steven Yablonsky, and for many years he was the Sports Page Editor for the Lansing State Journal. He wrote quite a bit about the flaws in the arguments used to defend the standard track arrangement and he went at it with Jordan Elgin in print just as fiercely as you did in person. Like you, he knew that something didn't add up. But unlike you, he was never able to define exactly what the hitch in the system was, or how it could be fixed. What you've done – or what you seem to be on the verge of doing – is sort of a culmination of his advocacy, his hope for a more fair system.
>
> I'm sorry to report that we lost our dad to Parkinson's a little over three years ago. Although he's not here to express his own appreciation, I want to do it on his behalf – maybe even in a practical way.
>
> I'm not in the field myself, but I do have connections to a few of my father's colleagues who are still with the paper. I realize this is WAY premature on my part – you've got a whole lot of college left to go, and for all I know, your mention of sportswriting as a potential career path might have just been an off-the-cuff remark. But if you decide, when the time comes, that it really is a possible direction for you, and you can manage to track me down, I promise I'll put you in touch with people who can at the very least offer you some valuable guidance.
>
> I'm fully confident that my father would approve.
>
> Sincerely,
> Shira (Yablonsky) Mills

Kevin slowly swiveled the chair away from the computer table, and sat staring at the trees just outside the library window for about four minutes, contemplating his future. He spent an additional three minutes contemplating the present, then got up and left.

When he returned to the house at about 2:30 that afternoon, a predictably large stack of mail awaited him. He decided to open the first five envelopes, see if any of the submissions merited a response, and hold the remainder for when he got back to campus. The second letter caught his attention, as he was familiar with part of the return address: It came from Apartment 174 in Enchanted Knolls, a local residential community for the elderly. Kevin had biked or jogged past it countless times over the years, and had seen the retirees playing croquet or socializing at their picnic tables.

He pulled out the handwritten letter, which read:

> To Mr. Kevin Wilkerson,
> I just wanted to let you know, that was one fantastic job you did on the Jim Newkirk Show. Those arrogant sons of bitches didn't know what hit 'em!
> And while I'm at it, let me also say congratulations on your decision not to wait for another earthquake.
> GO MUSTANGS!
>
> Sincerely,
> Burt Waldron (Monroe High, Class of '42)

CHAPTER 20
Danny

It was around 6:30 on a warm September evening in 2003 when Kevin pulled into the parking lot of the Richardson Park Community Center, which was hosting the ten-year reunion of the Monroe High Class of '93. Over the preceding two years, he had settled into a comfortable niche with the Lansing State Journal, writing a health and exercise-themed advice column and contributing additional articles on local or national trends in sports and fitness. He hadn't made a special trip back for the get-together, but its timing happened to coincide with his return home for a separate, unfortunate reason: His father had suffered a stroke about ten days earlier.

Mr. Wilkerson was recovering at an encouraging pace, but Kevin knew full well that the demands of caring for him would be heavily taxing on his mother without his assistance. His ability to continue his journalistic work online made his temporary move back home less disruptive to his livelihood. Even so, he took a two-week hiatus in order to devote his full focus and energy to his father's needs. He would be resuming his column in about five days, but he fully intended to forestall any return to Michigan until he was confident that his parents could manage without him being close at hand.

His concern for his father's predicament, in fact, was such that he had been leaning toward not attending the reunion at all. His mother was encouraging him to go, but it wasn't until he verified that at least two neighbors would be home – and available to help without the slightest delay in case of an emergency – that he consented to take a few hours' break from his caretaking responsibilities.

As he walked from his parking space toward the event hall and made his way up the stairs, he compiled in his head a quick list of fellow alumni whose company he would seek out, in the event that they were there. He knew the prospects would not include Jessica Mather, who had remained in Northern California after graduating from Berkeley. Now Jessica Quinn, she was four years into marriage, raising a young son, and teaching fifth grade in an Oakland suburb.

Also absent would be Billy Lloyd Beech, who now worked at Iowa State University as an assistant basketball coach and a career counselor for student-athletes. He and Kevin had stayed in regular contact over their first few years out of high school, when the task of defending their cause still fell almost exclusively on them. But as a progressively broader coalition emerged to help carry the banner and lighten the two founders' share of the load, their outreach to each other grew more sporadic.

Yet even as the paths of their lives diverged, Kevin never relinquished his gratitude for Billy Lloyd's willingness to stand with him in his fight for a fair arrangement. In one of their last email exchanges, about a year prior to this reunion, Kevin had told Billy Lloyd that whenever he happened to come across an instance of someone exemplifying real honor and integrity, he would amuse himself by commenting, "Now, ain't that a Beech?"

"Not the worst thing to be identified with," Billy Lloyd had responded appreciatively.

Staggered starting positions for mid-range running events were now the norm everywhere. Over a stretch of about four years, incremental shifts had taken place as one region after another came to see the merit of the adjustment and adopted it into its respective track & field programs. The states in the vicinity of Lake Michigan, where Kevin's original challenge to convention was of greater local interest, were the first to get uniformly on board. The West Coast and Northeast signed on shortly thereafter, followed by the Midwestern, Rocky Mountain, and Northern Appalachian regions. The tradition-steeped Southern States were more resistant, but by 1998 the last holdouts, Mississippi and South Carolina, had joined the fold.

The resultant opening of the doors to late-name athletes, who could finally see themselves as viable competitors in the 200 to 500-meter ranges, was lauded, reasonably, as the chief benefit of the revision. But commentators also naturally noted the increased excitement and intensity of the rush to the finish line, now that every runner in a given race, and not just two or three out of eight, stood a chance.

Even so, there were still those lingering choruses of discontent. Stuart Volk's prediction aside, many quarters did *not* view the old arrangement through any sort of what-were-we-thinking lens. Portrayals of the staggered-line mechanism as a vengeful plot against early-namers and/or a paternalistic babying of late-namers still emerged with regularity on one front or another. Some commentators suggested that, now that the adjusted starting blocks had brought about the desired increase in victories by late-namers, to the point where their chances were roughly equal to those of early-namers, they had "done their job" and could now be abandoned in favor of a return to the traditional, side-by-side starting arrangement. "Shouldn't the next logical step," they asked, "be to find out if they can win those races with a fair & square, universal starting line?"

Track & field associations in California, Washington, Vermont, and New York had reached a different conclusion regarding the next logical step, and had scrapped the custom of alphabetization altogether, opting instead to assign the lanes by a random drawing of the contestants' names. Their assumption that this should quash any lingering charges of favoritism was overly optimistic; Garland Bonham was quick to alert his viewers that the long-term goal behind this move was to secure both an inner lane *and* an advanced take-off line for late-namers. Most people outside of his loyal audience, however, seemed to grasp the concept that the starting positions would continue to correspond with the lanes themselves, not the competitors' names.

Kevin had navigated his fifteen minutes of fame in the aftermath of the Sports Nation panel, being approached by both admirers and detractors with some regularity throughout much of 1994. While he still fielded occasional inquiries or interview requests from one media outlet or another, he had, for the most part, let the validity of his cause speak for itself and generate its own momentum. He never envisioned himself, in returning to the scene of his struggle, as anyone's hero – or, conversely, as anyone's pariah.

While the impact of his advocacy had been profound, he always reminded himself that it had also been localized in its scope. In the big picture, the particulars and procedures of a handful of track events are only relevant to a tiny percentage of any given population. The regional spotlight that fell on the Monroe High School community as the epicenter of starting-block reform certainly caught the attention of virtually the entire student body, but it wasn't as if most of their lives were directly affected by it. A few might see Kevin as a symbol, but from his perspective, he was just a 1993 grad, here to catch up and have a good time with other 1993 grads.

Things got off to a slow start. There were a handful of casual, hey-how's-it-going exchanges with marginal former acquaintances, including Tristan Downing, who had managed to play a few years of pro football in Canada and was now back at home, segueing through a series of retail positions. Also present at the event was Kevin's old midfield mate from soccer, Terry Cressman, who was now on the faculty at the his own alma mater, running Monroe's computer center.

Kevin's most gratifying reconnection, early on, turned out to be with Peter Landreth – who, although a grade younger than him, was accompanying his wife, Melanie Culver-Landreth, who had graduated in '93 along with Kevin and the rest. Following college, Peter had returned to Richardson Park, where he now worked as a 911 dispatcher. He mentioned that he had maintained his close friendship with Brody Johnson, who had picked up enough clients as a personal trainer to open his own small gym in nearby Huntersville.

"Be sure to give him my best when you see him," said Kevin. "He was a cool cat. I really liked him."

"He'll be glad to hear that," Peter responded. "He still talks about it, the whole thing. You're like his idol."

Kevin instinctively turned his head to the side, as if to deflect the unsolicited praise. "Jesus Christ ..." he muttered.

"Well, yeah, he'd be up there too, I guess," affirmed Peter.

Kevin reacted to the joke with a slight chuckle, and then asked, "What about Mike? You know anything about what happened with him?"

"No – what?" asked Peter in a sudden tone of concern.

"Oh, no, I didn't mean – okay, that didn't come out right. I just meant, like, does anyone in your class know where he is these days, or what he's doing?"

Peter shook his head. "Not as far as anything I've heard," he said. "I figured if anyone was gonna stay in contact with Mike, it'd be you."

"Yeah, no ... I mean, we kept in touch for about a year – y'know, when you guys were seniors. But I think right around the time he went off to college, his dad's job ended and the family moved back to San Francisco. So we just kinda ... well, you know ... anyway. I'm sure he's probably doing fine, though, with whatever he's gotten into."

"Yeah," agreed Peter, "he was a winner, alright."

The reunions with these former athletic compatriots were interspersed with the usual civil nods between faces that were vaguely familiar – and, of course, those inevitable greetings from totally unrecognizable attendees, with whom Kevin tried to fake his way through brief, nostalgic conversations, as he wondered, *Who the hell is this guy? Am I supposed to know him?* He was already setting a time limit of about another forty minutes before he planned to duck out when he heard his name called: "Wilkerson!! Hey, Kevin!"

Craning his neck to peer through the crowd of partygoers blocking his view, Kevin saw a face from the past that took him at least a few seconds to assimilate.

"Danny!"

It was Daniel Hattenberg, the class valedictorian – and Kevin's old study partner.

"Get over here, man!" commanded Danny, already seated at a table with a plate of food from the buffet.

Kevin obligingly navigated his way through the crowd and settled in at the table, re-familiarizing his brain with an acquaintance he hadn't seen up close since they were both sixteen. They hadn't shared any classes over their junior and senior years, and Danny would have had no idea about Kevin's rebuke of the graduation-day hecklers, given that it took place a good distance from the podium, out of the honoree's earshot. They had no interaction that day, or subsequently. In fact, Kevin hadn't even thought to include Danny on his people-to-reconnect-with list. All the same, he found himself very happy to see him.

"You're lookin' great, man!" said Kevin.

"You, too!" responded Danny. Both compliments were sincere, but only Kevin's included an element of surprise in the mix. The transformation from the teenage Danny Hattenberg to the current incarnation was far more striking than any change that might have taken place in Kevin. The one who had frequently been described, with only minimal exaggeration, as "a blonde Pee-wee Herman, with glasses" now looked robust, strong-shouldered, and well styled – like someone who, in a younger incarnation, would have been thought of as quite a desirable catch among the available candidates on campus.

Danny initiated the catching-up process: "So what's going on with you?"

"Well, I'm – y'know what, hang on just a sec," said Kevin. "Lemme grab a little bite to eat, and I'll bring it over here." He draped his coat over the chair and hurried to get a plate, somewhat surprised at how eager he was to get back and find out what Danny was up to. He assumed the answer would involve sophisticated data analysis, or biogenetic research, or something in a comparable realm. He was scrutinizing the choices at the buffet table when he heard from behind him the voice of the one person he had hoped *not* to encounter.

"Hey, Wilkerson, how's it goin', buddy?"

Kevin reluctantly turned around to face Simon Addison.

He had learned from various alumni news briefs that Simon was making "serious money" as a stockbroker. Now, as he stood toe-to-toe with his former fellow athlete, he instantly learned something else about him: Only

45 minutes into the gathering, Simon's breath already reeked of alcohol. Kevin could see the effects of multiple years of heavy drinking in the streaks of pasty color on Simon's face.

"Hey, Simon, what's up?" Kevin responded with a very deliberate lack of excitement in his voice.

"You doin' alright?" asked Simon. "Still stayin' ahead of the game? Oops! Sorry, bad choice. Heh heh ..."

Unbelievable, thought Kevin. *He's been waiting seven, eight, maybe ten years to tell me that joke – that clueless, lame-ass joke.* His urge to return to the adult world where Danny Hattenberg resided was suddenly magnified. He gave a half-nod, half-shrug in response to Simon's quip, and set about filling his plate.

"Hey, I heard you helped Amanda Grayson get her job!" Simon went on.

"What the hell are you talking about?" asked Kevin, growing more annoyed by the second. The statement was so completely out of left field; Kevin scarcely remembered Amanda Grayson from their school days.

"Well, a few of us were talkin' about what we're doing these days, and she said she was working for, uh ... for Head Start! Isn't that your organization?"

"You get an A for that one, Simon," muttered Kevin, trying to look as unimpressed as humanly possible. Hastily leaving the buffet table, he repeated, "Yeah, man, you get an A. So I guess that means you have two of 'em now. Might make you an even faster runner."

As he vacated the immediate premises, he started thinking to himself, *What a world we live in. A guy can be smart enough to be a doctor, smart enough to be a lawyer, smart enough to run an investment firm or make a million in the stock market. And that same guy, that exact same person, can be just plain STUPID – hopelessly, terminally stupid. Bouncing through life with no clue how the world works, or whether anything he says even makes sense.*

Returning to Danny's table, and anxious to cleanse his mind of Simon's obnoxious spirit, Kevin asked, "So, were you about to tell me what's happening, or was I about to tell you?"

"Well, I'm fine either way, but I asked you," Danny responded.

Kevin brought Danny up to date on his advice column. He provided a few stock examples – someone might ask what he knows about the such-and-such fitness regimen, or what's the best way to rehab from this-or-that particular injury. Maybe a mother whose 11 year-old has never played competitive sports now wants to get him involved, but can't decide which sport would serve as the best "breaking-in" ground.

As he talked, the realization began to surface that Danny might legitimately *be* one of a handful of Monroe students who had absolutely no knowledge of Kevin's ordeal with the track & field politics, given that it had all taken place over their final two years at the school, after they had fallen out of touch. The whole story could quite possibly have evaded his awareness altogether. Danny had always stood entirely outside the social scene – not as a result of alienation or awkwardness, but simply as a reflection of his interests and priorities. He was in school to study and learn and get good grades, and that was it.

Danny, focused as ever, was now listening attentively to Kevin's description of his work. "That sounds wonderful, man, really cool," he responded when Kevin came to a pause. "So, when these people write in with their questions, do you already, like ... *know* what to tell 'em? Like, you've built up enough knowledge that you can just fire off an answer? Or do you have to go look stuff up, and then get back to them?"

"Both," said Kevin. "Some of each. Some of them I can just answer instinctively, but I'd say a little more than half the inquiries – maybe 60, 65 percent of them – are gonna force me to do at least a little research. But I know where to look. I know which sources are the ones you can trust, which experts – or so-called experts – have really done their homework, or haven't done it. So it's not hard for me to dig up reliable info to relay to someone, if I don't know how to respond off the top of my head."

"Hmmm. 'So-called experts.' Yeah, I'm sure there's a lot of quack science you gotta sift through in the health & fitness world, huh?" Danny surmised.

Kevin nodded. "Like pretty much anywhere else," he said with a slight shrug. "But yeah, you're right; I gotta sift through it. I definitely can't be casual about just parroting, y'know, 'something I read somewhere.' If I give someone bad advice – or, like, if I make a recommendation that I can't attribute to a qualified source – the paper could be liable if something goes wrong. So I can't ever sleepwalk through it. I've gotta stay on top of, y'know ... what's legit and what isn't."

"Sounds like you're doing that," affirmed Danny. "So is there any chance of syndication – like, beyond just the Lansing paper? 'Cause that's supposed to be where you can make some really nice bread, isn't it? When there's something like ten or twenty or fifty papers all carrying your stuff?"

"Nothing like that yet," said Kevin. "Well, actually, there's a handful of, y'know, little community papers that co-opt some of their material from the bigger ones, and I've been worked into a few of those. But as far as any big-time circulation, it's still way too early in the game, as far as really establishing myself. I mean, it's going well – I'm getting a good response, overall, and if that keeps up over a long stretch … well, we'll see. But tell me what's going on in your life!"

"Well, I'm kind of involved in politics now," answered Danny.

"Really!" Kevin's reaction included a slight rearing back of his head – not for dramatic effect, but out of genuine surprise. Hearing that Danny Hattenberg was into politics was every bit as unforeseeable as it would have been to learn that he was playing linebacker for the Steelers, or that he was hosting a beach party show for MTV. "What're you … I mean, are you running for office somewhere, or working on – well, what *are* you doing, and how'd you get into it? Tell me."

So Danny told him.

"Well, it goes back to when I got my degree at Penn, about seven years ago. Of course I'd convinced myself that there'd be endless options waiting for me in the software industry, or something like that. But a series of job leads fell through, and suddenly I found myself scrambling for some way to make ends meet. I got some referrals for – well, long story short, I found myself holding down a math and computer science position at this high school in Philadelphia – South Philly – working mostly with the freshmen. The pay was tolerable, and the benefit package was decent, but man, did I grow up in a hurry. It was so incredibly night & day from any experience I'd had, any setting I'd been in. I mean, they say 'inner city' these days, 'cause 'ghetto' sounds kind of outdated, or demeaning. But whichever term someone wants to use, *this* … where I was … was exactly what they're talking about."

"Were they pretty rough on you?" Kevin asked. An amusing visual popped into his head of his science-geek associate – again, not that Danny fit that prototype *now*, but he definitely did at an earlier age – desperately trying to implement various classroom-management strategies on a lively, boisterous class full of African-American kids.

"Some of them were … some of them were," said Danny, "but you know, what I learned is that you can take *any* group of 25 or 30 kids, at any age, in any type of setting anywhere, and I guarantee you, you'll have the whole range within that group – in terms of attitude, I mean. The grades and percentages won't necessarily match up from one school to the next, but the mindset that the kids bring in – you'll see the same types as anywhere else. There'll be those kids who come in every day knowing what's expected, who get down to business and give you the best effort any teacher could ask for. Then there are others who've already said 'screw it' and given up on their academic lives. You know the type. It's not like we didn't have some of those. On a test, they'll just jot down a bunch of random numbers, hoping they'll get something right by pure chance. Then you've got kids who are seriously capable of advanced thinking, and they show it in little isolated moments, but they don't quite have their priorities straight – they worry they won't look cool if they seem too enthusiastic about what the teacher's offering. And then there are the ones who might be behind the curve in terms of being able to grab onto the material, but who have a real, sincere desire to get themselves up to where they need to be. A lot of those kids, it's just a matter of support – at the point you first get them, no one's ever *told* them they can come out on top, or given them the tools to get there. When you see one of the kids in that category make a real breakthrough, like when they get their first score in the 90% range, or explain a certain concept back to you perfectly – man, that's when you know you're doing something worthwhile."

Kevin, who had never stood in front of a class except as a fellow student doing a presentation, nonetheless felt a vicarious jolt of satisfaction at the thought of an underserved student enjoying the unfamiliar glow of success. He was already engrossed enough in Danny's depiction that it didn't occur to him to interrupt and ask when the political content was scheduled to come into the story.

"But what got to me more than anything else," Danny went on, "was the conditions that I found out these kids were living in. It was such an eye-opener; I got more 'education' in my first three months teaching there than I'd got in my entire life as a student. It hit me over the head so hard. I literally don't think any of us would've *survived* if we were suddenly dropped into those circumstances. I mean, just for starters, I had a few kids who were nodding off in class. So you jump to the normal conclusions. They must be staying up too late, watching TV or playing video games or whatever. Until I started asking questions, and really looking into it. You know what it came down to? Malnutrition. Some of their parents had so little money, they could only afford to give them breakfast on alternate days

– so half the time, they're sitting in class, and they're too busy thinking about how *hungry* they are to worry about order of operations or factoring a polynomial. It got me thinking so much about *us,* back home, and how much we had going for us, how much was geared to – to work in our favor. How much was *given* to us, really."

The phrase "given to us" struck Kevin as mildly pejorative, as if the implication was that their achievements weren't legitimately earned. "Well, it's not like we were exactly rich kids or anything," came his mild protest.

"No, but see, Kevin, that's the point! That's exactly the point. We *weren't* rich. We weren't anywhere near the top levels of – y'know, within our demographic group. But we were *white.* We were white kids, at a white school, in a white community …"

For a split second, Kevin felt the urge to interject again and offer up the sprinter Kendrick Turner, of the Turner-Aldrich relay fiasco, as a counterexample. He stifled himself, however, realizing just as quickly that (a) the name would mean absolutely nothing to Danny, and (b) his ability to cite only *one* black Monroe student by name – one whose years of attendance didn't even overlap their own – pretty much served to reinforce Danny's assessment, rather than undercutting it. So he let Danny continue uninterrupted.

"And that meant," Danny went on, "that there were certain things we could count on. We never had to wonder whether they'd be there. That was never something that would even enter our minds."

"Like … give me an example. What 'things' are you talking about?"

"Gee, let's see," said Danny. "How about this? When we went to computer class, we knew that we'd actually get to work on a computer. We didn't have 28 kids – again, in a *computer class* – having to share *three* computers, 'cause that's all the school could afford."

"Please tell me that's a hypothetical example?" pleaded Kevin, having trouble envisioning it as a real scenario.

"No, dude, that's not hypothetical – I taught that class. That was *my* class. I couldn't believe it was real, either. I asked the administration how the hell I was supposed to teach a computer class with no computers, or just one for every ten kids. They just threw their hands up. Nothin' they could do, the funds needed to go to other priorities. So get this – I had to give the kids printed-out copies of the keyboard, so at least they could practice their typing skills on *pretend* computers while they waited for their six minutes on the real thing."

Danny went on: "That's one example. I could've told you, like, twenty others. Like the week-and-a-half during the winter when we had to hold five different classes – regular, academic classes – in different corners of the gym, all at the same time. The roof to one of the main buildings, which had six classrooms in it, was in such terrible shape, it was springing leaks left and right. Kids would've been trying to study and write with rainwater dripping down on their papers and books. So we had to herd about 150 kids into the gym every period, bring portable whiteboards to teach on, and hope that – that the kids taking math in the northwest corner wouldn't be distracted by the social studies lecture going on practically right next to them in the northeast corner."

"Damn," responded Kevin.

"And again, can you picture that happening to us? Anything like that?" Danny asked. Using his hands and arms to depict the scene, he continued, "I mean, imagine it: This is the multi-purpose room, and Miss Green's got her class over here, and Mr. Vogelson's got a separate group of students sitting right over there, and about ten feet behind all of us, Miss Searles is trying to demonstrate a chemistry process to *another* class – because no one, for months or even years, had the time or the funds to make sure the ceilings would hold up if the weather got bad. Would that be something we'd *ever* have to worry about?"

"I hear what you're saying," said Kevin. "I guess you kinda get locked into your own reality, and you don't think about what it's like outside that, unless something brings you face-to-face with it." As he said this, Kevin felt a sudden twinge of familiarity in his own words. It occurred to him that he could just as easily have been talking with Billy Lloyd about that eye-opening meet at Greenfield High. "So the 'into politics' you were talking about stems from all this, huh? That's what you're working on now – education reform?"

"Not quite," said Danny. "I mean, kinda tangentially, sort of … 'cause … well, like, the thing is, when you talk about 'education reform,' you're really talking about economic reform. It all comes down to what a state, or – or a municipality, is gonna prioritize. In the end, you're pretty much restricted by whoever's in power, and what their philosophy is. Either they give a shit about these kids, and they'll treat their education as something that matters, or they don't, and they won't – and you end up beating your head against the wall."

It struck Kevin that he had already adjusted to the new Danny Hattenberg well enough not to be shocked at his seamless incorporation of a term like "give a shit" into his dialogue.

"So what are you doing, then? What's your focus?" he asked.

"Well, what was getting to me the most," responded Danny, "was seeing the cases where some of these kids put in all the effort in the world – I mean, the ones who *did* care, who *did* have their act together – but when they were trying to get into decent colleges and stuff, they were coming up against competition that had all the advantages that they didn't. We had the college counseling, we had all the A.P. courses available to us – meanwhile, they had textbooks that they had to share with a classmate, where they'd rotate taking it home for the night. When you take a real honest look at these crazy differences in – in the amount of support for kids in different settings, it all adds up to a deal where, realistically, you've got *no* chance if you're trapped in one of these, these holding pens. And, see, for a lot of years, what's worked as a good countermeasure against that has been affirmative action. But now *that's* been under serious attack for a while – we've got one party doing everything it can to try to get rid of it, and the other being too chicken to defend it. So that's my main focus – trying to defend against these attacks. I'm working with a nonprofit called the Hand Up Foundation, and that's the main thing we're doing: We're going to places, regions where affirmative action policies are being threatened, and doing what we can to stand up for them. "

"I'm not as up on a lot of political issues as I know I oughtta be," confessed Kevin. "Affirmative action – I mean, I know the term, but I don't really know the history, or all the … well, I know it's when you give special preferences to certain–"

"Whoa – *whoa!* Sorry, gotta stop you there!!"

The suddenness and intensity of Danny's reaction caught Kevin totally off guard. Out of nowhere, Kevin saw his tablemate with his teeth clenched, his right shoulder scrunched in, and his arms thrust forward in a defensive posture. It was as if Danny had a lethal allergy to nuts, and someone had just offered him a cashew-pecan-walnut smoothie. Kevin made a mental note to never, under any circumstances, use the term "special preferences" as a connotation for affirmative action in Danny's presence. He had no clue as to *why* this pledge was necessary, but he had a pretty strong premonition that he was about to find out.

CHAPTER 21
About Context

"I'm sorry," said Kevin hastily, still in the dark as to the transgression for which he was apologizing. "I didn't know – I mean, I was just spouting off the – the only term I'd heard. I don't know what the whole issue's about, or what's the … like, the proper way of putting it."

"Yeah, no – I apologize too," said Danny, who had collected himself by now. "My reaction was a little … I didn't mean to … well, it's not your fault. I mean, you said it. Those *are* the only terms you've heard. They're about the only terms *anyone* hears on the issue these days. One side's propaganda, one side's talking points, they've gotten so much airplay that people take it in like it's just the accepted – like it's the definition of things. That's the first thing we're trying to change."

"Cool. Well then, start with me; set me straight here," invited Kevin. "The problem with it is … ?"

"Well, think about it for a sec – 'special preferences.' What does that mean, really, if you look at the actual words? It's like, playing favorites, isn't it? You get some sort of privilege, some kind of favored treatment, because you're 'special.' Because you're somebody's 'preference.' Because somebody *likes* you better than someone else. That's exactly the way they want to paint it, 'cause folks react in a negative way if it sounds like you're doing special favors for certain people — I mean, who *wouldn't* be turned off by that? So they make sure to keep language like that front and center, so they can build a total bullshit idea of what affirmative action's all about."

"I gotcha," affirmed Kevin. "So, but – so then, what *is* the idea – in your terms? Like, how would you characterize it, so people would get the point?"

"Well, I'd be way too optimistic if I said that people were anywhere near 'getting the point' right now," lamented Danny, "but I can tell you how I'd characterize it." As he was about to commence his characterization, he suddenly hesitated. "Well, but I dunno if I should, uh … I mean, when I get on this subject, I kinda lose track of time. I don't wanna monop– I mean, you got other people to see here too, I'm sure."

"Nah, man, it's cool," said Kevin, "I pretty much connected with everybody I wanted to see. I'll let you know if I need to take off or anything. So, affirmative action …" He gestured with his left hand for Danny to proceed.

"Well, uh … okay, well what we're saying," said Danny, "is that when you've got an imbalance, an unfair arrangement, built into the set-up where people are competing to get ahead, then you need to make some adjustments that take that into account. It's that simple. You need to look at people's achievements in *context*, not in a vacuum. You don't set up a rigged game and then pretend you're getting legitimate, meaningful results out of it. I mean, you're really just conning yourself if you think you are; ultimately, you're – it – is everything okay? You're looking kinda tripped out."

"Uh – it just kinda made me think about something," said Kevin, as he shook himself out of what had momentarily become a transfixed stare. "Go on."

Danny took a second to remember where he was. "So … so that's what affirmative action is. It's saying that we need to make those adjustments, because we did exactly that in this country – we threw people into a rigged game, and kept them there for centuries. We took certain groups and we subjected them to *negative* action, day in and day out, one generation after another. So now, all we're saying is, you gotta factor that in when you're considering how people have performed. It doesn't mean anything stupid, like, 'Oh, you hire someone just 'cause they're black.' You're talking about, when people *have* shown their worth, you weigh it a little bit in their favor if they've shown it with all that machinery stacked up against them. And it's not about *blaming* anybody. You're not assigning guilt to any one party, but you're recognizing that there *are* these patterns in history – and a lot of them still in full force today – and that when you've got a *systemic* problem then it demands a systemic response. So you need to–"

Kevin raised a hand to cut in: "You say 'systemic' problem – as opposed to what other kind?"

"As opposed to, like, just regular bad luck, like the kind of problems that could've happened just as easily to you or me. I mean, like, anyone could get in a car wreck and end up partially paralyzed or something. Anyone *could* have, uh … oh, I dunno, could've had a parent who was an alcoholic or who walked out on the family. We can all have bad things happen to us, right? And some get hit by more of it than others. It sucks, sure, and if I had any say over the priorities of our country, I'd want people in those situations to get whatever help they needed. But it's a different thing – those examples aren't cases of the *system* – the government, y'know, the official policies of your own society – telling you that you're a second-class citizen, and putting up all kinds of roadblocks that they don't put in front of other people, just 'cause you're in a certain category. You see the difference? We don't owe it to everyone to jump in and fix all their problems. But when the problem is – when the whole reason it's *there* is because the society decided that that was how they wanted things … well, then I say you damn sure *do* owe it to people to correct what you've done to them."

"That's like when they gave compensation payoffs to some of the Japanese who were put in the internment camps in World War II," offered Kevin, relishing the momentary feeling of being able to contribute some substantive content to the dialogue.

"That's a perfect example, exactly!" applauded Danny. "That's a case of facing up to our own history – we're saying that, yeah, we did this thing to this specific group, and it was *wrong*, and we owe them something a little more than just 'Oops – sorry; we won't do that again.' But it's easier to see the connection when it's something specific like that – like the Japanese internment, or the Holocaust … something singular and dramatic like that. But when it's a whole *history*, when it's patterns that just linger on year after year, and it's just 'the way things are' – then it's a thousand times harder to get people to recognize it. They don't want to face up to that history – it's too inconvenient, too threatening to their sense of patriotism or something."

Kevin sought clarification: "A whole hist– so, racism, you mean?"

"Yeah, that's the word," said Danny. "And hey – you're a good step ahead of a lot of people: At least you can *say* the word. Even *that's* farther than some of them can go. So many out there just don't want to hear it. They act like if we just don't *talk* about the problem, it'll go away – that the only *real* problem with racism today is that some people still have the nerve to bring it up."

Kevin thought it over for a second, and then volunteered, "Well, people see minorities succeeding in a lot of areas where they didn't before. So, they probably figure those – those roadblocks you're talking about are exaggerated, or brought up as a way of … I dunno. I mean, you've obviously dug into this way more than me over these years, so let me ask: Is it really *that* pervasive? I mean, I know there are still racist incidents, and there are all kinds of Rodney King-type cases that we *don't* hear about, 'cause no one caught them on video. But it seems like there are so many folks, black or Hispanic or whoever, who manage to break through anyway. Does it really hit everybody like that?"

Danny gave a deadpan shrug as he asked, "So should that be the measuring stick for whether something qualifies as a problem, as something we need to fix? Like, only if it's *so* imposing, *so* devastating that *no one* can overcome it? I mean, there are probably a good number of people out there who've overcome … who've overcome, like, being molested as kids – but I sure as hell don't know anyone who'd sign up for that. And I don't think you'd sound too empathetic if you … if you said, 'Well, we oughtta be able to cancel all those counseling programs, all those support groups, 'cause so-and-so was sexually assaulted when she was a kid, and *she* turned out okay.' Would you want to be the one saying something doesn't really qualify as a problem unless it wipes out *everyone* in its path?"

Kevin was caught. "No, but … well, like I said, you know more about this problem than me. I've been kinda insulated, like everyone else from around here, now that I think about it."

"Right," said Danny, readily, "and see, the problem with that is that the patterns and the ways of – the things that really make life *different* for one group versus another aren't gonna get noticed, 'cause you're not looking for them. Just a minute ago, you said 'racist incidents.' So, see, unless it's an *incident,* something that really catches your attention, it's like it doesn't exist. Discrimination ends up being defined for minorities by something that happens to them, but for us, it's defined by something that *doesn't* happen."

"Okay – you lost me there," said Kevin unapologetically. "Whattya mean, something that doesn't happen?"

"Alright, uh … okay, here's an example," said Danny. "You go to a bank to take out a loan for some business you want to start. So they tell you, 'Okay, for the loan you want, for that amount, you need such-and-such collateral.' So then you present them with proof that you've got the collateral, that you meet the requirements, and they give you the loan. Just regular business as usual."

Kevin nodded but maintained an uncertain look, to indicate that he was following the scenario, but didn't yet grasp the point, if he was supposed to have it by now.

"Just business as usual," repeated Danny. "It wouldn't occur to you, even for a second, that there was a *racial* component to what just went down – that your being *white* had anything to do with how things turned out for you. No, you were given some instructions, you followed them, and you got the result you were promised. What could be more simple?"

"I dunno," Kevin responded – referring not to the rhetorical question but to the overarching point that Danny still seemed to be counting on him to decipher.

"But it's not quite that simple," said Danny. "Because a couple hours later, a black man – let's say, the father of one of the kids I've been teaching – goes into the same bank, asks to take out the same loan, and presents the same collateral. But he *doesn't* get the loan. They find some reason to deny him, something buried in their policies. Trust me, it happens more than you can imagine. The bankers *themselves* probably don't even notice, aren't thinking consciously racist thoughts. But so many areas of our society work exactly like that, and it adds up. It adds up to a basic difference in our – in people's relationship with the world around them. It *does* impact everybody, to answer your question. We get a society that tells people like you and me that if we work hard, and play by the rules, we can be anything we want to be. Now, I *know* that doesn't mean it's guaranteed to work out that way – but that's the message we're given. And meanwhile, another race is told, from day one: You're suspect. You don't get the benefit of the doubt. We don't trust your abilities. We won't even assume that you're not a criminal. Check this out: I was also the advisor to some of the more advanced math students, and I was working with this junior who was off the charts – kid had around a 95 average, and he was the kind who, if he got 19 out of 20 on a test, he'd be kicking himself for the one he missed. You know the type I'm talking about."

"Yeah – *you* were that type," said Kevin, adding with a chuckle, "Well, except I don't remember you ever *getting* a 19 out of 20."

"It happened," Danny assured him. "What *didn't* ever happen, in my case, was missing finals 'cause I'd been thrown in jail the night before."

"Oh, shit ..." muttered Kevin.

"And so, your instinctive question is 'What did he do,' right?" Danny asked presumptively. As it happened, Kevin *wasn't* thinking that, because by this point in the dialogue, he gathered that an arrest for a legitimate reason wouldn't fit in with Danny's narrative. He declined to say anything, though, and just let the story take shape.

"Well, what he 'did,' was, he got out of school really.late one afternoon, 'cause he was staying for a tutorial, putting in extra time to make sure he was getting every detail squared away before the big exams. So he lost track of time, and he came out after his normal ride had needed to take off. So he's stuck walking home after dark, which is not a position you want to be in for any more time than you absolutely have to in this neighborhood. So he happens to see his cousin driving by, with a couple of friends in the car. His cousin offers him a lift, and of course he takes him up on it. But they get pulled over – not for a traffic violation, but for a little crack in the taillight. The cops search the car – again, over a *crack in the taillight* – and they search all four occupants. And they find a quarter-ounce of grass in one of the passengers' bags. So what do they do? They haul the *entire group* into jail for possession – not just the guy who had the shit on him. So Latroy calls me, totally distraught, telling me they're not letting him out for two days."

"They can *do* that?!" Kevin was stunned.

"Well, they couldn't do it – or, let's say, it would never *occur* to them to do it to you or me. But in a community like South Philly, it's par for the course; it's a reality you're forced to factor into your life. It jumps up to bite almost everyone, sooner or later. Now try comparing that to Jillane, Bibbs, and Matisse – you remember them, I'm sure."

Kevin nodded to affirm that he did remember, as anyone from the class of '93 would. On March 1st of the group's senior year – at the start of the exact same week as Mike's historic breakthrough in the 400 tryouts – the Richardson Park police had caught Tommy Jillane, his girlfriend Nicole Matisse, and their friend Jonas Bibbs in Jillane's car, parked off campus. The three were in the act of snorting cocaine, and they had a bottle of liquor that, as it turned out, the two boys had stolen from a local store. Bibbs, once determined to have been the instigator of the activities in question, had been expelled from Monroe, and Jillane and Matisse had received ten-day suspensions and the revocation of their off-campus privileges for the remainder of the year.

Danny continued: "Well, after this thing happened to this student of mine, it occurred to me to poke around a little bit, and follow up on our old classmates. You know, like, I wanted to find out, now that this Latroy kid has an actual juvenile arrest on his record for hitching a ride home, I thought I'd find out what kind of price you pay for the *serious* stuff – y'know, like stealing booze or doing hard drugs during school hours."

"So you found out something about the three of them?" Kevin asked, with genuine curiosity fueling the question at this point.

"That's Nicki Matisse right over there," said Danny, pointing toward one of a handful of well-dressed women socializing near the bar. "I don't know exactly where Jillane and Bibbs are right now, but I do know that all three of them went on to college, graduated, and they're in, y'know … respectable careers. That stuff they pulled, it's no factor in their lives, in affecting what opportunities they had or didn't have. There's no criminal record on any of them – and Bibbs and Jillane were both eighteen when it went down. For us, for any of us, something like that can just be a 'youthful indiscretion,' a 'kids-being-kids' kind of thing. You go on, you live your life, and it doesn't tail you around. That's night and day from these other places, where you've got such a huge percentage of young men walking around with criminal records, which'll play hell with them trying to get jobs, apply for social services, get housing, all kinds of things. And the vast majority of it's for minor little drug offenses, or wrong-place-at-the-wrong-time situations – the kind of thing that wouldn't follow any of us past the next morning."

"What happened with what's his name – is it Latroy?" asked Kevin. "I mean, he must've still been able to take his tests, right? Any school would give someone a reprieve for something like that, wouldn't they? I mean, I can't picture them not making up *some* kind of arrangement." His facial expression pleaded for a reassuring report.

"Uh-huh, yeah, they did. They let him take them two or three days late, the day after he got out," affirmed Danny. "And his record was expunged, eventually, after his grandmother raised enough of a fuss. Someone like him, I'm confident enough that he'll be successful in the long run. It's not gonna derail his whole life, although it *could* for someone without that same strength of character. But even for him, there was no way in hell an experience like that wasn't going to hamper things. He was literally shaking when he came back to school – I mean totally freaked out, traumatized. And since he'd been stuck in there, he hadn't been able to look things up if he needed a computer to do it, or anything like that."

"So he didn't end up doing anywhere near as well as he would've done if this little, this little 'mishap' hadn't happened to him," Kevin guessed.

"Of course not," confirmed Danny, "but who's gonna give that any thought, any consideration, when they're looking at his grades, or comparing them to the marks of a kid coming from Monroe, or wherever? Is anyone gonna look at those numbers in context? Will it matter to anyone that his showing was directly affected by an outside factor – one that would never in a million years happen to you or me? Or will they just say, well, so-and-so's one percentage point higher, so that's the most qualified person. That's who earned it."

"So, the cops, the court system, the banks ... school conditions ..." Kevin recited the list, already wondering if he was omitting something from it. "You've really tuned in to these situations where there's a real difference in how people – how they fit into the picture."

Nodding, Danny added, "And again, that's just the tip of the iceberg. Because none of these – well, basically, anecdotes – none of them really delve into the *effect* of being treated differently. I mean, really – how's somebody who society's basically given the finger to, how're they supposed to have any real faith in that same society's readiness to come through for them? How're they supposed to have the same confidence that whatever effort they *do* put in is gonna be recognized, that it'll pay off for them? How do we go around pretending that it wouldn't have any effect on someone's trajectory, on their drive? And hey, we're still just a generation, or maybe two, beyond the time when, if they lived in a certain part of the country, confidence and self-assertiveness could just as easily be a death sentence as it could get them ahead in life."

Kevin thought for a moment, then guessed, "You're talking about, what, the South?"

"Yeah. I mean, any of these kids whose ancestry traces to Mississippi, Alabama, Louisiana – their parents or grandparents had to tiptoe around knowing that if they even *looked* at a white person the wrong way, or spoke in the wrong tone – anything that could be seen as 'not knowing your place' – it could lead to murder, plain and simple. And there'd be no worry, for the people who did it, no worry of any legal penalty for the crime. Hell, half the time, the police might be participating in it themselves. We don't ever think about what it'd be like to live under that – well, *terror,* really. And then we can't imagine why they might not be quite as good at telling their kids, 'Hold your head up, don't let anyone stop you, be all you can be!' Yeah, it must just be their own lack of ambition."

"You build a good case," acknowledged Kevin. "So then, again, affirmative action is sorta saying, there's all this discrimination and unequal treatment going on, and there's gotta be something put in place to make up for ... for the effects of it."

"That's the basic idea, yeah ..." said Danny in an uneasy tone, "but I'm hesitant to use those words, even."

"Why?" asked Kevin.

"Because ... because 'make up for it' has kind of a cheap feel, sort of a tit-for-tat kinda feel to it – and that's not what affirmative action is saying.

When you talk about these policies that do place a certain amount of weight on someone's race, people react to them like, 'Well, wait a minute – why do *I* have to pay the price for something other people did? *I* didn't own any slaves.' It's so stupid. They don't realize how, even if they weren't the instigators of the problem, it still shifted things in their favor. There's no way they don't reap some of the benefits. I mean, if you were running a race against someone, and they had – like, some big metal brace around their ankle, wouldn't it occur to you, after you won the race, that maybe it wasn't just a matter of you being faster?"

"*I'd* figure that out," insisted Kevin, wearing the earnest expression of a student assuring the teacher that, while the rest of the class might be too dumb to get the answer, at least this *one* kid has his act together.

"Yeah, good – I mean, who the hell wouldn't notice something like that?" responded Danny, prompting Kevin to begin composing a mental list. "But when it comes to that same thing, that same situation in *society*, people just refuse to see it. They can't see how they come into very real advantages, relatively speaking, from *not* having had all that shit thrown in their path. They don't notice any imbalance, until the first moment that it's not giving *them* the advantage. That's when they freak out, these same folks who go for centuries saying, 'Hey, life isn't always fair – deal with it!' The moment they see something, a policy or a program, benefitting someone *else*, what do we hear from them? 'Hey, wait a minute! *That's not fair!*' "

"Yeah, they ... they do get that way, don't they?" Kevin agreed readily.

"It's crazy," affirmed Danny. "They'll paint it like it's the minorities who have all the advantages – like they just get this cakewalk. I was debating this woman from a conservative organization just a few months ago, and she pulled out the same card they always do, the one about how affirmative action 'cost her the chance to get into college' – or at least, into the specific college she wanted to go to. She spouted that line – I swear, these people are all reading from the same script – about her guidance counselor telling her that if she'd been black, she would've 'waltzed right in.' They always use that exact word, 'waltzed.' No one ever, like, 'tangos' or 'breakdances' into college; it's always gotta be the waltz."

"So what'd you say?" asked Kevin.

Danny, sidetracked by his own joke, needed a second to re-gather his narrative focus. "What'd I say? Well, I asked her whether it occurred to her that 'if she'd been black,' that would mean being black full-time, *every day of her life* – not just on the day she sent in her college application. I asked if *that* reality, and all the little details that went along with it, if that was really what she dreamed of, what she thought the sweet life was really all about."

"She offer any comeback?" asked Kevin in amusement.

"Not much – I mean, who's she kidding? She just kept reiterating how *wrong* it was, what a violation of the principles of fairness that we all believe in, that 13 minority students whose grades weren't exactly as high as hers got in at the same time she didn't. But she didn't count on me doing my homework ahead of time."

"Why – were their grades actually higher?" Kevin asked hopefully.

"No, she was right, technically. But what I pointed out – well, I asked her if she knew, in that same year, how many white kids whose grades *also* weren't as high as hers got in ahead of her. Of course, she had no idea, so I broke the news: It was more than a hundred! She'd been leapfrogged by at least *seven times* as many whites as the number of blacks or Hispanics. It could've been any kind of reason – connections, family legacies, financial status, geographical outreach, recruitment by one department or another – but it never occurred to her for even a second to accuse any of *them* of getting something they didn't earn, or of taking something that was, you know, 'rightfully' hers."

Kevin pounded the table in genuine excitement. "Oh, shit, that's brilliant, man," he said. "I wouldn't – I mean, that never would've occurred to me."

"Well, I wish I could take full credit, but it didn't occur to *me*, either – I mean, not originally," confessed Danny. "Neither did that first comeback I hit her with. I went to this lecture on racism a little over a year ago, just a little bit after I'd committed myself to work on this issue. And it hit me so hard that I set up a phone consultation with the speaker a short time afterward. White guy, interestingly, from Louisi– I mean, uh, Tennessee."

"So those were his ideas?" Kevin asked.

"Yeah. He hadn't talked specifically about affirmative action, but he raised so many examples that drove home, y'know, the disparities and everything, that I was pretty sure I'd be able to get some points and strategies from him. So, yeah, both of those were his suggestions. I dunno, he may have gotten them from another source himself. But the point is, really, the difference when it comes to giving people the benefit of the doubt. It's strictly the black students, the Latino applicants, where we keep hearing that they're not earning it, that they're getting the end results handed to them. But the one group that got to hold the cards for our entire history, the one that actually *did* get to position itself to receive all the 'special preferences' out there – no one thinks to challenge *our* qualifications. It just becomes – it's such a norm, that it just never comes up for questioning."

"Force of habit has a pretty strong pull to it in any society," said Kevin, wondering for a second whether he should similarly credit that observation's original source. It occurred to him that Jessica would have shared at least a few of the advanced placement courses that made up Danny's class schedule, but he doubted that her name would ring any bells, given Danny's lack of social interaction at the time.

"But I'll tell you one thing," said Danny, bypassing Kevin's input in his focused momentum. "If it's true, if it's really the minorities who have it so easy, the word sure as hell hasn't gotten around to the parents of my students. I've heard at least twenty times, in parent-teacher conferences, these folks tell their kids, 'You got to go twice as far to get to the same place.' "

"They say that? Those exact words?" asked Kevin, as he involuntarily lurched from a slightly slumped posture to a firm, upright position.

"Yeah. That, or some little variation of it – like, 'You got to be twice as good to go half as far.' But yeah, that's pretty much how *they* sum up being African-American, right across the board. I've never once heard one of them say, 'It's okay – you can just get *pretty* good grades, 'cause affirmative action'll carry you the rest of the way.' I don't think that memo ever made it to them."

"Uh-huh. Well, I've definitely known my share of people like that woman you were talking about," said Kevin. "You can't reach them by talking about fairness, 'cause 'fair,' to them, means they come out on top, where they just assume they're supposed to be."

"You got it," muttered Danny.

"So people like that are gonna try to keep the discussion in two areas," Kevin said with a suddenly authoritative delivery. "Either you're *punishing* the early– uh, I mean, uh, the white people, for having advantages to begin with, or you're 'lowering expectations' for the minorities, and saying they can't do it without some extra help. I mean, that's how *they* want us to look at it, am I right?"

Danny paused and looked at Kevin admiringly. "Yeah," he said, "that's … you just hit on the two themes that we keep hearing over and over again. Those two exactly."

Kevin went on, ever more confidently: "And dig this – she's gonna say that the minorities shouldn't use any of that whole history as an excuse, that they're just, what is it, like, 'playing the victim' if they bring up what's been done to them like it has anything to do with anything. But she won't expect any of that same resilience from herself, right? She won't tell *herself,* 'Hey, so you didn't get what you thought you had coming. Get over it – don't take on a victim mentality.' *She's* allowed to whine about missing out on stuff, but they're not."

"For someone who says he doesn't know anything about the subject, you catch onto things pretty damn fast," Danny observed.

"Well, I have some – there's kind of a – well, I can get into it some other time," said Kevin. "So you need, like, a different angle to come at people, so they'll get the real point of the whole thing."

"A different angle – that's a good way of putting it, yeah," agreed Danny. "That's why the case we're trying to make – and I don't think we've done a good enough job of it, by any stretch – is that, again, it's about *context.* It's saying, you damn well need to look at the circumstances in which people accomplish whatever they accomplish. It makes total sense that that should be part of the evaluation. Look at me – yeah, I got all A's in high school. You know what else? The only thing I had to *worry* about was getting A's! I never would have *thought* of it that way at the time, 'cause – well, 'cause my reality was the only one I had to refer to. But I had the inside track, all along. All the – what?"

"Nothing."

"Oh. Well, yeah, all the things these kids at Carver High have to deal with, none of that was part of the equation for me – for any of us, really. Again, that's not to say that people everywhere don't have problems, or struggles, that they don't, uh … y'know …"

As the pause in Danny's sentence lingered for an extra moment, Kevin happened to catch another glimpse of Tristan, who sat about six tables away, engaged in conversation with two other alumni. He recalled some of the minor pangs of empathy he had felt back in the day related to Tristan's academic struggles, and the *what-if-that-had-been-me* thoughts that his knowledge of those difficulties had occasionally sparked within him. The realization now struck him, with some accompanying satisfaction, that even in his apolitical teenage-hood, he had somehow managed to develop a basic awareness of the uneven cards that fate handed people – and of the modicum of humility for which that awareness seemed to call, as Mr. Bowerman had stressed at graduation. As he pondered this, he suddenly began wondering if there hadn't all along existed some sort of deeper psychological subtext, some inherent trait unbeknownst even to him, which had ultimately fueled his reformist endeavor within the sports world.

But it occurred to him, simultaneously, that Danny was not talking about Tristan, and the misfortune of being born with a minor cognitive impairment. He was talking about Latroy, and the others like him, and stressing that their neglect or persecution by the system was wholly inappropriate to categorize as mere "misfortune."

Danny wasn't through. "And even if they *could* – I mean, if there was someone who, by some miracle, *didn't* have to worry about any of that external stuff, they still wouldn't have had any kind of a fair shot, being where they are. It's technically impossible."

"What's technically impossible?" asked Kevin.

"To match up with a G.P.A. like the one I had, if that's the only thing you're gonna look at," explained Danny. "Because look – I could get all the extra points I wanted on my transcript for honors and A.P. classes. Hell, my junior and senior years, that's *all* I took."

"That is a lotta bonus points," affirmed Kevin. "And they can't get them there?"

"At G.W. Carver, they've got a total of *two* A.P. classes – Spanish literature and calculus. That's it. Nothing in English, science, social studies – no way any of these students, no matter how much they might want to, could equal my numbers. So I'm supposed to say, well gee, that must mean I'm *better* than all of them? That it could only mean I must've cared more, worked harder, than anyone in that entire school? And here I am, teaching kids – again, I'm not talking about all or even most of them, but definitely a handful – who have more determination and more resilience than I could've ever imagined having. Well, maybe we need to take a step back and say that, in context, a 3.8 from one of them might actually be a *bigger* accomplishment than a 4.8 from me! Maybe *they're* the ones who've really shown they deserve that spot in the university, or that position someone's hiring for."

"So why don't you think you're doing a good job at it – at making the argument?" asked Kevin. "What do you think it's gonna take?"

"What I think we need is some … some kind of symbolic representation that can drive the point home in terms that people can relate to, where they can see it clearly," Danny proposed. "Because, see, we're always trying build a logical argument, or a *moral* argument, but we're going up against one of the absolute toughest roadblocks in people's ... in their psyche. Nobody wants to be told that they've had an unfair advantage. They just can't handle that. They see it as someone trying to tear them down, or, like ... degrade their accomplishments or something. And again, a lot of the evidence that we build our case around isn't apparent to them, 'cause they stay in these protected circles where they don't have to hear about it. That brother who got turned down for the loan at the bank isn't their buddy, who they're gonna be getting together with at a barbecue this weekend, asking how his week went, and learning a surprising thing or two about the financial industry's habits. It's not part of their lives, so they have the luxury of not having to think about it. It just doesn't regis– you know, you're making that same tripped-out face again – is something wrong?"

The verbatim echo of Billy Lloyd's old phrase had sparked another sudden, dramatic widening of Kevin's eyes. Again, he shook his head to reorient himself

"No. Nothing – go on," he exhorted. "So, but then, if you *do* put the evidence in front of them ...?"

Danny took a moment to re-adjust from the slightly unsettling effect of Kevin's reaction. "Well, uh ... yeah, I mean, when they see the evidence, they're still totally closed off to it – maybe not to the evidence itself, but to the idea that it should have any effect, or that it calls for any ... like, y'know, any official response, or repair. They try to take the whole history, and the whole idea that our country has a record of actually *doing bad things to certain people,* and shove it all under the table. It doesn't matter how in-your-face all that evidence is; they'll still find a way to pretend it's all imagined, all made up – that it's just people whining about not coming out ahead. Some of them have said almost exactly that: They'll say that leaders like Jesse Jackson, or whoever, are just going around making other blacks 'think' that they're victims of racism. Did you happen to notice whether there were any wheelchair ramps at the entrance here, when you came in?"

"Umm, I, it, uh, wh– no. Why?" Kevin asked, in sudden, total bafflement over a question so far from the subject at hand.

"No, there weren't any, or no, you didn't notice?"

"I didn't notice," said Kevin, still completely in the dark.

"Yeah, neither did I. I just walked up the stairs without thinking about it."

"And ...?"

"Well, you see? We didn't *have* to notice. That's another thing this lecturer pointed out. It's not an issue in our lives, 'cause *we're* not handicapped – we can just walk up the stairs. But what if someone came in here with a wheelchair, looking flustered all to hell, and said they had to crawl up the stairs and lug their chair up along with them, and asked why the hell the place doesn't have a goddamn ramp? Would you trust that they were probably right about that? Or what if I said to them, 'Oh, there probably *was* a ramp, and you just didn't see it?' Wouldn't I come off like kind of an asshole?"

"Yeah, that'd be the word for it," agreed Kevin. "I think I'm starting to see where you're going with this …"

"Well, I'm making the point that we would *trust* that person. We'd treat them as pretty reliable when it comes to an issue that they've gotta deal with all the time in their life. We wouldn't think even for a second that maybe *we* were more tuned in to the situation than they were. That'd be insane. But these conservatives, they don't give any of that same credit when it comes to racism. They don't trust that black people might be, y'know … *cognizant* of their own experiences. No, apparently blacks need someone to inform them of what their lives are like – they must not be able to figure things out themselves. Oh, and they're being lied to by their spokespeople – they didn't *really* go through what they went through. They're just *imagining* that those cops roughed them up, or that the real-estate agents told them the house they wanted had been sold, when it really hadn't. Sure, they've had exactly the same chances, the same treatment we've had."

"Somehow, folks convince themselves, while they're at it," inserted Kevin.

"Which folks?" asked Danny in momentary confusion.

"I mean the ones who try to make the arguments you're talking about. It's like you said. No one wants to go around thinking they had an unfair advantage. People can overlook a hell of a lot when it comes to holding onto that – to that illusion."

"Damn straight. They deal with it by always bringing it back to the individual, and his – y'know, his responsibility for his own fate," clarified Danny. "You know the refrain – it's a 'free society,' you make your own way, and you should only blame yourself if things don't work out for you. Well, that might be comforting and reassuring for the ones who *have* had things work out well for them, but the one little problem is, it's a crock of shit. Factors from the outside *do* carry some weight – that's reality, even if you pretend it's not. It's like if you saw a football game where only one team was given the right gear – y'know, helmets, pads, everything. So you watch this game that's obviously a total farce all the way through, but you come away insisting that it was legit, that it was just a case of the better team winning. You say, 'Hey, the ref didn't favor one team or the other.' And it's like, 'Well, yeah, but – *hello?!*'" He gestured with one hand as if pointing out the sharp contrast in the teams' respective wardrobes from somewhere up in the stands

"That's a pretty good analogy right there," responded Kevin, as the thought began making its way to the forefront of his mind: *I think I might have an even better one, though.*

"But that's exactly how we operate in America," insisted Danny. "We can't face up to our own role in holding certain people back, so we just keep insisting that they're holding themselves back. I mean, how would you feel if you were thrown into a situation where you couldn't come out on top, where everything was *set up* so that you couldn't come out on top, no matter *how* much ability or effort you put into it – but then, when you *didn't* come out on top, all people told you was that you didn't try hard enough, that you must not have earned it as much as someone else?"

"Yeah, that … that would kinda suck," muttered Kevin, who was now leaning on his elbow and staring momentarily off into space.

Danny took Kevin's posture as a sign that he was losing him. "I'm sorry," he said, suddenly cringing in self-reprimand. "I know I'm going too long. Damn it … I know – I know I get on a roll, just like I warned you. I get so passionate about this that I just start rambling, and I don't check to see if I'm boring people. Hell, maybe *that's* our problem."

"A symbolic representation …" mumbled Kevin, the words buried too far under his breath for Danny to hear him clearly.

"Huh? What'd you say?"

Kevin took a few seconds to gather his thoughts, and then sat back upright. Still looking a bit askance, he simply said, "Danny."

"Yeah?" Danny responded, sensing some gravity in the moment.

"Danny, do you know – did you ever know anything about what happened with me during our junior and senior years? Like, after we stopped being in the same class together? Do you know about any of that whole deal?"

"That whole de– what hap– Oh! Right!" It suddenly occurred to Danny

232

that, on the periphery of his studies, he had, in fact, heard his ex-lab partner's name surface rather prominently in connection with some issue of school policy. He tried for a moment to recall whether he knew what the specifics were, and then admitted, "Well, no, not really. I guess ... I mean, I guess it involved – what, some sort of rules change in sports somewhere? Was it something like that? And I guess it must've been a fairly big deal, 'cause, yeah, I do remember now that there was a lot of ... a lot of media attention that came around the school. You'd see, like, TV news vans on campus. And it was you and, uh, umm – that really tall guy, Billy Ray or whatever. Y'know, the one Bowerman singled out at graduation. That was connected with you, wasn't it?" Kevin nodded.

Danny continued, "But no, I never really knew what the whole issue was all about. I mean, you know me. I was just buried in my books the whole time, so a lot of that stuff got past me."

"How long are you in town for?" asked Kevin in an all-business tone.

"Uh, for the weekend – I'm flying back to Harrisburg on Monday morning. Why?"

"Listen," said Kevin as he rose from his chair. "I gotta take off. My dad's dealing with some health issues, and I need to be there for him. But this is important: You and me, we're gonna connect over the next two days." He didn't so much propose this meeting as he *announced* it, speaking with a resolve that left nothing about it open to debate. "Either tomorrow or Sunday, we need to have lunch or something. Here." He dug a business card out of his wallet and handed it over the table to Danny. "Call me tomorrow morning."

"Umm ... okay, sure, man," said Danny, who had quickly traded in his political crusader's force of personality for an openly curious innocence. "I can make the time. But what – can you tell me what for?"

"I want to talk to you some more about this campaign of yours," said Kevin. "I wanna get involved. I think I might have some good ideas for you."

"You degrade us, and then ask why we are degraded. You shut our mouths, and then ask why we don't speak. You close your colleges and seminaries against us, and then ask why we don't know more."

Frederick Douglass